The Demise o

CW00377092

Richard

By the same author:

The Puglia series of novels
Dancing to the Pizzica *(2012)*
The Demise of Judge Grassi *(2013)*
Leonardo's Trouble with Molecules *(2014)*

The Commissario Beppe Stancato stories – set in Abruzzo
The Case of the Sleeping Beauty *(2015)*
A Close Encounter with Mushrooms *(2016)*
The Vanishing Physicist *(2017)*

Long Shorts
(A collection of amusing and unusual stories – updated 2015)

The Curse of Collemaga *(A novel. 2020)*
Puglia with the Gloves Off. Book1 – Salento
(A travelogue – 2019)

Published by nonno-riccardo-publications
richard_s_walmsley@hotmail.com

Cover design by Esther Kezia Thorpe

(The front cover depicts the silhouette of Lecce's magnificent 'campanile' in the Piazza del Duomo)

This book is dedicated to all those people who still believe in small miracles.

The group of musicians who figure in this story can be found on Youtube. Type in **Schiattacore Pe' tutti ui.**
The song, which plays a significant part in the story, is called (in dialect) Lu Scarparu, meaning The Shoe Mender.

Prologue

Am I speaking to Judge Grassi? Judge Amedeo Grassi?

That is correct, *signore.* Whom do I have the honour of addressing?

I am calling you from Rome, signor giudice. I am under-secretary to the Prime Minister, Sergio Balducci, who wishes to enlist your help in dealing with a problem he has encountered.

I cannot imagine what that might be, signore. I have never had the honour of dealing directly with the Prime Minister before.

I will not waste your time or mine on small talk. May I say, first of all, how distressed the Prime Minister was to hear of your recent double bereavement. It must be hard to lose both parents in so short a space of time - very upsetting for you, signor giudice.

I thank you for your concern, *signore.* Now would you be so kind as to come to the point of this call? I have an important appeal case to prepare for.

It is precisely that particular case which is of great concern to the Prime Minister. The gentleman on trial is a close friend of Signor Balducci and also an industrialist of great importance to our export drive.

I see. I trust that you will not be asking me to pervert the course of justice. I can hardly turn a blind eye in this case.

We are not asking you to turn a blind eye, signor giudice. Nor are we asking you to pervert the course of justice. Heaven forbid! But there are aspects of this case to which you are not privy.

Frankly, I do not like the way that this conversation is going. Political interference in the course of justice is clean against the constitution of our country. I cannot...

Listen to me carefully, signor giudice. We wish to protect your career and reputation at all costs. Judges like you are an invaluable asset to our beloved country and we would not want this matter to jeopardise your position in any way. But the Prime Minister has other priorities to consider. It is not in the interests of Italy that this gentleman be exposed to the public eye at this time. I am sure that a man of your intelligence can comprehend the delicacy of the situation.

With all due respect to the Prime Minister...

There is only one way in which you can show due respect, signor giudice. I trust that is perfectly clear to you. We will be at great pains to ensure that other parties affected by this case are adequately protected and recompensed. We are fully apprised of the details of the accusation.

I will not be a party to corruption, *signore* - not even for the sake of *Il Cavaliere Balducci.*

We shall ensure that the outcomes of the trial are handled satisfactorily, signor giudice, provided, of course, that you are willing to play your part. I trust that your dear parents will be able to rest in peace when they realise that their only son has been duly rewarded for his loyalty.

What is that supposed to mean?

Thank you, signor giudice, for listening and being so understanding. I shall convey your willingness to cooperate to the Prime Minister. He will, I imagine, be delighted and eternally in your debt. Arrivederla, signor giudice.

(Telephone conversation held on 23rd April 2002)

1: Ripples on the Surface

Amedeo Innocenzio Grassi sat down to read his Saturday newspaper in a coffee bar near his home at about ten o'clock. This agreeable ritual formed part of his recently established post retirement routine. He flicked through the first pages, taking in the usual items of local news. In the centre pages, his surprised glance at seeing a photo of himself turned to coffee-choking consternation as he began to read his own obituary.

The morning had started off normally enough. He had been lying in bed looking up at the high vaulted ceiling, wondering how he should spend his third post-retirement Saturday without resorting to switching on the television before midday. At the same time, he would have to resist the temptation to uncork another bottle of *Primitivo di Manduria* from his wine cellar – equally before midday - which would inevitably lead to a surreptitious, one-man wine-tasting session well before lunch was served. He sighed audibly at the star-shaped ceiling which stared brightly but impassively back down at him. At the age of sixty-seven, he had been looking forward to the moment when he would be free to enjoy his retirement, 'well deserved' in his case, he earnestly believed; time to devote himself to his immediate family and complete his comprehensive volume on the wines and vineyards of *Salento*. His book would be different to those run-of-the-mill books on wines. This compendium would also delve into the family history of each *viticoltore* – with photographs of the families included. The addition of the human element would, he considered, add appeal to an otherwise stale formula. His innovative idea had worked well in his frequent newspaper columns on the subject of local wines, which were published regularly by Lecce's regional newspaper, *Il Quotidiano*. But he had quickly realised that compiling such information inevitably required him to sample the fruits of the wine-producers' labours during his tours of their vineyards and some of the larger *cantine;* an enjoyable pastime, admittedly, but one which was in stark contradiction to the insistent injunctions of his doctor, who had subjected him to extensive and thorough *analisi* almost as soon as he had completed his last day in office. His wife had been the main instigator in this matter and she had brooked no procrastination on his part.

'You must cut down on your wine drinking, Amedeo,' his doctor had stated unequivocally. 'Or run the risk of developing liver disease. It's your choice! And your cholesterol level is currently 6.2,' he said piling on the agony. 'That's far too high, my friend.' Amedeo Innocenzio Grassi recognised, not for the first time, that doctors wielded a degree of power over his life that permitted them to address him, without fear of reprisal, by the intimacy of his first name. His title magically vanished as if by some medical sleight of hand.

Thus, there were elements of conflict in his life which he felt should not be present now that he was no longer actively engaged in passing judgement on the misdeeds of his fellow men. He had to acknowledge, at moments like this, that he missed the constant challenge of his profession. But what was much harder to admit, even to himself, was that he felt his status and self-respect were being eroded by his not having the opportunity to exercise power over other people. He had told himself frequently whilst lying in bed in the morning that he should have delayed his retirement until the summer months when they could transfer the household to their coastal home near Leuca, where they owned a spacious stone villa perched on a cliff-top high above the Adriatic Sea. But, in his more honest moments, he knew that putting off the inevitable event would not have made a significant difference to the way he felt when the time had come. No, he would have to learn to live without the sense of purpose in life that the exercise of judicial power had given him. 'How galling!' he exclaimed out loud to the ceiling above.

'What's galling, *mio caro*?' asked a voice in the corridor. The judge's wife opened his bedroom door and looked at him, smiling a broad smile which was framed by the doorpost.

'How does she always manage to display so much good humour at this time of the morning?' thought the judge ungraciously. He muttered something neutral to her and she, unperturbed, responded by saying that she would make sure that Marta prepared some strong black coffee in the moka pot for when he got up.

Amedeo's wife, Antonella, was a handsome woman in her late fifties. She was almost invariably in a good mood and was never at a loss for things to do. She was currently organising Lecce's annual '*Cortili Aperti*' event on behalf of those owners fortunate enough to live in the sumptuous inner city sanctuaries whose ancient courtyards and gardens were normally hidden from view behind massive, solid, wooden doors. Needless to say, Judge Grassi and his wife were privileged enough to possess such a dwelling. The ninety-thousand inhabitants of Lecce would be thronging the streets over that weekend in June – not to mention the teeming hoards of visitors who would descend on their provincial capital from the surrounding towns and villages. There was not just the opening of the gardens to organise; there would be student musicians from the University playing classical music, who would need to be assigned to each little hidden courtyard in the city. There were traditional costumes to supply to those acting as guides in this spectacular annual pageant. The volunteer guides themselves would have to be vetted. The organisation required would keep Antonella occupied for weeks to come. It was the first of April today. 'Just about enough time left to get things sorted out,' she had told her husband enthusiastically.

It had not been entirely thanks to Judge Grassi's income that he and his wife could afford to live in one of these secluded apartments with their luxuriant gardens. Antonella was a well-off lady in her own right. Her father had set up a pasta factory outside the city after the Second World War. The product was renowned for its superior quality, being made of the very best durum wheat, whilst the various pasta shapes were slow dried to retain their fullest flavour. The simple transparent packets proudly bore the family name, *Cavallaro*, in green lettering. It was now Antonella who was the driving force behind this successful family business. The judge stirred in his bed and uttered a noncommittal grunt. He had to admit a grudging admiration for his wife's energy. There was nothing for it but to get out of bed and shower in his en suite bathroom before donning his worldly attire and going down to the kitchen to have his first coffee of the morning - the problem of how to fill his day still unresolved. His wife's bedroom door was wide open, the space inside long since vacated. They had decided on separate rooms, without recriminations or undue ceremony, almost as soon as their two children, a son and a daughter, had finally left home in their early thirties.

Antonella smiled at Amedeo as he walked into the kitchen and sat down at the table. Marta, their almost full time housekeeper and cook, put a small cup of strong black coffee in front of the judge. He nodded at her by way of thanks.

'I have to go to the 'farm' this morning, *mio caro*. Don't get into any trouble while I am out, will you?' she said light-heartedly. Amedeo managed the first fleeting smile of the day in her direction. Antonella always referred to the family business as the 'farm'. He had also cottoned on to her covert reference to his tendency to sample the lunchtime wine before the meal was ready.

'You don't usually go down to Melissino on a Saturday,' he commented.

'I know - some case of unfair dismissal. The man is threatening to sue us,' she explained.

'What did he do?' asked the judge.

'He was caught lighting a cigarette before he had got outside.'

'Clear cut case, I should think,' said Amedeo.

'Should be,' added Antonella. 'And what are you up to this morning?'

'Oh, I'll go and get a paper in a minute,' he said. 'And then come back and write up a bit more about the *Cantine le Due Palme* for my book. Then I shall go round to Aurelio's house. He needs some help with a case he's handling.' Aurelio was their son. He had followed in his father's footsteps as regards his university studies but had decided to become a lawyer rather than a judge, specialising in the complexities of company law.

9

Amedeo downed a second cup of hot coffee and felt better disposed towards life. He went out into the courtyard and stood admiring the oleander trees whose flowers gave off a heady, fragrant scent which pervaded the communal gardens. There were nooks and crannies in every part of the carefully tended garden. You could hide and remain undiscovered for hours. His two grandchildren, one from each of their offspring, loved playing hide-and-seek outside in the safety of this enclosed, secret garden. Then he walked out into the narrow street stooping slightly to step through the little wooden door that formed a section of one of the heavy main doors. He was not particularly tall but he had a distinguished air about him. He had a head of wavy greying hair and a look of calm authority on his face. He walked along the narrow street with an unhurried, steady pace. He had cultivated his public image carefully over the years. People walking in the opposite direction usually stepped off the pavement in deference to his presence. Those who knew him still greeted him by his title.

'*Buongiorno signor giudice,*' they said as if in the hope that some of his authority and prestige would rub off on them if they addressed him by his title. The shadows of his early morning self-doubts dissipated as he walked up *Via Cairoli* towards the ancient city centre, dominated by its sixty-eight metre tall, 17th century *campanile*, soaring high above the *Piazza del Duomo.* He walked into the tobacconist where he normally bought his Saturday copy of *Il Quotidiano*. He never bothered with a paper on weekdays, preferring to watch the home-grown TV channel, *Telenorba,* for the local and national news.

'*Buongiorno, Carmela,*' he said addressing the woman behind the counter. Her expression changed in an instant. The judge could have sworn that her face turned paler. He thought he detected fear in her eyes.

'You look as if you have seen a ghost, Carmela.' he said with a wry smile.

She shook her head to dispel whatever thought had crossed her mind and immediately, she was smiling back at him. The split second impression was erased as soon as it had appeared. She accepted his €10 note and graciously held out the change as he took his paper. *'Buona domenica, signor giudice,'* she said as he walked out with a cheery wave over his shoulder. Amedeo heard a newspaper being opened impatiently behind him. He clearly heard the sound of paper tearing.

'She must have been reading something very intriguing,' he thought mildly amused. As he walked back towards home, he thought he caught a few strange looks from one or two vaguely familiar faces. He sketched a smile in their direction and strode on without giving it much thought. Another coffee was needed, he felt; at his usual bar. He much preferred *espresso* coffees made in the coffee bars by those majestic, polished steel machines, equipped with nozzles and spouts of hissing steam, which dispensed a preordained dose of coffee topped with a beautiful light brown *crema*. The girl brought his coffee over to him as he was spreading his newspaper open to read the front page. She carefully placed the cup on his table warning him that the rim was probably hot from standing on the warming-plate on top of the coffee machine. Nothing of particular interest on the front page: the usual sad catalogue of high speed motorbike accidents resulting in the premature deaths of their teenage riders. *The young man was not wearing a crash helmet,* the article added unnecessarily. A shopkeeper had been arrested in Lecce by the *Guardia di Finanza* for not supplying receipts for goods sold. He had thereby avoided paying VAT, amassing a personal fortune of €10 000, to the detriment of the Italian Treasury, all in the space of a single year. This same scenario, multiplied thousands of times over throughout the land, went a long way to explaining Italy's huge financial deficit he told everybody whenever he could. As if they did not know already.

Amedeo turned to the next page, and saw his photo and the article announcing his departure from this life. And so began a period in his life that would change his outlook for ever.

The waitress was alarmed to see that the judge's face had turned puce in colour as he struggled for breath. She must only have been about fifteen years old and was terrified that this customer was going to die on the spot. She called out in a panic to the *padrone*, who was talking animatedly to another customer at the far end of the bar. The customer had been pointing out a newspaper article to the bar owner. 'But isn't that the judge sitting over there?' he asked in puzzlement. At that moment, the girl cried out, 'Come over here quickly, PLEASE!' The *padrone* took one look at the choking judge and rushed over clutching a glass of water. He felt as if the world had suddenly become unreal. He had just been discussing the demise of Judge Grassi and here was the person in question seemingly living his final moments on this planet. The *padrone* slapped the judge on the back, only considering afterwards what a breach of social étiquette he had just committed. 'I'm so sorry *signor giudice,*' he said. 'I really thought that you were about to ...' He left the sentence unfinished.

The judge was beginning to recover, at least from the physical symptoms of choking on the coffee.

'...*crepare!*' he said, finishing the sentence for the *padrone*. 'Snuff it! Apparently someone thinks that I already have!' he continued angrily indicating the newspaper article.

The unfortunate *padrone* felt responsible for the situation and apologised profusely. Amedeo put a reassuring hand on the man's arm and thanked him for his concern. 'Perhaps you would be so kind as to tell as many people as possible that, as far as I know, I am still very much alive.'

'*Sì, signor giudice!* Of course I will. Without fail! I am glad that you are not ... that you are still with us,' he concluded as Amedeo got up from his seat clutching the offending newspaper, which was so crumpled up that it looked as if he was intending to light a fire with it. The bar owner refused to take money for the coffee and, without any intended irony, wished Amedeo a *buona domenica*.

All Amedeo wanted to do was to escape back to the sanctuary of his own kitchen and read the article properly. 'Somebody will pay dearly for this!' he threatened under his breath. He was still too shocked to realise consciously that this inexplicable episode had removed the onset of Saturday boredom in one fell swoop. His anger and bewilderment carried him forward on a swiftly flowing current – and deposited him, feeling drained, on to the nearest kitchen chair. He spread out the crumpled pages on the table and prepared to read the article properly. He needed the presence of Antonella to discuss the event that had overturned the predictability of his routine existence in the space of a few short seconds. But there was no chance that she would be back for at least two hours. At least, he considered, he now understood the reaction of the woman in the paper shop. A hint of a smile returned as he remembered his comment about 'seeing a ghost'. She must indeed have thought that he was some form of spirit treading the streets of Lecce after his untimely departure from this world. Or else, that she must have been dreaming when she had read the article on page three of *Il Quotidiano*. No wonder she had been in such a hurry to re-read the article as soon as he had set foot outside the shop.

Marta walked into the kitchen just as he was plucking up the courage to read his 'obituary'. She looked at him strangely. 'She knows!' said the judge to himself.

'Your son and your daughter both phoned while you were out, *dottore*. They sounded anxious. They wanted to know if anything had happened to you. They asked if you...' She stopped in embarrassment.

'I'll phone them immediately,' he said.

It had slipped his mind that he was due to go round to his son's house. He overcame his reluctance to talk about the newspaper article to them and said that he would see them in about thirty minutes. His daughter, Teresa, had immediately offered to come round to her brother's house so that they could discuss what had happened. In the end, the judge decided to put off reading the article and drove the short distance to where his son lived in the town of Monterone to the west of Lecce – a fifteen minute drive. He wore sunglasses – more to act as a disguise than to protect himself against the rays of the sun. His daughter was fond of expounding her pet theory that most Italians firmly believed that, by hiding behind a pair of dark lenses, the shadow-land that exists

14

in the world beyond the sun-glasses somehow rendered *them* invisible to the public gaze. 'Self-delusion, of course,' she would say to round off her argument.

Being with his family rapidly restored his sense of normality. His grandson, nine-year-old Alessio, was trying to get his grandfather interested in a book he was reading on aeroplanes. Teresa, who had read the article in the paper, made light of it. She pointed out that it was April 1st and concluded that it was some kind of elaborate April Fools' Day joke.

'In extremely poor taste,' was Amedeo's opinion. Nevertheless, he was happy to clutch at the straw that this new explanation offered him.

'Of course, *papà*, you must go in person to see the editor of *Il Quotdiano* as soon as you can. The very least he can do is explain why he did not check his sources before printing the article. And he will have to publish a second article to explain that you are not dead,' she added bluntly.

'You take after your mother, my dear,' he commented dryly.

'Have you read the article yet, *papà?*'

He admitted that he had felt disinclined to do so up till now.

'You should, *papà*. It's all very formal. It says all the things that you would expect about a distinguished career as a judge and how your contributions in praise of our wines will be missed. But there's a little twist in one of the sentences - a sting in the tail. Look! I've highlighted it for you.'

Amedeo looked as he had been told to do. The sentence that did not quite fit into the general tone of eulogy read, '... *of course, everybody praises Judge Grassi for his impartial handling of some notably thorny cases – but perhaps history will reveal that he was not always quite so impartial or virtuous as he might have wished to appear.'* The article then went on to express condolences to all his family. There was just that one sentence which rung a discordant note. Amedeo looked deeply thoughtful but passed no comment.

'I shall go and see the editor today,' he said. 'He has some explaining to do.' His son pointed out that he might now have to wait until Monday. Only the Sunday editor was likely to be there. The Sunday edition would be largely ready to go to the presses by this time. Amedeo summoned up sufficient detachment to help his son with the case he was engaged in. He drove back home in time for lunch. They had arranged to have a family lunch the following Sunday. It would be his daughter's child Emma's ninth birthday and the two families would come to the parents' house in Lecce.

When he arrived home, he drove the car directly into the garage, which was a converted stable from days gone by. Marta had laid the table. Antonella was back. Her usual cheerfulness was notably missing. She looked strained.

'I take it you had a difficult morning?' he enquired kindly.

Antonella shrugged the suggestion away. 'No, it was fine,' she answered.

'Ah!' he said. 'You've read the article then.'

She shook her head, puzzled. 'What article, Amedeo? What are you talking about?'

After a pause, she spoke again.

'Do you mean that you haven't seen the posters outside in the road?'

He shook his head.

'You had better come and have a look,' she added ominously.

2: Treacherous Undercurrents

Near their cliff-top summertime villa, there is a notorious spot in the Adriatic Sea, right at the very foot of a sheer cliff face, where the waters are so deep and treacherous that nobody dares to venture there. This part of the Adriatic has claimed countless lives over the years. The surface of the water looks unthreateningly calm. But below the surface, the swirling currents can drag the unwary swimmer – or even dinghies that have strayed into the area - into oblivion within seconds. Amedeo has stood in meditation on this spot many a time in his life, looking down with morbid fascination at the powerful surge of the sea. At this precise moment in his life, he is experiencing the terrifying sensation of being in the grip of such primeval elements and of being sucked down into a watery abyss. He has always suffered from a fear of drowning. Such a fate features regularly in his more disturbing, nocturnal dreams.

Antonella was there by his side. They were looking at one of those posters, so commonplace in the south of Italy, which inform everybody in the neighbourhood that a loved one has passed away. Antonella had often commented that, in a country which was corrupt and inefficient in so many ways, it was nothing short of a miracle that these posters announcing a bereavement appeared only hours after the departed souls had reached paradise. The posters usually stayed on the walls for weeks afterwards, becoming torn and tattered round the edges, until fresh posters, fresh departures from this life took their place.

Antonella and Amedeo were standing in front of a poster which had *his* face printed on it. They could clearly see another two identical posters further up the street. Even as they were looking, it was likely that a man was going round Lecce in one of those three-wheeler contraptions, powered by nothing more than a single cylinder scooter engine, putting up more posters informing the general public of the passing away of Judge Grassi.

'This is no April Fool's prank,' stated Antonella quietly to her rigid, tensed-up husband, who had briefly explained the contents of the newspaper article as they were walking out into the street. The posters bore the text of the much quoted words from the Gospel according to Saint Matthew:

Judge not lest ye be judged. For in the same way you judge others, you will be judged.

Judge Grassi's features had undergone a fearsome transformation. Gone were the composure and dignity that he normally assumed like a carnival mask for the sake of the world around him. The illusion of equanimity had disappeared, to be replaced by an intense and ugly puffing up of his features born of an interior rage. Antonella's face had altered too. She had seen this inner fury on her husband's face before, on the rare occasions when he allowed the hidden demons to take over. She had an enigmatic smile on her face that seemed out of place in the circumstances – as if she was drawing strength from her husband's discomposure.

Amedeo's hands, more like claws, reached out to rip the offending poster from the wall to which it had been pasted. Antonella laid a hand on his arm to prevent him carrying out his act of destruction. 'Wait!' she commanded calmly. 'Are you going to destroy the evidence, *mio caro?'* She had taken out her iPhone from her pocket and proceeded to take photos of the poster, including a close-up of the printer's name which was written unobtrusively at the bottom of the poster. The lithographic firm was a local one situated in the industrial zone of the city.

'Now you can tear it off if you still want to,' she said. But the judge had begun to reassume his everyday face again. He drew a deep breath and said simply, 'Let's go back inside.' She acquiesced. She took the crook of his arm – still rigidly held against his body as if to contain the rage that was threatening to erupt from within.

Lunch was on the table when they entered the spacious kitchen where the couple always ate when they did not have guests. Marta had prepared his favourite local pasta dish with *orecchiete,* bitter broccoli and anchovies. The judge picked at the food and even forgot to open the bottle of wine. Antonella secretly thanked the saints that she had found a means of reducing her husband's wine intake; all it required was for him to be deeply troubled. She was initially concerned that his anxiety would have the opposite effect. He sipped mineral water and did not seem to miss the wine at all.

'Long may it last!' she thought. Marta usually sat down and ate with them and conversation, although not scintillating, was normally spontaneous enough. Today, they ate in meditative silence. Amedeo looked at Marta thoughtfully. He realised that he had taken her existence in their household for granted for a long time. She must be only in her mid forties, he reckoned. He seemed to remember that she had grown-up children but realised that he knew nothing about them. She was really quite a striking looking woman, he thought, surprised by this minor revelation. She had always struck him as being a trifle dour, even melancholy. But today, she seemed to be more...*relaxed.* That was the word for it. Aware that he was staring at her, the judge made some apologetic comment about not being hungry. He was sure that she would understand why. 'Yes, of course, *dottore,*' she said with a brief smile. 'That is entirely normal in the circumstances.' She must have gleaned what was going on, he thought. She was, after all, an intimate part of the household by now. Another cup of coffee and the meal was over.

'Marta seems to be quite an intelligent woman,' he said to his wife afterwards, still somewhat surprised by his discovery.

'Why should she not be intelligent, *caro?*' replied Antonella with a certain glint in her eye. 'Not all cooks and housemaids necessarily have low IQs,' she added pointedly. 'Surely you are not committing the error of equating social standing with mental aptitude, are you?' Amedeo said he hoped he wasn't whilst admitting to himself that that was precisely the assumption he had been making until challenged by his wife. He winced inwardly when the words *'Don't judge by appearances'* sprang quite unbidden to his mind. He had been trying to keep at bay the emotions provoked by the wording on the poster.

Amedeo Grassi spent the rest of the afternoon in a state of frustration and introspection. He had tried to contact the editorial desk of *Il Quotidiano*, but there was nobody there who was willing to take responsibility for his unusual complaint. 'Can you call back on Monday morning, please *signore?*' was as far as he got despite all his attempts to persuade them that he was a force to be reckoned with. Even his threats were of no avail. Apparently, a judge who has retired and been declared dead loses some of his clout. He remained plain *signore*, despite the sympathetic noises

20

that his interlocutors managed to instil into their voices. He had marginally better fortune with the local TV station, *Telenorba*, who promised that they would look into the matter and 'react as appropriate'.

He continued brooding despite Antonella's attempts to persuade him that nothing bad had happened to him personally. She pointed out that a relatively small number of people would have seen the news – or the posters. The people who mattered knew that he was alive. 'After all,' she added, 'you have no reason to be anxious. You have nothing to hide, have you?' Even as she spoke, she knew that this assertion was questionable. *Everybody* in public office had *something* to hide. Amedeo was non-committal.

They usually went out together on Saturday evening, while Marta had the rest of the weekend off. Amedeo was reluctant to set foot outside their home. He would feel exposed, he explained. In the end, she persuaded him to go to the cinema with her to take his mind off the events of the day. 'The more people who see you acting normally, the better,' she said persuasively. 'In the cinema, you will be almost anonymous,' she added convincingly. They went to the Odeon cinema, right at the end of *via Libertini,* well known for showing high class films and having very uncomfortable wooden seats. The cinema hired out cushions to its clientele for the duration of the sitting. The film was about Giovanni Falcone – the anti-mafia magistrate who was blown up, along with his escort, by the Sicilian mafia, *Cosa Nostra,* in 1992. Not the best choice of film for the occasion, Antonella apologised afterwards, even if the production had been impeccable. But her husband replied that the film could have been about the latest sex scandals in Rome for all the attention he had been paying. But he kissed his wife briefly before retiring to bed and thanked her for her support. She left him to meditate on the significance of the day's revelations until he fell asleep in the early hours of Sunday morning. He feared that matters which had been laid to rest might be about to resurface, although for the life of him, he could not conceive how this could be. He dreamt that he was in the sea, struggling against a rising tide, clutching a rope held by some shadowy figure on the rocks above him.

* * *

Sunday morning. The judge and his wife always attended mass at the church of *San Matteo,* a glorious example of the many spectacular, baroque churches in the city. Apart from adhering to traditional beliefs and customs, Amedeo believed that attending mass was the public duty of a judge, even in retirement. He took pleasure in being seen walking arm-in-arm with his wife on their way to church. He was proudly aware of his public image as he and Antonella sat side by side, always near the front of the congregation, responding solemnly to the ritualistic mantras devised by Holy Mother Church to commemorate for all eternity the single historic event of Christ's Last Supper. During the sermon, he always managed to put on the appearance of someone listening intently to every word uttered by the priest whilst, in his mind's eye, he was choosing the wine that he would have with his Sunday lunch. It helped him endure the regurgitated menu of pious platitudes that was the usual fare.

On this Sunday morning, their walk to church was a furtive affair. They were helped by the fact that there was a light drizzle so that they could walk along under an umbrella. But, once inside the church, Antonella headed resolutely up the aisle to the place where they normally sat, leading her reluctant husband by the arm. People were so used to seeing them each Sunday that they aroused no curiosity. If anyone at all in the congregation had read Saturday's paper or seen the obituary posters in the street, they must have assumed that they had been mistaken – or had dreamt it.

The young priest who appeared in the pulpit high up above the worshippers that morning was unknown to the congregation at large. He had a beautiful face, topped with a head of curly black hair. He looked more like a celebrity than a priest. He smiled as he was making the sign of the cross. *'In the name of the Father...'* A kind of stifled gasp could be heard echoing round the church – whose congregation was at least sixty per cent female - as soon as the priest opened his mouth to speak. It was obvious to Judge Grassi that this was not going to be an ordinary sermon. And it rapidly became apparent that he would derive little consolation from the priest's beautifully modulated Italian.

'Judge not lest ye be judged. What amazing words!' began the priest whose voice sounded more like that of an incarnate angel. Antonella was not sure whether the jolt that she felt in her chair was because of a movement of surprise that she had made or whether it was due to the fact that her husband had started violently in *his* chair at the sound of the opening words of the sermon. She laid a calming hand on his arm and she could feel him trembling – or was it her arm that was trembling?

The young priest-cum-incarnate-angel was obviously not going to let the congregation slip into Sunday morning apathy. There were quite a number of young children present in family groups. He started off with them. *'Put up your hands if you still go to school.'* All the children's hands shot up spontaneously. *'How many of you LIKE school?'* asked the priest, changing the tone of his voice with each question. About three quarters of the children put their hands up. *'And how many of you would rather stay at home?'* The rest of the children plus some who had already voted in favour of school raised a hand in a more tentative manner. Little giggles ran round the children in the congregation. Their anticipation of boredom had been dispelled. Their eager young faces were turned upwards towards this unusual, smiling priest.

'Now!' he continued. *'Put your hands up if you have a teacher that you don't like all that much.'* A surprisingly large number of hands were slowly raised in response – after their owners had given a sidelong glance around the congregation to make sure that they were not the only ones. The priest nodded knowingly. *'I wonder how many of you are thinking about the same teacher?'* he asked in a hushed voice as if he wanted to be let into their mysterious and secret lives. Once again the children looked round, giggled a little and, recognising children in the same class, they nodded.

'Where does he think this is going to lead?' hissed Judge Grassi crossly to his wife. He had made a perceptible noise of disapproval. Antonella shushed him discreetly. She had been enjoying studying the perfect symmetry of the priest's face, his neat ears close to his curly mop of hair and the line of his jaw that descended past the kindly mouth down to a beautifully shaped, clean-shaven chin. The priest had noticed the tut of disapproval and was looking smilingly straight at the judge. *'Don't worry,'* said the priest in a mock stage whisper. *'You will soon understand.'* Judge Grassi wished that he had not drawn attention to himself.

'I'm just wondering about this teacher you say you don't get on with.' The invitation was irresistible. Hands shot up before parents could prevent the inevitable betrayal of the teacher whose reputation they were about to destroy. What a wonderful time they were having at mass today! Even better than being at home watching repeat DVDs. Antonella turned to her husband and whispered, 'I hope he realises that this teacher might well be here at the mass too.' The judge nodded but made no comment lest the sharp-eyed young priest singled him out again. But his performance was to be flawless. He was leading his 'audience' skilfully.

'Just a minute,' he said interrupting himself. *'I don't want to be perched half way up to heaven in this pulpit.'* Suppressed giggles from some of the congregation. *'I'm coming downstairs.'* And with those words, he disappeared out of sight. The fact that he reappeared almost simultaneously in the nave produced another gasp of surprise. 'Did you fly down, father?' asked one little girl. The priest laughed. *'Now where were we? Ah yes. The teacher you say that you don't like! Do you know what?'* He held up his arms in mock horror. *'I'm feeling sorry for your teacher already. Maybe she – or is it a 'he' - is having a hard time in life?'* There was a confused murmur about the teacher's gender. *'Perhaps her mum or dad is in hospital. Or it could be that her children are being disobedient and ungrateful. Did you ever think that she may be suffering more than you are?'* The children had fallen silent under the spell of the angel's voice. You could see them shaking their heads at this new idea. *'There you are! Now you know what Jesus meant when he said*

those words.' A dramatic pause allowed the words to register. *'What do you think is going wrong?'* There was a silence until one serious looking boy of about twelve years old said boldly: 'We've been judging our teacher too harshly, father.' *'What's your name?'* enquired the priest kindly. 'Giovanni,' the boy replied. *'You are a good boy, Giovanni.'* The priest's words were full of such warmth that the whole congregation began to applaud spontaneously. *'Now here's a question for you all. Do you think I'm a little bit crazy? Hands up if you think I am.'* A few people, adults and children, raised a hand uncertainly. But it was all so good-humoured that another titter of laughter ran round the congregation. Children who had been sitting further back got up and walked up the aisle to be nearer him. Nobody objected. In the space of two short minutes, he had captured the attention of the whole congregation and everybody, young and old, knew exactly what he was talking about. The priest laughed good-naturedly. *'Don't worry! I'm not crazy. Now I want you ALL to think very carefully. Can you tell me the name of just ONE person in this life – and I'm talking to the grown-ups too now – whom you never judge too severely? A person whom you forgive even if you know they have done something really wrong? One person whom you truly believe deserves forgiveness a thousand times a day - whatever they do? Can you think of anyone like that?'*

'My mum!' said a little girl. She got a hug and a loving word from her mother as everybody else smiled and applauded her briefly. *'I wish every child felt the same about their mum as you do, Agata.'* 'How did you know my name?' asked the little girl, surprised yet delighted. *'Because your mum just called you Agata.'* He was smiling warmly at the girl. But the priest was still after a different answer. *'But there* is *someone else special, somebody whom we find it very difficult to judge harshly.'* No answer from any of the congregation but they were all thinking hard. *'Giovanni? Can you think of this special person?'* The boy whom the priest had singled out previously looked at him and said:

'Yes, father. I think his name is Giovanni.'

'Come here, Giovanni.' The priest put an arm round Giovanni's shoulder and turned him round so that the whole congregation could see him – smiling shyly. *'Your mother and father must be so proud of you, Giovanni.'* 'Yes, we are,' said the mother with an expression of warm sincerity on her face. The priest held Giovanni by the shoulder throughout the remainder of his special kind of sermon.

'That special person is ME! It's each one of YOU! Think about it! How upset we become if people continually judge us and find fault with us. Now, I want you to go away after mass and think long and hard over the next week. Think of a person whom you have judged too harshly in the past; a person whom you have done a great wrong to; a person whom you have deeply offended. When we meet again you will be able to look at me – and Jesus – and say, 'I have done something to make amends to this person that I have wronged. Every one of you! Whether you are young or old, a postman, a bus driver, a nurse – even a judge,' he added. Once again, Amedeo felt himself singled out. He experienced a sensation of outrage that this priest seemed to be playing on everybody's sense of guilt. Or was it just *his* guilt?

'In the name of the Father and of the Son and of the Holy Spirit,' concluded the priest making the sign of the cross.

27

'Amen,' said nearly everyone. 'Thank you, father,' said a man in the congregation. 'In five minutes, you have given us an insight into ourselves and something real to think about.'

'What's *your* name, father?' asked the little girl, Agata, as the priest was walking away. Again the brief, infectious swell of laughter ran through the congregation. The incarnate angel turned round smiling and said, *'Gabriele'* and he vanished – behind a pillar.

Mass followed its preordained course. The young priest helped give out the hosts at communion. As Amedeo and Antonella stood up to leave after the blessing, Antonella thought she noticed a familiar figure leaving the church hurriedly.

'Look,' she said nudging her husband. 'Isn't that our Marta?' But the fleeting glimpse that she had caught was too brief and by the time they looked again, the figure had disappeared. 'Strange,' said Antonella. 'She told me that she was going home to Soleto.' The judge shrugged his shoulders.

'You must be mistaken, then,' he said indifferently. 'Ask her tomorrow if you want to satisfy your curiosity.'

To everybody's disappointment – including Judge Grassi's, who had intended having a quiet word with the man on the way out – there was no sign of their young preacher. The elderly parish priest was at the door shaking hands with his congregation as was his custom. 'Good morning, *signor giudice,*' he said.

'Who *was* that priest, father?' asked the judge rather more abruptly than he had intended – partly because he was afraid the priest would question his continued presence on the face of this Earth.

'Ah, you mean Don Gabriele! He is on loan to us from the Vatican for a few months. At his own request,' added the old priest. 'I think he hopes to teach us how to use computers, *and* how to deliver sermons, it seems.'

'Apparently so,' said the judge gruffly.

The couple walked home. Members of the congregation were in the street discussing animatedly the topic of the unusual sermon that they had been treated to.

'How did he know I was a judge?' asked Amedeo. The thought had been troubling him ever since the priest had ended his sermon.

'I *think* you are being a bit paranoid, *mio caro*. I am certain it was merely an accidental choice of profession.'

The judge grunted, unconvinced, even if he would have liked to believe it.

Amedeo and Antonella decided to go out to lunch instead of eating at home. They drove down to Nardò and ate at their favourite restaurant, *La Corte Santa Lucia.* They both felt the need to get out of the city.

The *padrona* looked in wide-eyed surprise at Judge Grassi. 'I do not wish to seem indiscreet, *signor giudice*. But ....'

'I am not dead,' replied Amedeo aggressively, 'if that is what you mean. It seems to be some kind of bad April Fools' Day hoax. Tomorrow, *cara* Claudia, heads will roll, I can assure you.'

The food was excellent as usual - and Amedeo drank water. 'I drink wine to celebrate being alive and kicking,' said Amedeo in answer to his wife's anxious enquiry. 'Not to commemorate my demise.'

Antonella drank nearly a half litre carafe of wine all on her own.

'Quite a reversal of custom,' she said with determined good-humour. The judge did not appear to be appreciating his food as much as he usually did, but ate with a kind of fierce resolution. Antonella refused to allow her husband's state of mind to detract from the joy of eating the *Santa Lucia's* superb cuisine.

'Ah well,' she thought. 'Tomorrow is Monday; the day when 'heads will roll'. That should prove interesting!'

3: Encounters of an Unexpected Kind

Judge Grassi was ready for action by seven o'clock. For once, he was up, showered, shaved and dressed before his wife had even stirred. He had put on his most formal looking dark suit to add weight to his mission. He was acutely aware nonetheless that, before his retirement, his impact on those around him would have been instantaneous, even if he had walked into a room with his pyjamas on. He meditated upon the illusory nature of power. His thoughts returned to *that priest* who, inexplicably, had succeeded in touching a raw nerve. Amedeo had failed, however, to identify which particular nerve it had been. 'I bet that if I met him in the street, he wouldn't be so sure of himself!' thought the judge uncharitably. Amedeo, determined not to be intimidated by his walk to the city centre, set off looking defiantly at every passer by as if challenging them to doubt his continued presence on Planet Earth.

As chance - or destiny - would have it, the first person whom the judge ran into on the way to his prime port of call – the offending local newspaper – was the equally offending priest. It was a disconcerting experience in several ways. In the first instance, the young priest recognised the judge before he realised who was greeting him. So he made the tactical error of returning the greeting with a smile on his face – quickly mutated to a scowl as soon as he became aware of his mistake. But it was already a little late and it put the judge at a moral disadvantage. His initial failure to recognise the young priest had been partly due to the fact that he was wearing jeans, a T-shirt and trainers instead of a cassock.

'You seem to know who I am,' said the judge with a touch of surliness in his voice.

'Oh, yes, indeed I do!' replied the priest in an annoyingly cheerful manner. 'You are the gentleman who disapproved of my sermon yesterday. I recognised you immediately.'

'Your performance could hardly be graced with the word 'sermon', surely,' retorted Amedeo uncharitably. He had been irked by the priest's overt friendliness and wished to diminish its impact, behaving as if he had been back in the *tribunale,* discrediting a witness who had obviously evoked the sympathy of those in the courtroom. If the judge had hoped to disconcert the priest, he was instantly disillusioned.

'I agree with you entirely, *signore*,' he replied, grinning cheerfully, whilst looking the judge straight in the eye. 'Delivering sermons is quite definitely the prerogative of those who assume that they are always right.'

The implied criticism did not escape Judge Grassi, who instantly felt the familiar surge of anger swelling up from inside; a rage which he had great difficulty in keeping under control. The raw nerve had been touched again by this young priest for whom he had conceived such an inexplicable aversion. 'How dare he presume to pass judgement on *me!*' he thought indignantly and was instantly shocked to recall the message conveyed in this priest's sermon. He looked thunderously at his adversary – whose face displayed a benevolent expression of genuine sympathy.

'Look at you!' snarled Amedeo. 'You are not even dressed appropriately, young man. I do not believe that you really *are* a priest.' Any notion that Amedeo entertained of provoking an indignant response was foiled yet again. The priest seemed genuinely amused by the judge's outburst.

'I suppose you are right, strictly speaking, *signore.* In fact, I am more accurately speaking a monk. But I *am* ordained. I belong to the order of Saint Benedict. And you know how the expression goes: *L'abito non fa il monaco. 'Wearing a habit does not make a man a monk.'* I guess that I am taking that saying to its literal conclusion. I can still be a monk *inside* without having to wear the habit on the *outside*. Thus you see me as I really am,' he added with amused conviction.

Judge Grassi had had enough of this repartee – an exchange that was leaving him increasingly at a disadvantage. He put on what he hoped was his most judicially scornful demeanour and turned his back on the monk and made as if to walk away. The young Benedictine reacted by uttering a few quiet words with an intensity and kindness that came from deep within him. 'I hope sincerely, *signore*, that you will soon be relieved of the millstone round your neck. Inside you, I believe there is a good man waiting to get out.'

The judge made a rasping sound, almost like a snarl, turned tail and walked off with all the dignity that he could muster. After twenty steps or so, he turned round to see the effect that he hoped he had had on 'that upstart of a priest'. But the earthly angel, Gabriele, if that was his name, was nowhere to be seen. 'The impertinence of the man!' he later said to Antonella. His wife, however, would look increasingly thoughtful as he continued to relate the unfolding events of the morning.

After his encounter with this unusual representative of the Catholic Church, the judge soon reached the editorial offices of *Il*

Quotidiano in Via dei Mocenigo, still not able to identify the reason why this young monk should arouse such feelings of antagonism in him. His battered ego quickly began to recover as soon as it became apparent that he was going to be treated with the respect and deference that he was convinced was his birthright. The receptionist greeted him by his title and offered to accompany him in person upstairs to the editor's office. The editor, Claudio Sabatini, knew Judge Grassi well – by sight and by reputation. He had been warned by his staff that the report of the judge's demise, which had appeared in his newspaper in the Saturday edition, might have been an immense journalistic *faux pas.* He was naturally anxious to safeguard his newspaper's reputation – not to mention his own. He had, consequently, put his staff on full alert and told them in no uncertain terms to treat the judge with the greatest diplomacy and sympathy should he arrive at their main offices.

The editor, who was about the same age as the judge's son, Aurelio, leapt to his feet and came round to the other side of his desk with his hand held out, well before the moment he reached the point where the judge was standing. This gesture gave Judge Grassi a few seconds grace in which he could decide how to react. He certainly was not prepared to be caught out a second time that morning by committing the error of being affable to a potential adversary. He took the editor's hand and shook it firmly and briefly whilst managing to look accusingly into the newspaper man's face. He withdrew his hand immediately and launched into his verbal attack without delay.

'You owe me a very cogent explanation, young man. I hope that it will prove to be a satisfactory one,' he added pointedly. The editor was not about to attempt to justify his position.

'*Signor giudice,* I can only apologise profusely for this very disturbing lapse in our editorial security - for which I accept full responsibility, it goes without saying. I promise you that a full apology, rectifying the facts, will be published in tomorrow's edition; on the front page, of course. That is the very least we can do.'

'Yes, I agree that is the least you can do,' replied the judge, not yet wishing to relinquish the moral high-ground. 'You also need to investigate how such an outrageous oversight could have occurred.'

The editor, who refused to be provoked by the judge's verbal aggressiveness, indicated the comfortable swivel chair that was in front of his desk and gestured to Amedeo to sit down. He went round to his side of the desk, sat down and opened a yellow file.

'I've been thinking about the matter ever since I came in at seven o'clock this morning, *signore,*' he stated carefully, in the hope that the judge would at least give him credit for taking a personal interest in the matter of the damaging article. 'Would you like some coffee before we begin, *signor giudice?*'

The judge shook his head briefly, dismissively. Amedeo did not wish to allow the editor even a second's remission. The judge was certainly an imposing figure, considered Claudio Sabatini, looking at his steady grey eyes, the strong mouth and slightly Roman nose. 'I would not like to be on the wrong side of this man!' he thought, followed by the realisation that he already *was,* in point of fact. He needed to remain business-like, however, if he was to survive the next fifteen minutes unscathed.

'*Allora, non meniamo il can per l'aia,*' said the judge in peremptory manner.

'Indeed not, *signor giudice*. I have no intention of beating around any bushes, I can assure you. Allow me to explain to you in the first instance, sir, how the system usually works in cases when a well-known celebrity such as yourself...' The journalist hesitated.

'You don't need to mince your words, young man. You mean, when someone passes away, dies, *crepa!*' exclaimed the judge – not mincing *his* words.

'Thank you, sir. I am grateful that I can speak so frankly with you,' replied the editor, allowing himself a brief, hesitant smile. 'What usually happens is that a close member of the family, or occasionally a priest or family lawyer, will compose the obituary in advance of a well-known person's death and bring it to us in written form – but, increasingly, in some electronic form such as on a memory stick.' Claudio Sabatini paused to make sure that Amedeo Grassi had understood exactly what he was saying. The judge grunted and nodded with a single downward motion of his chin to show that he was following perfectly well.

'We call it, in newspaper jargon, *un coccodrillo.*' The judge's eyebrows went up in surprise despite his determination to maintain control over all his reactions.

'Why on Earth should it be called a crocodile?' he asked, his curiosity getting the better of him.

'I'm really not sure, judge. I suppose it has to do with 'crocodile tears'; tears shed when the person concerned is still alive - thus expressing a false emotion. It was a Roman journalist who invented the expression, I believe.'

'Well, at least I suppose I have learnt something that I did not know before,' said the judge with heavy irony. 'But it does not explain how you came by – and acted upon – this false information.' A horrible thought had just occurred to Judge Grassi.

'The original text; it wasn't brought in by a young person claiming to be a priest, by any chance? You just mentioned that these things are sometimes compiled by priests.' Even as he uttered the words, he was perceptive enough to realise that he was becoming paranoid about the young monk.

The editor was looking puzzled.

'No, judge,' he replied cautiously. 'As I understand it, the original text was handed in by ...' Claudio paused to select his words carefully, '... by someone claiming to be your son.' The editor held up one of those cheap, coloured plastic-coated memory sticks. 'On this!' said the editor.

Amedeo experienced a shock of surprise. He had seen his son using an identical gadget on several occasions. 'When was this brought to you?' he asked.

'According to my sub-editor, about three weeks ago,' replied the editor.

'And you say that this person claimed to be my son. What did he look like?'

'I... I don't know, judge. I'm sorry. We can ask my colleague in person, if you like.'

Judge Grassi reflected for an instant but decided against such a step whilst their conversation was in full swing. It would probably be counterproductive. If it had really been his son, then he would find out by asking Aurelio directly.

Instead, he looked at the editor and asked the other question that had been troubling his thoughts.

'Signor Sabatini. How can I put this?' he began.

But the editor, who was sharp, had anticipated that he would be asked a further question about the text.

'I believe that you are about to ask me if the text that we inadvertently published on Saturday had undergone any modifications from the original.'

Amedeo nodded his confirmation that this was precisely what he had been about to ask.

'Yes, is the answer to that question,' said the editor nervously, knowing that any explanation he gave would run the risk of being complex and reflect badly on his newspaper. But there was no point in attempting to dodge the issue.

'The original version on the *coccodrillo* did not include that very untypical section of the text that seems to cast aspersions on your career. That was added afterwards,' said Claudio looking uncomfortably at the judge, almost appealing to him not to delve any deeper into the issue. But, inevitably, the judge pressed the point home.

'So...' continued the judge, 'how did that extra sentence find its way into the final article? That is what *I* need to know.'

Claudio Sabatini had no alternative but to comply with such a reasonable request.

'Either someone on my staff added the offending sentence at the time the obituary went to print...which I have almost ruled out as a possibility, knowing as I do the person involved. Or...' Claudio took a deep breath before continuing,

'...someone has hacked into the newspaper's editorial system just prior to the article being printed and inserted the extra sentence.'

'Is it possible to do such a thing?' asked the judge, now completely out of his depth.

'It would have to be someone who is a very good hacker indeed. Someone who is well versed in the process involved in producing the copy. And it would have to have been done at just the right moment too; very early on Saturday morning. But yes, *signor giudice*, I regret to say that it can be done.'

At this point, the editor failed to tell Amedeo that there had been an incident of hacking into the paper's editorial system on a previous occasion, some years earlier. By coincidence, the judge had been directly implicated in this episode too. Except that Claudio Sabatini did not believe too readily in coincidences. However, he did not want to complicate life unnecessarily at this juncture without being sure of his facts.

Amedeo remained deep in thought for a few moments. Amidst the confusion of impressions that he had formed in his mind as a result of the editor's revelations, there was one aspect of the affair that remained to be cleared up.

'So *signore*,' he said finally to the editor. 'Who contacted you to tell you that the time was right to print my...obituary?'

'Once again, *signor giudice*, I can only tell you frankly that the person who phoned in purported to be your son. He was very upset. My colleague who took the call was very struck by that fact. Unfortunately, it was not the same colleague who accepted the original electronic version of the text, so it was impossible to say whether or not it was the same person in each case just by the sound of his voice alone. I am inclined to think that it must be. The whole affair suggests very careful and subtle planning.'

'Did the man who was claiming to be my son ask when the article would be published?' asked Amedeo shrewdly.

Claudio Sabatini looked at the judge with renewed respect.

'*Sissignore*,' he confirmed. 'Now you mention it, he did. And we told him that it would appear in the Saturday edition.'

'Then it would appear that your surmise about a hacker is correct, Signor Sabatini.' The judge had, to the editor's relief, ceased to patronise him with the title of 'young man'.

'Just one more thing for now; I think I *would* like to speak to your colleague after all - the one who met 'my son' when the original text was delivered - now that we have clarified the matter as far as we can. It would be interesting to know what this man claiming to be my son actually looked like.'

The editor had anticipated the request. But Amedeo learnt very little. The man who had delivered the *coccodrillo* on the memory stick had been in his late twenties or early thirties, wore a business suit, and spoke good Italian. The junior editor's description could easily apply to almost any young professional male in Lecce. That was all he could remember, he said apologetically.

Judge Grassi thanked the editor for his time, shook him less formally by the hand than when he had arrived – and left the offices of *Il Quotidiano* in thoughtful frame of mind.

* * *

His next port of call, as he was in the city centre, was his current account bank, just opposite the *Castello Carlo V.* He felt the need to re-establish some sense of normality in his life after the events of the morning. Up to this point, the judge had suffered little apart from a certain degree of embarrassment and humiliation. He had been buoyed up and carried along by the surge of his own anger and a sense of outrage that anyone should dare to invade his personal domain in this way. But matters were about to take a turn for the worse. By the time he left the bank, the full impact of what was happening to him would have struck him with the force of a bolt of lightening. A shadowy, unidentified figure had set about the task, deliberately and calculatedly, of bringing him to his knees.

The process of waiting to be served at one of the bank's *sportelli* was normal enough. The bank had been obliged to introduce a system of numbered tickets to avoid the perennial Italian problem of queue-jumping. Before the system was reluctantly introduced, a free cashier's desk was immediately targeted by a host of Italians, tired of waiting in what was intended to be a patient queue, making a bee-line for the next available counter. The clients tended to wait in a horizontal line, rather than waiting one behind the other. As soon as a cashier had become available, the more athletic – or ruthless – clients had elbowed their way to the vacant position with muttered excuses that they had elderly mothers to attend to, or young children who needed to be picked up early from school. The result was that the elderly or more courteous customers had had to wait indefinitely for their turn. Arguments amongst the waiting customers, whose patience was finally tried to the limits, had become more and more frequent as the length of time required to cope with the bureaucratic processes involved in dealing with each client's individual financial transactions had become increasingly protracted. The bank had become the great social equaliser, Judge Grassi had often thought to himself after he had plucked his numbered ticket from the dispenser near the entrance. Of all the places that he had occasion to visit, even before his retirement, the bank had been the one place where his importance and social standing meant nothing. He had had to wait his turn like anyone else and ceded his rightful place to the humble refuse collector or primary school teacher.

Thus, his feeling on this occasion was one of patient resignation. After all, the matter of the newspaper article could soon be put behind him and life could resume its usual course.

The first hint that all was not as it should be came as soon as he asked the pretty, young brunette behind the desk for an up-date of his current account. She had keyed in the details which the judge had given her on to the computer. A puzzled frown appeared on her flawless features.

'Something wrong?' asked the judge anxiously, as the first hint of alarm sent a wave of panic through his body.

'The account seems to have been blocked, *signor giudice.* I don't understand.'

Amedeo Grassi understood only too well. As soon as someone dies, their account is automatically frozen. 'I think that I should see the manager, *signorina,*' he said simply. His secret fear had just become reality; a fear that he had, up till now, succeeded in suppressing. The manager, whom he knew well, agreed to see him immediately. Amedeo spent nearly an hour with him. The judge had never particularly liked Signor Giovanni Cataldo, who struck him as typical of a man in this position; slightly overweight, a vaguely superior and bombastic manner and a voice that was too loud for comfort. *'Judge not, judge!'* he heard himself saying to his alarm. At least, the manager was efficient and listened to the story that Amedeo was forced to relate in some detail. He confirmed what the judge already suspected. His considerable pension, due to have been paid in on the last day of March, had been stopped.

'It could be that your expert hacker has been at work there too,' said the manager. 'You will need to get in touch with the INPS and try to sort out with them what has happened, *signor giudice*. This is really the first time that I have ever known such a case. This appears to be a finely tuned and malicious campaign against your person. I am truly sorry that I cannot help you more ably, *signor giudice*,' concluded the bank manager with something approaching genuine sympathy in his voice.

The INPS, as the judge was fully aware, was the body with the responsibility of administering the pensions of those who were employed by the State. The last thing that he felt like doing at that moment was trudging to the outskirts of Lecce, where their offices were located, and going into the details of this crushingly humiliating experience yet again with some junior employee. He made his way home on foot, wanting more than anything else to hide from the world and seek comfort from his strong, smiling wife. He felt suddenly bereft of all strength and support. He was a little boy again, walking home from school in his native Abruzzo after he had been mercilessly ragged by a group of older children. All he wanted was to reach home, be hugged by his mother, hide in his bedroom and lick his wounds in private.

Antonella listened to the events of Amedeo's morning with growing alarm, sitting round the kitchen table as they always had done. It never occurred to either of them to conceal what they were saying from Marta. She had silently witnessed so many of their family discussions whilst preparing coffees, lunches, dinners, piling dirty plates and cutlery into the dish-washer, usually with her back turned to them, that her presence was simply taken for granted. Her discretion was never doubted for an instant.

It came as a great surprise, therefore, when, during a very subdued lunch, Antonella had turned to Marta and said cheerfully: 'By the way, Marta, we thought we saw you in church yesterday.' They were astonished to see their housekeeper shake her head wordlessly and burst into a flood of uncontrollable tears. She ran out of the room followed immediately by a very concerned Antonella.

The phrase *'crocodile tears'* sprang to Amedeo's mind. But even as the inappropriate echo of the words that he had heard so recently faded from his mind, he had the unusual, intuitive impression that her tears had been, in some inexplicable manner, shed out of sympathy for him. *'Judge not, judge!'* he heard himself thinking again. He was forced to regard their housekeeper in a different light. She was a woman with hidden emotions which needed to be taken into account. The revelation came as a shock to him.

Antonella came back into the kitchen five minutes later, explaining: 'She said she was sorry about the outburst. She'll be alright again soon. It's just a family problem, she says.' It was apparent by the expression on Antonella's face that she was only partially convinced by this explanation.

For a brief minute or so, Amedeo forgot his own problems. He was not the only person who was suffering, it appeared. The judge had once again forgotten to open a bottle of wine. But Antonella opened a cupboard in the sideboard and poured them each a little glass of orange liqueur, setting one of the glasses in front of her husband without asking him if he wanted a drink.

'I shall telephone Aurelio and Teresa later on,' she said resolutely. 'Time for an emergency family meeting, I feel.'

What an amazing sense of comfort Amedeo drew from these few consoling words. He briefly took hold of Antonella's hand and squeezed it affectionately. He was surprised to see her give a little, secret smile and to notice the hint of tears gathering in the corner of her eyes. He recalled the words of Oscar Wilde – a writer whose pithy sayings the judge greatly appreciated. *'Women were created to be cherished, not to be understood.'* The reactions of the two women in his immediate vicinity had left him perplexed. But he was too preoccupied by his own situation to grasp the nature of the emotions that he had just witnessed – so he gave up trying, thereby delaying by several days, revelations that might have spared him some of the pain that was still to come.

4: Family Matters

Since Amedeo refused to leave the confines of his own home, *(Could he even truly consider it his 'own' home any longer, he wondered, bereft as he was of his main source of income and his status reduced to that of an itinerant ghost?)* it was decided that Aurelio and Teresa should come to their parents' apartment in Lecce the following morning while the children were at school. But there was still a whole night to be endured before Tuesday arrived and Amedeo was not expecting the passage through the early hours to be easy to bear.

He and Antonella delayed the moment of going to bed for as long as possible. They sat together on the sofa watching whatever was on the television until, at about half past eleven, their eyelids grew too heavy with sleep to resist the need to retire for the night. Telenorba had spent a creditable three and a half minutes of local news time dealing with an unusual item about a certain Judge Grassi who had suffered the disturbing experience of finding his own obituary in the local newspaper. The TV station had telephoned Amedeo earlier to tell him what to expect. He had declined their invitation to appear live and so they had had to content themselves with a brief video clip of him which they had found in their archives. The newsreader had put forward a number of possible motives to explain this 'vindictive act'; an April Fools' Day hoax, an individual or a family with a personal grudge against the judge as the result of the perceived injustice of his verdict. The news report even hinted that the hand of the local mafia might be behind the affair. It was a well known fact that

Judge Grassi had once handed out a protracted prison sentence to a cousin of the local *boss*.

Amedeo had reached for the remote control and would have changed the channel, but at that moment, Marta had come into the room to bid them goodnight. She had begun to watch the news item too, so it would have seemed churlish to turn it off.

'Are you feeling alright, Marta?' asked Antonella kindly, as soon as the report had finished and the judge had turned down the sound.

Marta apologised to them both for her tearful outburst. She said that she would tell them about the family problem very soon and then they would understand. She had said 'goodnight' with a sad, half smile on her face before she had left the room. Amedeo was struck anew by the perfectly balanced features of her attractive face, not to mention her shapely rear view as she had turned round to leave the room. His thoughts were not lascivious but rather registered surprise that he had not taken proper notice of this third member of their household before. There was also something about her features that reminded him of someone else. But that other person's identity eluded him and he dismissed the thought as fantasy.

Marta had a comfortable en-suite bedroom on the second floor of the spacious apartment. They had heard her footsteps walking along the tiled hallway and ascending the marble stairway with an agility that did not appear to match the sadness of her smile. Antonella looked quizzically at her husband, but he seemed unaware of the discrepancy. 'I read too much into everything,' she considered and put the intriguing thought out of her mind.

Amedeo had done all he could to make sure that he was weary enough to fall asleep almost as soon as his head touched the pillow. There was very little that he could do, however, to prevent the vivid images of his dream world invading the tranquillity of total oblivion like an alien army of his own personal demons. He witnessed his own son, disguised as a hooded monk, entering the darkened offices of *Il Quotidiano* and saw him, quite unequivocally, handing over an orange memory stick to the editor. They were both smiling at each other in conspiratorial manner. Without any transition, he found himself once again in deep water struggling to reach the shoreline where his wife was stretching out her hand to help him. But as he was about to take her hand, she withdrew it with a serene smile on her face as she uttered the words: 'No, *mio caro.* Not until you have begged my forgiveness for all the times you have been unfaithful to me during our married life. Starting with that little brunette tart who used to be your *secretary!* And look, *amore mio,'* continued the image of the wife whom he thought he knew so well. 'I've got *your* pension as well now,' she finished off triumphantly, waving what looked like a gold-plated credit card in his face.

Amedeo felt himself thrashing around in the water as his head sank below the surface. His feet searched for the sea bed but he was out of his depth. 'PLEASE HELP ME!' he called out as he swallowed the first mouthful of black, salty sea water. He woke up, gasping for air. He was the scared little eight-year-old boy again reliving the time when he had nearly drowned in the Adriatic Sea on holiday with his parents - an only child, who was about to leave his parents for ever and be sucked down to a watery grave. It was another holidaymaker who had saved him, only a few metres from the beach, and led him white-faced and terrified back towards his parents. As if by instinct, Amedeo, the adult, got out of bed and crept into his wife's room, for the first time in ages, seeking the comfort of her warm sleeping body.

Feeling the movement of an unaccustomed presence next to her, Antonella stirred in her sleep and then began slowly to regain consciousness. She turned round so that they were facing each other in the darkness.

'Bad dreams, *amore?*' she asked in a sleep slurred voice. He just nodded, not thinking that the wordless gesture would be lost in the darkness. She seemed to understand by the slight movement in the shadows that his answer had been 'yes'. She put her arms round him and pulled him closer. More to Amedeo's surprise than even to that of his wife, he began to feel aroused. She responded with a secret feeling of happiness inside her. The dormant volcano of her husband's passion had come to life after an eon of sexual slumber. The eruption was not on the scale of Mount Etna but Antonella was not complaining.

In the quiet afterglow of their intimacy, Amedeo spoke softly to his wife.

'I'm sorry about all the times I have been unfaithful to you, *amore mio*. Even though it has been a long time since...' The time remained unspecified even though he remembered exactly when the last time had been. 'You did not deserve that treatment. I am ashamed about the number of occasions ...' That sentence too was left unfinished. 'I don't know how many times ...' he began yet again.

'Oh, I *knew* on every single occasion, *mio caro!*' interrupted Antonella quietly but without malice. 'Only men are naïve enough to believe that they can conceal their wayward behaviour from us women.'

'*O Dio*', said Amedeo, 'Every time?'

'Yes, *every* time'

'But how...?'

'A different smell, a furtive shower, an unscheduled cleaning of the teeth, a sudden loss of appetite because the stomach cannot take a second meal, suddenly taking to using aftershave - there are a myriad little indications,' said Antonella with something resembling the glee of a tormentor expressed in the forcefully uttered words.

'You put me to shame, *amore*,' said Amedeo humbly. 'And to think that you have remained so faithful to *me*. I do not deserve a wife like you.' The words could have sounded hackneyed and false had it not been self-evident that they had been said in complete sincerity. The sheets rustled as Antonella changed her position with a sudden gesture, preceding a change of mood.

'*Mio caro Amedeo!* I put up with it all because I love you. I always have, despite, rather than because of, the way you are. But what makes you so certain that I have always been so faithful to *you?*' she added quietly after the briefest of pauses. 'How do *you* know that I do not have a lover *now?* You may have just noticed that I still enjoy the act of *sex.*' The last word had been spat out emphatically. It had come out more forcibly than Antonella had intended - the verbal equivalent of waving the proverbial red rag to the bull. Her *toro*, however, had fallen silent. It was taking Amedeo some considerable time to digest the blow to his male pride. In the end, he said in breathless disbelief, not without a hint of fear in his voice:

'*Amore,* you surely cannot mean that you have been making love to someone else? I mean...'

Antonella was almost enjoying herself. 'Do you mean that you don't think I am still attractive to men?' she asked, with that menacing edge to her voice that only a very rash man would have dared to ignore.

'No, of course not, *amore,*' replied Amedeo, drawing back from the brink of disaster. 'You are a very desirable woman. I just meant ...' What *did* he mean exactly?

His wife was in no doubt whatsoever as to what he had meant.

'Surely you cannot be assuming, in these days of equality, that it remains the prerogative of the Italian male to be unfaithful whenever the fancy takes him, whilst the unfortunate woman has to languish in a state of sexual frustration and emotional rejection?' As usual, Antonella had succeeded in cornering her husband by expressing precisely what he had, in point of fact, been assuming.

'But *have* you been unfaithful to me?' he asked fearfully, not knowing at all how he would react if she answered in the affirmative.

Antonella pulled the husband that she loved towards her again and said: 'I leave *you* to work out the answer to that question, my beloved husband.' And that, was all she would say. She kissed him firmly on the mouth in the intimate darkness of the room, turned over and fell into a peaceful slumber until the morning light entered 'their' bedroom.

Whereas his wife had succeeded in putting aside all other issues in favour of sleep, Amedeo was left to stew in his own juices for the remaining hours of darkness. He lay on his back, staring up at another vaulted ceiling, just as he had done a few days previously. This time, the ceiling was shrouded in darkness, as was the drift of his sombre meditations.

His wife's closing words had left him in a state of confusion. At first, he managed to dismiss the thought that his wife would ever make love to another man. 'She would never do that!' he tried to convince himself. She was merely asserting her right to be loved by *him*, and him alone, he reasoned. But then, he got to thinking that it was just his wounded pride that refused to allow him to accept the very likely possibility that other men would find her attractive, and, furthermore, that the hurt that he must have occasioned her in the past, would be quite enough to push her into the arms of other men, if only to correct the emotional imbalance.

Suddenly it occurred to Amedeo that all her trips down to Melissino, purportedly to visit the pasta 'farm', had been a skilful ploy to cover her tracks. Yes, that was it! She *did* have a lover - in Melissino. It was so obvious now. He would not stand for this. He would leave her tomorrow and go and live ... But where? How? He could not even gain access to his own bank account any more. His dependence on his wife was absolute. He managed to perceive dimly that the true source of his suffering was not so much the fact that Antonella might be having an affair, although that was bad enough. No, what wounded his pride even more was the realisation that *his* frequent affairs had been totally transparent to his wife, whereas *she* had succeeded totally in hoodwinking him. It was *that* that rankled more than anything else. He wanted to wake her up there and then so as to face her with the accusation and let her know that he was not so easily duped. 'You are guilty not only of infidelity,' he would say. 'But of deception and disloyalty.' That's right! He would pass judgement on her and only later would he consider forgiving her.

Naturally enough, the word *'judgement'* triggered off in his mind memories of the priest and his wretched sermon. Judge Grassi got angrily out of his wife's bed and returned to his own bed. But it was cold and unwelcoming and his thoughts continued to torment him. He was haunted too by the image in the dream of his son furtively visiting the offices of *Il Quotidiano*. Of course! That too was obvious. Aurelio had always been on his mother's side if there had been any disagreement, however slight. It was a conspiracy, he decided. Aurelio was in cahoots with the editor. They were all in this together to punish him. What - even his daughter? Why not, he thought. Thus the seeds of paranoia were sown in his overwrought mind. He slept for maybe an hour before he was woken up by Antonella, smiling kindly at her husband, carrying a small cup of morning coffee to revive him. His muffled thanks were all tangled up with his inner conviction that he was a victim of a family plot. When he finally entered the kitchen to find Antonella waiting for him at the table, indicating the chair next to her with an inviting smile, he sat reluctantly down beside her. She was holding an official letter from the INPS, offering their condolences for the family's loss and informing her that she would be receiving 60% of her husband's pension from the end of the month.

'Don't worry, Ame.' She had not used the affectionate abbreviation of his name for *years*. 'We shall sort this matter out together when the children get here.'

Amedeo Grassi was fighting off another attack of paranoia brought on by his newly hatched family conspiracy theory.

* * *

The first member of the family to arrive was their daughter, Teresa. She hugged her father affectionately, as she always did when she saw him. Amedeo felt instantly reassured. There surely could be no guile hidden behind that spontaneous gesture – unless, of course, she was an accomplished actress. But then, unbidden, came the thought that her mother had displayed the ability to conceal her true feelings over many years, as their conversation in the early hours had shown; his feelings of reassurance consequently diminished by a few degrees, based on nothing more substantial than the presumed similarity in character of mother and daughter.

'Who's looking after the shop this morning Terri?' asked Antonella.

'Oh, Laura can cope admirably,' replied her daughter. 'She loves the opportunity to play at being the expert in fashionable clothing.' Teresa had, with the help of her mother's money, opened up a fashion boutique in Lecce's well-to-do modern district in one of the many busy streets around the *Piazza Mazzini*. The boutique had developed a healthy reputation and appealed to the fashion conscious ladies, young and not so young, of the city. Teresa took after her mother in this respect. She had shown no desire to follow an academic path. She possessed her mother's business acumen in large measure. Her husband, Leonardo, was the academic. He was a physicist who had recently been appointed professor in the University of Salento's well-established nanotechnology department. One academic in the family was enough, Teresa had decided as she had thrown all her excess energies into making a success of her business.

'And little Emma?' asked Antonella. To Amedeo, the question seemed unnecessary. Obviously, she was at school. But Teresa knew that the simple question carried a more covert message.

'*Little Emma'*, as you are fond of calling her,' replied *Little Emma's* mother with a touch of ill-concealed pride in her voice, '... is under threat of having to eat plain pasta for a month if she ever indulges in the luxury of correcting her teacher in public ever again.' Antonella laughed at the turn of phrase. Young Emma had, on repeated occasions, told her primary school teacher that her sums were wrong, that her spelling was not accurate and that her hair needed washing.

'She takes after her mother when she was that age,' said Antonella with vivid memories of her own daughter's outbursts of uncensored home truths at inopportune moments – all that at the tender age of seven.

A morose Judge Grassi was listening to this exchange with gloomy fascination. Yet more evidence of shared information to which he was not privy.

His son, Aurelio, arrived soon afterwards. It was evident from his body language that he would rather have been elsewhere but he was determined to put a brave face on it. He gave his father a peremptory hug and muttered a few words of consolation about the problems his father was facing. Amedeo had the distinct impression that Aurelio secretly thought that his father had brought his troubles on himself. Aurelio hugged his mother for a significant fraction of a second longer than he had hugged his father. He excused himself for seeming abrupt but explained that he was due in court later on that morning.

Down to business round the kitchen table. Marta served them coffee and *biscotti* and asked whether they wished her to leave the kitchen. Amedeo shrugged his shoulders and looked round the table. 'No, you can stay if you want, Marta,' said Antonella warmly. She had decided that any departure from their normal rapport with their housekeeper would give the impression that they had something to hide. Marta came and went at regular intervals as she started to prepare lunch or went upstairs to tidy the bedrooms.

Amedeo related everything that had happened to him the day before, including his encounter with the monk in jeans. Marta had briefly turned round with a smile on her face when Amedeo had repeated the priest's comment about sermons. Once again, Amedeo experienced that brief stab of recognition. Aurelio was mildly shocked when his father had told him that the well-dressed young man who had handed in the memory stick had pretended to be him. The unconscious look of appeal on the judge's face prompted Aurelio to say:

'Don't look at me like that, *papà*. I would never dream of presenting a newspaper with your obituary without consulting you first. I am not expecting you to depart this life for another twenty or more years.' Amedeo's father had lived until he was nearly eighty-eight.

When the judge had finished telling them about the previous day's events, the group became thoughtful for several minutes before Teresa broke the silence.

'Well! I have refused to pay my *pizzo* to the local mafia gang who are supposed to be 'protecting' my shop premises,' she declared and was greeted by a stunned silence. 'Not just *me*. I'm not *that* brave! No, all the *commercianti* in and around the *Piazza Mazzini* got together about two weeks ago. Nearly all of us agreed that enough was enough. They have been extracting something like 20% of our takings for the privilege of not having our shops torched in the middle of the night.'

'*Bravi tutti voi!*' said her brother. Reaction against this intrusion, by a handful of ruthless mobsters, into the daily life of those trying to run businesses had been steadily growing in the 21st Century - especially after a shopkeeper, who had been working late behind the scenes in his shop, carrying out a routine stock check, had suffered severe burns when his shop had been set alight by those who dared to call themselves *The Protectors.*

A case had been brought by the *carabinieri* against the fairly obvious culprit, who had been fleetingly identified by the shopkeeper. He was a cousin of the local *boss.* Judge Grassi was well aware of the case. By the time the trial had reached his final court of appeal, funded by the seemingly bottomless coffers of the local clan, the *mafioso* cousin had been in custody for three years. Judge Grassi had been roundly and publicly censured by the press for delaying the final decision for two weeks and then reducing the 15 year sentence to a mere additional three years. He had justified his decision with consummate ability, pointing out the weaknesses in the prosecutor's case, which had depended almost entirely, he argued, on the victim's brief identification of the arsonist. The judge had been covertly accused of colluding with the local mafia boss – an accusation which he had always calmly and convincingly denied.

Nothing was said by anyone sitting around the family table for a seemingly protracted period of time, but Amedeo knew what thoughts were passing through the minds of his children. It was Antonella who broke the silence, coming loyally to her husband's defence.

'Your father came to the only possible legal conclusion in the circumstances,' she said firmly. There had been no need for the reason for their silence to be explained in words, since this scene had been played out on a number of previous occasions around the same family table.

'Besides which,' said Teresa coming to the rescue in her turn, 'we are not here to dwell on the past. And I cannot see a link between what is happening to *papà* and our campaign to stop paying the *pizzo* to the local mob. This campaign smacks of something far more intimate and personal. It is just not the mafia's style. In any case, from the mafia viewpoint, *papà* seems to have acted in their favour. *Scusami, papà.* But you know what I'm saying.'

Amedeo nodded in acquiescence but added no comment. The whole case of the *mafioso* cousin had been a nightmare.

'No,' continued Aurelio. 'We should be looking for an explanation much closer to home.'

Another significant pause before anyone dared to put thoughts into words. Marta, who had been putting clean plates back in cupboards, clearly understood which direction the discussion was going to take and tactfully decided to go out and do a bit of extra shopping.

'You have to admit, *papà*, that there have been *indiscretions* in the past. You were a bit of a Casanova in your younger days. Maybe we should be looking in that direction?' This, from the ever pragmatic Teresa! Aurelio nodded in agreement, giving his mother an apologetic glance.

The turn that this conversation had taken was not to the judge's liking and he was looking increasingly uncomfortable. The old familiar anger was stirring inside him, tempered by a realisation that what his offspring were saying might well be true. Only *he* knew to what extent this might be true. Once again, it was his wife who came to his rescue.

'Let us not make this a personal issue,' she said. 'Your father and I have come to a far greater understanding of each other during the course of last night. There are many other possible avenues to explore before we jump to conclusions.'

'Thank you, *amore*,' said Amedeo quietly and with a degree of humble gratitude that took his children by surprise. 'Nevertheless, it has to be admitted that the explanation might well lie in that direction.'

They had nothing to go on, in reality. The events through which Amedeo had lived over the past few days did not seem to fit exactly into any of the categories that they had discussed. The whole scenario was shrouded in an aura of mystery. It had been more like a theatrical performance put on for Amedeo's benefit.

'It's like a *giallo.* An Agatha Christie plot,' said Teresa – who else – with a look of girlish merriment on her face which transformed the atmosphere of growing gloom around the table into something lighter and more manageable.

'Come on *papà*. I'm going to take you to the INPS office. Sorting out your pension is a practical step that needs to be taken at once. Let's wait and see if anything else happens. Otherwise, we will be speculating *ad nauseam* but getting nowhere.'

Amedeo hugged his daughter and the family meeting broke up amicably.

'Don't forget to take all your ID and documents with you, *papa*,' added Aurelio. Amedeo was grateful to his family for their support. But, in his heart of hearts, he knew that there was some darker element upon which they had not yet touched. He did not try to express any of this to his daughter as they drove to the outskirts of the city, round the chaotic ring road where vans, buses and helmetless scooter drivers dodging round badly parked cars, were all trying to fight for the few metres of free space in front of them to enable them to go about their daily business. What a contrast to the historic city centre where traffic was mercifully restricted to the limited number of vehicles displaying a resident's permit.

Going to the INPS office did not turn out to be straightforward. Not that Amedeo was expecting an easy ride from this highly bureaucratic State body. This was, after all, his beloved Italy, where the least important transaction – even paying an electricity bill – can involve the work of several minutes and the signing and duplication of a multitude of bits of paper and counter receipts. The people employed in such establishments seem to take a perverse delight in observing every single bureaucratic rule down to its last dotted 'i'.

Thus, Amedeo and his daughter rapidly discovered that it was much easier to convince them of his demise than it was to persuade them that he was still alive, over the age of sixty-five and a genuinely deserving recipient of a State pension.

'But I have a death certificate from your doctor!' exclaimed the young clerk in his twenties. This revelation provoked a jolt of disagreeable surprise. His persecutor was being alarmingly thorough.

'Then it must be a fake. As you see with your own eyes, I happen to be very much alive. There has been a slight misunderstanding. I am, quite simply, not dead,' he attempted to explain to this disbelieving youth. In the end, the youth was dispatched to seek out a superior ranking manager.

'Ridiculous!' commented Teresa. 'So much for Holy Mother Church's credibility in asserting the resurrection of the dead,' she commented ironically.

In the end, they had to agree to come back on Thursday to see a committee of managers, whose minds could not readily cope with this unprecedented situation. There was no written instruction *anywhere* in the building which covered the eventuality of a pensioner returning from the grave.

'And could you please bring a certificate from your doctor stating that ...'

'Yes, we will do that,' interrupted Teresa to pacify the youthful bureaucrat. 'You mean a kind of non-death certificate, I suppose,' she added sarcastically. Her irony was wasted, however. The youth merely nodded in appreciation of her grasp of the situation.

Outside, a despondent and frustrated ex-judge, ex-member of the human race, thanked his daughter and gave her a warm *bacio* on each cheek. 'You get back to your boutique,' he said. 'I'll walk home through the old town. I need to calm down. And be careful about crossing the local mob,' he added, anxious about his daughter's defiant stance against paying protection money.

Twenty minutes later, he turned into the narrow road that led from the park into the walled city, under an archway. He felt drained and demoralised, and increasingly inclined to allow events to take their course. He was not interested in rooting around in his past to find out who bore him such a grudge that they would go to these extreme lengths to vent their resentment and anger. He must have, quite inadvertently, done something really bad, something of which he was totally unaware. He was just about to feel relief at his decision to ignore his problems – even though he knew that Antonella would never accept this defeatist attitude – when he happened to notice a new, white plaque on the wall by the side of two big wooden doors that led into another antique building similar to their own. The wording caught his eye immediately. 'Alessandro GRECO – private investigator. *We guarantee an expert service and complete discretion.'*

Judge Amedeo Grassi stood looking at the plaque with its neatly formed blue and red lettering for at least five minutes before deciding that, at the very least, he had nothing to lose by going inside and gaining a first impression of the unaccustomed and slightly shady world of the private investigator. If he gained a positive impression of this Alessandro Greco, he could leave the solving of this mystery to a third party. What a blissful sensation of relief he would feel!

He rang on the intercom bell and a beautifully modulated female voice invited him upstairs – to the third floor, second door on the left.

5: Alessandro Greco's Detective Agency

Alessandro Greco's qualifications for opening a private investigation bureau were practically non-existent. He had completed his university degree at Lecce University – the renamed *L'Università del Salento* – studying *Beni Culturali,* which is the course that many students, without a specific vocational aim in life, study with a view to becoming art critics, restorers of old masterpieces, museum curators or, more ambitiously, sculptors, painters or musicians in their own right. As a consequence, at least fifty per cent of graduates from this praiseworthy discipline end up without employment. It takes three or four years to complete the degree but existing museum curators, art critics and restorers of old paintings generally remain in their posts for the whole of their working lives. Thus, saturation point in this job market was reached some considerable time ago.

In his favour, Alessandro Greco was a prepossessing young man of twenty-seven, intelligent, computer literate and a very good communicator. More significant was the fact that he had a rich, retired uncle in Lecce who had agreed to let his nephew use his former architect's studio in the city centre rent free. He had had his arm twisted by his brother, Alessandro's father, to *'give the lad a chance'.* The uncle had allowed himself to be persuaded to accept no rent for the studio in the firm belief that the arrangement would only be temporary. In the uncle's view, people who studied *Beni Culturali* at university were automatically destined to spend the rest of their working lives slaving away over a hot griddle in a McDonalds or becoming hospital porters – the latter only if they were *really* ambitious. It galled the uncle that

Alessandro was still occupying his studio, free of charge, after one whole year had elapsed – and in addition, that he was making a success of the business. That was the last straw.

Business had been very sluggish in the first few months. His bread and butter income had been earned by dealing with husbands, wives and engaged couples who were convinced that their partners were being unfaithful. In one case, he had been separately approached by the same couple to investigate the misdeeds of the other partner. In point of fact, he had succeeded in demonstrating that both partners were being unfaithful to each other. It had required skilful diplomacy and exact timing to avoid husband and wife finding out that they had unwittingly employed the same agency. But generally speaking, and to Alessandro's mild surprise, in only three cases out of ten, statistically speaking, had he been able to show that any infidelity had taken place. In most of the other cases, Alessandro had discovered nothing more serious than unfounded suspicions, jealousy or fear of betrayal.

Then Alessandro had hit upon a brilliant idea. His reputation was greatly enhanced and the scope of his remit broadened when he set himself up as a specialist agent offering to help the numerous English and American people who came to Puglia to buy properties in the almost permanent sunshine. It was all too frequent for unsuspecting and ill-prepared foreigners, whose ability to understand and speak Italian was limited to ordering their daily pasta dish, to fall foul of devious lawyers, crafty vendors who failed to tell them about structural faults and local builders who automatically doubled their estimates as soon as they sniffed the presence of a foreigner. Alessandro had set up his own website and gradually attracted a small but faithful clientele.

His reputation grew by word of mouth or, just as likely, by word of Twitter. He had understood that English-speaking house-buyers would be more than happy to pay him the fee out of the money that he had usually saved them. He was very glad that he had taken pains to acquire a good level of spoken English, thanks to good teaching at his high school and a memorable Englishman called Adam, who had taught him at university.

It had soon become apparent that he had more work than he could cope with on his own. He had wisely decided that his business required a female assistant to help him carry out investigations where a woman's touch was needed. So he had put an advert in the local paper, on the web, and also used the local employment agencies to spread the net as far as possible. He had been surprised, even overwhelmed, by the response that his advertisement had produced.

He had had to devote the best part of two afternoons to interviewing prospective candidates. The process of selection might easily have taken him many more sessions had it not been for the arrival, at 15h30 on the second afternoon, of a beautiful woman in her late thirties, who insisted that she be called Elena Camisso – even if that was not her real name, she had added.

'Just for the records, *signorina,* may I know what your actual name is?' Alessandro had asked his prospective candidate.

'Thank you for the *signorina,'* she had said. 'But I suppose *signora* would be more appropriate. I have two young children and a partner. My real name is Rosaria Miccoli. But I have found that, in this line of business, it is safer not to go around telling everybody who you really are.'

Alessandro had been stopped in his tracks for a whole five seconds while her words sank in.

'Do you mean to say that you have done this kind of work before?' he asked holding his breath in expectation.

'Elena Camisso' had gone on to relate how she had helped her friends find stolen purses in discos, caught out unfaithful partners, unearthed insurance and tax-dodging scams, revealed several fraudulent attempts by dishonest clients who sought to borrow monies on the basis of incomes that they did not have. She had rounded off her non-stop catalogue of achievements by telling Alessandro a fantastic tale of how she had, with the help of her English partner, tracked down and 'dealt with' a Calabrian *mafioso* in London who had murdered her cousin and best friend.

Alessandro had decided on the spot that he had just found a suitable assistant. He had just stopped himself saying 'partner in crime'. The other girls that he had interviewed had all been attracted by the glamour of being a mere secretary to a private detective. Elena-Rosaria had actually *done* the things which would be required of her – and more besides.

For form, he asked her about her computer skills. 'Very advanced, *dottore,*' she had reassured him with a significantly conspiratorial gleam in her eyes, which left Alessandro wondering about the extent and nature of her skills. 'And do you speak English, Ros... Elena?' She told him about her English partner called Adam and there then ensued a conversation during the course of which it transpired that her Adam was the same Adam who had taught *him* at university.

'But, excuse me, Elena,' he began. 'Isn't Adam a bit ...'

'Older than me, you are about to say,' she said finishing the sentence for him. 'Is that going to constitute grounds for not offering me this post?' she added in a charming but challenging tone of voice.

'Certainly not!' he replied quickly. 'When can you start?'

'Give me a few days to sort out child-minders and partners,' she said with a radiant smile. 'How about next Monday?'

And thus it had been settled between them. A monthly salary of €1400 had been decided with a bonus added for each case solved. Elena-Rosaria had been delighted. So was Alessandro's twenty-four-year-old *fidanzata*, who had not been at all happy about the prospect of her fiancé spending his working hours in the presence of some sweet and single young thing from the provinces. Alessandro forbore to tell her that Elena/Rosaria, in her late thirties and blessed with two children, was ten times more attractive than anyone else that he had interviewed. He would cross that bridge when the time came.

* * *

It was 'Elena Camisso' whom Judge Grassi first set eyes on after he had walked up three flights of stairs and arrived slightly breathless at the studio belonging to Alessandro Greco's uncle. She smiled at him as soon as he set foot in the doorway, her eyebrows raised in mild surprise.

'Good morning, *signor giudice*,' she said brightly. 'Welcome to our studio.'

In the first few seconds, Amedeo Grassi was flattered that he had been instantly recognised and addressed by his title, reassured by the friendly welcome and attracted to the simple

69

beauty of this smiling *salentina* woman, who had managed to convey, in no time at all, the perfect balance between youthful charm and intellectual maturity.

'Ah,' he said. 'I see you know who I am and, therefore, you can probably guess why I am here.'

'I only know the little that I have gleaned from the TV and the local newspaper,' she replied politely. 'I would not want to make any assumptions as to the reasons for your visit. But we will be delighted to help you if we can,' she added, rounding off her perfect performance with a dazzling smile that dissolved any remaining doubts that the judge might have been harbouring about having to climb laboriously up three flights of steep stairs each time he needed to consult with Alessandro or his assistant.

Alessandro Greco came out of his adjoining office, whose door had been ajar, as soon as he heard Elena talking to someone. On seeing Alessandro for the first time, Amedeo gave an involuntary start of false recognition. This was simply because Alessandro corresponded exactly to the image that he had created in his own mind as to the appearance of the young offender who had handed in the memory stick containing his 'obituary' at the offices of *Il Quotidiano*. Alessandro experienced a similar reaction on seeing Amedeo. But this was because the judge reminded him of his uncle. Alessandro lived in daily expectation that his uncle would arrive out of the blue and demand that his nephew should start paying rent on his premises. As soon as they had both recovered from their respective shocks, Alessandro ushered the judge into his office. The sunshine was streaming in through the blinds. It was a nice, bright, efficient business environment, thought

Amedeo, without any sign of pretentiousness. His expectations were becoming more positive with each minute that elapsed.

Instead of sitting behind his desk, Alessandro indicated a sizeable, round, wooden table which had six chairs around it. 'Let's sit here to discuss matters, shall we, *signor guidice?* A round table is more democratic, don't you think?'

'So,' thought Amedeo. '*He* recognises who I am, as well.' It was doubly reassuring. He felt that he was about to be treated seriously.

'I would like my assistant, Elena, to be present too, *signore,* if you have no objections, of course. She often sheds light on matters that other people miss.' The judge acquiesced with a fleeting, business-like smile and a slight shrug of his shoulders to indicate … what? Indifference? Lack of opposition? Alessandro could not be sure. Elena Camisso came in with a notepad and pen in hand and sat down between the two men. They could see each others' faces without having to crane their necks round.

'So would you like to tell us all the details of these unusual last few days, *signor giudice?* I am, of course, assuming that that is the reason why you are here,' he added smiling. 'From what we have read in the papers and seen on the local TV, it is certainly a very unsettling affair.'

Again Amedeo Grassi merely nodded. He had had a reputation for maintaining an enigmatic lack of expression on his face when he was presiding in the *tribunale.* He found it difficult to drop the mask whenever he was in public.

'Don't leave anything out, please, *signor giudice.* Any little detail might prove to be significant later on,' added Alessandro. And so the judge told them everything from the outset, leaving out nothing. He even went into details about the Sunday sermon and the fact that the young priest – or monk, rather – had used the same text about judging others as had appeared on the posters in the street. Alessandro exchanged the briefest of glances with Elena, who was writing cryptic little notes as she was listening. But, despite his innate ability to sum up the facts, Amedeo did manage to omit certain details which his mind had filtered out of the narrative because they did not seem essential to *him*.

'So you live on your own with your wife, *signor giudice?* Is that the case?'

'Yes,' replied Amedeo. 'There's Marta, our housekeeper, of course,' the judge added as an afterthought.

Again there was that brief but meaningful exchange of glances between Alessandro and Elena.

'Ah,' said Alessandro. 'Does your housekeeper live with you under the same roof?'

'Yes, but surely ...' the judge left the sentence unfinished.

'We just do not know, at this stage, what may or may not have a bearing on what has happened to you,' added Alessandro. 'Try not to leave anything out, please *signore.'*

'How long has this Marta been with you?' asked Elena, speaking for the first time. Amedeo could not remember precisely. She had just appeared one day when he had come back from the courtroom. Antonella had dealt with the appointment when their previous housekeeper had left one day and never returned.

'It seems like quite some time,' he answered. 'But in reality, I suppose she came to us only about nine months ago.'

'A suitable gestation period, I suppose,' said Elena as if she had been thinking out loud.

'Pardon?' said the judge.

Alessandro laughed quietly. 'It's just her sense of humour, *signor giudice,*' he said. 'Do you know what her surname is by any chance?'

'Surname?' said the judge in a surprised voice, as if it had never occurred to him that Marta would need such a thing.

'I can find out for you, of course,' he said looking puzzled at both Alessandro and Elena. 'But why all the importance attached to this woman?'

'No reason probably,' replied Alessandro. 'The significant thing was that it did not occur to you to mention her without prompting – naturally because she is such an integral part of your household. You must both trust her implicitly. No, *signor giudice,* it is probably nothing at all. But we have to be meticulous. I mean Elena and myself, of course. It is our job and we wish to be thorough. The thought has occurred to both of us that this campaign against you seems to have a very personal element to it. It is just possible – although unlikely, I admit – that there is someone closely linked to your daily lives who has a hand in this plot, which seems to be designed to …'

The judge's mobile phone rang at this moment. 'My wife,' he explained. 'She probably wonders why I am not home yet. Excuse me a minute, will you?'

While he was out of the room, Elena said something rapidly and quietly to Alessandro who nodded in agreement. 'I told her where I was,' said the judge and I asked my wife what Marta's surname is. According to Antonella, it's *Vollaro.*

'Did your wife check the name on her ID card?' asked Alessandro.

'Yes, I'm sure she must have done. She is very efficient in all things.'

'I don't suppose you asked your wife if Marta has any children – or a husband?' asked Elena with a bright smile on her face. She was irresistible. To his annoyance, Judge Grassi found himself apologising to her for the oversight.

'All I know is what I told you, I'm afraid. She has 'family problems' and goes down to Soleto in her free time. I'm sorry I cannot be more precise.'

'Don't worry, *signor giudice*,' said Alessandro smiling. 'First of all, you need to decide whether you want to engage our services.

'I do,' replied the judge, solemnly. 'I do not have the will to sort this out on my own. I suppose I should ask you what your fees are likely to be?'

By way of response, Alessandro handed the judge a printed card. His eyebrows went up in surprise until he started to calculate mentally what *he* would have earned in one day when he had still been working. It was considerably more than the amount that the private detective was asking.

'It is quite a lot of money,' said the judge. 'But I suppose your overheads here are quite high.' Alessandro nodded and shrugged his shoulders modestly to show that this was the case. Elena nodded too, thinking of her own salary. Nothing was said about Alessandro's uncle, naturally.

'The question is, therefore,' said the judge. 'How long do you reckon that it will take you to solve my 'case'?

'With a bit of luck, we should be in a position to know who is responsible within a week,' replied Alessandro. 'We try to be efficient.'

The judge calculated that the expense involved would be well worth the risk. These two people appeared to be highly intelligent. Just how intelligent and focused they were, he was yet to discover; they would have his whole life dissected in a matter of days. He pointed out that his bank account and pension were blocked.

'Ah yes! May I make a suggestion, *signor giudice*? If you would care to make me temporarily executor of your estate, I am sure I can get your pension and bank account unblocked within the week – merely by pointing out that I cannot do the job I have been appointed to do by you, because you are not ... dead! I will willingly do this within the cost of the fee that we are charging you. What do you think?'

'Why not?' replied Amedeo – to his considerable surprise. The prospect of this couple working on his behalf had inspired his confidence – especially since the alternative would involve weeks of self-examination and tiresome research into a past that he was not sure he wanted to delve into too deeply.

'Another question, *signor giudice*,' said Elena. 'When your wife phoned you just now, do you think that Marta was present?'

Yet again, this insistence on their housekeeper, he thought. Elena could see the hint of irritation on the judge's face. 'It really could be important,' she said with a smile.

'I would say almost certainly yes. I could hear the sound of saucepans and plates in the background,' he replied mollified by the smile.

'And did your wife repeat out loud the name of this agency when you told her where you were?' Elena was pressing this point home. He looked at her with a degree more of respect for the astuteness of her line of interrogation. He nodded silently.

The judge spent the next few minutes sorting out the formalities of signing a straightforward contract that could be renewed after a period of one week.

'A few more questions if you don't mind, *signor giudice,*' said Alessandro. 'I imagine that you have another bank account apart from your current account?' The judge nodded looking slightly guilty. 'Yes, I do,' he said.

'Is it an online account?'

'Yes, it is,' replied the judge now looking decidedly cagey.

'Don't worry. We are not prying into your personal financial life,' said Alessandro lightly. 'But it may be worth your while checking to see if that has been blocked too – although I doubt it,' added Alessandro shrewdly. He knew far more about the manner in which the Italian *magistratura* handled their cosy financial dealings than he was letting on to his new client.

'I hope that you have a very secure password to access your internet site,' said Elena. The judge looked at her again in bewilderment. 'I don't know,' he replied. How was it that the younger generation were so savvy about everything to do with the cyber world, just like his own two children. 'I just...came up with a password that would be easy to remember, that's all,' he said defensively.

Alessandro looked sympathetically at the judge. 'This is Elena's field, *signor giudice.* She is about to surprise you, I believe.'

Elena smiled her brilliant smile at their client and said: 'May I ask you a couple of semi-personal questions, *signor giudice?*' Amedeo nodded, looking slightly perplexed.

'You told us that your wife's name is Antonella, I believe?' The judge nodded. 'And when is her birthday?'

'The fifteenth of April.'

'Are you very fond of your wife?' asked Elena, all innocence.

The judge bridled at this question but answered, huffily: 'Yes, of course I am!'

Elena disappeared into her office. Alessandro smiled reassuringly at Amedeo. 'Don't judge her too soon,' he said and wondered why his new client's face had registered a spasm of alarm.

Elena came back into the room holding a piece of paper out to the judge. 'Is that your password, *signor giudice*?' she asked. Amedeo merely looked at Elena with his mouth wide open. The expression on his face bore a revised level of respect for her.

On the piece of paper, she had written the numbers and letters: **15nella04** – his exact password. Elena had even split Antonella's birth date around the familiar form of her name. And he thought that he had been so clever.

'I should reset your password, if I were you,' said Alessandro. 'If you are not sure how to do it, we can help you. At present, anybody who has a minimal acquaintance with your family situation could work it out for themselves – just as Elena did.'

* * *

Judge Grassi had a great deal to think about as he walked home past the magnificent local council offices which were housed in an ancient *palazzo* with its cobbled courtyard – unfortunately filled with parked cars. He hardly spared a glance at the *Santa Croce* church next to the *palazzo*, whose elaborately carved stone facade ranked among the most beautiful in Italy, in Amedeo's opinion.

Amedeo was amazed that he had put so much trust in these two young people – a sign of how desperate he had become, he told himself. Before leaving the Greco studio, he had supplied his mobile phone number and that of Antonella, on Alessandro's insistence. 'You never know,' the investigator had said. 'According to Murphy's Law, if you don't give me the numbers, I am bound to need them.' The judge had made the young man temporary executor of his will. It was, in any case, a harmless step that could be reversed whenever he saw fit. He was anxious that his wife would disapprove of the action that he had taken in involving a third party. But the relief that *he* felt more than compensated for any criticism that he might have to face from Antonella.

His mobile phoned bleeped three times; a text message. No doubt Antonella was worried that it was past lunch time and he still had not returned home. He looked at the screen, which was difficult to see in the sunlight. There was no name or number on the screen. He stepped into the shade provided by a porch and read the words: ***Fear not, Amedeo. Your redemption is nigh.*** He scuttled home and dived into the safety of the shaded, flower scented garden, as if he was being assailed by some marauding spirit from the Underworld.

6: Another Turn of the Screw

Judge Grassi found a hidden, shaded part of the garden where he took in deep breaths of the flower-scented air in order to compose himself before entering the apartment. He took out his mobile phone and looked again at the strange, anonymous, message in the vain hope that it was no longer there or that, maybe, he had just misread the words, which might merely have been saying, 'Hurry up, Ame. Lunch is getting cold'. But, of course, the original message was still there staring defiantly back at his disbelieving eyes. Without thinking, he scrolled down and was shocked to see that the message was *not* exactly anonymous after all. He had revealed two letters that looked exactly like someone's initials. **A.G.** he read. They rang a bell somewhere in the back of his mind. Amedeo was feeling just a little bit embarrassed by his recent, paranoid panic attack. Now the sense of relief was palpable and he went quickly into the house and headed for the kitchen, where he found Antonella and Marta half-heartedly picking at a dish of thin slices of chicken breast covered with shavings of parmesan cheese, rocket salad and balsamic vinegar - a simple dish that he particularly loved. He smiled vaguely at them both, muttered an apology for his lateness and helped himself to the chicken. To his surprise, he had found his appetite again. Antonella had even put out a bottle of white wine from the cooler in the fridge. The little droplets of condensation on the outside of the bottle were irresistible, carrying as they did the promise of the tangy, citrus taste of the wine inside. It was a local wine from Matino produced by a young couple who had just started to produce wine commercially. Amedeo recognised the label and remembered that he had been disparaging about their wines in one of his articles for *Il Quotidiano*. Amedeo poured himself his first glass of wine for days. He sipped it tentatively and discovered that it was very good. Perhaps he had been too harsh in his judgement of this young couple's endeavours, he thought.

The choking fit which followed his first sip of the wine was generated by the simultaneous presence of three elements. First of all, his unwitting use of the words *judgement* and *harsh*, occurring mentally within seconds of each other, had struck a chord in his conscience. Secondly, came the awareness that he had just identified someone who might well have a serious grudge against him. And thirdly, was the realization that the initials **A.G.** were his own. When he had recovered, he thanked his wife – presumably because she had patted him energetically on his back – and Marta for fetching him a glass of water. He really should try to avoid swallowing his drinks down the wrong way. It was the second time in just a few days, after all.

Marta looked so genuinely concerned for his state of health that Amedeo decided to throw caution to the winds. If Marta was in some way involved in the conspiracy to derail his life, as Alessandro Greco had suggested, then it would be better not to let her know that she was under suspicion. In any case, seeing her in the flesh, looking so anxious about his state of agitation, made her involvement in the plot seem highly implausible. So Amedeo launched into an account of his visit to the Greco *studio*, leaving out references to Marta. He wanted to ask her questions to find out about her children but felt that he could not do so in the context of Alessandro Greco's private investigative agency without it being obvious that he had talked about their –

decidedly *simpatica* - housekeeper. It was obvious that the matter of the strange text message was preying more on his mind than his visit to the private detective. So he showed them what had appeared on the screen of his mobile and asked them what they thought of it and the initials **A.G.**

'Well, I certainly did not send myself a text message!' he said with heavy humour in answer to a sardonic comment from his wife.

'I can think of at least two more people with the same initials,' said Antonella. 'In your state of mind, my dear, I think you have missed the obvious!'

'Tell me ...' said Amedeo urgently.

'Your son and your grandson, Ame,' she said.

Aurelio and Alessio Grassi! How obvious it had been! How stupid of him to have panicked!

'But Aurelio would never send a message like that. And Alessio doesn't have a mobile. He's too young. Besides which, the person who sent the message thought it necessary to conceal their number,' argued Amedeo, who was not convinced by this engagingly obvious explanation.

Marta was looking at him with some strange light shining in the depths of her brown eyes. It occurred to the judge that she was *enjoying* herself in some inexplicable way. It was as if she *knew...* But knew *what* exactly?

'What did you say the name of this investigator was?' asked Marta. 'Didn't you say it was Alessandro Greco?' There were a few seconds of stunned silence while the implications of her simple statement of the obvious sunk in; four people with the initials **A.G.** It was bordering on the uncanny.

'But in the text message, it was my *first* name that the sender used. If it was … this Greco man, then he is playing tricks on me even before he has started investigating. If it turns out to be him … or his assistant…' But even as he felt the familiar tide of anger rising up, he had dismissed the notion that the detective agency was the source of the message as highly improbable, if not ridiculous. The look of fear had crept back into his eyes and he could feel his face muscles contracting in tension.

Antonella came up and gave her husband a hug. Amedeo wanted to talk to her alone about what had been discussed at the Greco *studio* but Marta was still there. She seemed to have something that she wanted to say. Amedeo looked at her. It was impossible to believe ill of this woman, he thought. There was a natural kindness behind the mask of solemnity which she had adopted during the time she had been with them. The judge raised a quizzical eyebrow as if to invite her to speak if that was what she wished to do.

'I see a look of fear on your face, *signore*,' she began hesitantly. 'But, if I may say so, there seems nothing threatening about this message. It is almost as if it has been sent by a well-wisher.' She had finished saying what was on her mind but continued to look at the judge steadily. 'Don't you think so, *signora*?' added Marta appealing to Antonella.

'I don't know, Marta,' she replied with a sigh. 'If it is a well-wisher, then why couch the message in biblical language? And why not say outright who has sent it? No, it seems to be part of the wider plot to make sure my husband is discomforted as much as possible. Although I cannot for the life of me fathom what is behind it all.'

'*Sissignori*, I am sorry. You are right, of course. I spoke out of turn.' Both Antonella and Amedeo reassured her hurriedly that they had not taken her comment amiss. Marta bowed her head ever so slightly in a simple gesture of gratitude. She excused herself and said she was going out for a while. But, they both noticed, she was managing to shed the image she had projected for so many months of being an unobtrusive, subservient member of the household. She had a life and a personality of her own beyond the confines of their apartment, they realised.

Amedeo wasted no further time before telling Antonella what had transpired at the agency, adding the comments that Elena Camisso, in particular, had made regarding their housekeeper. He expected Antonella to be vociferous in her objections. It was to his surprise, therefore, that she said:

'It seems that you have not wasted your time this morning, *amore*. Without being able to put my finger on anything definite, I have had the growing sensation that there is something going on in Marta's mind that has nothing to do with cooking our meals and making our beds. It is as if she has a hidden agenda, some mysterious motivation for continuing to be here that I just have not managed to fathom out. This Elena Camisso has merely sharpened the impression that I have. We have both taken Marta so much for granted over the months that we have in some way failed to perceive the real person concealed below the surface. We may have misjudged ...'

Antonella looked at her husband's face and decided to leave the sentence unfinished. Any grammatical variation of the word *judge* seemed to trigger a nervous spasm these days.

'And I've been thinking back to the day she first came here,' continued Antonella. 'It was ever so slightly unusual.'

'How do you mean?' asked Amedeo.

'Well. You do remember our previous housekeeper, don't you, Ame?'

'A rather stout, sour-faced individual whose ability to cook was a trifle limited, if I remember.'

'If you say so, *caro,*' replied Antonella who just stopped herself from saying that maybe his judgement was a bit severe. 'But her parting words were something like: 'I'm sure you will get on very well with my replacement, *signora'.* It was as if she knew who would be coming in her place. I checked with the agency and asked them why Micaela - that was her name - had decided to leave so suddenly. They were as much in the dark as we were but said they had someone in mind who was very keen to come and see us. I didn't think anything of it at the time. But Marta seemed to know in advance that we would be needing a new housekeeper. It's all very tenuous, Ame. But, recently, I've noticed little things that, on their own, mean nothing but added together ...'

'Like the time when she burst into tears,' said Amedeo.

'Yes. And afterwards, when she apologised and said that she would soon tell us about her family problems. You remember. Well she sort of tripped lightly up the stairs – as you do when you are in a happy mood. It seemed incongruous at the time. You didn't notice, *caro*, but I did.'

'But have you ever asked her about family, husbands, that kind of thing?' asked Amedeo, remembering that he was supposed to convey the information to the Greco establishment.

'Yes, a long while ago. She hinted at a marital break-up. I got the impression that her husband was a rather undesirable character. He went up north to Milan or somewhere. She told me that she has a son who lives in Rome and a daughter who is slightly handicapped.'

The judge looked thoughtful.

'Well, she knows about my visit to the Greco Detective Agency now. By the way, did she hear you telling me that her surname is *Vollaro*'?

'No, I don't think so. I went into the hallway before telling you.'

The judge reflected for a few minutes before adding, pointlessly:

'I still cannot think of *any* connection between Marta and what is happening to me. To us,' he said, amending the statement when he caught a look on her face that implied she was, by association with her husband, in the firing line too.

'Neither can I,' concluded Antonella. 'I suppose we shall have to wait and see what transpires. According to your text message, if it is not just a joke in poor taste, we shan't have long to wait.'

And on that slightly chilling note, they went about their separate business.

* * *

Amedeo picked up that day's copy of *Il Quotidiano*. It had slipped his mind that today was the day when the newspaper was supposed to print the article retracting the report of his demise.

At first glance, he felt quite satisfied with his treatment by Lecce's principal newspaper, which prided itself on its impartiality in matters local and national. The editor, as promised, had printed an apology for the erroneous report of his death on the front page. Claudio Sabatini had briefly explained how the error had occurred but had played down the manner in which the rogue sentence had found its way into the obituary. Instead, he had undertaken to ensure that the provenance of future articles of this nature would be meticulously screened even at the risk of offending members of the families concerned.

'Presumably he is going to check people's identities more carefully in future,' Amedeo muttered to himself.

The article was rounded off with a sentence apologising for any distress caused to members of his family, whilst wishing the judge a long and happy retirement. The article was even accompanied by a flattering photo of Amedeo – obviously taken some years previously. Amedeo was vain enough to feel appeased by the photograph but not so naïve as to be unaware of the additional grey hairs and wrinkles round his eyes that a glance in the bathroom mirror revealed every morning while he was shaving.

He was slightly less pleased to find an advertisement for Alessandro's Investigative Agency sharing *his* space on the front page. But why should he be upset by that, he considered. Possibly because it displayed a bit of opportunism on the part of the young investigator to whom, naturally enough, Amedeo had related the fact that an article of apology was due to be included in that day's edition. But a moment's reflection told him that Alessandro Greco would not have had time to get the advert inserted in the newspaper to appear the same day. Unless...

The young investigator and his assistant, who were reading the article around about the same time, could not help thinking that the juxtaposition of their advert alongside the mysterious report of the judge's demise might trigger off some association in the public mind. 'Very fortuitous, Sandro!' said Elena-Rosaria with a malicious glint in her eye.

Judge Grassi's paranoia was at work again. 'What if this young man was in cahoots with the editor, Claudio Sabatini?' he thought. He expressed the suspicion to Antonella who was passing through the kitchen at that moment. She merely shrugged and told him that the timing was wrong. 'Besides which,' she added, 'it hardly constitutes a breach of trust, *mio caro*.' She obviously did not believe in her husband's paranoia-induced conspiracy theories. She must be right, as ever, conceded the judge who continued to read the inside pages of the newspaper.

He was brought up with a start by an article in the editorial section of the paper. On reading it, any pleasure that he had derived from the article about his resurrection was instantly cancelled out. It had been written by a popular journalist who called himself Umberto Incazzato, *'Umberto-the-Pissed-Off'*.

He tended to write pieces about any issues that annoyed him and got under his skin. He prided himself that he said publicly what his readers secretly wished to say out loud but did not dare. The judge forced himself to read the article merely so that he could indulge in a feeling of self-righteous indignation. As usual, Umberto 'Incazzato' launched without preamble into his favoured style of cynical irony.

'What on earth do people see in such cheap journalism?' he muttered to nobody in particular, apparently unaware that he was sharing the same morbid fascination as everyone else on reading about the public denigration of another member of society – with the sole difference that, for once, *he* was the object of this journalist's vitriolic humour.

Dear Readers,

It is with great pleasure that we learn today that our favourite judge, Amedeo Grassi, is not, after all, the late Judge Grassi. What an uplifting experience it must be for him to learn that he is not deceased! I am overjoyed that we can share with him the happy sensation that he is still numbered among the (living) noble citizens of Lecce. Did I say 'noble'? I believe I meant 'distinguished'. I am not personally convinced that our judge will ever merit any variation of the word 'nobility' on his final epitaph. It is not, I hasten to add, that we can reliably point the finger of accusation at any particular incident of malpractice in our judge's career.

'You can bet your life you can't!' exclaimed Amedeo to the empty kitchen.

I am sure that, should there have been any irregularity in his professional dealings, he would have been far too skilful in the art of obfuscation for ordinary mortals such as you and me to have discovered any betrayal of public trust. Our judge is, of course, an upstanding, tax-paying member of Italian society. But let us not descend into the murky world of personal insinuations.

'As if you haven't done that already!' the judge thought indignantly.

We all know, or suspect we know, about the capacity of the judiciary, in our land of open democratic procedures, to conceal the true extent of its personal financial gains – and the means by which they have been procured.

So let us, for the sake of argument leave our Judge Grassi to examine his own conscience in the tranquillity of his own – exclusive – home. We shall talk instead about a fictitious, wholly Platonic form of judge. Let us call him Augusto Garibaldi, for the sake of argument. '**A.G.** again,' thought Amedeo with a renewed twinge of alarm.

Our Judge Garibaldi has retired at the age of 67, let us say. Quite early for a judge! Perhaps Augusto feels that he has drained the public coffers sufficiently to allow himself a comfortable retirement? Or maybe he has seen the writing on the judicial wall? In these times of economic straits, the blind generosity of the State is being closely scrutinised – at long last, some may consider. Let us say that our Judge Garibaldi has an annual income of €120 000. That means, for those of us who cannot visualise such heady sums of money, €10 000 for every month of his life. And this figure does not include any additional benefits to which our man is entitled which, thanks to our beloved country's lax financial controls, may never show up on Judge Garibaldi's official pay slip. We can safely assume that his final annual salary is in the region of €150 000 – all this for a workload amounting to only 1560 hours per year. Let me remind you that there are 8760 hours in one year. So our dear judge has an average working day of less than five hours. No wonder that Augusto has a self-satisfied smile on his face.

But, our judge will argue, cogently no doubt, that such a vast salary is necessary to guarantee impartiality. A very high price for us to pay for simply being honest, I would suggest. But what measure of impartiality are we talking about? Our Judge Garibaldi may be suspected of behaviour in his younger days that fell well short of even his own ideals. He remembers, guiltily I trust, of occasions when his impartial judgement might have been clouded by the insidious, nocturnal presence of the local mafia boss, not to mention suitable inducements from the same source, 'requesting' him to look favourably on the accused. A catalogue of not dissimilar incidents, now forgotten by the public, may also be weighing on Judge Garibaldi's mind.

Of course, none of this necessarily applies to our own distinguished citizen judge. But, nonetheless, I am relieved for Judge Grassi's sake that he still has time enough on the face of this earth to reconsider any transgressions of the law for which he may have to account at the hour of Final Judgement.

If I have said anything in this article which I should regret, then I am most gratified.

Your humble literary servant. **U.I.**

Amedeo was not sure exactly *how* he felt by the time he had reached the final sentence of this ambiguous, but clever piece of journalism. Exposed! Publicly exposed, furthermore! Alarmingly, there came to his mind the frightful memory of the time when, as an over-sensitive fifteen-year-old adolescent, his mother had caught him in the act of masturbation in the privacy of his own bedroom. She had threatened to expose him to his father unless he undertook without delay to present himself to the local parish priest in the confessional. He would never forget the acute humiliation that he had suffered. And now, he was experiencing a similar feeling of being exposed in his nakedness to gloating public disapproval.

He expected to feel the usual sensation of outrage welling up from inside. But instead, he just felt emotionally drained. Even more alarmingly, he realised that he was feeling an obsequious kind of respect for the public executioner of his reputation. It had been skilfully carried out and, protest as he might – and he would, when he next met the newspaper editor face to face - he had the sense to realise that he had no real grounds for bringing a libel charge. He would publicly deny the implied accusation made against him in the article, even if he had to admit its truth to himself. Quite unbidden, there came to him the new sensation that the time was ripe for a thorough searching of his own conscience. He feared that the task might be too onerous to carry out alone. 'What am I saying?' he thought, scared by the newness of this idea. 'I shall end up by going to a psychoanalyst – or even worse, a priest!' He entertained the facetious and ignoble notion that the latter alternative would cost him a great deal less financially. His reverie was interrupted by Marta coming into the kitchen and telling him that she had finished cleaning his study and the other upstairs rooms.

'Thank you, Marta,' he said distractedly. 'That is very kind of you.' She looked almost shocked by the change in attitude of the master of the house towards her. Amedeo had the impression that a shadow of something resembling guilt had crossed her face. He suddenly wanted to ask her about herself, her past life and her family circumstances. But all he could summon up the courage to ask was whether she was happy working for them. Strangely, she let out a deep sigh, smiled sadly at him and said simply: 'Of course, *dottore.* How could I not be happy?'

Amedeo was quite taken aback by her reaction and was searching for the right words. In the end, he said feebly:

'Good. I too am happy that you are with us, Marta.'

The mixture of emotions that crossed her face in that instant was such that the judge regretted his comment, fearing that he had been too familiar. He could feel a flush of embarrassment on his own face. But it was nothing to the blush that appeared on Marta's face, which expressed a fleeting look of guilt replaced by a struggle not to look pleased at the compliment that this normally severe-looking man had just paid her. In the end, she uttered the words 'I'm so sorry, *dottore*', turned away from him and began to lay the table again for the evening meal although it was still hours away. The judge simply failed to understand how his comment could have provoked such an emotional response. He was struck, yet again, by the sensation that the workings of their housekeeper's mind were hidden from his view. He knew that, if he tried to apologise for his choice of words, he would merely increase her embarrassment. So he said simply: 'I shall be in my study, Marta. By the way, do you know where Antonella is?' he added in a voice that was meant to be reassuring, but in an attempt to sound natural, his voice seemed to catch in his throat.

'I believe she went to see her mother, *dottore*,' she replied without interrupting the unnecessary task with which she was busying herself. Antonella's mother was in her eighties and lived in her own flat nearby. She was fiercely independent and refused 'to be a burden' to her family.

'Will you tell her where I am when she returns, please, Marta?'

With that, he left the kitchen thoughtfully and retired to his study upstairs, wondering why on earth Marta should have used the words '*so sorry*'. Sorry for *what*, he wondered? For being embarrassed, he supposed.

He felt the need to talk to someone – his daughter, maybe. But he knew that he was merely delaying the moment when he would have to switch on his computer and check his e-mails, something which he had not done since the disturbing events of the previous Sunday. His reluctance to use his computer was usually induced by nothing more serious than a wariness of modern technology. On this occasion, there was the added knowledge that he should check up on his second bank account which had lain dormant for years on end. The article that he had just read had made him feel threatened and increased the sense that his private dealings would somehow be rendered public by the words of *that* journalist. Guilt can play havoc with normal behaviour patterns, thought Amedeo.

Like any other ordinary mortal, the judge, sitting in the security of his own study, suffered from the common delusion that his actions were protected by the privacy of familiar surroundings, unaware that, at a touch of a key, our private lives are instantly transferred into the invisible public domain of cyberspace. And so the judge switched on his computer with the aim of bringing up his secret bank account. Instinctively, he looked round the room to assure himself that he was alone. He was aware of a niggling sensation that there was something slightly different about the room but he could not put his finger on what had caught his notice. He shrugged. It couldn't be anything important, he decided. Maybe books that Marta had rearranged while she had been cleaning. He tapped in his code to gain access to the account. He could feel his heart pounding whilst he was waiting for the details to appear. He was relieved to see that the account was intact, revealing the magnificent and untouched sum of €756 000 – plus the accrued interest.

The money in this secret account was, officially, the sum that he had inherited on his father's death. But he knew that well over half of this sum had been surreptitiously added to his inheritance money by a third party with the sole purpose of disguising its true provenance. His feeling of guilt was acute but was now aggravated by the fear that some mysterious stranger might know about it and could hold him to ransom.

There seemed to be nothing amiss, however. He closed down the page and returned to the less stressful task of reading his e-mails. There was only one, he noticed. But the single new item was enough to throw his soul into turmoil yet again.

The moment of your reconciliation is upon you, dear Amedeo. Please look at the attached video file. Do not be afraid. A.G.

With trembling fingers, Amedeo opened up the attachment. There was an old circular stone granary set amidst a grove of ancient olive trees. There appeared from nowhere a girl of fifteen, maybe sixteen years old, dressed in a traditional Salento costume, dancing the lilting, springy steps of the *pizzica.* The music was haunting, ancient, pagan in the sentiments that it evoked. The girl herself was beautiful and the perfectly executed steps enhanced her beauty ten-fold. She had a secret smile of enjoyment and an intense look of concentration on her face that held Amedeo spellbound. He knew that there was something familiar about the girl's face, but he realised, too, that the memory was too old and elusive to recapture. And yet, and yet... the image *did* recall some more recent experience. Yet again, he failed to make a connection with the present.

His reverie was interrupted by a discreet knock on the door. It was Marta looking very apologetic. 'Excuse me for disturbing you, *dottore.* Your bank manager is on the phone. Apparently, it is very urgent.'

7: Disturbing Disclosures

Amedeo ran downstairs to take the phone call from his other bank, forgetting that there was an extension in his own study – with the ringing tone turned off so as not to disturb his train of thought. He left Marta standing on the landing looking perplexed. When he had reached the ground floor, she took out her mobile phone, dialled a number and talked quietly to someone. The conversation was very brief. Marta looked relieved.

Downstairs, Amedeo picked up the receiver in a panic knowing that this bank would never have contacted him unless it had been an emergency. He was already anticipating more bad news.

'*Pronto?*' he said breathlessly into the receiver.

'*Buona sera, signor giudice,*' said a calm female voice on the other end of the line. 'My name is Annamaria Santucci. I don't believe we have met. I am the new *direttrice* of this branch of *La Banca Salentina.*

Amedeo was taken aback; A *woman* in charge of a private bank – *any* bank, come to that - seemed to fly in the face of the natural order of things. But Amedeo checked himself and remembered just in time what Antonella might have said had he expressed such a sentiment out loud. Her reaction would have been scathing in the extreme.

'*Buonasera, Signora Santucci.* No, I am sure that I would have remembered,' he said with only a hint of aloofness designed to preserve a vestige of male superiority. 'Is there a problem?'

'I hope not, *dottore*. May I ask if you have logged on to your private bank account in the last fifteen minutes?'

'Yes, I have,' said the judge, feeling a surge of rising panic.

'Just as well it was you, *signor giudice,*' said the lady director perfectly maintaining her business-like manner. 'However, I am very dubious about the level of strength of your password. I would respectfully suggest that you change it to something more secure. There is a far greater risk nowadays of a breach of security than when you opened up the account all that time ago.'

Amedeo could not quite bring himself to admit to this woman that he had no idea how to set up a new password. So he said stiffly: 'I would have thought that it was the *bank's* duty to ensure the security of my account, *signora.*'

The new *direttrice,* however, had read the signs with perfect accuracy and replied smoothly: 'Precisely, *signor giudice.* That is why I would like to suggest that you come in to the branch at your earliest convenience so that we can set up a new password.'

'Tomorrow morning, then,' suggested the judge, who felt that to have rushed over to the other side of Lecce so near closing time would have looked undignified. The lady director hesitated, but in the end, did not think it was worth insisting. After all, she had fulfilled her obligation and the telephone call would be logged in the event of any infiltration of the judge's account before tomorrow morning.

'Shall we say nine o'clock tomorrow, then?' she said. 'It is very important. There is a significant amount of money involved,' she added unnecessarily. And so it was agreed.

Amedeo tripped lightly upstairs, painfully aware that his moods and emotions were entirely dictated in response to the rapid changes in his exterior circumstances. Yet he felt compelled to re-read the e-mail accompanied by the poignant video clip of the dancing girl. It had to mean *something* but he could not for the life of him think exactly what. He heard Antonella coming home, talking to someone else. He realised with pleasure that it was his daughter, Teresa. Reluctantly, he decided to share the strange electronic missive with them. What was happening to him was so personal and seemed to be so intimately bound up with some forgotten event in his past life that he hesitated to share it with anyone else; he felt that he was exposing some weakness to those whom he believed trusted in his invincibility - which thought indicated a certain amount of wishful thinking on his part.

The two women read the message and watched the video clip totally enthralled.

'Do you recognise the girl?' asked Elenora.

'No, I don't. Yet I have the tantalising impression that I *ought* to recognise her.'

'Well, it could be one of your past conquests, *papà*,' said Teresa cruelly. 'But otherwise, it could simply be one of the hundreds of beautiful girls with which Puglia seems to be blessed.'

The judge looked furiously at his daughter but had the grace to blush quite visibly.

'Grown up by now, of course,' added Teresa, by way of mitigation, but with a hint of sarcasm to match the cruelty of her earlier words.

Antonella had remained very pensive but she gave an ill-supressed snort of laughter at her daughter's cutting humour. To her husband, she said more kindly:

'I don't know what it means yet, Ame. But one thing is absolutely certain. The person who has sent you this video clip is the same person who is responsible for everything else. Of that, I am certain.'

As they were discussing Antonella's comment, Amedeo was surprised to see yet another e-mail arriving. But this time it was from the Greco private investigation agency. They were anxious to see him as soon as possible to keep him abreast of events. Teresa said that she was curious to see what this couple were like and that she would accompany her father the next day. So she sent a reply to the e-mail on her father's behalf making an appointment for 10.30 the next morning, without mentioning that she was coming too.

'Only if you want me to come too, of course, *papà*.' added Teresa. Amedeo smiled an affirmative, ready to forgive his daughter's unkind comments. He was more than happy not to have to go on his own. The door to Amedeo's study had remained open and the family were surprised to see Marta standing there. She had coughed politely to attract their attention. She was wearing an outdoor coat and carrying her handbag. Her eyes were dilated and there was a look of nostalgia on her face that the whole family noticed.

'Marta!' exclaimed Antonella. 'Come in, please. You don't have to stand on ceremony with us.'

'I was just going to ask you if I could pop out for thirty minutes,' she said making an effort to speak unemotionally. 'I need to go to the post office.'

'That's alright, Marta. Of course you can! You are free to go where you like without permission. You know that.'

Marta smiled back with a look of gratitude on her face. 'Thank you, Anton... *signora*.' She darted off before her unconscious slip of the tongue could embarrass the whole family group.

'Now that is really interesting!' said Antonella thoughtfully.

Amedeo slept with Antonella again that night. He needed the physical comfort of her body even more than before. Thoughts of his wife's infidelities were far from his mind. The need for her by his side during the wakeful hours of night time was far more immediate than the volatility of his previous fearful imaginings about her extra-marital relationships. They made love quite convincingly this time and Antonella complimented her newly found lover on the hardness of his erection. 'Have you been taking those little blue pills, by any chance, *mio caro?*' she asked mischievously and with her usual candour. Amedeo admitted that he had considered doing so but told her that he thought that the rest had done him good. She laughed and drew him towards her for a long embrace. What comfort he drew from this renewed contact with his wife! In the midst of this strange assault on his private life by an unknown being, the rediscovery of intimacy with his wife was the single, unlooked for silver lining to the cloud of uncertainty that engulfed him during his waking hours.

They had lain there in the semi-darkness discussing what little they had to latch on to in this inexplicable affair. The only aspect about which there seemed to be any clear indication was that their mysterious housekeeper knew more than was apparent. But they both remained convinced that there was no malevolent intent in Marta's presence in their midst.

'She almost called me by my first name this afternoon. Did you notice that Ame? It's as if she regards herself as my friend but is not in a position to admit it. And I am quite convinced that she saw the video clip while she was standing outside the study door. Did you see the expression on her face?'

Amedeo nodded in the darkness. 'But should we tackle her about it?'

Antonella paused while she considered the validity of a direct approach – from which she would not have shied away if she had thought that it would prove productive.

'No, *mio caro,* we have nothing concrete to go on. And since we are employing *Signor* Greco and company, we might as well leave the investigating to them. If they are as good as they claim, then we can leave the detective work in their hands.'

Soon after that, Antonella fell into her usual deep, untroubled slumber, leaving her husband behind to tread the tortuous paths of his dreamland all on his own. He spent what seemed like ages trying to work out whom he knew with the initials **A.G.** He had even realised that he might be wrong in assuming that **A.G.** was a man. But nobody of either gender came to mind. When, finally, he fell asleep, he dreamt, not of devils pursuing him, but of his adolescent years walking the mountain paths of the *Gran Sasso* on his own, back in his native *Abruzzo*. He felt peaceful but lonely. But he was not on his own, he realised. He was holding the hand of a girl that he could not see distinctly. The hand belonged to the dancing girl, her dreamy, concentrated look focused on the distant blue peaks. The 'Pizzica Girl' had got under his skin. The dream faded before he could ask her what she was doing there by his side. He woke up the following morning after Antonella had already gone downstairs to organise the coffee. Marta was there and smiled at the lady of the house, relaxed and confident again. No, there was no malice there, thought Antonella, which made her potential involvement in the professionally executed campaign against her husband appear unlikely – even highly improbable. Antonella shook her head silently as if to clear her mind from confusing speculation.

* * *

The following morning at nine o'clock, Amedeo presented himself at the branch of *La Banca Salentina,* and asked to see the *direttrice.* 'Yes,' he said sharply to the casual young man at the counter. 'I *do* have an appointment. Tell her that Judge Grassi is waiting.' The young man scuttled off suitably chastised. A little voice inside was trying to tell him that his harshness towards the lowly bank employee had been uncalled for. Thus, when the young man returned and ingratiatingly offered to usher him to the bank's inner sanctum, he smiled and thanked the lad courteously. 'You're getting soft, Amedeo!' he thought. 'About time too!' said another more gentle, interior voice that was not his own. He thought about the dancing girl who had accompanied him in his dream. He had even gone back to his study in secret that morning to see if the e-mail was still there. In a slightly calmer state of mind, he had noticed that the missive had been sent by someone called simply *The Messenger.* The accompanying e-mail address had been a confusing jumble of letters, numbers and symbols. He had tried to send a message back saying: 'Who are you?' but he had received an immediate 'non-delivery' reply, saying that the e-mail address was non-existent.

'Come in, *signor giudice,*' said an elegant young woman who was about the age of his daughter. 'I am Annamaria Santucci. Thank you for coming in so promptly.'

She held out a hand to the judge, who was slightly put out by the fact that this attractive woman was two or three centimetres taller than he was. 'She's wearing heels, of course,' he said to himself. The 'other voice' inside his head let out a soft sigh of mock despair. Amedeo shook his head as if to dispel this new intruder. Annamaria Santucci misinterpreted the gesture and added: 'Well, fairly promptly.' She had a forgiving smile on her face. The judge muttered something to the effect that he had been thinking about another matter.

'*Signor giudice,*' she began as soon as she had sat him down in front of a computer screen and sat down beside him in a second swivel chair. 'I know from the news that you have been going through some unusual experiences recently.' She paused and looked at Amedeo's face to gauge his reaction before continuing. 'You may, therefore, be less surprised when I tell you that this account was... compromised, only minutes after I telephoned you yesterday.' There was a look of shocked horror on the judge's face before he said in a strangulated voice: 'Compromised? Do you mean...?'

'Yes. I mean that someone hacked into your account.' She took one look at Amedeo's blood-drained face and added quickly: 'No, don't worry, *signore.* The account was automatically blocked until we reset it with a new password and PIN number. The strange thing was,' she began again slowly until she had her client's full attention, 'there was absolutely no attempt at transferring any funds out of the account – which could easily have been the case.'

'You mean...' began Amedeo thoughtfully. 'It was as if somebody just wanted to see the details? That there was no intention to steal?'

'Precisely so, *signor giudice.* Does that make any sense to you?'

Amedeo merely nodded thoughtfully. Unfortunately, it *was* beginning to make sense to him in some obscure way. *Fear not. Redemption is nigh!* There was an absence of malevolence in this whole series of events. He was not being threatened, but ... *warned, prepared, softened up.*

By the time the business with the bank had been concluded and his account rendered 'impregnable' – the words of the employee who had helped him reset his secret password – he felt very differently about beautiful women being bank managers and had shaken Annamaria Santucci's hand warmly in both of his. 'Until next time, *signor giudice!'* she said with a mildly sardonic smile on her face.

Amedeo walked briskly back to the old town centre where he was to meet his daughter outside Alessandro Greco's agency. His head was crowded with a multitude of speculations, none of which gelled into a coherent pattern.

Teresa was not there waiting for him. Her father was not surprised. She, in common with Italians in general, had a flexible notion of punctuality which varied according to the demands of the moment. A text message arrived from her, suggesting that her father go on up and that she would join him in ten minutes – at the most. He looked at his watch and decided not to wait for her outside. He arrived *chez* Greco slightly less out of breath than before. His reduced alcohol intake was obviously having a beneficial effect on his health. He was greeted with a business-like smile from Elena and ushered directly into Alessandro's office. They sat round the table as before and Amedeo told them to expect his daughter to arrive very soon. The news was greeted positively, with only the briefest of conspiratorial glances between the two investigators.

'Well, what progress have you made?' asked the judge, who was not expecting there to have been any major break-through after so short a time had elapsed. He was agreeably surprised, therefore, when Alessandro Greco announced that they had managed to convince the INPS office to reinstate his pension. He raised an eyebrow in surprise, tinged with not a little admiration and relief.

'How did you manage that so soon?' he asked.

'With the help of your doctor, *signor giudice,*' replied Elena.

'But I do not remember giving you the name of my personal doctor,' stated the judge, disturbed by yet another manifestation of the invasion of his private world.

'It is a matter of public record,' Alessandro quickly reassured him. 'It was an easy step for my assistant – my partner,' he said, amending the title quickly when Elena had given a polite cough. 'She is very adept at using the internet to her advantage,' he added with a professional smile. 'Your doctor was very helpful,' he continued. 'Even the staff at the INPS have managed to digest the contents of yesterday's front page of *Il Quotidiano*. Incidentally, *signor giudice*, I apologise for the appearance of our advertisement alongside the editor's letter. It was purely coincidental, I assure you.'

The judge nodded in understanding but did not deign to smile.

'So, will I have to go to the INPS tomorrow?' he asked.

'A mere formality, but yes,' said Alessandro. 'They will need the inevitable series of signatures in triplicate on myriads of documents, I suspect.'

'Thank you for that,' said the judge more graciously this time. 'You have saved me a lot of trouble. But have you made any progress on finding out who is responsible for...?' He seemed reluctant to put the matter into words, realising that his perception of events had been radically altered in the period of time that had elapsed since his first visit to this couple.

It was Elena Camisso who took centre stage at this point. The judge was soon reeling with surprise at the amount of ground that she had covered. He found himself enraptured by the vitality of her expression, the light in her eyes and the movement of her lips as she told him what she had discovered in such a short time. He had to make an effort to concentrate on the actual words she was saying rather than on the person who was uttering them. Alessandro was smiling secretly as he, in his turn, studied the face of the judge.

'In the first place,' Elena had begun. 'We can rule out any involvement with the local mafia. I have it from the horse's mouth, so to speak, that they have no grudge against you for the sentence you passed on their family member. I understand that you and the *signore d'onore* in question came to an amicable settlement at the time.' Her words were accompanied by a knowing, conspiratorial smile that said: 'It's quite all right. I am a woman of the world. I know how these things work.'

The judge, however, was attempting to recover from the shock of yet another intrusion into one of the more shadowy incidents in his past life. First the journalist, Umberto Incazzato, and now this warmly smiling woman whose breasts were modestly exposed to his mesmerised gaze.

'How on earth did you manage to ...' he began.

'Oh, I used to go to convent school with his daughter,' she said lightly. 'Shall I continue, *signor giudice?*' The said judge nodded distractedly. He wondered what else this couple had discovered to his detriment.

'I went to the printers outside Lecce who were responsible for the posters announcing your... demise. It appears that it was the same young man who took the memory stick to *Il Quotidiano* who came to order and pay for the posters. The description matches well and the person claimed to be your son. They did add something interesting though,' said Elena modulating her entrancing voice to emphasise what she was about to say. 'They had the impression that the man spoke like an actor. They couldn't say why precisely. And they said that they were struck by the fact that he made the sign of the cross as he told them that his father had passed away. He even had tears in his eyes! It was a very convincing performance.'

Amedeo was thinking to himself that this young woman could charm her way into the *Palazzo Chigi* without an ID card if she had a mind to do so. He realised just in time that she had stopped talking and he managed to drag his mind back to reality. Elena was enjoying herself. Alessandro was congratulating himself – not for the first time – on recruiting Elena.

'Elena would like to ask you a question, *signor giudice*. She suspects that ...' Alessandro made a gesture with his head inviting her to proceed.

'I am not sure, *signore*, but I believe that it is possible that your computer has been hacked.'

Amedeo, once again, sat there with his mouth half open in surprise and a large measure of respect. 'How did you know?' he asked.

'It is just a suspicion,' she said. 'Have any of your personal affairs been compromised?'

Amedeo had to tell them about the infiltration of his second bank account and his visit to Annamaria Santucci before he had come to see them.

'Did you notice *anything* unusual while you were logging on to your account?' asked Elena.

Amedeo was thoughtful for a minute but shook his head in answer to the question. But there *had* been something, he remembered. 'It's nothing,' he said, 'but I did have the briefest of impression that something was out of place.'

'Had anyone else been in the room before you went in?' pursued Elena.

'No. Well, only Marta the housekeeper – to clean the room.'

Alessandro and Elena exchanged a very meaningful glance on hearing this piece of information.

'Did she by any chance go back into the room again?' asked Alessandro as casually as he could. Amedeo thought back to that moment.

'It's possible, I suppose,' he said. 'But only in the brief minute or so that I was downstairs taking the phone call from the bank.

'One more question, *signor* giudice,' said Elena. 'Did Marta stay in the house afterwards?'

'No,' replied Amedeo. 'She asked us if she could go out to the post office for half an hour. But why is this so important?'

'It may be nothing,' said Alessandro. 'But if your account was hacked into soon afterwards, then it might just be that a device had been planted in your study and then removed immediately after you had checked your bank account.'

'There are some very sophisticated gadgets out there nowadays,' explained Elena. 'They can pick up and remember minute electronic signals emitted by the keys that you use to access your bank account – or anything else, come to that.

'Whoever hacked into your computer is a real professional, *signor giudice*.' added Alessandro.

Amedeo remained silent and pensive. In the end he muttered, 'Just call me *signore* from now on. I seem to be well out of my depth here.'

The two of them smiled sympathetically at this shift in Amedeo's perception of their standing in his eyes.

'Apparently, there was no attempt to transfer any money from my account,' Amedeo informed them. 'Do you think, as I do, that this could be significant?'

After a long pause, Alessandro replied: 'It does seem strange, doesn't it? There seems to be a lack of criminal intent in all of this.'

'It is as if someone wants to teach you a lesson, *signore*,' added Elena.

'Did anything else unusual happen yesterday?' asked Alessandro Greco after a pause.

The judge did not want to tell them about the video of the dancing girl. The appearance of this girl in his life evoked even darker secrets from the past which he was reluctant to share with this couple, who had already managed to penetrate areas of his life that he had considered inviolable. But at that precise moment,

Teresa breezed into the office and introduced herself. She sat down comfortably at the remaining 'corner' of the round table. Elena Camisso took one look at Teresa and realised that she had found an ally in the camp.

'Has he told you about the e-mail and the video clip yet?' asked Teresa without preamble. With intuitive perception, she had guessed correctly that her father would find it difficult to bring up the matter of the dancing girl. The cat was out of the bag. The judge shrugged his shoulders in resignation. There were to be no secret stones left unturned before this affair was over.

'I implore you, *signore*,' began Alessandro Greco after he had listened to the account of the video clip accompanied by the haunting strains of the *pizzica*. 'Please tell us about *everything* that happens to you without reservation. *Anything* could prove to have a bearing on this strange case.'

'I need to look at this video clip myself,' added Elena Camisso. 'It might be possible to trace it back to its source.'

'I'll send it to you as soon as we get home,' promised Teresa. 'Yes, *papà!*' she said to her father. 'You must not keep any of this to yourself.'

Elena did not waste her breath or reveal her hand by telling them that she was quite able to find her way into the judge's e-mail account without help. She would be examining this video clip well before father and daughter had reached home. The concept of 'ethical hacking' might be stretching their new clients' faith a bit too far, so she said nothing.

'Should we tackle Marta face to face, in your opinion?' asked Teresa.

'No, not for the moment,' replied Alessandro emphatically. 'We have virtually nothing to go on. We shall be concentrating our investigations in that direction from now on. But if she suspects that we know about her involvement, then we may find the door closed before it can lead us anywhere.'

'And please text us immediately if you receive other messages from this person calling himself – or herself – **A.G.** won't you, *signore*?' said Elena.

'He will!' Teresa assured her. 'Won't you *papà?*'

The judge and his daughter walked home discussing their session with Alessandro and Elena. 'That couple are *in gamba, papà,*' stated Teresa categorically. Really bright! Teresa had obviously been impressed by her encounter. 'You should listen to what Elena tells you,' she continued, 'rather than staring at her breasts when she is talking!' Why was it, thought Amedeo, that he took his daughter's outrageous comments on the chin without protest?

'Ah well,' added Teresa as if addressing herself. 'Old habits die hard, I suppose!'

There was a double electronic beep from Amedeo's mobile phone. Apprehensively, he took the phone from his pocket and read the text message. He silently passed the device to his daughter so that she could read what it said.

Take one more step towards your salvation, Amedeo. There is a new e-mail for you. A.G.

'Come on, *papà.* Let's get home!'

8: Elena Camisso on the Case

Rosaria Miccoli, alias Elena Camisso, did not waste any time after the judge and his daughter had left the office. She was glad that she had briefly managed to corner Teresa while her father was having a last word and hand-shake with Alessandro. 'This has got my mobile number on it,' she had said to Teresa, handing her a business card. 'Can you send me a text message so that I've got *your* number?' Teresa Grassi had smiled and nodded recognising, as Elena had done, that there was already the promise of a bond of friendship between them.

'Do you think that your father knows more than he is saying?' asked Elena in an urgent whisper.

'No, I think he is as puzzled as we are,' replied Teresa. 'He is desperately trying to link what is happening now to some incident in the past. I think he's terrified that something bad is going to happen to him and...' But Teresa was unable to elaborate because her father was approaching. The conspiratorial look between the two women said plainly that they would arrange to meet up soon.

As soon as she was on her own, Elena switched on her computer and set up the programme that she had used the previous day to hack into the judge's computer. She had had the impression that she was not the only one attempting to do the same thing. A quick flash of some number-covered page, which should not have appeared on *her* screen but which had disappeared again in a trice, had alerted her to the possibility that she was not alone in taking an interest in the judge's personal affairs. She had seen the first video clip sent by *'The Messenger'* and felt emotionally moved by the poignant images of the dancing girl. The pizzica song and music was being performed by a group that she recognised from last year's *Notte della Taranta* at Melpignano, near Soleto. The male singer's voice had had a ring to it which bordered on the sinister, perfectly conveying the essentially atavistic quality of the dance, Elena recalled.

Soleto - hadn't she heard the name of this town to the south of Lecce in another context recently? She was sure she would make the mental connection again shortly if she didn't try too hard to remember what it was. Meanwhile she was impatient to open a second e-mail that she noticed had been sent to her client by the same hand as the first one; an individual who, enigmatically, had chosen to call himself 'The Messenger'; not 'The Blackmailer' or 'The Prince of Darkness', as one might have expected. She and Alessandro had both come to the conclusion that the sender was driven, not by revenge or money, but by a desire to scare their client into believing that he was in danger. If this was revenge, then it was a very subtle form of it.

The second video clip was accompanied by another message which was couched in the same enigmatic language:

Amedeo, fear not for yourself. Your time of waiting is nearly done.

The attached video clip lasted little more than half a minute and showed images of the same girl as before. But she appeared to be distressed. She was running from room to room in a sparsely furnished old *masseria* somewhere in the Puglian countryside, whose old stone courtyard and garden could be glimpsed as she ran into the kitchen and sat down at the table, her head in her hands. She was wearing a diaphanous dress which revealed her figure through the flimsy material. With a sharp intake of breath,

Elena saw clearly that she was several months pregnant. The clip was accompanied by music played and sung by the same local folk music group as before. This time, it was not a *pizzica* but had a slower more plaintive note to it. The words which accompanied the song were in dialect, which Elena had learnt as a child, and spoke of a girl who had been abandoned by the sea shore by a heartless lover. The music and images brought tears to Elena's eyes.

'Sandro,' she called out to her boss. 'You had better come and have a look at this.'

'How do you do it?' he asked in admiration, obviously referring to Elena's computer skills.

'It's not very difficult really,' she said modestly. 'I'll show you one day.' Elena knew that, while she was the only one to possess such skills, she would remain indispensable to the Greco agency.

Alessandro was mesmerised by the images of the pregnant young woman. 'This is serious, Elena. If the judge was somehow involved with this girl...' He left the sentence unfinished. 'Is there any way that the sender can be traced?'

'I'll try,' said Elena. 'But this hacker is very good. I doubt whether he has left any obvious footprints.'

Elena tried for nearly an hour to retrace the origins of the e-mail. The sender had been very skilful in concealing the devious electronic paths that he or she had followed. The message had been sent via three separate computers before it had arrived on Judge Grassi's screen. The last step backwards on its journey through cyberspace had revealed such a preposterous result that Elena laughed out loud in disbelief. On hearing her outburst of mirth, Alessandro rushed into her office assuming that she had achieved success.

'Well?' he asked.

'No, I don't think that can be right,' she said.

'Tell me anyway,' said Alessandro persuasively.

But despite all his efforts, Elena was too embarrassed to say what she had come up with.

'It has to be a mistake. I thought I was nearly there but I must have gone wrong on the last step. Let me have one more go later on, Sandro, and then I'll tell you anyway,' she said with pleading in her voice. 'It just can't be right.'

They discussed the case together in detail for another twenty minutes or so and decided unanimously that they should follow up the tenuous link between the housekeeper, Marta, and the events that had filled their client's last few days.

'We need a photograph of Marta,' stated Elena.

'Why do you say that?' asked Alessandro, who had, by now, learnt the sad truth that his assistant was often one step ahead of him when it came to perceiving connections between events.

'Intuition, Sandro,' she answered with exasperating conviction. 'We need to know where she goes and whom she sees when she leaves the Grassi household.'

'But we would have to stand outside in the street waiting for someone whom we assume to be Marta to come through the main gates. It's a very hit or miss method. And we don't really have the time or the resources,' he added in case his assistant was proposing that *he* should be the one who had to stand for hours in the streets of Lecce taking photos of every forty-plus-year-old woman who came through the big wooden doors which lead out of the garden on to the street. Elena could see what was going through his mind. She smiled her most dazzling smile, leaving her boss to admire the perfect whiteness of her teeth, and said:

'Leave it to me, Sandro. There's a simpler way. And when it comes to shadowing Marta, I have just the man who can help us – my partner, Adam. He will be delighted to be involved in something like this again. Marta won't suspect him for a minute.' She spoke with a conviction that she did not entirely feel but was confident that Adam would play along as long as it did not involve the risk of being murdered by a Calabrian *mafioso* as had happened while they had been tracking down her cousin's assassin all those years ago.

'All right,' sighed Alessandro. 'But we must start looking back over the judge's cases to see if we can find a plausible connection with what is happening to him now.'

'This afternoon, Sandro, I promise. I already had it in mind.'

'I'll help you as soon as I've cleared up the Mosca affair,' he promised. He had undertaken to help a well-off lady called Liliana Mosca, who owned two shops in Lecce which sold very expensive wedding presents to the city's upper middle-classes. While she was managing the main shop in the old part of the city, she left her other shop in the hands of three part-time girls who came at various times of the day or on certain days every week. One of them was helping herself to money before it even reached the till. Liliana could not be sure but the money she had found in the till did not seem to correspond to the electronically printed receipts. She reckoned she had lost something in the region of €500 in the space of three weeks. Alessandro had told her that it should be easy enough to trap the offending shop assistant and had given her a price for his services. 'It should take me only three visits to your shop at the most, *signora*.'

Alessandro had devised the simple plan of going into the Mosca shop and buying something 'small' - there was very little for sale under €30, he noticed. He would pay for the item with a €50 note which would have a tiny mark on it that only the two of them would know about. The first girl had been a surly, rather overweight girl who had sold him some piece of *bric-à-brac,* which was marked up with a 200% profit margin, Alessandro reckoned. Being young and susceptible to female charms he had mistakenly assumed this unprepossessing girl must be the culprit. He would be able to charge the agreed fee for a mere one hour's work. Unfortunately, the marked bank note had duly been retrieved by the rather haughty *Signora* Mosca. His second visit had been equally fruitless. Alessandro was inwardly crossing his fingers as he stepped into the shop later that same afternoon to buy his third coloured glass fruit bowl – made in China. The sales assistant was a pretty brunette with pert breasts who smiled as if she was pleased to see him. Alessandro's heart sank. He was sure that he would be returning Liliana Mosca's advance fee to a condescending scowl from this snob of a woman. As he was paying for the item, the girl smiled sweetly at him and asked: 'Did you need a receipt, *signore*?' He was immediately on the alert. Shopkeepers were under extreme pressure, thanks to the government of Mario Monti, to issue till receipts for everything from a single carrot to a complete dining room suite.

'No, there's no need to bother,' he replied with a knowing wink. He left the shop thinking that he had done a good job. 'What a pity - she seemed so sweet-natured,' he thought.

It had been quite a fruitful day, financially. He had received a very generous cheque that morning from the judge's wife, well in excess of the sum he had specified. 'A bit extra so that you know how much we appreciate your help', the enclosed note had said. 'In other words, don't you dare take on any other work until you have solved this case,' Alessandro had accurately interpreted Antonella's pointedly chosen words.

Back in Alessandro Greco's *studio,* Elena had started her research, still half annoyed with herself and yet amused too at the false step she must have taken while attempting to trace the source of the e-mails sent to the judge. She could only hope that 'The Messenger' would send a third e-mail over the next couple of days. Then she could try again. She had been pleased to see that Teresa had sent her a text message so that she had that number on her mobile. She immediately sent Teresa a text message asking her to try and take a photo of Marta, the housekeeper, without arousing her suspicions. 'I am sure that she will find a way,' thought Elena confidently. Her faith in Teresa's intelligence was vindicated within thirty minutes. She had taken a photo on her iPhone by holding up the gadget at arms' length and getting a head and shoulders image of herself, Marta in the middle and Antonella on the other side. Marta's smile was not very convincing, but it would do. Elena downloaded the image on to her computer, enlarged the image of Marta's face and printed it off so that her unsuspecting helper, Adam, would have no trouble recognising Marta.

She spent the rest of the day fruitlessly going through the available court case files in which Judge Grassi had been involved. She had started with his recent cases and worked backwards. She had reached 2006 when she gave up for the day. They had all been routine cases and the outcomes all seemed to be perfectly unequivocal. She decided that it might be more profitable to have a word with a lawyer cousin of hers who had been working in the *tribunale* for nearly ten years. He would know from gossip if there had been any dubious decisions made by the judge in the past decade. She had an intuitive feeling that the case that she and Alessandro had become involved in was going to be solved by more direct means. Before leaving the *studio*, she sent another text to Teresa asking for details as to when the housekeeper began her time off. Instead of simply giving Elena this piece of information, Teresa Grassi had suggested that they meet up for a coffee near the *Santa Croce* church the following morning at about 10 o'clock. Teresa said she would bring a memory stick containing the *two* video clips which her father had received. 'Yes, there has been a second one,' said the text message. Elena would not be revealing the fact that she had hacked into the judge's computer. Nor that her name was not Elena. Not just yet, in any case.

Elena-Rosaria was pleased that she had judged correctly that the two of them had the potential for being friends. She shut down her computer with a sense of relief. Alessandro came in at that moment looking relatively pleased with himself after his visit to Liliana Mosca's gift shop.

'Not *another* coloured glass fruit bowl!' she exclaimed mockingly.

'I feel sure that this one will be the last,' said Alessandro. A telephone call from his client soon confirmed that the €50 note had not ended up in the till. The haughty lady thanked Alessandro without warmth and even requested that he be present when she confronted the girl next week. 'Certainly, *signora,* if I am available,' he had replied. The offer of a further financial inducement was made; obviously Liliana Mosca did not want to be on her own for this confrontation with her employee. Elena had told Alessandro about her lack of success in identifying any case tried by Judge Grassi that might have a bearing on the current events in his life. She told Alessandro that she intended to spend the following morning at the law courts. He agreed that it was a good idea.

'I agree with you, Elena. This case is more likely to be solved through personal contacts,' Alessandro said. Elena told him about the plan to follow Marta wherever she went when she had her time off. Alessandro approved and told his 'assistant' to go home. He would continue to go through the judge's cases for another hour or so.

* * *

How good it felt to be home again, to be greeted with a kiss from Adam and to be called 'Rosy' instead of Elena. The children, Anna and Riccardo, ran up to hug their mother who fussed over them for ages. Adam just went on cooking dinner. Rosaria, at home, decided to tell Adam all about Judge Grassi, in order to ensure that he would become as fascinated as she was by the unusual circumstances surrounding this investigation. After the children were in bed, she came up close to him and stood with her body pressed up against his. After all this time, it still aroused her partner who, nevertheless, suspected that there might be an ulterior motive.

'You are being *very* nice to me this evening, Rosy.'

'I'm *always* nice to you, Adam.'

'Yes, but I mean extra specially so. I take it you have a favour to ask?'

Rosaria was always pleased that their love still had a sharp edge to it. Adam would respond to her seductive advances but was never entirely taken in. He had half guessed that she wanted him to take part in this investigation, so he said outright:

'If you imagine for one minute that I am going to pursue another mafia gangster, Rosy, you can think again.'

'Oh no, Adam! It's nothing like that. I wouldn't even put myself through that kind of experience again.'

'Well, *that's* reassuring,' he said sarcastically.

So Rosaria told him about her plan to have Marta shadowed to see where she went and who she spoke to.

'She will never suspect anything if she is being tailed by an Englishman in his fifties,' reasoned Rosaria. Adam did not like being reminded of his age - even if nobody ever believed him on the rare occasions when he had to divulge his age.

'So, do you know if she has a car?' asked Adam.

'No, we are not sure. But we think she takes the local train down south.'

'Well, it will make a change, I suppose. You know how I love travelling on those pre-Second World War trains, Rosy.' This was not sarcastically meant. Those lumbering diesel trains, shipped down to Puglia when they had become too ancient and graffiti-laden to operate in the 'respectable' northern Italian provinces, wound their way through olive groves, fruit orchards and herds of scraggy sheep, rattling past white-painted farm houses on a single line track that joltingly and noisily linked all the little villages and towns together. It was a journey through a Salento that had not changed for hundreds of years.

'Do you know where she will be heading?' asked Adam.

'Soleto, I think.' That was it! The connection that she had been trying to make had come to her out of the blue. Someone had mentioned Marta's home town whilst they had been discussing the Grassi case. She kissed Adam and they made their way to bed. The children were fast asleep. 'How angelic children look when they are sleeping!' remarked Rosaria. *'L'apparenza inganna!'* said Adam, quoting his favourite all-purpose phrase about everything Italian – how easy it is to be fooled by appearances. There was something tantalisingly applicable to the Grassi case in the phrase which Adam had just used, she thought. She put the matter out of her head and they went to bed and slept. Rosaria always slept deeply. Adam eventually fell asleep after lying awake wondering how he had been inveigled into spending his free time traipsing around Salento in pursuit of a forty-year-old housekeeper. 'Chained to love, soul-bound to Rosaria', he concluded reluctantly, falling asleep with a hand resting on her stomach.

* * *

The following morning, Rosaria became Elena again and went to meet the judge's daughter in the coffee bar near the *Santa Croce* church at ten o'clock – ten past ten in Teresa's case.

'I'm so sorry I'm late again, Elena,' she began. 'I had to have a word with my daughter's head teacher. Emma is in the habit of telling her class teacher home truths to her face. It's quite embarrassing at times.' Teresa outlined some of her daughter's past comments to an amused Elena.

'What did she say this time?' asked Elena.

'She asked her in public what her boyfriend was called.'

'That's not so bad, is it?' suggested Elena.

'It is when her teacher is a lesbian,' replied the mother, who could not suppress her amusement.

'Our daughter tends to be outspoken too,' said Elena.

'Out of the mouth of babes, sucklings and educated middle-class children!' said Teresa. 'The trouble is, I threatened to put her on a diet of plain pasta for a month – or was it three months – the next time she embarrassed her teacher. I suppose I shall have to punish her this time.'

Elena loved the way the judge's daughter spoke. She was having to stop herself saying: 'Call me Rosy, please!' But with *cappucini* and *cornetti* on the table in front of them, they got down to business. Teresa handed over the memory stick on which she had recorded the two video clips of the unknown girl. Elena was sorry that she had to continue the deception and pretend that she had not seen those poignant images. It would not be right to reveal immediately that she possessed advanced computer hacking skills – especially since they had not produced any positive results. Thus, Elena encouraged the judge's daughter to describe the contents of the video clips and the accompanying messages.

'How has your father reacted to the images?' asked Elena.

'He is deeply upset, of course, and still desperately attempting to link the images to some incident in his past life.'

'But do you still not think he may be concealing something that he knows?' asked Elena.

'On second thoughts, almost certainly, yes.' replied the daughter. 'But I am sure he has not succeeded in convincing himself that he is on the right track. He is becoming increasingly afraid that something catastrophic is about to happen to him, as I said before.'

The two women agreed that this was precisely the effect that the unknown 'assailant' was attempting to achieve.

'It's such a strange name for a would-be blackmailer, or vengeful assassin, to call himself – or herself, I suppose,' commented Teresa.

'You mean, *The Messenger?*' said Elena. 'Yes, always the religious overtones! *The Messenger* has calculated the effect with extreme precision.'

Elena told Teresa what her plans were for today. She would nose around the law courts and talk to a cousin that she knew. She explained what she had done the previous afternoon and told her companion that she had achieved nothing.

'I think we can safely say,' said the judge's daughter, 'that whatever it is that happened goes further back in time. I reckon we should be looking at events of ten years ago.'

Elena had the same impression as Teresa and asked if she could identify any event in her father's life which had taken place round about that period of time. Teresa thought back carefully and her eyes suddenly had an alert look about them. 'It's about ten years ago that my grandparents died – my father's mother and father, I mean. The two deaths occurred very close together. But I cannot for the life of me see a connection.'

'I believe that you might have discovered a link which could prove to be significant, Teresa. But I have to say, it's is a purely intuitive feeling.'

'*Always* trust intuitive feelings, *mia cara* Elena! Especially as we are women,' she added. Teresa attracted the attention of a passing waiter who came over immediately and presented them with the modest bill.

'*Grazie, Teresa. Tienimi al corrente! Mi raccomando!*' said Elena, using the familiar form of address for the first time to her new friend.

'Of course I'll keep you posted, Elena. We will meet again soon, I just know it.'

As they were about to part company, Elena asked: 'Isn't it this morning that your father has to go to the INPS about his pension?'

'Yes, that's right. He's going there with his doctor, his lawyer and my brother – who is also a lawyer, by the way. He's taking no chances with Italian bureaucracy,' replied Teresa laughing. Their first *bacio* on the cheek to establish the sense of familiarity which they both felt and the two women went their separate ways.

* * *

Elena Camisso spent the morning nosing around the *Palazzo di Giustizia,* looking up the judge's old court cases. She gained the impression that the judge had been disappointingly fair in most of his dealings. A number of cases had been tried with two other magistrates present, which was the general rule if the case was likely to be contentious. The outcome of many of the cases was decided without a jury; nothing unusual there. Her cousin, Savino, had promised to take her out to lunch somewhere busy so that what, if anything, he had to reveal would be covered by the noise of people talking and the clatter of cutlery.

'Ah, your Judge Grassi was more notorious for his alleged affairs with a series of beautiful young secretaries than for a lack of impartial judgement,' Savino had said. His cousin looked crestfallen. 'But...' he continued, '...there were rumours about a number of earlier cases. There was the case where he cut the sentence of a supposed *mafioso* gangster, a cousin of the local *boss*. You remember that, I am sure; the case of the shopkeeper who received severe burns when his shop was torched with him inside it, because he had refused to pay his protection money. The judge cut the sentence to three years arguing that there had been no intent to kill since nobody knew that the owner was inside the shop at the time; plus the fact that the mafia cousin had already served three years in custody.'

'Yes, I know about that case,' said 'Elena' to her cousin. 'It doesn't appear to have a bearing on the judge's current predicament.'

'I agree, Rosy,' said Savino. 'But it is rumoured that your judge received some 'favour' in return for the reduced sentence.'

'Other cases?' she asked. 'About ten years ago?' She felt that she was groping in the dark.

'There were a couple of strange cases round about 2001, or maybe 2002, which aroused attention,' continued Savino. 'A case of a farmer who had been accused of adulterating pig feed. The unusual aspect was that it transpired that your judge was having an affair with the farmer's younger sister, who was his secretary at the time. Many people believe that he got off lightly with a mild reproof from Grassi, who stated publicly that the case should not have come to court. Then there was, if I remember correctly, a case of a wealthy industrialist who was involved in a case of sexually abusing his daughter. Judge Grassi appeared to simply quash the sentence at the final appeal stage in the *tribunale*. The man concerned just disappeared up to Milan or somewhere and the case petered out. Oh yes, and then there was the rumour – nothing more – that the judge had seduced an underage girl who had come to him for help because her family was insisting on her marrying an older man whom she was not in love with.'

'I don't suppose you remember any names?' asked, Elena-Rosaria, whose senses had been alerted by her cousin's uncertain recollections.

'No, I don't remember exactly. She was a very beautiful girl, dark hair, olive skin and so on. The judge was seen with her in a restaurant outside Lecce. But... there was one strange thing that the more cynical members of the public made great play of at the time, I seem to remember; the girl had the same initials as the judge, A.G. The humourists even suggested that the girl was related to the judge in some way and there were crude jokes about incestuous relationships flying around.'

Savino could not possibly understand why his cousin's expression had changed to one of wide-eyed absorption, or why she stood up and kissed her cousin firmly on his cheek. 'Please try to remember the girl's name, Savino,' she pleaded. 'It could be very important.'

9: The Day of Reckoning

It was Friday morning and Amedeo had received no further e-mails or text messages from his 'persecutor'. The trip to the INPS the day before, to sort out his pension, had been successful. The employees had been suitably apologetic and had handed him a cheque for the amount that was due to him for the current month – minus the sixty per cent which had already been earmarked for his wife that month. His lawyer demurred but Amedeo had laid a hand on his lawyer's arm and said, 'It's alright, Enzo. Don't worry.'

'Things will be back to normal in May, *signor giudice*,' the employee had reassured him, secretly thinking that he wished he could earn even the remaining 40% of the judge's pension every month.

Amedeo remained deeply disturbed by the video clips that he had received and was suffering from a paranoid conviction that he was about to pay the price for some forgotten sexual misdemeanour. He was suffering from a potent mixture of guilt, fear of punishment and the same unpleasant sensation of having been publicly exposed that he had experienced whenever his mother or father had caught him out in some activity of which they morally disapproved or which fell short of their expectations of him.

Amedeo took the coward's way out by not attempting to analyse his past misdeeds. If he stayed at home, he reasoned, nothing untoward could happen to him. If only he could get through Friday and Saturday without any more text messages or e-mails from his shadowy pursuer, it would be Sunday in no time at all. He would then be surrounded by his whole family, assembled for Emma's birthday. Apart from a family trip to church, where there would be safety in numbers, there should be no exposure to the outside world at all. He believed that whatever was going to happen to him was imminent, so by staying indoors or, at least, being in company if he ventured out, he could ward off danger for the next few days. He would not even begin to think beyond the following Sunday, which would already mark the beginning of the second week of private terror that seemed to be measured in years rather than days. Antonella took pity on her husband.

'I have to drive down to Melissino and settle the matter of the cigarette smoking employee, *mio caro.* Why don't you come down with me, Ame? It will take your mind off things. And I could really do with a second opinion from a judge's viewpoint.'

The appeal was irresistible and the alternative was to stay at home and torment himself with fears about his immediate future. So he agreed, with alacrity, to accompany Antonella to the pasta factory. They went downstairs arm in arm to retrieve Antonella's new Citroën DS from its 'stable'. They left Marta busy preparing *antipasti* for the Sunday lunch. Young Emma had decided that she would rather celebrate her birthday in the secure environment of her grandparents' 'secret garden' than go out to a restaurant where she would be constrained to sit for hours at a table while the adults gorged themselves with food and wine. Her idea met with universal approval – which made a pleasant change, thought Emma.

'Apparently, Emma thinks that Sunday lunch may be her last meal on earth,' said Antonella, who had been highly amused by her granddaughter's latest indiscretion. 'She will be eating plain pasta until she writes a letter begging her teacher's forgiveness coupled with an undertaking signed in blood that it will never happen again.'

'Emma's Last Supper, so to speak!' said Amedeo amused – and not a little envious – that this child was able to grow up without fear of retribution from morally over-zealous parents.

'Changing the subject, Ame, Marta has asked if she can have next week off. She wants to spend time with her daughter. I take it you don't have any objections?'

'None at all,' replied Amedeo. 'She has never once asked for time off, as I remember, in all the months she has been with us.' Her potential involvement in the judge's troubles was still hard to take seriously.

When the couple had arrived at the 'farm' in Melissino, they found the whole work-force assembled outside the factory. One of the longest serving workers acted as spokesman. He was a very dignified man of about fifty-five. He spoke quietly and respectfully to Antonella explaining that the offending employee was under stress at home. 'He has a teenage son who has been arrested for possession of drugs by the *carabinieri*,' explained the man.

'In return for Mauro's reinstatement, *signora*, we would like to propose that we have a total smoking ban during working hours. A number of us feel that this would avoid future misunderstanding – and, incidentally, help us to give up our own bad habits,' he concluded with a wry smile.

Antonella looked at the judge. He knew that his wife was a little afraid of showing weakness when faced with her workforce. He just nodded his approval and turned to the spokeman and said simply: 'But this ban must be total and be observed rigidly,' he said putting on his best judicial manner.

So the matter was settled within ten minutes. Amedeo and Antonella decided not to go home immediately, so they drove towards the west coast and then down south towards Leuca. They would go and visit their holiday home for the first time this year and then go and have lunch somewhere overlooking the Adriatic Sea. The judge looked around the house. He always felt a tinge of guilt when he saw how beautifully it had been restored. He wondered if Antonella guessed that the finances for the renovation had not come directly from his pocket.

* * *

Elena Camisso decided that she would be spending her time better, not sitting in front of a computer digging up old court cases, but visiting the archives of *Il Quotidiano*. She had made an appointment to see the editor, Claudio Sabatini, on the following Monday explaining that the Greco agency had been employed by Judge Grassi to investigate the unusual attack on his privacy. Claudio had heard about Elena and was curious to meet her, so he had readily agreed to see her.

She had spent too much time the day before pursuing the matter of the girl who had had purportedly been seduced by a younger Judge Grassi. Elena's lawyer cousin had remembered that the initials **A.G.** had stood for Aurora Gaetano. Elena had quickly tracked down the girl – who was nearer thirty than twenty years old by now – and had driven north out of Lecce to Trepuzzi where Aurora was now a slightly haggard-looking mother of two children. Aurora had been highly embarrassed to be reminded of the rashness of her desperate attempt to enlist the help of Judge Grassi.

'It was my fault, entirely, *signorina*,' she told Elena. 'I seduced him. It wasn't the other way round as all the newspapers said. And as far as I know, the judge and I are not related – as some of the nastier-minded journalists tried to imply. In fact, he was very helpful and persuaded my parents not to be so rigid about my getting married to the husband of their choice.'

'Well, I hope you married the person of *your* choice in the end,' said Elena kindly, looking at the two rather undisciplined children eating their lunch and arguing between every mouthful.

'I sometimes think my parents might have been right, after all,' replied the girl sadly.

Elena left the flat feeling depressed in general for the fate of humanity. At least the visit had eliminated one avenue of research in a matter of minutes. Now, she would have to concentrate on… what exactly? The industrialist accused of sexually abusing his daughter? She would start researching the case that afternoon. Back at the Greco *studio*, she spoke of her frustrations to Alessandro, who reassured her that they would unearth something sooner or later. They agreed that the judge should come in to the studio on Monday when they would persuade him to be a little more 'open' about his past life. Elena remembered that Adam was going to follow Marta as soon as she left the Grassi household the following day. With any luck, that trail might lead somewhere.

* * *

It was Saturday evening at about seven o'clock. Marta had completed her preparation of the picnic lunch for Emma's birthday round about two o'clock and had bid the family a fond farewell. When Antonella had thanked her and complimented her on her mastery of Salentino *antipasti*, Marta had smiled radiantly and performed a half-humorous bow of gratitude with her arms crossed in front of her, oriental style, in thanks for the compliment given. Antonella had been left with the impression that Marta had wanted to kiss her on the cheek but that she had checked the impulse.

'It's almost as if she isn't intending to return,' said Antonella thoughtfully after their housekeeper had left.

'You're reading too much into her reaction,' said Amedeo. 'She probably feels as if she is on holiday.'

'Mmm,' was his wife's unconvinced rejoinder.

Amedeo was just beginning to hope that his persecutor had decided to give up. He was beginning to relax and look forward to a Sunday spent with his family. He lowered his emotional guard for the space of five minutes. That was precisely the moment when his mobile phone bleeped, revealing the arrival of a text message. His heart was pounding in his rib-cage within seconds. The expression of dread on reading the message was clearly visible in his eyes.

Amedeo, you must look at one more e-mail. Tomorrow, the scales will fall from your eyes. Do not be afraid. A.G.

He went up to his study on his own. Antonella quietly continued to work around the kitchen, getting picnic plates, cutlery and glasses out ready for the Sunday party. The third video clip was the most shocking of all. It showed the dancing girl again. She looked blankly at the camera, devoid of all recognition and emotion. Her eyes were staring vacantly into a space behind the lens. There was no background music this time, but there was the distressing sound of someone sobbing uncontrollably. Antonella came upstairs and watched the brief video clip. She was visibly affected by the images that she saw. She phoned Teresa who, in her turn, phoned Elena. Adam had just returned from his tour of Salento on the slowest and most antiquated *Sud-Est* train that he had ever ridden on.

'It sounds as if we might have something more concrete to go on after tomorrow,' was Teresa's pragmatic comment.

'Yes, it does look that way,' replied Elena. 'And yet, there is still an absence of any threats.' Teresa promised to phone Elena should there be any developments.

Amedeo spent a tormented night, only falling asleep in the small hours. He slept fitfully, haunted by the images of the girl with her distant, unblinking eyes staring at him in the semi-darkness. Not for the first time, he had the impression that he had met this girl before, but for the life of him, he could not think under what circumstances. In the end, he decided that it was merely a false impression that he had gained born of his alarming familiarity with the images projected from his computer screen. He sought the physical comfort of his wife's presence. He was reassured by the pressure of his back against Antonella's. Reassurance was not Antonella's principal sensation that night; it was more a feeling of discomfort. She did not have a very peaceful night.

* * *

Sunday morning dawned bright and clear with no hint of impending doom as the rays of the impartial sun streamed warmly through the half closed shutters of the bedroom. There was nothing for it but to get up and get ready to go to mass as if nothing was wrong, thought Amedeo Grassi. The fears of the night had been dispelled by the morning sunshine and, soon after, by the arrival of his family. Fear of the unknown is more potent and insidious than fear of something as ordinary as being attacked in the street. The eight people who walked to the church of *San Matteo* that morning looked like any other unperturbed family group, drawing strength from their shared identity.

In the church, Amedeo was seated at one end of the row nearest the aisle with Antonella down the other end. There was a hush of expectancy as the whole congregation waited to see if it would be the young monk of last week whose figure emerged from the pillar and appeared high above them in the lofty pulpit. There was an audible sigh of relief when the familiar face of the monk-priest materialised before their eyes, wearing the full regalia of alb and chasuble. He smiled at the people below him but it was more like a broad grin that encompassed the whole assembly.

'In the name of the Father ...' he began, making the sign of the cross. Everybody in the church found themselves spontaneously copying this symbolic gesture of the Christian faith. Even the judge, to his great surprise, caught himself in the act.

'First of all, I want to thank the children here for being so good to the teacher that we were talking about last week. She tells me that she is feeling much happier than before. Only one young person

upset her just a little bit this week by asking her a question about her boyfriend. But I am sure this person did not mean to be unkind. It just shows how careful we must be when we choose the words we use.'

Emma felt her face going a bright red and tears pricking her eyes. How did he know? This priest seemed to know everything. Teresa, a bit shocked herself by the priest's apparent insight, put a comforting arm round her daughter and gave her a quick hug. 'I promise never to do it again, *mamma*,' she whispered. In point of fact, Emma had noticed how much happier her teacher had seemed and thought that a friendly question about her boyfriend would cheer her up even more. What a miscalculation of an adult's reaction *that* had proved to be!

'What shall we talk about this week, I wonder? Ah, I know! Some words from Saint Matthew since we are all together in his church today. Here we go: 'But many that are first shall be last, and the last shall be first'. Let's think about what these words of Jesus mean.'

The monk-priest was interrupted unexpectedly by the voice of the little girl who had asked him what his name was at the end of his sermon the previous Sunday.

'Please come down from heaven again, Angel Gabriel!' she called out to the general amusement of everybody in the church.

'Of course I will, Agata. Thank you so much for reminding me.'

There was another sharp intake of breath when the priest re-emerged from behind the pillar, only seconds later, wearing jeans, sandals and a simple T-shirt. His only concession to his office was a simple wooden cross hanging round his neck on a length of brown cord. He was smiling mischievously again. Judge Grassi was stupefied to realise that he no longer felt antagonism towards this man of God. 'You *are* getting soft, Amedeo!' he thought.

'I'm going to tell you a story – a parable – that you may not find in the Bible. One day, at school, a teacher called Jesus decided that all his pupils looked a bit fed up with doing sums and Italian grammar.' The usual titter of mirth ran round the church. *'So today, we are going to have a race. Jesus took his class and led them in crocodile fashion to the recreation ground in Lecce where there were nice white lines running round the outside forming a running track. All the children wanted to take part in this race except Tommaso who had been filling himself up with crisps and Fanta fizzy orange.* There was not a single child and hardly an adult who was not looking at the preacher. *'I'll just watch, Jesus,' offered Tommaso. 'To make sure there's no cheating' 'Oh no, Tommaso. I'm sorry, but EVERYBODY has to run in this race. It's called the race for life!' So, all the children lined up as near the starting line as they could. The first boy to pull ahead of all the others was called Massimo. He was a very strong, athletic boy who all the girls were in love with whereas most of the boys wished they looked like him. Massimo easily reached the finishing line before all the others. He did a kind of victory dance and flexed his beautiful arm muscles on the finishing line. 'We are the champion!' he boasted. Tommaso, who was a little bit overweight, came last of all puffing and panting as he collapsed on the grass. He had made it all the way round the track without stopping! But nobody cheered HIM. 'Now I have a bit of a problem,' said Jesus. 'Who do you think I should give this lovely gold cup to?' None of the children had noticed that Jesus was holding a cup in his hands. If anything, they had the impression that it had been a chequered flag. 'Massimo!' called out Massimo, in*

answer to Jesus's question. 'Yeah, Massimo,' called out a few of the children a little half-heartedly.

The priest turned to the congregation and asked them if they thought that the gold cup should be presented to Massimo.

'No!' came the half-hearted response from the children – and some of the adults too. *I see you are becoming too clever for me. So who should Jesus give the cup to?* 'Tommaso!' they said almost in one voice. *'Why do you think that?'* 'Because Massimo is a show-off who thinks he is better than everybody else,' came the reply from one child to the general amusement of the rest of the congregation. 'Yes, Jesus should give the cup to Tommaso, father,' said one little voice. *Tommaso? So why do you think that?* There were a few muttered answers but nobody wanted to say out loud what they thought because it wasn't their place to know better than the priest.

Is my friend Giovanni here this week? Ah, there you are Giovanni. What would we do without you? Who would you give the cup to, Giovanni? 'Well father, I think I would give it to Tommaso because he came last but he tried really hard to please Jesus.' A little cheer went up for Giovanni and a few children clapped their hands.

Thank you again, Giovanni. Yes, Jesus gave the cup to Tommaso because he had had to work very hard to keep up with all the other children. He probably gave up eating packets of crisps...'

'And he stopped drinking Fantas, didn't he father!' piped up Emma from the Grassi row of seats. She had obviously forgotten about her former humiliation. The laughter that ran round the congregation was less restrained this time. Once again, the priest had succeeded in arousing everybody's avid curiosity and he had conveyed a clear, simple message to everyone present.

So now I hope you understand just a little of what Jesus was saying. It doesn't matter if you think you are an important person in this life because in God's eyes it will be the people who have tried to overcome their difficulties, the people who have done their best to show love and sympathy to those who are vulnerable who will be rewarded when the final day of judgement comes.

Amedeo was feeling uneasy again and squirmed a little in his seat.

In the name of the Father and of the Son and of the Holy Spirit. I am sorry to tell you all that I shall not be able to see you next Sunday. There followed an audible sound of disappointment from the congregation. *But I promise you that I will be back the Sunday afterwards.* There were choruses of relief, and a little outbreak of cheers at this news. 'Thank you father, you are an inspiration to us,' said someone in the congregation. '*Bravo, bravissimo!*' said the congregation echoing the sentiment. The priest looked at them all and smiled warmly in gratitude. He crossed his arms in front of his chest and bowed his head slightly in a gesture of self-deprecating humour. Judge Grassi would have joined in the general applause that followed but he was suffering from the impact of mental shock as the scales did indeed fall from his eyes in that instant of time. He had seen that identical gesture, the self-same smile on the self-same face in his own kitchen the day before. '*O mio Dio!* He's Marta's son!' he thought with an inspired flash of recognition.

Almost immediately afterwards, whilst the rest of the congregation was settling back into the routine of giving the habitual responses required by Holy Mother Church during the saying of Mass, Amedeo understood something else with a blinding clarity akin to that of Saul on the road to Damascus. 'What was it the little girl, Agata, had said to the priest when he was high up in the pulpit? *'Please come down from heaven, Angel Gabriel.'*

'It's HIM,' he said loud enough for his grandson to turn his head and look quizzically at his grandfather. 'Angel Gabriel - the Messenger from God!' thought the judge. He had found out whom the initials **A.G.** belonged to. He looked down the row of chairs in Antonella's direction but neither his wife nor his daughter appeared to have cottoned on to the young priest's identity. Indeed, they both had a slightly celestial smirk on their faces. 'Obviously, mesmerised by the man!' thought the judge whose sense of male superiority briefly surfaced again. As the service proceeded, other fragmented memories fell into place. When Amedeo had asked the old priest the previous Sunday about the identity of the new preacher, he had answered something about him being 'on loan' from the Vatican 'to teach us how to use computers', he had said. And then there was the identity of the young man who had presented himself at the offices of *Il Quotidiano* as well as at the printer's on the outskirts of Lecce. The description fitted perfectly and it was obvious that this monk from the Vatican was happy to discard his priestly robes whenever he felt like it. In addition, he had made the sign of the cross at the mention of his 'deceased' earthly father – something that would come naturally to a Catholic priest. But what Amedeo could not determine, however hard he wracked his brains during the rest of the service, was *why* any priest – even any normal layman – should go to such extraordinary lengths to achieve whatever his secret purpose might be. 'What have I *done* to deserve such treatment?' he wondered.

As soon as mass had ended and the priests had filed out, disappearing into the vestry somewhere in the nether regions of the stately old church, the judge was on his feet. He called out to his astonished family with an intensity that left them totally bewildered: 'I've got to talk to that priest.' And with those words, he shot up the aisle and without hesitation, disappeared into the hallowed precincts of the priests' private domain.

Antonella and Teresa led the way out and the family sat on the church's stone steps and waited. When the judge failed to reappear after twenty minutes, they began to become anxious. After half an hour, Aurelio was dispatched off to the male preserve of the vestry to track down his father. He came back looking mystified. '*Papà* has disappeared,' he announced. 'Apparently, he got into a large car with smoked glass windows in the company of Don Gabriele and two other priests and drove off down a side street.'

The whole family looked bewildered. They became increasingly alarmed as they walked back home without the head of the family present. Antonella tried to call her husband on his mobile but, frustratingly, all she got was the announcement that stated impersonally: *La persona desiderata non è al momento disponibile.*

'What does all this mean?' asked an anxious Cinzia, Aurelio's pretty wife. The hint of some danger or mystery hung over the family group, affecting even the two young children.

'Has granddad been kidnapped?' asked Alessio, Aurelio's son, in wide-eyed wonder and more than a hint of fear.

'It rather looks that way,' said Teresa after a tense silence as the shocking reality of Alessio's innocent interpretation of events sank in. 'Whether he went willingly or not,' said Teresa as if thinking out loud, 'he seems to have been abducted by a priest.'

10: The Abduction of Judge Grassi

The family, minus one, wended its way home in almost total silence, walking close together, the children holding hands with whoever was nearest to them. The obvious thing to do was to phone 112 and tell the *carabinieri* what had happened. But what sort of reaction might they expect when they tried to explain that the head of their family had apparently been abducted by a bunch of monks? It would certainly bring a little comic relief to the police officers on duty, helping to alleviate the tedium of their Sunday routine. But they were unlikely to leap into their Alfa Romeos with sirens blaring to scour the countryside for three monks and a retired judge.

When the family reached home, the children were hungry. There was a mass of food to eat which had been prepared by Marta. None of the adults felt like eating or drinking. In the end, it was decided to let the children go out in the garden and pick at food as they felt like it. Cinzia accompanied by Teresa's husband, Leonardo, volunteered to keep the children company in the garden. The two adults could not have lived in more diverse worlds; Cinzia was an expert *pasticciere* who made superb cakes at home for private clients whilst Leonardo was the head of the nanotechnology department at the university. Everybody called him by his nickname, *Einstein*, even though he tirelessly pointed out that he was a mere technician who played around with nanostructures. After they had exchanged their bewildered thoughts about the disappearance of the judge, their conversation sunk to the level of the banalities of their daily lives. In the end, Leonardo hid himself in a corner of the garden and smoked a pipe, a pastime which was totally banned at home by his wife – and daughter.

In the meantime, Antonella, Teresa and Aurelio were indoors in a state of perplexity. They had recovered from the initial shock of Amedeo's disappearance. They had begun to reason that the head of their family was probably not in danger – in fact, as far as they knew, he might well have accepted an invitation to be driven off with the monk and his companions. What made no sense at all was why Amedeo had suddenly taken it into his head to rush off with such urgency to see 'that priest'. The fact that his mobile phone was switched off was decidedly ominous, thought Antonella.

'He probably switched it off during mass,' suggested Teresa. 'And then forgot to turn it on again.'

'That's right, *mamma*,' added Aurelio in an attempt to reassure his anxious mother.

They decided that it would be right to notify the police as to what had happened and risk an adverse reaction. To their relief, the *carabiniere* officer who took the call sounded genuinely concerned. Most people in Lecce who read a newspaper or watched the TV had gleaned the little information that was available to the public as to the unusual circumstances that had interrupted the retired judge's routine existence. The police officer consulted his *capitano* and promised the family that they would send an officer round to their home within the hour. It was reassuring to know that the police were taking the matter seriously even though there was little evidence of abduction and none at all of criminal intent. Indeed, as soon as the telephone call to the police was over, Antonella heard her mobile phone bleep twice. She seized the phone with visibly shaking hands and read the anonymous text message. Instead of reading it out loud, she simply passed the gadget to her son and daughter without a word. ***Do not be alarmed. Amedeo is quite safe with us. A.G.*** When she attempted to reply, she was told that the number had not been recognised.

While they were in deep discussion, the two children had come unnoticed into the kitchen having eaten all they could manage within the space of a mere ten minutes. 'But *why* would Amedeo want to talk to the priest just at that moment?' asked Antonella to nobody in particular.

'Because he suddenly recognised who he was,' interjected Alessio from behind them. The three adults swivelled round as if they had all been powered by one single muscular impulse.

'What do you mean, Alessio?' asked his father.

'It was exactly as I said, *papà.* Granddad was looking at the priest when he did that funny kind of bow and granddad said, '*It's HIM!'* Just like that,' concluded Alessio.

'Are you sure that is what he said, Alessio?' asked Teresa, digesting the implications of these few words.

'Of course I'm sure, *zia!*' replied the nine-year-old with a look of indignation on his face. 'Otherwise I wouldn't have said it.'

'Auntie' Teresa looked suitably chastised.

'Thank you, Alessio,' said his father proudly. 'You have just given us a very important piece of information.'

Alessio was still young enough to experience that uplifting feeling of joy in the heart when he found himself on the receiving end of a compliment from an adored parent. Young Emma was mildly stung that *she* was not the one who had been sitting next to her *nonno* in the church – particularly as it was supposed to be *her* birthday. She decided that it was time for *her* to make an intelligent contribution to this conversation and win a few credit points for herself – especially after being embarrassed by the monk's gentle chastising of her well-intentioned gaffe over her teacher.

'So all you've got to do is find Angel Gabriel and you'll find granddad too!' she proclaimed, little expecting the stunned silence followed by the look of total admiration on her mother's face. She earned the biggest hug and the sloppiest kiss she had had from her mother in years.

'You wonderful children!' said Teresa. 'What would we do without you?'

Teresa wanted to telephone Elena immediately but the *carabinieri* arrived just at that moment – a young *maresciallo* accompanied by an equally young female officer, her long dark hair tucked tightly under her official *kepi*. The three adults looked at each other thinking that they were taking part in the TV police drama, *Don Matteo*. '*Another* priest,' thought Teresa. 'How appropriate!'

The children decided that they had both earned the right to a second round of food and ran back out into the garden.

The three adults were able to furnish the identity of the judge's 'abductor' and identify the priest known as 'Angel Gabriel' as the one who had been responsible for staging the elaborate, theatrical production of the last eight days. The two police officers agreed that the judge did not appear to be in immediate danger but pointed out that, if indeed he had been abducted, the police would certainly be pressing charges.

'You must phone us immediately if there are any developments, *signori*,' they urged as they were leaving. 'Meanwhile we will alert all our units to be on the look-out.'

As soon as they had left, Teresa phoned Elena, excusing herself for disturbing her on a Sunday. They agreed to meet first thing the following morning. Elena was very excited and promised to fill Teresa in on the details of her partner Adam's excursion to the remoter parts of Salento the day before whilst pursuing the enigmatic housekeeper. The Grassi adults had still not made the connection between Marta and the priest which had precipitated Judge Grassi into his impetuous pursuit of the Angel Gabriel. Elena had an inkling of the truth but had not yet made the obvious link. In the excitement of the moment, they had all lost sight of the fact that the motives behind this elaborate charade were still shrouded in mystery.

The comparative relief felt by all the adults in the family was followed by the realisation that they had become very hungry. There was a subdued toast, with a bottle of chilled *Tenuto Marini,* to the safe passage of their absent head of clan while the girl whose birthday they were celebrating was happy playing somewhere in the garden with her cousin.

That night, Antonella slept on her own for the first time in days. She ought to have been relieved but was forced to admit reluctantly that she missed her husband's presence. It irked her to think that her husband had made some intuitive mental leap that she had failed to see. She finally fell into a deep slumber having grown weary of trying to picture where he was and how he was being treated. In the moments before slumber took over, she had even pictured him being made to wear a hair shirt as a penance for his past misdeeds and had been disturbed to discover that she had found the image amusing.

The following morning – Monday – Teresa met Elena at the same bar as before. It was only minutes past 8 o'clock. Husbands and partners were dropping the children off at school. The atmosphere was charged with a cross between excitement and fear. That circumstances had drastically changed since they last met was undeniable. The shadowy threats that they had been dealing with had become substantial. Yet, outright fear for the judge's safety seemed to be uncalled for – at least for the time being. As soon as the girls had their *cappucini* and *cornetti* in front of them, Teresa related to her companion everything that had transpired the day before. It took her a good ten minutes to go into all the details, ending up with her daughter's innocent and unwitting revelation of the startling identity of the owner of the initials A.G. When she had finished, Elena made her go over some of the details again.

'Do you remember exactly what the priest was doing when your father uttered the words, *It's him?'*

'According to my nephew, he had made a funny little bowing gesture with his arms crossed in front of his chest. He was modestly thanking the congregation for the compliment that they had just paid him.'

'I wonder why it was *that* gesture that triggered recognition?' said Elena thoughtfully.

'So, did your partner, Adam, discover anything on Saturday?' asked Teresa as her breakfast companion seemed to have fallen into a pensive silence.

'Poor Adam!' replied Elena. 'It was a long afternoon for him. I'm still not certain whether he achieved anything or not; maybe something that will prove to be significant later. He was loitering outside your parents' house for over an hour before Marta emerged. He followed her to the station where she took the train down to Soleto. It's quite a long walk from the station - which is stuck out in the countryside thanks to the planning of Benito Mussolini - into the town. He trailed her to a tiny house in the old town centre and took note of the address. He loves playing at being the sleuth, so he walked up the street and picked out the name of a couple further up – from the intercom doorbell. Then he went back and rang on Marta's door pretending to be looking for the people up the road. He said she was very kind and began telling him that she thought they lived at number 42 but that she wasn't sure. Adam said that the only other piece of information that he gathered was when her mobile phone rang while she was still talking to him. He could hear the anxious cry of a young woman on the other end of the line but could not hear any words. Marta said, *'Non preoccuparti amore mio. Mamma sta arrivando fra 10 minuti'*. With that, she excused herself and walked up the road to where a blue Renault Twingo was parked and she drove off in a northerly direction. Obviously, Adam was on foot so there was no way he could have followed her. But...'

'Do you still believe that Marta is involved in all this?' interrupted Teresa, not impatiently, but because she was not entirely convinced.

'Well, you can always tackle her directly when you see her this week,' suggested Elena.

'Eh, no, I can't,' said Teresa. 'She is on holiday all this week, apparently.'

At this point, Elena decided not to point out that, among other things, the text message that her friend's mother had received reassuring her as to the judge's safety clearly indicated that her mobile number was known to the Angel Gabriel. Elena was also convinced that the device which had enabled the priest to hack into the judge's bank account must have been planted by the housekeeper. She adopted the strategy of not giving Teresa the benefit of her more complex assumptions about Marta, at least until she had had time to investigate further. She was very aware that the Greco agency had done very little, to date, to earn the €7000 retainer that the Grassi family had parted with. At least, Elena Camisso, in her role as investigator, wanted her agency to be able to take the credit for discovering the whereabouts of the judge and, more importantly, what was behind this elaborate plot. She had a very incomplete theory forming in her mind, which she was not ready to divulge to anyone, except possibly to Alessandro Greco. The news that Marta was taking a holiday at the same time as the judge had been spirited away was, for Elena, stretching coincidence too far.

'Well, *mia cara* Teresa. Today, I am going to go to the church of *San Matteo* and see what I can find out about the priest, and then I have a lead to follow up at the offices of *Il Quotidiano*. I hope that I shall have something to tell you by tomorrow.'

The two women embraced and Teresa promised faithfully to phone her if they had any messages from the judge or from the enigmatic monk who seemed to be called Angel Gabriel.

* * *

Judge Amedeo Grassi had been so inspired by his discovery that he strode with single-minded purpose into the vestry scattering priests, altar boys and lay helpers in a state of confusion all around him. He was surprised at how many people there were in the restricted space of the vestry but disconcerted to notice that his quarry did not appear to be among them.

'I must speak to the Angel Gabriel!' he declared publicly. There were polite titters of amusement. Fingers were pointed to a half open side door that led directly on to a side street.

'He has just left,' said the elderly priest, 'with a couple of his friends. I think he might have been expecting you.'

Judge Grassi was outside in a flash. There were two unusually muscular monks standing by the open door of a modern-looking people carrier with darkened windows. The monks were smiling at him and beckoning him over towards the vehicle. Any incongruity in the sight that greeted his eyes was ignored by the judge who was driven solely by the desire to meet his adversary and confront him with a demand for valid explanations. The Angel Gabriel was sitting in the driver's seat next to the pavement. He gave a disarming smile of pleasure and said:

'Hop in, Amedeo. I was expecting you. I'll take you home. I am sure you must have a number of questions you would like to ask me.'

Amedeo was ushered into the back seat and the other monks walked round the other side of the car and got in, one next to the driver and the second settled himself next to the judge with a cheery smile. The Angel Gabriel slipped the car into gear and drove off with unsaintly alacrity.

'I thought you said you were taking me home,' were the judge's first words, tinged with alarm, as it became obvious that the little group was heading south out of the city.

'Ah,' said the Angel Gabriel blithely. 'I apologise for misleading you slightly, Amedeo. I meant *my* home, rather than yours.'

'You are abducting me, aren't you?' said Amedeo fearfully.

'I was hoping you would consider being my guest for a while, Amedeo. I'm quite sure you want to find out the reason why I have gone to such theatrical lengths to catch your attention; for which I humbly apologise to you. I needed to prepare your mind a little for what is in store for you.'

'Are you going to punish me for something awful that I have done?' asked the judge tremulously. He was terrified of the thought of being tortured and having to endure physical pain.

'Amedeo!' replied the monk. 'I am an ordained priest with only good intentions in my heart, I promise you. You may well suffer emotionally when you understand why I have...shall we say, snatched you from your familiar surroundings. Now, would you mind very much if we save up our conversation until we arrive, Amedeo?' concluded the Angel Gabriel kindly. 'I should be concentrating on the road.'

The judge was so relieved to find out that he was not going to be stretched on the rack or burnt with hot pokers by this young priest who had set himself up as a private, twenty-first century inquisitor that he felt emboldened to add in a more aggressive tone:

'You call me Amedeo as if you have known me personally for years – just like my doctor. I am quite sure you are not really called Angel Gabriel.'

For the first time during the car journey, the two monks sitting silently in the car let out a subdued chortle. 'His name really is Angelo Gabriele,' said the monk sitting next to him. He spoke with a distinct country voice with a strong local accent. He sounded more like a farmer than a monk. 'Would you be so gracious, *signor giudice*, as to give me your mobile phone? Gabriele wants to be sure that you won't be distracted over the next few days.'

Judge Grassi might have been relieved that the prospect of torture had receded, but it was eminently plain to him that his abductors meant business. The man sitting next to him, be he monk or farmer, was quite capable of taking his only means of communication with the outside world from him with minimum force, so Amedeo complied with the request without demur.

'I shall send a message to Antonella to reassure her that you are safe, Amedeo, just as soon as my hands are free.' These were the Angel Gabriel's last words during the forty minute car journey down south. The Salento countryside tends to look the same wherever you are – quite flat, covered with vines, olive groves, scattered with flocks of scraggy sheep that look more like wild goats and little clusters of houses coated with flaking white paint. Thus Amedeo had only a vague notion as to where they were going.

They finally pulled into the entrance of an old *masseria*. The judge had recently read an article in *Il Quotidiano* about these splendid old farmhouses dotted around the *Salento* countryside – many of them abandoned – waiting for some rich entrepreneur or film star to rescue them from total dereliction. The car stopped outside the massive iron gates, whose bars had been covered over with sheets of painted metal to prevent prying eyes from seeing inside. The monk sitting in front with the Angel Gabriel got out and unlocked the gates and pushed them open. As soon as they were open sufficiently, the car was driven quickly inside to prevent an exuberant and very large German shepherd dog from getting out. The judge's eyes were greeted by the sight of a large, two-storey, rectangular house whose exterior walls were painted deep pink. The double front door, wide open in welcome, was set back behind a shady veranda whose roof was supported by ornate stone pillars. From the roof, arose a number of traditional Salento chimney stacks, shaped roughly in the form of an inverted, bulging cone. A lazy plume of white smoke arose from one of them; the kitchen supposed Amedeo. The garden was vast and stretched invisibly beyond and behind the house. There were ancient olive trees, fruit trees of various kinds, a huge vegetable garden and newly planted vines surrounding the house. It was an idyllic setting in which to be held captive. Amedeo noticed, however, that a five metre high stone and plaster wall surrounded the whole estate.

'Welcome to our country home, Amedeo,' said the Angel Gabriel with a genuinely happy smile on his face.

'Mmm,' said the judge torn between wishing to appear morose in protest at his abduction and delighted to find himself in what seemed to be a country retreat akin to an earthly paradise. 'For a prison, it doesn't seem to be too disagreeable.'

'Amedeo,' replied the Angel Gabriel simply. 'I don't want you to escape just yet, it's true. But I am sure that you will not want to run away when you understand why I have brought you here.'

There were so many questions to be asked that Amedeo did not even know where to start. The Angel Gabriel was looking at him with an expression of appeal as if he was willing his captive to trust him. In direct but unconscious response to this, Amedeo said: 'I can't keep calling you Angel Gabriel every time. What should I..?'

'Just call me *Gabriele*. It *is* my name, after all,' interrupted the monk smiling. 'I don't think I am an angel by any stretch of the imagination, although Angelo is the first name my parents gave me. Come on, Amedeo. Let's get out of this car. And, by the way, don't be frightened by the dog. He wants to be *everybody's* friend, contrary to appearances. *L'apparenza inganna!* This is true about our dog as much as so many aspects of life in Italy.'

It was uncanny how this young monk seemed to read what was going through his mind. Amedeo had always been very wary in the presence of dogs ever since, as a five year old, he had been leapt upon by an over affectionate Labrador which had pinned his young body down to the floor and licked his face all over, until he had been rescued by its owner, who had had the audacity to find the whole experience highly entertaining. Amedeo had suffered humiliation rather than physical pain but what had hurt him most was that neither of his parents had offered him any comfort. He had cried and sulked for hours not because of any physical injury but a sensation of being abandoned emotionally. In the end, his father had banished him to his room with the injunction that he should 'pull himself together'. As soon as Amedeo stepped out of the car, he was assailed by the enthusiastically friendly hound. He raised his arms out of the dog's reach. A stern word from Gabriele and the dog did not jump up as instinct dictated. Amedeo felt a tinge of envy that this young monk seemed to exude a quiet authority that extended to the animal kingdom too.

'Just hold out your hand to him, palm upwards, Amedeo,' he advised the judge gently. 'Dogs have a sense of smell roughly one hundred times more sensitive than ours. Argo will recognise you for the rest of his life once he has noted your scent. He will be your friend for life too, if you like.' Amedeo tentatively did as he was bidden.

'Dogs really are Man's best friend, Amedeo. They are a marvellous creation. They will offer you eternal love and devotion in exchange for a friendly word. I learnt a lot of English at school and I was always amused that the English word *dog* is the exact reverse of the word *God*. It's as if the English language recognises that dogs are a pale reflection of the creator.' Amedeo wanted to ask the monk how Rottweilers fitted into this scheme but he had the impression that Gabriele was not making a serious theological point. So he merely smiled at him, checking himself immediately afterwards as he remembered that he had just been abducted by this unusual monk, who did not seem to attach too much importance to a priestly dress code. Gabriele understood precisely how his 'captive' was feeling.

'Come on Amedeo. Let's go inside. I'll show you to your room.' It was as if he had just arrived at a hotel.

'Is your mother here?' he asked brusquely without meaning to sound so abrupt.

'Yes, of course she is, Amedeo. *Please* believe me when I tell you that she feels very guilty about deceiving you, as she sees it. After a few days, she really began to feel at ease with you and Antonella. So, you will be understanding, won't you? It was entirely at my instigation that she came to live with you.'

'Of course,' replied Amedeo. 'We were very fond of her. I shall reserve my judgement,' he added with a wry smile, looking at Gabriele for the first time without any hint of ill-will in his eyes. The change was duly noted by Gabriele and a look of great relief passed across his expressive face.

'Come on Amedeo. Let's go inside,' he repeated ushering the judge through the double front door into the cool interior of the old *masseria*. Gabriele showed him to his room. Amedeo was amazed to find that it was spacious, simply but adequately furnished in rustic style with a double bed made up with fresh bed linen and covered with a brightly coloured duvet. Gabriele opened the shutters and revealed the full extent of the garden which stretched back a good five hundred metres. There was a separate shower room leading off the bedroom. He was even more surprised to find a few of his own clothes hanging up in a big, green wardrobe. There was a new tracksuit, which he had never once worn and had completely forgotten about, laid out on the bed waiting for him.

'The work of your mother, I guess,' said Amedeo with a touch of irony in his voice. Gabriele shrugged and smiled disarmingly by way of apology. In point of fact, Amedeo had to admit that he felt reassured by the sight of his own belongings in this unfamiliar room. 'Your preparation has been meticulous, Angel Gabriel,' said

Amedeo with grudging respect. Again, the monk performed that half ironic bow with arms crossed in front of his chest.

'*That* is what gave you away,' exclaimed the judge. 'Your mother made the identical gesture in our kitchen the day before.'

'Yes, I know,' replied the Messenger from God. 'Both mother and I are fond of our oriental bow. I knew at once that you had made the connection. I was so relieved, Amedeo; so very pleased.'

The judge looked out of the window at the soothing sight of greenery and the patches of warm sunlight which were joyously occupying every little space that the shade cast by the old olive trees had left free. There was an ancient, stone bench under one of the trees that beckoned invitingly as it had done for centuries. 'I fear you might be lulling me into a false sense of security, *caro Gabriele,*' said Amedeo with just a touch of apprehension in his voice.

The monk in young man's clothing replied seriously: 'You have only your own past shadows to fear, *caro giudice.* Now I shall leave you in peace until you feel ready to face the rest of our little family, which includes the brothers who accompanied us on the car ride from Lecce.'

When he was on his own, Amedeo stood still for a while looking out on the Garden of Eden beyond the window frame. He could see the two 'brothers', now without their monks' clothing, working busily in a second small vineyard that he could make out beyond the olive grove. 'I don't believe that they are really monks at all,' he said out loud. He had a shower, put on the track suit and a new pair of trainers that had been left for him. Naturally, they fitted his feet exactly. He lay down on the bed just to think over what had happened to him in the last nine days. He fell into a profound and dreamless sleep, emotionally and physically exhausted by events and secretly relieved that the doubts and fears of the past week had finally come to a head. The sun was low in the sky when he finally woke up in a strange bed, in a strange room, in an even stranger household. 'Time to face the music, I suppose.' He set foot nervously outside his bedroom and walked along the corridor towards the sound of voices and the smell of cooking. He felt just as he had on his first day at school when he was six years old, the fear of the unknown exposing the fragility of his protective shell. *'Coraggio!'* he said to himself as he made himself step over the threshold into the lighted kitchen.

11: Elena in Hot Pursuit

As soon as Elena had left Teresa, she headed for the church of *San Matteo* after the usual debate with herself as to whether she should walk or risk taking the car through the narrow streets of Lecce and then be unable to find a suitable – or legal – parking place. She might then find that she had to walk the same distance back to the church as she would have done from the bar where she had just had her coffee. As usual, the car won the debate. She probably saved herself five minutes after manoeuvring her Lancia Ypsilon into a space half the size of her car, down a side street some three hundred metres from the church. Frustratingly, she discovered that the presbytery was about the same distance from the church as she had just walked - but in the opposite direction. Feeling slightly ruffled as she rang on the ornate doorbell whose strident tones she could hear in some distant part of the building, she waited impatiently for someone to come and open the door.

Even before the door was opened, Elena had guessed correctly that she would be greeted by a frowsty, middle-aged *zitella* of a housekeeper who would see it as her mission in life to protect her little brood of men-of-the-cloth from any invasion from the outside world. Elena had already prepared her most ingratiating smile before the door was opened a few suspicious inches. The sour-faced spinster took one look at the beautiful young woman standing on the doorstep and determined immediately that it was her duty to protect the priests in her charge from the temptations of the flesh.

'Good morning, *signora*,' said Elena sweetly. 'I need to talk to a priest. It is very urgent.'

'That won't be possible, *signorina*. They are having their breakfast. They cannot be disturbed.'

Elena considered her options – which included pushing the door wide open and elbowing her way past the housekeeper. She decided she would have one more attempt at subtle persuasion.

'When did you last read your bible, *signora?*'

'This morning, young woman,' replied the housekeeper in indignation. 'Why do you ask?'

'Then you will remember Our Lord's words from the Gospel according to Saint Luke, chapter 21, verse 10,' continued Elena sweetly. '*Whosoever shall come knocking at my Father's door shall never be turned away.*' Despite her convent education, Elena could not even be sure that there *were* twenty-one chapters in Saint Luke's gospel. She was quite sure, however, that Jesus had never uttered those precise words, but they seemed to fit the general spirit of his teachings. Evidently, the housekeeper thought so too since she deigned to open the door sufficiently for Elena to squeeze past her before the housekeeper changed her mind.

'Wait there!' ordered the housekeeper sourly indicating a spot about one step away from the doormat. Elena took no notice of her and followed her along the corridor to the kitchen where she could hear the sound of voices and clinking coffee cups. She stood in full view of the three clergymen just beyond the confines of the kitchen wearing her most dejected looking face. The embittered housekeeper was whispering her discontent into the old parish priest's ear. The two younger priests were looking at the newcomer with rapt attention, but it was the old priest who stood up and came out to speak to Elena.

'I'm so sorry to have disturbed your breakfast, father,' she began. The priest made a dismissive gesture with one hand and wiped crumbs from his mouth with the other.

'How can I help you, my dear?' he said kindly.

Elena put on her most embarrassed expression. When it was firmly in place, she said:

'I am Judge Grassi's niece, father. We are very worried about my dear uncle's disappearance, as I am sure you can imagine. We haven't heard anything from him since he... since after mass yesterday. I believe you saw him just before...' She left the sentence unfinished as she allowed a tear to trickle down her cheek.

'I am quite sure your uncle is safe,' said the priest kindly. 'I believe that Don Gabriele just wanted to have a long talk with the judge.'

'But who *is* this priest, father? Can you tell me something about him?'

'Not a lot, I'm afraid. He was seconded to us from the Vatican for a few weeks. He has been teaching my two priests how to use computers. Apparently Don Gabriele has very advanced skills. He was somehow involved in investigating our wayward brothers in Belgium and Ireland. You understand what I am saying, don't you? The shameful incidents of priests abusing children...'

'Yes, father. I do understand! It is something too painful to talk about, isn't it?' Inside, Elena was feeling jubilant. When she had been trying to track down the provenance of the e-mails sent to Judge Grassi, she had traced them back to a computer apparently situated in the Vatican. What she had regarded in total disbelief at the time had turned out to be true. Her level of self-respect as to her computer skills had just increased tenfold.

'But have you any idea where Don Gabriele might have taken my uncle, father?'

'He told us very little, *mia cara*. I think his family has a house near Soleto. He was telling us about an old *masseria* where they live. He said he wanted to be with his mother for a time. Oh yes, and spend precious time with his poor sister.'

'His *poor* sister?' asked Elena, her ears pricking up.

'Apparently, she is emotionally very disturbed. The unfortunate girl has suffered some psychological trauma in the past from which she has not recovered. Don Gabriele never went into great detail. He seemed to need your uncle's help. I can't tell you any more, I'm afraid.'

The girl in the video clips, thought Elena, suddenly enlightened.

'Thank you so much, father,' she said in genuine gratitude. 'You have put my fears about my uncle to rest. I'm now sure that he is not in danger.'

'I am happy to have helped you, *figlia mia*,' said the old priest as he led her to the front door and showed her out. The housekeeper had retired to her room and was busy looking up Luke chapter twenty-one, verse ten. She failed to find the words that Jesus was supposed to have uttered, according to that 'young harlot' and resolved to redouble her efforts to keep evil at bay for as long as she possessed the fortitude to protect her priestly charges. She would pray to the Blessed Virgin Mary for the necessary steadfastness of purpose.

Elena felt elated as she trudged back to where she had left the car. For the first time, she had made positive progress in this strange affair. She had to phone Adam and share the news with someone. He cautioned her immediately about saying too much on her mobile phone and told her to save up the details until they saw each other that evening. Instead, he told her how Anna had refused to drink milk at breakfast. 'I think she has an aversion to the stuff. She says she prefers coffee.'

'I guess she's old enough to have aversions,' she agreed, 'even if she is still too young to overdose on caffeine. *Ciao amore. A dopo.*'

'Ciao Rosy - keep up the good work. And remember to pick up the kids,' concluded Adam.

Elena, back in her professional skin, deliberately drove the wrong way up a one way street simply because it was a logical short cut back to the *Piazza Sant'Oronzo*. She decided it would be better to park legitimately this time since she might well be spending a long time at the offices of *Il Quotidiano*. As she was climbing the stairs, a vital piece of this jigsaw fell into place. She suddenly understood the significance of the house near Soleto and the words spoken by Marta, overheard by Adam. If the girl in the video was the Angel Gabriel's sister, then that must mean that Marta was the priest's mother. *'O Mio Dio!'* exclaimed Elena. 'It's so OBVIOUS!' No time to think; she had arrived at the editor's office.

She took to the young editor, Claudio Sabatini, immediately just as she had felt instantly at ease with Teresa. Claudio had no difficulty in relating to Elena either – although he was her junior by a few years. He had to make a considerable mental effort to distinguish between his professional interest in the Judge Grassi case and the sudden appearance of this woman who had just walked confidently into his office radiating physical presence and intelligence in one dangerous concoction.

Elena explained briefly why she had come to the newspaper for help. She talked about the Grassi case, with which, of course, the editor was familiar. She explained that she wanted to look up details of a case that the judge had been involved in about ten years ago.

'Ah,' said Claudio, disappointed, 'I'm sorry to say that I was still in my journalistic nappies in those days.' Elena laughed at the turn of phrase.

'However,' continued the editor, 'I know someone who *can* help you.'

Claudio picked up the phone and asked for someone called Giacomo. After a brief conversation, the editor put the phone down and said that his colleague would be up in about fifteen minutes. Meanwhile, Claudio sent his secretary down to fetch cups of coffee. 'From the machine or from the bar next door?' asked his secretary, Gloria, who was one of the rare blondes in that part of the world. 'From the bar, today, Gloria, please.' That meant the coffee would be of good quality but only lukewarm by the time it arrived; an important decision that needed to be made several times in a day. During the interval, Claudio asked:

'So, Elena, what have you discovered so far?' Elena was going to play hard to get in editorial terms, aware that she would stand a better chance of finding out what she needed to know if Claudio was motivated by the thought that there was a story that he could print. So, she replied, tantalisingly:

'Oh, I know who abducted the judge and, as of this morning, I have a very good idea as to where he has been taken.'

Claudio's eyebrows had shot up in outright astonishment. After a pause, he asked: 'Well, are you going to enlighten me?' He tried and failed to convey the impression that he was only mildly curious. Elena laughed and teased him openly.

'Somehow, I am not convinced that a newspaper editor would be able to resist the temptation to print the story at once. I'm afraid that might seriously jeopardise our investigation. It might even put the judge's life at risk.'

Claudio was acute enough to perceive that, despite her choice of words, Elena did not believe that the judge's life was under threat. Nevertheless, he could see that there was a story of great public interest in the offing.

'Just a hint, maybe?' he pleaded.

'Alright,' conceded Elena. 'You can print that the judge appears to have been abducted in broad daylight, without a struggle, immediately after mass yesterday morning. The police have been informed but, so far, they have no leads. There has been no communication at this point from the abductors. There, does that satisfy you?'

'Not really!' replied Claudio smiling.

'I am sure you that you will be the first to know once there have been concrete developments. And that will happen sooner rather than later if you can help me piece together the next part of the puzzle,' she rounded off triumphantly. Claudio stretched out his arms in a gesture of surrender.

'So be it, *signora!* Ah, here is Giacomo,' he said as a pleasant looking, fifty-five year old man walked in. He had greying hair and, in contrast, a moustache that was still jet black. He smiled at Elena.

'Giacomo, let me introduce you to Elena Camisso, who has totally convinced me that it would be in all our interests to look into our Judge Grassi's past life.'

'Ah yes! Judge Grassi! A very interesting personage – with an equally intriguing past,' said Giacomo in a quiet voice. 'It will be a pleasure, *signora.*'

Elena had grown quite familiar with the *signora/signorina* routine over the past few years since she had given birth to her children – the covert glances from the opposite sex to see if there was a ring on her finger. She didn't mind at all. Indeed, it was quite flattering.

'How long ago are we talking about, Elena? May I call you Elena?'

Elena nodded. She had no objections at all; for the umpteenth time in her present job, she was thankful that nobody knew her real name.

'I think we are talking about a case that may be ten years old; possibly something to do with a case involving child abuse.'

She had been worried that the journalist would try to look intelligent, put on a thoughtful expression of deep concentration and say: 'Mm, I do recall some such case.' Instead, the grey-haired man looked at her with clear blue eyes and said:

'I knew you were going to say that.' How good it was to be dealing with professionals, thought Elena Camisso, thankfully.

'Come on, Elena. We'll go down to the archives and print off all the relevant articles for you...if that's alright with you, *capo?*' added Giacomo, who had caught sight of his boss's expression. Giacomo could not be sure whether the chief editor was reluctant to miss a piece of the action or whether he was loath to entrust this engaging woman to another man.

Claudio Sabatini merely waved them away with a rueful smile and said: 'I hope we will meet again soon, Elena.' The chief editor's words clarified Giacomo's mind instantly.

Thirty minutes later, Elena was holding a large brown envelope containing the articles she needed. Giacomo had outlined the case as they went along.

'I remember the trial as if it was yesterday. It was as blatant a case of a senior judge overruling a previous verdict in the appeal court as anyone had ever seen – *and* it was tried without a jury,' Giacomo explained. 'The man's name was Antonio Aprea, if I remember correctly. He had been found guilty of repeated indecent acts against his fifteen-year-old daughter – full intercourse was never suggested. The girl's name and the mother's name were withheld for obvious reasons. This Aprea character was an important industrialist in Milan. He was – still is, in all probability – an arms manufacturer. Therefore, of course, the State could not afford to have him involved in a scandal of that nature.'

'Was he a local man though, this Antonio Aprea?' asked Elena, holding her breath in suspense.

'Oh, there is no doubt about *that!* He originated from our part of the world - Galatina, I believe, or a village quite nearby.

'*Soleto,*' conjectured Elena to herself.

'He had a son as well; I remember that. Well, the father was let off the hook completely by our Judge Grassi. Most of us, at the time, who were involved in reporting the case, were convinced that Grassi had received a generous payment, either from the

171

State or directly from Aprea in person. But amazingly, nobody ever managed to prove anything and there was no visible trace of any illegitimate sum of money being received by Grassi. Those who were better disposed towards our judge pointed out that the appeal trial coincided with the death of both his mother and father in Abruzzo. They claimed his judgement must have been clouded by this double personal loss. *Nobody*, however, was ever quoted as saying that the outcome of the appeal had anything to do with justice – even by those who were on the judge's side, so to speak. There, I hope that all this will help you, Elena.'

Elena was sure that she must be on the right track. There were too many details that tallied to amount to pure coincidence and Elena had just perceived a way in which the judge might have received financial compensation without anyone being able to trace it back to its source. To Giacomo's great surprise, Elena Camisso gave him a warm hug. He tried to look embarrassed but failed to do so.

'Thank you,' he said beaming. 'That made it all worthwhile! I don't think I shall tell my editor in chief about the hug though,' he added mischievously. 'Just a minute, Elena; I've suddenly remembered some other detail that struck us all at the time. In one of the articles that we published about the judge, at the time of the trial, there was a sentence inserted that nobody on the editorial staff could remember writing. The sentence was quite different in tone to the rest of the article. It went something like, *Judge Grassi will himself be judged by a higher court that will not be of this world.* Just the same as happened when we published the judge's obituary last week! Does that make any sense to you, Elena?'

'It confirms what we already suspected,' she replied evasively.

'You should find that sentence in one of the articles in that envelope, by the way,' added Giacomo with a final smile. '*In bocca al lupo!*' Best of luck! Elena responded with the customary word, '*Crepi!*'

Elena thanked him again warmly and went back upstairs to pay her respects to Claudio Sabatini, promising that she would be in touch as soon as she was certain that she was on the right track. Then she was off in a fever of excitement to report what she had found out to Alessandro Greco.

'Now there are only two more bits of information that we need by way of confirmation,' she said. 'Can we go down to Galatina together, Sandro? We need to find out if there is a *masseria* near Soleto in the name of Aprea – or possibly Vollaro. That's Marta the housekeeper's surname. But I strongly suspect that the property deeds will be in the husband's name.'

'Of course,' he said. 'But I suggest we telephone the town hall first to let them know that we are coming. You know what local council officials can be like. Leave that to me. I think I know someone who works for the local council in Galatina. And what about the other piece of information that we need?' he asked.

'Oh,' Elena replied vaguely. 'I should be able to find that out on my computer.' She declined to be more precise and Alessandro had learnt from experience that if his assistant wanted to be secretive, he could spend the whole day asking questions to no avail.

As it turned out, Alessandro's 'friend' in the local council offices, who was in point of fact a second cousin, was not in that day. So Alessandro made their appointment for the following morning giving the cousin a general notion of what they needed to know. 'It's really important, Luca,' he stressed. Alessandro had to put his cousin in the picture about the investigative agency that he had opened and succeeded in arousing his relative's curiosity to such an extent that he offered to be there as soon as the offices were open at 8 o'clock the following morning. Elena protested that a day's delay might be putting their client's life at risk, but in the end, she had to accept that, in Italy, nothing ever happens just at the moment you want it to.

'Besides which,' added Alessandro. 'I have an appointment later on this morning with some English TV film actress who is buying a *masseria* near Tricase. So it has probably worked out for the better.'

'Name?' asked Elena.

'Pardon?' asked Alessandro, thrown by the abruptness of the question.

'The TV actress, of course!' snapped Elena. Alessandro understood that his assistant was taking her frustration out on him because she had wanted to solve the mystery that day. So, he replied patiently, ignoring her tone of voice:

'She's called Angela Swan. Apparently, she is famous for playing the role of both Queen Elizabeth and a very determined lady police inspector. Not in the same film, I would guess.'

Elena was interested in spite of herself and determined to contain her impatience by using the rest of the day to find out the other piece of information that she needed concerning Judge Grassi. The first step was to phone Teresa, who was astonished by the direction of Elena's enquiry.

'What my father inherited from his parents?' she asked aghast. 'Why do you think that is important?'

'You must trust me, Teresa. I think I am on the point of discovering the reasons behind your father's abduction. I don't suppose you know roughly what figure was involved?'

Teresa's friendship was being tested. In the end, she could only trust that Elena knew what she was doing. 'I'll ask my mother, Elena, and I'll let you know, but she is probably just as much in the dark as we are.'

'It might help to know the name of the solicitor who dealt with the will as well,' added Elena. 'I'm not prying, Teresa. We have made a lot of progress already this morning.'

'Leave it with me, Elena. I'll send you an e-mail as soon as I have spoken to my mother.' Teresa had decided that her new friend was to be trusted and was secretly optimistic that the mystery surrounding her father's abduction would soon become clear.

'By the way, Teresa, I believe that we will discover that Marta is the priest's mother - and the mother of the girl in the video.' Elena had slipped in this little gem of information at the end of the conversation for dramatic effect. She could tell by the gasp of surprise at the other end of the line that the revelation had had the desired effect.

'Of course, Elena - it makes perfect, logical sense. That's the connection my father must have made in church. How clever you are! Just wait until I tell my mother! She'll be delighted that her hunch about Marta's involvement was correct.'

Elena waited on tenterhooks for the e-mail to arrive. She became increasingly convinced that the Grassi family had drawn in its defences and no longer wished their private life to be pried into. But, finally, over an hour later, the e-mail arrived. Not only had Teresa supplied the solicitor's name and address in the small hilltop town of Loreto Aprutino in Abruzzo, but she had contacted the solicitor and authorised them to supply any information that was requested by the caller.

Nevertheless, when Elena contacted the solicitor, she had the impression that her call was not particularly welcome. The secretary who took the call had told her to hang on a minute. She had obviously cupped her hand over the telephone mouthpiece and was speaking to her boss in urgent tones. After a good thirty seconds had elapsed, she spoke stiffly to Elena: 'The *dottore* will speak to you now, *signorina*.'

'I understand you require information about a former client's assets,' said the solicitor in a voice that clearly implied that he was being asked to betray a trust.

'It would be a great help at the present moment, *dottore*,' said Elena as ingratiatingly as possible. 'We are acting on behalf of the Grassi family in an investigation involving their father.'

'I fail to see how the details of my client's will can possibly be of help to you now, ten years after his parents' death,' the solicitor added officiously. Elena was tempted to point out to this pernickety lawyer that the content of a will is - surprisingly for such a secretive country as Italy - in the public domain. But she chose not to rise to the bait and did not reply to his comment, thereby obliging the man to continue speaking.

'However, since it is apparently the wish of the judge's daughter that you should have this information, I can tell you that the judge received €306 000 from his parents' estate. There was an additional sum involved paid to the judge at the same time through our legal studio, but I am not at liberty to divulge either the source or the amount involved. I regret that is all I can tell you, *signorina.*'

Elena thanked him profusely, swallowing the words that she would have liked to have used to this stuck-up, small town lawyer; after all he was probably protecting himself from the risk of exposure to an illicit procedure to which he had been party ten years previously. She put the receiver down with a renewed feeling of elation. She had been right. The judge *had* received an extra payment round about the same time as the trial of Antonio Aprea. The *tangente* had been skilfully disguised as part of the judge's inheritance. The method of payment of this 'favour' implied official involvement at the highest level.

A normal person would have been quite content with what Elena had just achieved. But, as her partner Adam knew from past experience, once she had a problem to solve, she became as tenacious as a bulldog and would not let any matter rest until she had evinced the last, minute detail. Her curiosity needed to be satisfied as to the amount of the back-hander that Judge Grassi had accepted to justify having skewed the verdict in the industrialist's favour in what appeared to have been such a clear-cut case of sexual abuse.

She knew that the operation would not be straightforward. The judge's covert bank account would be impossible to access with her limited skills as a hacker. She felt sure that she would be overstepping the mark if she were to ask Teresa such a personal financial detail – if, indeed, the judge's daughter knew what amount was involved. So, Elena – who clearly recognised that it was 'Rosaria's' personal curiosity that was being satisfied over and above the requirements of this investigation – thought she would try the one avenue that might possibly be open to her. If this 'Angel Gabriel' had succeeded in accessing the judge's account, could she possibly discover what she wanted to know by hacking into *his* computer again, as she had succeeded in doing a few days ago? It was worth trying. It took her a total of two hours, tracing the priest's e-mails to Judge Grassi as she had done before, and then learning how to gain access to the other items on his series of computers. With a cry of success which brought Alessandro in to her office, she pointed to the itemised transactions of the judge's account. The total transaction paid through the solicitor's office in Abruzzo amounted to €756 000.

'That means our dear judge received €450 000 inducement to get this Antonio Aprea off the hook, Sandro. Just think of that!'

'You won't forget that he is our client, will you, Elena? We have to be very circumspect and keep this *entirely* to ourselves.'

Elena Camisso would have treated her boss to some very acerbic comments but for the fact that her mobile rang at that precise moment. It was the children's head teacher anxiously enquiring why she was not there to pick up Anna and Riccardo.

'*O Dio!*' she exclaimed. 'I'm terribly sorry. I shall be there in ten minutes.' She had forgotten that Adam was teaching a new English course at the University and that the arrangement had been for *her* to fetch their children.

'I'll see you tomorrow morning, Elena,' said Alessandro Greco. 'As early as you can.' Elena had almost forgotten in her excitement that they had arranged to go to Galatina to find the *masseria* which belonged to the Aprea-Vollaro family; the last link in the chain so far as their part in this investigation was concerned.

As she was driving, too fast, towards the children's school, where she could become Rosaria Miccoli once again, her mind was busy trying to fathom out in what way the Angel Gabriel could possibly use the information that he possessed to reshape the life of his unwilling, or maybe willing, captive – who also happened to be their far from innocent client.

Rosaria hugged her two children lovingly as soon as she found them standing like abandoned orphans in front of the school under the watchful and disapproving eye of the head teacher.

'I'm so sorry,' she apologised to all three of them. 'I just lost track of time.' In the car, she made Anna and Riccardo promise not to tell their father that she had forgotten to pick them up.

'Why not, *mamma*?' asked an innocent Riccardo.

'Because you don't want mummy to get into trouble, do you?' said his elder sister, scornfully stating the obvious.

12: The Veil Lifted

Amedeo stepped tentatively into the kitchen that Sunday evening. There were five people sitting at a long, rustic table with wooden benches on each side. The setting sun still cast a bronze light in the spacious room as its rays were filtered by air, sea and olive groves before falling on the five faces turned in his direction to greet him.

'You must have slept well,' said Gabriele standing up to usher him to the table. 'We were waiting for you before we had supper – not the last one, of course,' he added with a grin. He took Amedeo by the arm and did a tour of the table introducing the other four people. The judge felt in awe of the situation despite the apparent normality of the welcome.

'This is my cousin, Enrico,' said Gabriele introducing the younger of the two 'monks' who had driven down in the car from Lecce. 'And this is my uncle, Dario. I'm sorry about the deception, Amedeo, but as you have probably guessed, they are really farmers in monks' clothing.' The two men half stood up, looking a little sheepish, to shake Amedeo by the hand. 'We produce our own olive oil but we have been hoping this year to produce our own wine, too, with Enrico and Dario's help,' added Gabriel with obvious passion for the project. The judge uttered the customary word *'piacere'* as he was introduced to the two men. 'My mother you know already, even though you have only known her as my mother for a few hours.'

Amedeo had walked round to the other side of the table to shake hands formally with Marta. But she stood up and faced

Amedeo squarely with the simple words: *'Mi dispiace tanto, Amedeo.'*

'I don't fully understand why I am here, Marta,' replied Amedeo, speaking his first words in this unfamiliar environment with an emotional lump in his throat. 'But I am sure you do not owe me an apology.'

'That is so kind of you, Amedeo. I am just very happy that deceit is no longer required,' replied Marta.

Gabriele had moved round past his mother and was standing behind the last person in the group with his hands placed gently on the shoulders of a beautiful, dark haired young woman whose age it was difficult to guess with precision. She must have been in her twenties but there was something careworn in the slight frown that she wore. The judge recognised her immediately and felt no shock of surprise. He had known deep inside himself that he was destined to meet the dancing girl as inevitably as the sun was setting behind the old stone wall surrounding the *masseria*. Thus, his surprise was restricted to a feeling of awe at the beauty she had inherited from her mother coupled to the almost expressionless look on her even features.

'And this is my wonderful sister, Chiara,' said Gabriele with warmth and sincerity. Since the girl was looking at the judge without any hint of emotion, Amedeo noticed with a feeling of immense relief that Chiara had briefly placed her hand over that of her elder brother. The simple gesture made Amedeo smile at her even as he felt warm, uncontrollable tears welling up from within. The girl did not return the smile but Amedeo thought he perceived a brief flicker of movement in her brown eyes which had been staring at him as if she was looking through him out into the garden beyond. Amedeo was lost for words. None of the standard forms of Italian greetings seemed appropriate so he just said 'Chiara' quietly, hoping to catch some response in her eyes. In some inexplicable way, this silent girl must be the key to why Amedeo was here. He could not ask the questions that he wanted to with Chiara present. Reading his thoughts accurately, as would happen frequently over the following forty-eight hours, Gabriel said: 'We'll go on a tour of the estate after supper, Amedeo.'

Marta put soup on the table which had pasta and big chunks of various meat and vegetables mixed up with it. There was even a pitcher of red wine on the table and bread that looked wholesome and homemade. The judge's hungry and impatient spoon was already half way to his mouth when he heard Gabriele saying some words in Latin. Of course, it had been years ago that Amedeo and his entourage had abandoned the age-old tradition of saying grace before a meal. His spoon hovered half-way between bowl and parted lips as Gabriele quickly completed the small ritual; quickly, because to everybody's surprise but the judge's embarrassment, Chiara had quite distinctly giggled at the sight of their new house guest, sitting in the place opposite her. The next second, everybody else was chortling too – including Amedeo. The ice was broken as if by magic. 'We should have house guests more often,' said the cousin called Enrico. But Judge Grassi had the distinct impression that their laughter had sprung from astonishment at Chiara's reaction rather than amusement at his gaffe.

The conversation turned naturally to the quality of the wine.

'What do you think of our attempts, Amedeo?'

'It is good, really good,' replied the great judge of wines. 'If you want to produce it on a commercial scale though, I am not sure you should be combining *Negroamaro* grapes with *Aglianico*. *Negroamaro* is a very selfish grape, in my opinion. It hates sharing a bottle with other varieties – except possibly with the *Malvasia* grape.'

The two farmers looked at Amedeo with the dawning of respect. There followed a conversation about blending grape varieties, which had obviously been discussed on previous occasions. 'I tend to agree with you, Amedeo,' said Uncle Dario. 'But Gabriele and Enrico think we ought to experiment a little before we go public, so to speak.' Amedeo made some light-hearted comment about the age old tradition of monks producing wines and liqueurs. 'Including champagne, of course,' said someone.

'Danger! Danger!' said a small voice inside Amedeo's head. He was allowing himself to be lulled into a sense of security – not false, but real, which was far harder to combat.

When they had finished eating, Gabriele turned to the judge and said: 'Come on, Amedeo. Let us walk together in the garden.' The judge experienced a stab of apprehension at these words. He would soon be turned inside out at the hands of this young man. *Angel Gabriel, the messenger from God.*

The first words that Gabriele spoke were quite enough to make him aware that he was not in the presence of a simple man but one whose understanding of human nature was mature well beyond his years. The effect on Amedeo served to convince him further that the young priest possessed the gift of mind-reading.

'The simple fact that you are feeling apprehensive about talking to me now is proof enough that you are a good man at heart, Amedeo; just as I said to you when we first spoke in the streets of Lecce. Do you remember?'

'It seems a life-time ago already. I am sure that this question is not relevant to what I am about to learn, but why the elaborate charade over the last week? I just want my curiosity to be satisfied, Gabriele.'

'I think you have already unwittingly answered your own question.' The judge looked quizzically at the priest. Amedeo could not quite recall what he had just said. 'You have the feeling that last week was a lifetime ago,' explained Gabriele. 'I believe that this shows plainly how far you have travelled in such a short space of time.'

Gabriele was silent for a few seconds while Amedeo digested the implications of what he had said. 'When you think back to how you were when you first sat and listened to me amusing the children in church... yes, I know how you felt... and the way we are talking together now, on first name terms. Even my mother could see a big change in you in that short space of time.'

Of course, thought the judge in some embarrassment. Marta would have realised that he had started sharing a bed with Antonella again.

'And, by the way, Amedeo, you will not have appreciated what happened back there in the kitchen. That was the first time in a decade that Chiara has shown an appreciation of something amusing happening. We were all so amazed that we did not dare to react. That moment was a magical one for us all and we did not want to break the spell. It was the first time, too, that Chiara has responded to being touched by me. So you see, Amedeo, you have done some good already.'

'But why did you need your mother – Marta - to live with us as our housekeeper? Not that it wasn't a pleasure,' he added hastily.

'In the first place, she really needed the money - even though she hated leaving Chiara with relatives. This place does not quite run itself yet. And I needed someone on the inside - to get the lie of the land so to speak; someone who would come to understand you and tell me when the time was ripe. I need your help, you see.'

'Quite apart from needing somebody to plant that gadget in my study so you could hack into my bank account,' interrupted the judge with a touch of asperity which left him surprised at his own temerity.

'*Touché, signor giudice!* I deserved that,' exclaimed Gabriele with gleeful delight that he had been so pointedly challenged. It was, Amedeo decided, impossible to discountenance a person who never took offence at what was said. At this point, the judge felt a firm pressure behind his knee in the growing darkness that was falling. He turned round to find that the dog had appeared from the shadows of the garden and was pushing its muzzle into the crook of his knee joint.

'Ah! We have company, Amedeo. Don't be concerned. Argo will recognise you from now on. He stays out in the garden all the time. Should you ever wish to walk around the grounds at night time, you will never be alone. We hardly ever shut the front door to the house.'

There was a comfortable lull in the conversation as they continued to walk through the scented night. They had been right round the front of the house and had, by then, arrived at the old

186

stone bench that the judge had seen from his bedroom window. A nearly full moon had risen and was bathing the garden in a silvery light. Amedeo stopped to breathe in a lungful of the unpolluted night air and inadvertently let out a sigh of pleasure at the long-forgotten sensation of being far from traffic and city noise.

'I love being in the country, don't you, Amedeo?' said Gabriele quietly by his side. 'In my opinion, God created nature but Man built towns and cities. It is a tragedy that most people go through their lives without once experiencing how beautiful nature is. It is a sad indictment of the mistaken direction that mankind has taken.'

'I never really thought of it in those terms before,' said Amedeo. After a pause, Gabriele took up the lost thread of their conversation:

'I suppose I must apologise to you, Amedeo, for all the theatrical tricks that I played on you last week. I have to confess to a love of drama. I was an actor for a time before I went to Rome and even acted a bit while I was a seminarian. I came to realise that acting in a theatre is not part of the real world but, as I am sure you have noticed, I believe that drama has its place in our daily lives.'

'Well, it certainly works as far as your sermons are concerned, Gabriele. You clearly believe in audience participation.'

'Children are so spontaneous, aren't they?' laughed Gabriele. 'But I think that adults respond to drama too. I certainly managed to catch *your* attention, Amedeo.'

'As long as you don't expect me to acknowledge that in so many words, young man!' retorted Amedeo in a tone of mock rebuke.

'You really *have* come a long way, *signor giudice*. And now, if you don't mind, I am very tired after today's dramatic events. I did not have a siesta this afternoon as you did. May we leave the painful part until tomorrow?'

'Yes,' said Amedeo. 'But just one more question before you retire for the night. How did you know that I would come running after you this morning after mass?'

'The power of prayer, dear Amedeo,' replied the priest in total seriousness. 'I knew that my prayer had been answered as soon as that lovely little girl in the church asked Angel Gabriel to come down from heaven. You should have seen the expression on your face when you realised what the initials **A.G.** stood for. It was a real picture!'

Gabriele took his leave without uttering another word. He had briefly clasped his hands around the judge's arms and squeezed them for a second before turning round and heading back to the house. 'The Brotherhood of Man,' was the unbidden phrase that sprung to the judge's mind. He *was* going soft. *'You have already come a long way, Amedeo,'* echoed the words in his head. He had the humbling impression that his young captor was reshaping his soul, like a skilful potter moulding a clay vessel with strong but precise hands.

Amedeo had lost track of time and had left his watch in his bedroom. He wasn't feeling tired and had a myriad conflicting thoughts spinning round in his mind. He went for a walk through the olive trees as far as the little vineyard at the far end of the estate. There was a wrought iron gate set into the grey stone wall. On the other side of the gate, he could see more vines and the flat Salento countryside stretching away in the moonlight. A sturdy padlock on the gate prevented him going any further. He told himself that it was to keep intruders out rather than to keep him inside. Was he a prisoner? Yes, effectively he was being held here with no recourse to his familiar world. Whether he minded being imprisoned was another matter. He could not quite decide what he felt about that. He walked back towards the house, still not ready to return to his room. There was no noise except distant owls ranging over the countryside calling out to their mates and the occasional sound of Argo snuffling around somewhere in the dark. He sat down on the stone bench to meditate on what had transpired throughout that unusual Sunday. He felt a core of dread about what he would learn the following day. One thing was certain – he would not be feeling proud of himself by lunchtime. What the priest did not know already, Amedeo would feel morally obliged to confess to him. Never mind, he thought. He had carried the weight of guilt around with him for too long.

So deeply was the judge immersed in his thoughts that the ghostly apparition did not immediately register on his conscious mind. When it did, his first instinct was one of almost numinous fear. The figure was dressed in a long transparent white nightdress. The girl was dancing nimbly towards him, twisting and stepping in time to an inaudible tune, without apparently being aware that she was not alone in the garden. When Chiara was near enough to see plainly, Amedeo realised that she was holding a small gadget in her hand and was listening to the music through a tiny headset. He sat stock still waiting with apprehension for her to notice that he was there. The last thing he wanted to do was scare her out of her wits. When Chiara was about three metres away from him, she saw him for the first time. She stopped dead in her tracks and whipped the headset from her ears. She looked startled and fearful. With a presence of mind that took him by surprise, Amedeo clapped his hands together in gentle applause and said: '*Brava, Chiara.* You dance beautifully.'

Was that a brief smile he caught in the moonlight? It was too brief to be certain. Reassured, she put the tiny headset back in her ears and danced in front of him again, totally absorbed in the music. He could just discern that it was a group of local musicians, the muted strains of a *tarantella* or *pizzica* escaping from the headset. Amedeo was mesmerised. To his initial embarrassment, she finished dancing and came and sat next to him. She sat there for perhaps five long minutes without uttering a word. Amedeo took hold of his emotions and did his utmost to relax, resisting the social pressure to utter pointless words when they were not required. After a while, Chiara turned towards him and whispered: '*Grazie ca si turnatu, tata!*' And then she was off again heading back to the house. Amedeo thanked the deities of that magical place that he had not instinctively denied being her father but had simply said: 'I am glad to be with you, Chiara.' It struck him a few minutes later as strange that she had spoken to him, not in Italian, but in dialect.

Half an hour later, Amedeo stood up and walked deep in thought back to the house and lay down on his bed. He was touched to find that his mobile phone had been returned to him with a brief hand-written note which said: *If you call anyone, it will probably bring the police here. It's your choice, Amedeo.* He realised that this was the last thing in the world that he wanted and he eventually fell asleep until dawn.

* * *

'Before we begin, Gabriele, there is something I must tell you about what happened last night after you had left me...'

'You're going to tell me that you saw Chiara dancing in the garden, aren't you?'

'Yes, but that's not the end of it...' And Amedeo told his captor what his sister had said. *'Thank you, papà, for coming back home for me.'*

Gabriele's face had been transformed as if by some inner vision. He was looking upwards towards the blue sky above the olive branches and had a beatific smile on his face. *'Grazie Signore,'* he whispered. And then he looked at Amedeo who had been studying the handsome young face with a look of curiosity mingled with amused affection.

'It is an answer to my most fervent prayers, Amedeo. I knew I was right to bring you here.'

'Frankly, Gabriele, I am not sure whether I understand you.'

'Frankly, dear Amedeo, neither do I. But there is something wonderful going on inside my sister's mind – the first hesitant signs of recovery. It is nigh on miraculous! If you feel ready, I will tell you everything about the years of darkness and distress that my sister has suffered.'

'For which I share responsibility.' It was not a question but a plain statement of fact. Judge Grassi had always known that his monumental departure from honesty on that day more than ten years ago, his weakness in the face of outside pressures would inevitably catch up with him one day. A forgotten memory had come back to him, elbowed into existence with a painful emotional jolt; he had briefly and dismissively met Chiara at the time of the trial.

191

Gabriele made no comment in reply to Amedeo's statement, but started talking quietly and with intense concentration. Amedeo felt increasingly dejected, contrite and contemptible as the priest's story unfolded, taking him step by painful step through the dark night of Chiara's soul.

It started when Chiara was only about eight or nine. He, my father, used to come down from Milan every weekend. She truly adored her father and wanted to be with him every minute of the day from dawn to dusk. At first, my mother thought that he was just being an affectionate father. But as the months passed by, she became uneasy about the amount of time he spent alone with her, especially when it was bedtime. He would try to monopolise my sister's getting washed or having a shower and then begin to shut himself in the bedroom with her. He claimed he was reading her bedtime stories but they sometimes went on for hours. My mother confronted him one evening and accused him of becoming obsessed with his daughter – to the detriment of his family. He reacted defensively and blocked any suggestion that he was becoming fixated. 'I have a loving relationship with my daughter, that's all. How dare you imply anything else!'

But, of course, he began to neglect my mother bit by bit. She was convinced that my father had other women on weekdays up in Milan. Her suspicions were confirmed when she checked his mobile phone and read some graphic text message from someone called Beatrice. When she confronted him with this, he lost his temper and told her to keep out of his 'professional' life. Things just went from bad to worse. He told my mother that this house was his and that if she didn't like the way he behaved, we – that is my mother and myself - could leave whenever we wanted. He would 'make arrangements' for Chiara. My mother has a loyal family down here, but she had very little financial independence. She had little choice but to endure his constant and unnatural desire to be with Chiara.

I'm sure you remember my father. He is a very good-looking man, even now. He can appear charming, affectionate and be as persuasive as the devil incarnate. But he is quite ruthless. When I was old enough to understand matters of character, I realised that he is totally egocentric and self-indulgent. He is, I believe, bordering on the psychopathic; he displays no feeling for, and no moral awareness of other people. I understood this when, one evening, I challenged him about the factory that he owns. 'Do you know what happens to the guns you manufacture, the land mines that you churn out by the thousand, papà?' I shouted at him. I was about fifteen when Chiara was nine and I was full of a teenager's sense of the injustice in the world. 'Innocent Africans get killed and maimed,' I went on at him. My mother would look steadily at my father whenever I accused him like that, willing me on without ever saying anything herself. She was dominated by him, conditioned by years of his insidious bullying. Do you know, my father laughed and shrugged his shoulders. 'I don't care what happens to the weapons I manufacture, Gabriele. My mission in life is to sell as many guns as possible. What people do after that is their business. They need weapons, I make them. It's a simple as that. And I get very rich.'

After that evening, I waged a constant war on my father in my rebellious adolescent way. I was tall enough not to be intimidated by him and he knew it. Once, I barged into Chiara's bedroom when he was supposedly reading her a story – just to disconcert him. He was sitting on the bed and I could see clearly that he hurriedly withdrew his hand from under the bed-clothes. 'What are you doing *to my sister?' I asked accusingly. 'She had a pain in her tummy. I was rubbing it better, wasn't I, tesoro?' Chiara looked uncomfortable but she nodded her head. But after that, I knew that things were not right.*

But my mother and I felt powerless at that stage. Chiara was still infatuated by her father's attentions. That's the trouble, Amedeo. At that age, if a child knows no other way of life, then she, or he, assumes that this is normality. She wasn't being physically hurt and she seemed normal enough during the week. Only one teacher ever had the perception to understand that Chiara was abnormally withdrawn from other children, and told my mother so at a parents' meeting. Amedeo, I'm sure you are beginning to understand, so I'll try and move on to the next stage.

The judge just waved a hand in an invitation for his companion to continue talking. He was deeply involved in the narration of these events and did not want him to stop. They had been walking round the garden slowly with Argo following in their footsteps. Marta had taken Chiara out in the car to go shopping in Galatina. Chiara had not spoken at the breakfast table, but she had followed Amedeo with her eyes. It had been difficult to tell whether she had any memory of the previous evening. She had managed a brief smile in his direction as she was leaving with her mother.

When Chiara reached adolescence, she had the makings of a very beautiful woman – as you can imagine. My father began to take her away in his car and come back late at night. On returning, he would 'supervise' her going to bed and sit and talk to her until past midnight. Or else, they would listen to music together. He fitted a lock to the door to prevent anyone interrupting them. 'A girl of her age has a right to privacy,' he had the hypocrisy to inform us. There was a huge row when my mother, who had been holding back for years, launched into a cold, controlled verbal tirade. 'Then you will admit that Chiara has the right to lock YOU out so that she can enjoy becoming a woman in her own right.' Chiara was present and became visibly upset. She ran out of the room crying – and actually locked herself in her room. Of course, my father blamed my mother for upsetting her. It was all mine and my mother's fault, he said, 'for being over-protective and jealous of the relationship he had with his daughter', he claimed.

If my father had not returned to Milan every weekday, things might have come to a head much sooner. As it is, matters dragged on until she was fifteen years old.

'But surely Chiara herself must have begun to rebel against him?'

It is so difficult for normal families – such as yours - to comprehend, Amedeo. The influence that a man such as my father had over Chiara was insidious and invasive. It builds up slowly over the years. From Chiara's viewpoint, her father's 'friendliness and affection' were normal signs that her father loved her in return - simply because HE had ensured that she knew no better. For HIM, it was an easy matter to win over a vulnerable adolescent; he was used to persuading hard-nosed African despots to part with millions of dollars to buy his guns and rockets. He reinforced his hold over her even when he was back north in Milan by phoning her and texting her every day.

In fact, round about that time, she acquired a boyfriend. He was five years older than Chiara, the lead singer in a local folk group whose sister she had met at school. Chiara was - no is - an outstanding dancer as you saw for yourself. She became the band's

dancer whenever they played in public or at private parties –
usually on a Friday night before her father came home. They even
made a video here in our garden. You know the one, Amedeo.

The judge nodded. 'Indeed I do, Gabriele. The difference is that now I understand all too well the context in which it was set,' he added, increasingly distressed by what he was hearing. At that moment, they heard the car arrive back from the shopping trip. Cousin Enrico, Marta and Chiara were unloading the shopping and carrying it into the house.

'Come on, Amedeo. Let's go and see how the shopping trip went. We'll carry on talking later.'

Amedeo felt at once frustrated at the interruption of the narrative, so near its climax, and relieved that he could put off the moment when he would have to face up to his shameful contribution to this family's tragedy.

'I suppose we have plenty of time, Gabriele. There is no hurry,' he said suppressing his impatience.

The priest smiled at him wryly and said: 'I'm not so sure about that, Amedeo. I have a feeling that the two detectives that you employed are going to discover very soon where you are. My mother had the impression that they are a pretty smart couple. I would like to bet that they will arrive with the *carabinieri* in tow, let's guess, no later than Wednesday. As far as the outside world is concerned, you have been abducted. They will be looking for you right now.'

'Well, *caro* Gabriele,' said the judge firmly. 'I am not ready to be rescued from this place just yet.'

And the jean-clad priest and the track-suited judge at his side made their way back to the house. The mood in the kitchen was jubilant. Chiara was putting all the items away in their right place, without a word, a look of rapt concentration on her face. Sometimes, she would show Amedeo items that she had chosen with a look on her face which was plainly asking whether he approved of her choice; cheeses, salami and even a bottle of wine.

'She has never enjoyed shopping as much as she did today, Amedeo,' said Marta seriously. 'I am glad that you are with us.' Judge Grassi shrugged his shoulders modestly and spread his arms out in a self-deprecating gesture. 'Thank *you,* dear Marta,' he said simply. It was dawning on him that he was about to embark upon a new journey which would demand a level of commitment from which there would be no shirking. *'La resa dei conti, Amedeo Grassi,'* he said to himself. The time of reckoning has arrived.

13: Chiara's Story

It was not until later that afternoon that Amedeo and Gabriele found themselves alone again, able to resume the morning's gruelling narrative. Lunchtime had been a success. With bated breath, everyone had sat down to taste a pasta dish which Chiara had prepared. Thirty minutes previously, she had looked at her mother and said four simple words in dialect: *'Nci pensu ieu, mamma.'* *(I'll take care of it, mum.)* Marta had been so surprised at hearing her daughter's voice that she had set the plates down too heavily on the table, cracking one of them. She had left Chiara in the kitchen and run out in search of Gabriele and Amedeo. She had found them in the cellar looking at the rudimentary wine press and bottling equipment and told them what had happened in the kitchen.

Gabriele looked at the judge and said: 'You see, Amedeo? A little, slow miracle is taking place.' Five minutes before lunch was ready, Chiara rang the old-fashioned bell outside the front door – as they always did – to summon the family to the table. They need not have held their collective breath, ready to compliment Chiara on her cooking however it tasted; she had prepared a perfect *tagliatelle ai quattro formaggi* followed by pan fried chicken breasts and salad. They raised their glasses and toasted her with whatever they were drinking – wine or water. Gabriele hugged his sister warmly. There had definitely been a smile on her face and a brief look of radiance in her eyes this time; the small miracle at work.

After lunch, they had all gone to lie down, according to custom, to await the cooler air before starting the second half of the day.

By mutual consent, Gabriele and Amedeo had agreed to curtail their siesta and meet by the old stone bench. Gabriele took a deep breath and reluctantly launched into the most painful part of Chiara's story. Amedeo closed his eyes and listened to his companion's voice, enclosed in his own dark world.

When my father learnt that his daughter was out, in the company of a boyfriend, he went beserk. Unfortunately, I had been delayed in Lecce that evening. I was studying for a degree in psychology at the university in that period of time and I had stayed on to finish a thesis. My mother phoned me. She sounded frantic. She had been manhandled by my father in his jealous rage. He had shaken the information out of her as to where Chiara was and rushed off in his car to reclaim her. It was terrifying for all of us, but for Chiara most of all. I found her distraught, being 'comforted' in the arms of her father. She was promising him always to be there for him when he came back home and sobbing out a promise not to see her boyfriend again. Unfortunately, Enrico and Dario did not come and live with us until after the trial – after your trial, Amedeo, when you…

He left the sentence unfinished but Amedeo was looking deeply embarrassed and had screwed his eyes up tight to control the strong emotions that he was experiencing. Gabriele continued talking.

That was enough for us. We spent a miserable weekend trying our best to shield Chiara from her father's dangerous possessiveness, which came so close to outright depravity. I was fierce in my condemnation of my father throughout that horrendous weekend and he was wise enough not to cross my path. He left Chiara alone most of the time, contenting himself with pleading with her to be forgiven. When he had gone back to Milan, my mother and I resolved to take him to court – on the flimsy evidence that we had. Flimsy, from a legal point of view, I mean. Our first step was to go to the local carabinieri, who were very reluctant to get involved from the outset.

Well, the next part you know already, Amedeo. Against all the odds, we managed to convince the judge to place an injunction on my father to prevent him seeing Chiara. She was too mortified to go into details in public but the court accepted the fact that she was obviously deeply shocked by what she had endured over the years. She did manage to describe the night when he had publicly removed her from the stage where she was dancing. Her then boyfriend, the musician, had tried to restrain my father and reason with him, but he had physically dragged my sister off the stage and bundled her into the car. But it was my personal suffering at the hands of my father that convinced the judge that there had been a real problem of sexual misconduct.

'You too?' said the judge in an awed whisper. 'Do you mean that your father…?'

Yes I do, Amedeo. Forgive me for being blunt. I woke up one night to find my father bending over my body. He was touching me and fondling me. I'm not sure what was going through his perverted mind. Maybe he thought he could win me over if he treated me in the same way as he treated my sister.

Amedeo was looking deeply shocked and outraged.

Don't worry, it didn't last long. I kicked him hard and sent him sprawling across the room with a bleeding nose. I was only fourteen years old when it happened. But he never did it again – with me at least. Of course, by the time we took him to court, I was twenty-one and I found it easier to talk in public about what had happened

201

than when I had been a self-conscious adolescent. But my telling the court what had happened in graphic detail was enough to ensure that he would never have been allowed near us again. He stayed in custody for only a short period of time. He had found himself a high-powered lawyer from Milan who saw to it that he was released from prison to be able to continue 'helping Italy with its export programme.' We were staggered and dismayed when my father had the temerity to take the matter to the Appeal Court – your court, Amedeo.

The brief period without her father interfering with her life and with her body, gave Chiara a welcome breathing space. My father did not dare to come near us but stayed in Milan. We took the simple step of buying Chiara a new phone so that his text messages and calls came to an end. But, as you now know, Amedeo, her period of tranquillity was about to be shattered into a myriad tiny fragments, which only recently, we are beginning to piece laboriously and painfully together again.

'But, I still don't understand…' began Amedeo. What he did not understand was how his admittedly cowardly and base act of quashing the court's previous sentence, under considerable pressure from a highly placed and influential figure in Rome, could have resulted in the complete mental breakdown of a fifteen year old girl in Salento.

Ah, Amedeo! The worst part is still to come. Even now I find it very painful to think about the terrible months and years that followed your reversal of the conviction. Chiara came to you during the appeal trial to plead with you not to release her father. What chance did a frightened child like her have of moving your heart to pity! She came out in tears saying that you dismissed her in under two minutes, telling her not to interfere with 'adult matters'. I expect you had already received the promise of a very substantial sum of money by that time to overturn the previous verdict, helped by convincing arguments that an important man such as my father was needed to promote the industrial wealth of our country. The trial was a farce. The high-powered lawyer from Milan was there to add credence to the sentence that you were already expected to give. He made mincemeat out of mine and my sister's evidence and ate our small time provincial lawyer for breakfast within minutes. Oh Amedeo! If only you had stood firm on that day! How much suffering would have been avoided!

Amedeo's shoulders had become hunched, his head hung low in shame as God's Messenger continued to chide him gently. If only Gabriele had raged in righteous anger, it might have been easier to bear. The judge remained in the same posture throughout the rest of Gabriele's heart-rending account, until, near the end, his shoulders began to heave as he finally released the pent up tears of a decade. By the time Gabriele had finished talking, the judge knew that there would be no chance of his life ever reverting to its former comfortable and false equanimity. Gabriele continued speaking - bringing the events that had destroyed Chiara's life to their horrific conclusion.

My father had revenge in his soul after his court appearance. Truly, Amedeo, he was driven by the dark, satanic forces that rule his life. He followed us back home and gate-crashed with demonic energy into Chiara's bedroom, crying out that she had betrayed the father who loved her. He forced her on to the bed and he raped her. He left her weeping uncontrollably and bleeding over the white sheets. He drove off and never returned. If he had come back, my mother and I would have killed him.

We discovered soon afterwards that she was pregnant. She miscarried quite late on in the pregnancy. She remained totally traumatised by the experience, Amedeo. It was heart-rending, soul-destroying to see her. She never spoke a word after the departure of her father and remained locked in her own silent misery. Can you imagine it, Amedeo? She had lost her virginity to her own father then lost a child that should never have been conceived. She relapsed into a catatonic state from which we thought she would never emerge. At times, she would rush frantically around from room to room, or dance feverishly around to music that only she could hear in her head as if to expiate the devil from her mind and body. Most of the time, she remained withdrawn and silent as if lost in some subterranean maze, totally out of our reach and beyond our help.

Amedeo had, by this time, broken down and his shoulders were shaking in silent remorse. It was obvious too that Gabriele was close to tears himself, having had to relive the tragedy that had blighted his sister's life.

'There, Amedeo! It's all over now. I'm sure you would never have allowed my father to get away with this crime if you had known what the consequences would be. But isn't it frightening how decisions that we take can so catastrophically affect other people? But now, we must all be positive and concentrate on giving Chiara back her life. By some miracle, it appears that her recovery is underway. You can help her climb this mountain out of the valley of darkness. Please, Amedeo! We really need your help in so many ways.'

Gabriele put his arm around the judge's shoulder and hugged him. That gesture of forgiveness and warmth was the last straw for Amedeo; the tears came flooding forth in a rush and he wept out loud for the first time since his distant childhood. 'You *are* a good man, Amedeo,' said Gabriele. The judge had been judged – and pardoned. He shook his head from side to side, sobbing out the words: 'No, no, no! You are mistaken, Gabriele. I am *not* good. I do not deserve your kindness.'

Gabriele stood up and walked away, leaving Amedeo to his private grief. He needed to be alone to recover from his self-loathing and remorse, the priest understood. Time and not words were what counted now.

Amedeo did not move from the bench for a very long time. His mind was numb from the shock of coming to terms with the part he had played in Chiara's horrifying ordeal. Hours later, he heard the bell ringing to summon the family to the table for supper. He couldn't move from where he was. He felt too deeply ashamed to look Chiara in the eyes.

Round the kitchen table, Chiara cast rapid glances at the empty space opposite her. There was a questioning look in her eyes as she looked at her brother anxiously.

'It's alright, Chiara. Amedeo is fine. He needs to have a little time to himself. Don't worry.'

As darkness fell, Amedeo finally stood up and walked around, but he instinctively headed further into the olive grove away from the lighted house, as if the shadows of the ancient trees could hide his wrong-doings. Now it was dark. The moon had risen again, casting its ghostly light throughout the olive grove, silhouetting the conical chimney stacks sitting astride the *masseria*. Amedeo had the unnerving sensation that the house was moving slowly through space and time carrying him away on a journey into another realm. He sat down on the stone bench again and began to ponder, rather than wallowing in remorse. He went into a deep reverie. At some point, Argo came up and sniffed around the seated figure. Amedeo put out a hand and patted the animal distractedly. He felt his hand being licked and the German shepherd dog trundled off again to go about his canine business. The place began to have a soothing effect on the judge's mind.

A sensation of tranquillity descended on him in which his image of himself as a sixty-seven year old man, locked into a single, painful moment of existence, began to dissolve into an eerie perception that he was sitting astride eternity. He became once more the child who lived in the shadows of the mountains of Abruzzo, the student determined to succeed in the profession that his father had wanted him to follow, the man who finally got married and had children. But he was equally aware that he had a future stretching ahead of him which must somehow encompass a priest, his mother and a troubled but beautiful young woman, who apparently needed *his* guiding hand to help her along the parallel track of her life. He grasped with startling clarity that the workings of other people's minds are inextricably linked to one's own consciousness. He had read in an article recently that the quality of human consciousness is still a largely unexplained phenomenon. The author, a physicist, had tried to explain that it was all bound up with the effects of quantum mechanics and the non-locality of particles which can simultaneously influence others, even when separated by astronomical distances. The scientist had expounded the notion of a kind of collective cosmic consciousness. For a brief moment, Amedeo had grasped what the scientist had been saying, although he would have been hard-pressed to explain it to anyone else. His flash of metaphysical inspiration left him quite shaken. The revelation, like a bright light in his mind, merged seamlessly into the next step in his spiritual rebirth.

He looked up from his meditations to see Chiara walking towards him. It was quite unlike the experience of the previous evening if only because she seemed to have a purpose in her step; the purpose was, apparently, to come and see him. As she drew nearer, he could see that she was carrying a portable CD player. Amedeo experienced a moment of panic which he quickly smothered. It could be fatal to show fear or agitation and scare away this fragile girl. 'Just relax,' he told himself.

Without a word, Chiara set down the CD player on the stone bench and switched on her favourite dance music – played by the same local group as before. Why had she not brought her palm-sized gadget as before? It was obvious that her intention was to share the music with him. She began to dance, unselfconsciously, in the space in front of him. He could not just sit there passively and say nothing. Then, he had an inspired idea, which required a certain amount of his new-found courage to execute. He stood up slowly and said quietly to the girl:

'Why don't you teach me to dance, Chiara?'

She registered immediate pleasure and nodded. In fact, in his younger married life, he had given in to Antonella's persistent nagging to do something about his wooden performance when it came to moving in time to music and enrolled on a course where he learnt passably well how to dance the *pizzica* and other popular folk steps. At first, he felt clumsy and did not have to pretend to be an amateur in front of Chiara's easy and graceful movements. She indicated how he should move his arms and showed him the rudimentary steps of the tune that was playing. He was getting into his stride when the tune came to an end. The next dance was a *pizzica*. Chiara obviously loved dancing the *pizzica* and turned up the volume so that she could throw her whole being into the skipping, gyrating steps. Amedeo managed to play his part well enough but was totally out of breath five minutes later when the music came to its frenetic end. In the shadows beyond them, four people began to applaud enthusiastically. Amedeo wagged a mock admonishing finger in their direction. The emotional bridge had been crossed. The pangs of self-pity and remorse had left him. He was astonished to hear Chiara's voice next to him. She had turned off the CD and was standing close to his side. *'Te sai balli propiu bonu, Amedeo!'* she said in a quiet but normal voice. Simultaneously to the glow of pleasure that he felt at Chiara's gracious compliment about his dancing, he understood something vital about what was happening in Chiara's mind. It was only the second time that she had spoken to him and, on both occasions, she had spoken in dialect. He had a question that he would ask Gabriele as soon as they were alone.

The four spectators approached and, after a brief whisper in her ear from her brother, she put on another track of the CD. It was a slow ballad to which everyone knew the words – except Amedeo, since they were entirely in the local dialect. Not that it seemed to matter. The six people danced round in a slowly turning circle in the moonlight, arms linked.

'Luna d'argentu quante cose viti quandu la notte sula sula stai?'

(Oh silvery moon, how many things do you see when you are up there all alone?)

Amedeo was content to feel truly and unequivocally part of a vibrant, close-knit family for the first time in his life, with every vestige of guilt about his past finally out in the open. As they were dancing, he was intrigued to receive confirmation of his discovery about Chiara; she was singing the words with the others in a crystal clear voice with a happy look of concentration on her face.

As they walked back towards the house, Amedeo found himself side by side with Marta. She had placed her arm through his. He could ask her about what he had been wondering.

'Marta, did Chiara and Gabriele use to speak dialect when they were young children?'

'Yes, we did. It is the children's first language. I think I know what you are going to say, Amedeo, because I was just having the same thought. Chiara is beginning to talk again. But she says everything in dialect – the language she used to speak at home before her life was destroyed.' Amedeo felt the pressure of Marta's arm tighten in her suppressed excitement of this shared discovery.

* * *

The following morning, Tuesday, Amedeo was awake bright and early. Only two days had elapsed since his 'abduction' and yet it already seemed eons ago that he had stepped impulsively into Gabriele's car outside the church of San Matteo. He had a long shower and a shave with the razor which had been provided for him. His stubbly growth of two days was scraped away leaving him looking a bit younger - or so his reflection in the old, stained mirror told him. There was probably a change of underclothes sufficient for another couple of days before he would need to worry about becoming socially unacceptable. He had woken up after a deep slumber, with the vivid sensation that he was in the springtime of his life.

For the first time in forty-eight hours, he thought about Antonella and his own son and daughter. They must be anxious for his physical safety, he supposed. He was tempted to use his mobile to put their minds at rest. On balance, he considered, their temporary concern for his safety would not be too acute. There were still important issues to be discussed with his accuser – and saviour. He tiptoed into the still deserted kitchen and made himself a coffee, a sign of the extent to which he felt at home in this vast old farmhouse buried somewhere in the Salento countryside. He felt immensely comfortable in trainers and track-suit and wondered why he had always felt the necessity to don a shirt, tie and suit whenever he had got dressed. The truth was that he did not wish to leave this place, not just yet at any rate.

14: Elena and Alessandro Close In

'Stop trying to pick up every individual cornflake with your fingers, please, Riccardo,' said Adam patiently in English to their second born child. 'God invented spoons so that we would not have to continue living like little savages.'

Anna giggled. *'That's* not right, *papà!'* she replied in Italian. *'God* invented our fingers, so Riccardo is probably just following God's orders.'

Adam sighed. Their daughter was showing her mother's characteristic trait of having an apt response to every situation. Try as he might, his children refused to speak in English. He had to console himself that at least, they understood every word he said in his own language.

'Unfortunately, Anna, God also intended that we should arrive at school by half past eight every day. So a man-made spoon might help us to accomplish this.'

His daughter had the grace to smile at his joke.

'Where's *mamma?'* asked Riccardo with his mouth full.

'She drove off with another man,' pronounced Anna with some glee.

Alessandro had arrived some thirty minutes ago and whisked his assistant off after a brief handshake with Adam and a promise that he would stay longer when they came back after their trip to Galatina. Adam was used to Rosaria's dogged determination to see a problem through to its bitter end. He had come within an inch of losing his life all those years ago in London at the hands of Enrico, the mafia boss, thanks to Rosaria's pertinacity. The visit to Galatina that morning was, the love of his life had assured him, the

211

last link in solving the case of the disappearance of Judge Grassi. Adam did not suppose that this trip was life-threatening.

'Hurry up Riccardo,' sighed Adam. 'Let's go and clean your teeth properly, shall we? You've got more cornflakes stuck between your teeth than in your stomach.'

Thank goodness, tomorrow was the last school day before the short Easter break, he thought. They would be able to fit in a trip to the beach and get a bit of sea air. Adam bundled them into the car and set off on the trip to their schools – fortunately next door to each other.

'Why have you got grey hair, *papà?*' asked Riccardo out of the blue.

Adam had been wondering how long it would be before the inevitable question came up – for the second time. Anna had been through the process of getting used to the fact that her dad was older than all her friends' fathers some time ago. Adam debated whether he should give the question a serious answer or try to pass it off with some witty comment. He was spared the trouble when Anna intervened:

'Because, Riccardo, that's the way *mamma* likes her men.'

Adam was amazed at her daughter's perceptive psychological analysis of her mother's intimate preferences and laughed out loud.

'Thank you, Anna. There, Riccardo! Always ask your sister in future if you want a straight answer to difficult questions.'

He got a rapid *bacio* on the cheek from them both before they ran off through the school gates. A few hours of total peace. But Adam knew that he would be missing the amicable conflict of their diverse personalities within thirty minutes.

On the way to meet Alessandro's friend at the municipal offices in Galatina, Elena had updated her boss as to her latest research. She had succeeded in contacting the leader of the group of musicians whom she had met all that time ago.

'How did you know who to contact?' asked Alessandro.

'I recognised the music on the video clip that Judge Grassi was sent. You know, Sandro, the first one where you see the girl dancing the *pizzica*. I remembered the name of the group. It took me some time on the computer to find out the group leader's name and contact details.'

'And what happened? Did you find out anything useful?'

'I asked him if he remembered making a video of a girl of about sixteen dancing in an olive grove.'

Alessandro did not say anything, so Elena continued.

'Well, he did... remember, that is. He said he would never forget the episode. They went to her house – a large *masseria* near Soleto and made a video of this girl whom he had met at a *festa* in Galatina. They had been so amazed at the way she had been dancing that they asked her if they could film her. She became his girlfriend for a time although 'nothing happened' between them, he claimed. I believed him, Sandro – he sounded genuinely disappointed at not making a conquest. Anyway, he went on to tell me that this girl was dancing up on the stage at a concert in Collepasso one night when her father turned up, furious with everyone in the group. He had rushed on to the stage and dragged her off in tears. The group leader, Maurizio, had tried to calm the father down but he had continued to yell at him that he had no right to take his daughter away from home without his permission.

Alessandro looked at his 'assistant' in envious admiration. She seemed to be able to find out *anything* – so effortlessly, too.

'And did he remember where this *masseria* was, and what it was called?'

'Maurizio told me that it was somewhere just north of Soleto. He remembers going down a country track off a minor road. He said he remembered that the house name began with the letter 'M', but he couldn't recall the full name.'

'Well, I suppose that will narrow it down a bit,' said Alessandro with a shade too much sarcasm for Elena's liking.

'What it does, Sandro,' she replied with a degree of asperity in her voice, which usually made her paymaster quake a little in his shoes, 'is to confirm what we already suspected about where the judge is being held. Remember what my Adam found out last Saturday.'

'Alright, well done, Elena,' Alessandro said in placating tones. It was better to keep the peace whenever Elena felt that she was being challenged. Besides, he had to admit, she was usually right.

When they arrived at the municipal offices in Galatina, after the habitual problem of finding a parking space, which had left their car bumper to bumper, wedged between two other vehicles, they discovered that Alessandro's friend, Luca, had not yet arrived, despite his previous assurance that they could arrive at eight o'clock if they wanted; the first inevitable frustration of the day.

'Why does nothing ever go smoothly in this part of the world?' muttered Alessandro. What had annoyed him was the fact that *he* had organised this encounter and not his assistant, and,

214

inevitably, there had been a hitch. Elena shrugged resignedly and said that they were not in such a hurry.

'I'll give him a ring,' said Alessandro. It sounded as if his friend Luca was speaking another language altogether. 'Dish ish Ooka. Ah kan shpee... gauwa klam in mow ... Haga kook aik ...gengish ... she yoo akeng... shorry!'

'I can't understand a word he is saying, Elena. Can you understand him?' said Alessandro handing her his mobile. Elena listened and nodded, smiled, said *'grazie'*, and handed the phone back to Alessandro.

'Luca says he's sorry but he had a toothache, so he went to the dentist. He can't speak because he's got a clamp in his mouth. He'll see us at 10 o'clock,' said Elena in an annoyingly matter-of-fact voice.

'How the devil did you manage to understand all *that*?' asked Alessandro, slightly peeved.

'Because his dentist just told me, Sandro,' replied Elena trying and failing to keep the smugness out of her voice.

She could be so annoying, thought Alessandro, who gave a sheepish grin in her direction whilst realising that he often felt like throttling his assistant. 'You're worth your weight in gold, Elena,' he said between gritted teeth.

They had a coffee in the nearest decent-looking bar. It was just past nine o'clock. One hour to go before Luca would appear. They decided they would go to the municipal offices and try to make a start looking up the official property sales records in the Soleto area. As soon as they presented themselves, they knew that they would not get very far without Luca. The middle-aged woman, who sat behind the barricade, which was skilfully disguised as a reception desk, said curtly and without a smile, *'Sì?'* by way of encouraging introduction. Why was it, thought Elena, that every single council office – or post office - in Italy was fronted by some disagreeable woman who reacted instantly as if she was about to be asked to hand over all her money, reveal why her lot in life was a continuous round of drudgery, or worse, have to explain why her husband no longer made love to her. Elena's instant desire was to tell her bluntly that she was among the fortunate minority in this part of the world to have a guaranteed, life-long job with a state pension at the end of it – despite not having the intelligence or imagination to sweep a floor properly. Realising what was going through his assistant's mind, Alessandro laid a restraining hand on her arm and patiently set about explaining to the harridan why they were there.

'I'm too busy at present,' she snapped. As she had been doing absolutely nothing when they had arrived, their fears that they were wasting their time were confirmed. Nevertheless, Alessandro and Elena stood their ground, declining the suggestion that they should sit down. Their immovable presence did, in the end, make the clerk realise that her usually successful technique of repelling boarders was not going to work.

'What exactly do you want to know?' she asked ungraciously. Alessandro explained carefully that they needed a list of *masserie* and their legal owners in the Soleto district, which fell under the jurisdiction of Galatina.

It was quite a tall order even for someone with real computer skills. The woman did not bother to show them the screen at any stage so that it was impossible to see what she was doing. In the end, she printed off a list and handed it over the counter in a manner which stated that she had done all that was expected of her. They sat down and studied the paper. It was impossible to tell what the woman had omitted since they did not know how she had set about extracting the data. There were certainly a number of *masserie* on the list beginning with the letter 'M' – too many, in fact. *Morigino, Malapezza, Merine, Massiva, Marelica, Morello, Moderna* – a contradiction in terms, said Alessandro to an unimpressed Elena. *Manieri, Monacelli, Mosto* and *Madonna delle Grazie.* It was amazing how many *masserie* there were, let alone how many of them began with the letter M, said Alessandro to Elena, who nodded absent-mindedly. The names of the proprietors appeared by the side of each *masseria*. None of them was what they were expecting or hoping to find. One of the owners was listed simply under the initials S.I.M.

'Very unhelpful,' sighed Alessandro.

It was nearer 10.30 when Luca finally arrived, attempting to be apologetic as far as his injection-frozen tongue and face would allow him. Elena and Alessandro forgave him readily as soon as they saw him. His manner was in stark contrast to that of his colleague; friendly, open, affectionate and welcoming, a man who would be happy even in Siberia. The sort of person who restored your faith in humanity in general and *Salentini* in particular, thought Elena.

'Don't worry, Alessandro,' he said. 'We'll find out what you want to know, even it takes us all day.' In point of fact, it did just that. By lunchtime, they had been through all the computerised information available. They had had to assume that Elena's contact had incorrectly remembered the initial letter of the *masseria* that he had visited ten years ago, and they had gone through a further fifty or more properties in and around Soleto. Over lunch, which Alessandro insisted on paying for, the Greco agents felt that they could trust Luca implicitly. They regaled him with the details of the case to satisfy his undisguised curiosity as to why this research was so important to them.

Luca was frowning at some thought that had occurred to him. 'I wish you had told me this before, Sandro. I might have been able to save you a lot of time. I'm just trying to remember something I heard about … about ten years ago. Aprea, you said?' Elena and Alessandro sat with bated breath.

'Ach! It'll come back to me soon, I'm sure. I'll tell you what,' he continued brightly, the effects of the injection wearing off. 'We'll go through the original paper documents in the archives after lunch.'

They began with the letter 'M' properties again, thumbing through all the pages in search of a signature that even looked remotely like Vollaro or Aprea. There was one signature that looked more like a straight line than a person's name. It belonged to the *masseria* called 'Masseria Marelica' which they had found on the original list supplied by the lady upstairs. It was the one where, instead of a name at the head of the document, there appeared the initials S.I.M.

'Ah!' exclaimed Luca, the light dawning in his eyes. 'I knew it would come back to me. Didn't you say that this Aprea character is an arms manufacturer?' Elena and Sandro nodded in expectation of the forthcoming revelation. 'That's it then!' said Luca triumphantly. 'S.I.M stands for *Sicurezza Internazionale Milano* – the most blatant euphemism for a weapons manufacturer that you could imagine. The property must be registered through his company.'

When they rechecked the signature, one could just imagine without too great a stretch of the imagination that it read Antonio Aprea – at least the two capital letters were almost recognisable. Elena embraced Luca warmly with a beaming smile all over her face. Luca led them back upstairs, all three of them talking vivaciously. They shook hands warmly as they left. 'Let me know the outcome, Alessandro, won't you?' said Luca.

The harridan scowled disapprovingly at them, so Alessandro went up to her and thanked her for all her help. The brief smile that she gave him must have demanded a supreme effort on the part of her face muscles before they resumed their natural position of antipathy once again.

'Off to the *carabinieri,* I think,' stated Alessandro firmly in case his assistant had been entertaining notions of charging off on the rescue mission all on her own.

They went directly to the local *carabinieri* post in Galatina. A young man in uniform greeted them with a complete absence of the usual surly scowl that was the norm in Alessandro's experience of such things.

After the preliminary courtesies, Alessandro came straight to the point.

'We believe we know where Judge Grassi is being held,' he stated to the amazement of the junior officer, who raised his eyebrows in involuntary surprise. To his credit, he did not need an explanation and had realised the importance of this information instantly.

'I'll go and fetch our *capo,*' he said.

Alessandro shook the senior officer by the hand and said: 'This is my assistant, Elena Camisso.'

'Rosaria Miccoli!' declared the *carabiniere* officer immediately. 'What a pleasant surprise after all this time! Why did your companion call you...?'

'It's the name I use when I'm working,' she explained hurriedly. 'This is my boss, Alessandro Greco. Alessandro, this is *Capitano* – no sorry, *Colonnello* Marco Scarpa,' she said, amending his title when she looked more carefully at his insignia.

Alessandro smiled ruefully at the colonel. Yet again, his assistant had managed to upstage him. 'This is the officer who helped me when Adam and I tracked down the *mafioso* killer who took my cousin Diletta's life. You remember me telling you, don't you, Alessandro?'

'Elena' and the colonel swopped news for the next twenty minutes whilst sitting in *Colonnello* Scarpa's office sipping coffees which he had sent his junior officer out to get from the nearest bar.

'I won't insult you both by offering you coffee out of our machine,' he had stated. Then, finally, they got down to the business of the missing judge.

'To the best of our knowledge,' explained Alessandro, 'our judge is not in danger of his life. It is a very unusual case indeed.'

'Yes, as far as one can gather, he was abducted by a monk, if I have understood the situation correctly?'

'It seems that way, *colonnello*. But there has been no communication with his family since Sunday, apart from a brief text message from the priest saying that he was in no danger. So his family has no idea where he is or whether he has indeed been harmed in any way. We are fairly certain that he is being held, against his will or with his compliance, in a *masseria* near here. So, we have come to you for help.' Elena went into the details of their research at the local town hall. The colonel was thoughtful for a few minutes.

'If you don't object,' he continued, 'it would make life easier if we delayed presenting ourselves at the *Masseria Marelica* until tomorrow morning. The judge will then have been officially missing for well over 48 hours. I am also very short-staffed today. My men are all out looking for a missing child.'

'It would be very helpful if we came with you, *colonnello*. I think the judge would be reassured by our presence. Would you mind?'

'As usual, Rosaria, you have a perfect way of expressing yourself,' laughed the colonel. 'Of course you must come too. But if the judge is really in danger, you may have to stay in the background.' He had understood that it had become yet another personal mission for Rosaria – he could only think of her as Rosaria – to be present when her distinguished client was rescued from his captors. The colonel had wisely decided to err on the side of caution; in his experience, members of the clergy were not always what they seemed. He could be dealing with a set of spiritual terrorists or religious inquisitors for all he knew. Thus it was agreed that Alessandro and Elena would present themselves at the police station the following morning, Wednesday, at 8 o'clock.

'You aren't suffering from toothache by any chance, are you, *colonnello?*' Elena asked an uncomprehending senior police officer.

The next person, after Amedeo, to walk into the kitchen of the *Masseria Marelica* on that Tuesday morning was Marta. She came up to him, gave him a *bacio* on the cheek as if he had been part of their household for years. She put croissants on the table and made some fresh coffee in a big, coffee-stained *moka*. She looked more alert as soon as she had swallowed a mouthful of the reviving black liquid. She smiled at him. Amedeo took a deep breath, threw his customary caution to the winds and said to her:

'Oh Marta! How could a beautiful woman like you ever have got involved with a man like *him?*' Marta seemed to understand exactly what her house guest meant. She smiled a rueful smile but was looking into the mental realm of her past ordeal as she answered:

'Ah, Amedeo, we all make mistakes in life, don't we? I was young, naïve and in love at the time. The strange thing about it all is that I have two beautiful children from the union, so there will always be a part of me that cannot regret my choice – however traumatic it has been.'

The judge nodded silently – taking on board the comment about making mistakes in life with a brief gesture of acknowledgement with his hand.

'I am so pleased that Chiara seems to be showing signs of recovery. I am not sure if my arrival has played a part or not, although I should be overjoyed if that were the case.'

'It could be a coincidence, I suppose. But I do not think so. Gabriele was always convinced that you would play some part in Chiara's life. He has the gift of prescience, by the way - as you will probably find out in due course,' added Marta smiling mysteriously.

Amedeo looked at her and replied: 'I am sure you are right, Marta. I have seen some evidence of that already. But what puzzles me is the question of who Chiara believes me to be in her perception of things. I hope she does not really equate me with her father.'

'No, Amedeo. I am sure she does not. She has banished the memory of her biological father to the nether regions of hell. I'll get her to show you the paintings she did some time ago to give you some insight into the way she thinks. Chiara is a brilliant artist as well as a dancer – hopeless at maths, though. No, I think you are her father substitute. She is in desperate need of a true father figure as you can imagine. You look a kind person – you *are* a kind person even if you have only just realised it yourself. Poor Amedeo! What a responsibility we have laid on your shoulders!'

Amedeo looked at her. 'It was high time,' was all he said. He might have enlarged on the thought but the other members of the household had begun to arrive. They sat down round the table and discussed the plans for the day.

'Excuse us, won't you Amedeo, if we speak in dialect,' said Gabriele.

The judge waved a hand in acquiescence. It was quite easy to understand the local dialect even if the words sounded strangely different from his own childhood dialect in Abruzzo. He recalled a TV documentary that he had seen a year or so back in which the reporter declared that, thanks to education and the media, 49% of all Italians now spoke Italian at home – as if she was announcing a major breakthrough. Just a minute, the judge had thought; *that* means that more than half of the population still communicate in dialect when they are at home. Quite a revelation!

Chiara drank milk and spoke a few words in dialect in reply to questions. Gabriele looked at the judge meaningfully as if to reinforce the fact that this was a new and miraculous development.

'Why don't you show Amedeo your paintings, Chiara? He would love to see them, I'm sure,' suggested Marta. Amedeo nodded and smiled at her in encouragement. She beamed at him and ran off to her room to fetch her folders down. Amedeo realised that he had not yet seen the first floor of the *masseria* and was promised a guided tour later on in the morning.

Amedeo gasped in amazement at Chiara's paintings. It had obviously been a source of great emotional release to her over the years, enabling her to escape some of the pain she was suffering inside. One poignant painting in particular showed a young woman lying broken at the foot of a high cliff, her legs splayed out at an unnatural angle, whilst a dark, sinister figure of a man looked down scornfully at her from the cliff top. It took his breath away with its stark simplicity. Not all of the paintings were so black in their mood, however. One painting showed a girl (Chiara?) dancing against a backdrop of an olive grove with the sun's rays casting a golden sheen over the whole scene. She had captured the movement of the dance with uncanny precision.

Amedeo made enthusiastic noises of admiration throughout, uttering genuine words of praise, whilst Chiara herself pointed out various aspects of the paintings which she was particularly proud of, or which she felt were relevant to herself in some way.

Where Amedeo got his next idea from, he would never know. It was inspired by whatever new-found spirit that had come to inhabit his soul. He asked Chiara if she had any more drawing paper and pencils. He sat down opposite her at the table and explained that he was going to draw a picture on his sheet of paper and then describe exactly what he had drawn without her looking at his sheet of paper. She was to draw the picture that he was describing on to *her* sheet of paper. She became totally absorbed in the details of drawing snow-covered mountains, churches, flowers in a valley and a man fishing by the river until Amedeo ran out of ideas. They then compared the two pictures. Chiara's was an artistic treat compared to Amedeo's rudimentary representations of the scene he had described.

'*Adesso, Chiara, tocca a te!*'

It was Chiara's turn to draw a picture and describe it to him. The suspense in the room was palpable. Gabriele and Marta pretended to go about their business as if nothing out of the ordinary was going on. Enrico and Dario had gone outside in the garden. Slowly, hesitatingly, Chiara began to describe her picture to Amedeo. There was a young man walking a dog along a road. The young man was *beddru*, she said – 'handsome'. She was speaking in dialect but one or two words like 'church' and 'tree' came out in Italian. When Chiara showed her intricate picture to Amedeo and compared it to his, she burst out in a peel of laughter.

'I wouldn't go out with *your* young man,' she stated in amusement.

Marta was in tears that she could not disguise by busying herself with the kitchen chores and Gabriele had that beatific smile on his face again as he looked heavenward. Amedeo and

Chiara carried on until they had run out of drawing paper. Reluctantly, Marta dragged Chiara away to take her shopping again with the promise that they would buy another drawing pad while they were out.

Amedeo had his conducted tour of the upstairs floor by an Angel Gabriel who could not stop showering his guest with praise. Amedeo soon realised that the potential of this house had not been fully exploited; more than half the rooms on the first floor were unused.

'Eventually, I would like to turn this house into a hostel for kids in trouble and give them some purpose in life again,' explained Gabriele. 'There are so many lost souls in Salento crying out for help that nobody gives them, Amedeo; the permanently unemployed, drug users, kids from broken homes, the sexually abused... The list is endless.'

Amedeo asked how the Catholic Church viewed his apparent preference for following his own path.

'I think they realise that I am something of a loose cannon,' he laughed. 'But I have friends in high places.' Amedeo was not sure whether he was referring to God or the Pope, but thought it should amount to the same thing.

'And now I have to ask you seriously, Gabriele,' said Amedeo when they had gone back downstairs and were sitting at the kitchen table again. 'What do you want me to do to make amends? I mean in the immediate future, to help Chiara.'

'What you are already doing,' said Gabriele simply. 'But there is a wonderful private clinic outside Rome where people who have suffered sexual trauma are helped back to life. We would love to send her there for a while when she is ready. But, it is very expensive...'

'Ha!' exclaimed Amedeo. 'I shall have to pay a ransom after all!'

The Angel Gabriel turned to Amedeo smiling innocently as he said:

'Well you know what Jesus said in Matthew Chapter 19 verse 24, don't you *signor giudice? It is easier for an Audi Q7 to pass through a keyhole than it is for a rich man to enter the kingdom of heaven.*

Judge Grassi tried hard not to laugh at the Angel Gabriel's clever anachronism but failed to suppress his amusement, which emerged in a splutter of mirth.

'Well, Gabriele,' he said finally. 'It's probably just as well that I had already made up my mind to give you the lot anyway. I have spent ten guilty years wondering how I could get rid of it in some meaningful way. Now I have found a good cause at last. I guess you already know the sum involved,' he added caustically.

Gabriele looked apologetically at the judge. 'If you have decided to use this money to help Chiara, then all I can say is, God bless you a million times over, Amedeo.'

'Well, Gabriele. Considering where the money came from in the first instance, I guess there is a good measure of poetic justice in settling matters in this manner. I am sure that there will be enough money left over to fulfil your other plans too. You might even consider modernising some of your wine making equipment – and you could do with investing in a machine to print off some decent wine bottle labels too.'

The rest of the day was spent discussing the details of transferring the funds to Gabriele's family. The member of the order of Benedictine monks pointed out that they would need to transfer the money into Marta's bank account since he was not allowed direct access to money by the rules of his religious order. The family discussed how they could renovate and refurbish the parts of the *masseria* which were not yet habitable – with a view to putting into practice Gabriele's scheme for providing a refuge for lost or wayward teenagers. They did a tour of the estate and discussed what would be needed to make a success of producing wine and olive oil on a modest commercial scale. Chiara, equipped once again with paper, got out all her paints and an old easel which she set up by the old stone bench and persuaded Amedeo to sit while she sketched the beginnings of his portrait. Marta and Chiara produced a celebratory dinner with local antipasti, a huge dish of pasta with porcini mushrooms followed by a local lamb casserole dish cooked with celery, chilli, tomatoes, bay leaves and the unusual addition of *pecorino* cheese, all cooked without oil in a traditional *pignata* – a stoneware cooking pot that sat in the oven for three hours while the meat stewed in its own juices. Amedeo claimed that it was the best lamb dish he had ever tasted in his life.

Gabriele was looking pensive towards the end of the meal and Amedeo asked him what he was thinking.

'I fear that the spell may be temporarily broken tomorrow, Amedeo.'

'How do you mean?' asked the judge.

'I think that the outside world will catch up with us again. I believe your detectives have been busy trying to track you down.'

Amedeo intercepted a knowing look from Marta and he recalled what she had said about his gift of prescience. The judge was not ready to leave this place just yet and, in any case, he did not see how it would have been possible to track him down to this remote *masseria* in such a short time.

The evening finished off with the group walking round the garden to digest their meal by the light of the eternal moon. Amedeo slept soundly.

The following morning, after a late breakfast, Chiara led Amedeo to her room where she had been deeply engrossed in painting his portrait. She had an arm through his as she proudly showed him the half-finished picture. He gasped in awe at the image of himself that was emerging on the paper. 'This, I shall frame and keep for ever, Chiara. It is brilliant.'

Chiara looked radiant and whispered a simple *'grazie papà'*.

It was in that moment of simple intimacy with this fragile woman standing by his side that Amedeo heard the distant sound of a police siren. It was coming nearer and nearer. The car finally stopped outside the massive gates of the *Masseria Marelica* a reflection of the flashing blue light catching in the window pane. Gabriele had been right in his prediction. Amedeo's heart sank slightly before he decided to take control of the situation. He hugged Chiara and led her back downstairs saying to her: 'Do not be scared, Chiara. There's nothing to worry about.'

15: Startling Revelations

Gabriele, Chiara, Marta - plus one German shepherd dog with lolling tongue - were lined up side by side with a white-faced Chiara in the middle. The human element was standing with arms linked. Out of the front door strode a purposeful Judge Grassi, fully dressed in the clothes he had been wearing on the day of his abduction. Without a glance at the little group, he marched steadfastly towards the main gates, clutching the hold-all which he supposed had been used by Marta to bring his few belongings from their house in Lecce. Dario and Enrico were opening one of the main gates as Judge Grassi reached the entrance. As soon as the gate was open sufficiently wide to let him pass, he was outside. He was faced with Alessandro and Elena smiling in welcome.

There were three *carabinieri* nervously fingering their pistol grips in their holsters. He looked at the fourth officer, obviously in charge, and spoke severely to him.

'For heaven's sake turn off that ridiculous flashing blue light and tell your men not to look so trigger-happy. There's a young woman in there already quite traumatised enough by life without you terrifying her even more with your ostentatious arrival.'

Colonnello Scarpa made a gesture to his men to obey the judge's wishes and he told them to get back into the car.

'I take it you have come to no harm, *signor giudice!*' said the senior police officer with a rueful smile, 'and that you are not being held here against your will.'

The expression on the faces of the people inside the grounds of the *masseria* was telling. Marta looked terrified at the prospect of being taken away by the police and having to leave Chiara behind. Chiara was trembling and close to tears. 'Is Amedeo leaving us?' she kept on saying. Gabriele's expression had turned from a look of curiosity to one of growing concern that he had miscalculated the judge's character completely and put his mother's and sister's safety in jeopardy. For the first time, he had lost that look of serenity and firm belief in the powers above.

Ten minutes of unbearable tension elapsed during which the judge could be seen in deep conversation with the group of people outside. He seemed to be talking mainly to the couple whom Gabriele assumed must be from the private detective agency. And then, letting out an audible sigh of relief, the little group saw Amedeo Grassi step back inside the garden and walk towards them as the police car drove away. He was no longer carrying the hold-all. He stopped in front of Gabriele, Marta and Chiara and said without a smile on his face:

'Well, I take it you are not kicking me out just yet? But I do need some fresh clothes. Those two good people have not yet earned the fee that they charged and are very happy to organise things with my family. I also told them that, on penalty of death, no details as to my whereabouts must be communicated to the media. I said that they could promise the newspaper editor a story which would rock the whole of Italy when I next come to see him.'

'Oh Amedeo!' said Gabriele with a deep sigh of relief. 'You had us worried just then. We really thought for a moment that you were going to abandon us.'

Amedeo tapped Gabriele playfully on the chest with a forefinger and said:

'Judge Grassi's little act of revenge, young man.'

The monk laughed with pleasure at having been caught out by his 'captive' and hugged Amedeo warmly. 'Well done, Amedeo! You carried it off like a true professional.' The family group went back inside arm in arm, with Chiara holding on tightly to the judge's arm. Marta went to a cupboard and took out a bottle of some homemade *aperitivo* which she poured into six little glasses. They drank to each other's happiness and to Chiara's tentative return to the real world. Even a sip of this aniseed flavoured liquid was enough for Chiara, completely unused to alcohol. She spat it out immediately into the kitchen sink. Amedeo put a concerned arm round her shoulder. She managed a smile and a shake of the head and said: *'Mai più!'* Never again!

'And now, I really must phone my wife,' said the judge. 'I wonder if you would be so kind as to wash that tracksuit for me?' he asked Marta graciously. 'I have become strangely attached to it – and I think that the attachment will soon become very noticeable to all concerned.'

* * *

Judge Grassi spent the next few days as if time had been suspended. The passing of the hours was measured by the changes of light in the trees and the lengthening of the shadows as the sun went down. His being was imbued with a sense of community and closeness to the people with whom he was sharing this corner of the world - a sensation which he had rarely experienced before. Nothing that he did was dictated by the pressure to be doing something else. This was the magic of the place, he decided. Yet, by the end of the day when he had finally retired to his room, he could look back on a rich array of activities and human contact in which he had become totally immersed. The old Amedeo Grassi had indeed passed away. The new one had a mission in life that would last until the end of his time on Earth. He had rejected the formality of a starched shirt and tie. He reckoned that he might well spend the rest of his days in a track suit. In point of fact, this was not to be the case, as he himself intuited. But this transformation was still, mercifully, a few precious days away in a future of which he himself would be the architect.

Before falling asleep he went back over the events of the last two days. Chiara had been totally engaged in completing his portrait and had shut herself in her room, put on her favourite music and painted until her colours ran out. The judge, Chiara and Marta had gone shopping in Galatina where, in a pokey back-street art shop known only to regular local artists, they had restocked Chiara's supply of paints. It was a wonderful thing about this part of the world, Amedeo considered, that little shops like this still managed to survive the onslaught of the modern world, simply because their owners – inevitably in their sixties and seventies - loved what they did and had no illusions that they would ever be rich. Marta agreed with him – and immediately drove them off to the out-of-town *Conad* supermarket, a latter-day Aladdin's Cave of Italian culinary delights. Amedeo had insisted on paying for everything and had profoundly enjoyed the sensation that he was parting with money that he no longer needed to hoard like a miser counting his ill-gotten gains.

Later on, round about midday, Elena Camisso had arrived with Adam and their two children with the hold-all containing fresh clothes, including a brand new silver-grey track-suit which Amedeo put on immediately.

'Why does your... partner keep calling you Rosy?' asked a bewildered Judge Grassi.

'Because, *signor giudice*, Rosaria is my real name. And I am relying entirely on your discretion to keep it a secret.'

'You can trust Amedeo utterly,' said Gabriele coming to his rescue with a smile in Rosaria's direction.

But the remarkable thing about that lunchtime and early afternoon was that, while the 'adults' talked about what had happened, Chiara led Anna and Riccardo off by the hand and began with a tour of the *masseria* that kept them engaged for ages. They could not be precise, later on that day, as to whether Chiara had spoken to them in Italian or in dialect, but they had come back full of enthusiasm after an hour or more, bubbling over with glee at the discovery of an ancient communal toilet down one end of the building, which Amedeo had never quite reached.

'And did you know, *mamma*,' said Anna, 'that in olden times the whole family did their poos sitting next to each other so they could gossip to each other as they did it?'

'I would be holding my nose and not talking at all!' exclaimed Riccardo. *'Che schifo!'* How disgusting!

They then showed their parents some rudimentary printing that they had done under Chiara's guidance. She had got them to cut simple designs in a rolled out sheet of Plasticine, covered the sheet with a layer of ink and then pressed a sheet of paper on to the ink.

'Look!' said Riccardo. 'I did a beetle.'

'And I did an angel,' said Anna.

'I hope you thanked Chiara for everything, children,' said their father.

They had gone up and kissed Chiara and been hugged in return. Chiara looked happy and relaxed.

'*Il piccolo miracolo va avanti,*' whispered Gabriele to Amedeo, who nodded.

Amedeo took 'Elena' to one side and had spoken to her in hushed tones. He had thanked her for what she had done. She had protested that they had not done nearly enough to justify their generous fee. Amedeo had told her that the Greco agency would soon have the opportunity to rectify the situation.

'By the time I have finished, you will be able to make up for any over-payment, Elena. In fact, you will have earned another fee after I have finished revealing matters which should have been made public ten years ago. Believe me when I say that I shall be making enemies in high places. I suspect that I shall be needing your help again - especially your advanced computer skills,' he concluded ominously.

Apart from that, Amedeo had learnt how to prune back the vines, had managed to distinguish between Negroamaro and Primitivo vines, flourishing in the red-coloured, iron rich Salento soil. He had discovered to his surprise how much land there was behind the *masseria* by opening the little gate at the bottom of the garden. He had held lengthy discussions with Gabriele, Dario and Enrico about what new equipment they would need to store the young wine while it fermented. 'We could buy some French oak barrels,' he suggested enthusiastically.

He had devoted time to walking around the grounds with Chiara, who still said very little in words. She seemed to be trying to adjust her mind to all the things that were happening to her as she began to blossom like a flower in springtime. She showed Amedeo his nearly completed portrait. He talked to her about the possibility of exhibiting some of her paintings in Lecce; he told her about a friend of theirs who owned an art gallery just a stone's throw from the *Piazza del Duomo*. She had looked at him disbelievingly as if such a goal was far beyond her artistic aspirations. Together, they had looked at all her paintings again. Amedeo said that he wanted her signature on his portrait. She had looked embarrassed until Amedeo had realised that she had not written a word for nearly a decade. They had practised writing her name and after fifty or so attempts, she managed to write *Chiara Aprea* in a way which pleased her. They decided on a title for each one of her paintings. When they had come to the poignant image of the girl lying at the foot of the cliff with the dark and sinister figure towering above her, Amedeo had made a few suggestions for a title. Chiara had shaken her head at each one of the judge's tentative suggestions. In the end, she had looked at him and said quite clearly in Italian: 'No, *papà*, it's called *Nelle grinfie di Satana* – In Satan's Grip.' He had put an arm round her shoulders and given her another hug. He found the gesture reassuring and thought how absent it had been in his own childhood.

In the evening, the whole family, which now included Amedeo, walked round the garden together. Chiara brought her CD player and they linked arms as they had done before and danced round singing their signature tune: *Luna d'argentu cosa viti....?* It was for Chiara a means of reasserting her new found awareness of life, they understood. She even managed to teach them all new dance steps so that they were not merely shuffling round in a circle more or less in time to the rhythm. It was nearly midnight when they walked back towards the *masseria,* a dark silhouette swinging slowly in the heavens on its nocturnal passage round the moon.

On Friday morning, Amedeo was up early and was joined in the kitchen by Gabriele. The judge had had another idea. 'You could get Chiara to design your wine labels for you, Gabriele. She would love to do that.'

Gabriele looked in amazement at Amedeo. 'I say it again, Amedeo. You have worked miracles with Chiara since you have been here. You must come back soon,' he added.

'Well, I wasn't intending....' But Gabriele had that certain look on his face as if he was peering into a future that he had just perceived.

'I believe that you will have a phone call today, Amedeo, which will take you away from us for a time,' the Angel Gabriel stated without drama. There was a subdued silence as they drank their coffees.

'But there are still so many unanswered questions that I want to ask you, Gabriele.'

Gabriele smiled and said: 'There's no time like the present, Amedeo. Don't worry. I'll enlighten you as long as I know what the answers are myself.'

'I was wondering if your choice of university subject had a direct bearing on what happened to Chiara – and yourself to a lesser extent.'

'Yes Amedeo. I became fascinated by the complexities of the human mind, horrified by what led men – and women – to inflict

238

pain and torture on others. Not just on human beings but on all living creatures. And the more I studied, the more I became convinced that the Church, for all its outdated notions and naïve concepts of the material and metaphysical universe, was right to insist that our very souls are a battle ground between good and evil; a battle which it often appears Satan is winning. To my mind, the explanation that Satan is constantly trying to tempt us down the path to hell and personal damnation presents a far more accurate explanation of our behaviour on Earth than the volumes written by Freud and his successors – however valuable their analysis of the intricacies of the human mind might be.

Of course I wanted to understand better how my father could have justified to himself the manner in which he destroyed his own daughter's happiness. How he had not one tiny jot of remorse for what he did to her. So, yes, I learnt that he was a psychopath devoid of conscience and moral sense. But I still believe even now that the evil in him is fostered by some alien spirit determined to reduce God's amazing creation to the burnt out ashes of Hell. That is certainly what drove me to taking holy orders. Besides, I loved the idea of wearing monk's robes.'

Amedeo shook his head in gentle irony at this man's inability to resist the temptation to make light of the path he had chosen; a kind of spiritual modesty, Amedeo supposed.

'But, forgive me asking this, Gabriele. You are a very good-looking young man – my wife used the word *beautiful*,' he added almost grudgingly. 'How could you renounce all things carnal, the love of a woman, to embrace celibacy for the rest of your life? It seems such a waste in your case.'

Gabriele smiled broadly, totally unperturbed by the implications of such a personal question. 'Oh, I am no virgin, Amedeo. I enjoyed all the sins of the flesh while I was a student at Lecce. In fact, I met a beautiful girl during the course of my degree studies. I even have a daughter somewhere down south – near Tricase. Yes, I am sorry to shock you, Amedeo. Like Saint Augustine, I enjoyed the pleasures of intimacy frequently before I decided to take holy orders. I made a conscious choice to make that sacrifice, unlike those sad clergymen who are ordained before they truly understand how powerful sexual urges can be – until it is too late.'

'And what about the computer hacking and your time working in the Vatican?' asked the judge, his curiosity unabated.

'Well, I haven't really finished in Rome, Amedeo. If we take Chiara to this clinic in the hills outside the city, I shall need to be near her anyway. We shall try to persuade her that she is going on holiday for a few weeks – which is what it will be, I hope. It's run by the Catholic Church. The clinic is run by Carmelite sisters but there are also very devoted Catholic lay doctors and psychologists there too. We shall need to reassure Chiara that she has not been abandoned in any way.'

Amedeo was wondering if he himself was included in this collective 'we'. He hoped he was.

'As to my computer skills,' continued Gabriele, 'I hope I have only ever engaged in ethical hacking. It is all too easy to probe into other computers once you realise that the whole world-wide system is linked. In reality, privacy does not exist. Most people who use computers imagine that they are operating in a little private universe of their own – and the illusion is maintained

240

simply because their activities are largely innocent and of no interest to a computer 'invader'. I developed the ability to manipulate the system bit by bit while I was at university. I even added a line or two in an article published by *Il Quotidiano* about that trial – just for practice, I have to confess, although I did feel a lot of anger towards you at the time.'

'I can well understand *that*,' said the judge.

'In the Vatican, I was asked to identify the sad handful of priests involved in cases of suspected paedophilia in Ireland and Belgium in particular. Contrary to what the media in certain countries tries to persuade us, it *is* only a tiny minority of priests who have tragically become victims to the corrupting power of sexual temptation.'

'But the Catholic Church has appeared to cover up the incidents of child abuse amongst its clergy, Gabriele. It has been most reluctant to see the offenders brought to justice.'

'But whose justice are we talking about, Amedeo? From God's point of view, these men - usually men - are endangered souls who desperately need redemption and reconciliation. Justice on Earth is more concerned with punishment and public scandal – very often the media is guilty of dwelling with morbid curiosity on sexual details in order to increase newspaper circulation or audience ratings. They wish to vilify a Church which they do not believe in, whose mission on Earth they certainly fail to understand. Neither do they accurately distinguish between *paedophilia*, which is a sexual interest in prepubescent children, *hebephilia*, a preference for eleven to fourteen year olds and *ephebophilia*, which is love for a person in late adolescence – which is not even considered to be a pathological disorder. The vast majority of cases which I have come across belong to this latter category. Please do not think for a moment that I am condoning such relationships, but there is not a man on this planet who can honestly say that he has never felt attracted to a young person in this age group. Most people, thank God, recognise the moral pitfalls of putting such thoughts into action. But imagine what it must be like for a lonely priest, who has never known the joy of making love, never held another living person in his arms. What a frightful discovery to make at this stage of one's calling! Only the truly committed have sufficient moral strength to resist.

Yes, it is true that, on occasions I have uncovered the real perils of this evil, where groups of priests have got together and shared their experiences – and physically shared young children – using the internet. There should be no protection from earthly justice for such individuals. *'It would be better for him to have a large millstone hung around his neck and to be drowned in the depths of the sea.'* And those were the words of Jesus himself, as you know, Amedeo. I could tell you fantastic tales of secret signs and symbols used by these people to denote their sexual preferences on line. It is horrific, Amedeo!' said Gabriele close to tears as he spoke.

'I have talked for hours with our pope, Clement, about these matters. He is truly a good and holy man, Amedeo, like Pope John-Paul before him. He has to attempt to resolve the impossible dilemma between seeing things from God's point of view, reconciling his desire to save a sinner's soul whilst placating the moral outrage felt by the world at large. It's a difficult path to tread.'

Amedeo was thoughtful for several minutes. He sat at the table shaking his head gently from side to side.

'Truly, Gabriele, you are an uncommon monk. Here we two are talking in a place that is akin to paradise on earth, yet as far as the Church is concerned, it is Good Friday.'

Gabriele laughed and said with that twinkle in his eyes:

'Why so it is, Amedeo - how remiss of me to forget!'

Judge Grassi was still not entirely sure if Gabriele was pulling his leg. The young monk saw the puzzlement on Amedeo's face and added:

'I believe that what is happening here is far closer to the Good Lord's plans for us now than the annual ceremonial observance of an event that I carry in my heart every day of my life.'

Amedeo nodded in agreement but added in playful tones:

'But you cannot call yourself a conventional priest by any stretch of the imagination. Why, next you will shock me to the core by telling me that you do not believe in the Virgin Birth or something like that.'

Gabriele gave his soft laugh, laden with acute awareness of the subtleties and complexities of his true thoughts.

'It's funny that you should say that, Amedeo!'

Amedeo looked at the Messenger from Heaven with eyes wide open in alarm and disbelief. What shocking heretical conviction was Gabriele about to reveal next?

'You don't mean to tell me ...?' began Amedeo.

'If God decided to make Mary pregnant with Jesus without the help of Joseph, so be it. I am willing to believe it. But if it were ever proven that Jesus's birth was like yours or mine, I would say that the creation of another human life inside a woman's womb, from nothing – just like the creation of the Universe – is already miracle enough for me. And it would not diminish my belief in Jesus by one iota. The trouble is that the Church, since medieval times, has hammered home the theological point that God made the ultimate sacrifice in sending his only son to be a human being on Earth. Yet somewhere else, it describes *us* as being sons of God, made in his image. I do not believe that Jesus humbled himself by becoming a human being. I believe rather that by being a mortal man, Jesus showed us how people like you and me could be elevated to a level of divine awareness. We can aspire to becoming sons or daughters of God in our own right. I think that the Church has placed a wrong emphasis on human life, treating us all as fallen creatures rather than helping us to see ourselves as spiritually more like angels trapped momentarily in the flesh and blood of human form.'

At some point during this conversation, Gabriele had led Amedeo into the garden when he heard the sounds of the rest of the household stirring. They had returned to the house and Amedeo was standing thoughtfully near the door. He was nodding sagely to himself.

'Do you know, Gabriele, it seems to me that I have always believed the truth of what you have just said. But I have never heard it expressed so poignantly – never dared to put the thought into words. But if you ever repeated from the pulpit what you have just told me, you would be defrocked – and probably excommunicated.'

Amedeo was quietly shocked by the monk's next words. 'I have already told Pope Clement what I have just told you. He replied that he has entertained similar thoughts to mine, but begged me not to preach in public what I believe in my heart. '*The world is not quite ready for such revelations as these, Gabriele,*' were his words to me. He said that we could not risk destroying the faith of millions of simple Christians around the world, who cling to traditional beliefs like drowning children in troubled waters. It would be an act of mass spiritual assassination.'

Judge Grassi wanted to discuss a host of other theological points with the Angel Gabriel, but the rest of the family were emerging from the kitchen after breakfast. Chiara led Amedeo upstairs to see his completed portrait. He expressed delight at what he saw and exclaimed with pleasure when he saw that she had managed to paint her signature at the bottom of the painting in black letters.

'We shall take it to that little art shop when we go shopping today to get it framed,' said Amedeo. And so another day began. Amedeo had forgotten completely about Gabriele's assertion that he would receive a phone call from the outside world. Chiara was enjoying giving him his first art lesson in the kitchen whilst Marta was preparing lunch. The sudden sound of his mobile phone ringing had startled him.

It was Antonella. She spoke in an urgent whisper attempting to keep the shock out of her voice. 'Ame, you must come home. Teresa's shop has been set alight. She has received threats from… certain quarters, for refusing to pay her *pizzo* to the mob.'

* * *

Alessandro Greco had driven down with Aurelio to pick up the judge, since the *masseria* was too tucked away to give clear instructions to someone who had not been there already.

There had been emotional good-byes. Chiara had clung to Amedeo because she was not ready for this separation. Gabriele had reassured his sister that they would soon see each other again. 'We shall see each other this Sunday, Amedeo, Easter Sunday. We shall all come to our church in Lecce. I have spoken to the priest there to tell him that I have completed my mission here. Don't worry about Chiara, Amedeo. I'll explain to her why you must leave us for now."

Amedeo embraced them all in turn with a special hug for his new-found daughter. She had whispered something in his ear and kissed him on the cheek. *'Ti voglio bene papà.'* Then it was the Angel Gabriel's turn to embrace Amedeo.

'Don't be too long before you return, Amedeo. You may not have realised this, but Chiara is not the only one who is happy to have found an earthly father.' And with that startling revelation ringing in his ears, he was driven back to Lecce at speed.

16: Back Down on Planet Earth

More than a week later, well after the Easter break was over, Amedeo, Gabriele and Chiara were comfortably seated in an Intercity train speeding across Italy on their way to Rome. Amedeo had not needed much persuasion to accompany them after Gabriele had told him that Chiara had expressly wished her *papà* to be there on her journey into the unknown. She sat next to the window looking at the unfamiliar scenery rushing past. She had never seen mountains before except in her imagination. The prospect of seeing Rome excited her and terrified her a little in the same breath. Occasionally, she would look at her brother and her adoptive father and give a nervous little smile. But the anxiety on her face was belied by the hint of excitement in her eyes. She was, Amedeo realised with deep sympathy, like a child on her first outing to an unfamiliar place.

No, Amedeo had left Lecce behind him very willingly in order to be present on this important mission of mercy. He had been extremely busy in the intervening week, upsetting many preconceived notions of what people expected of a retired judge and setting in motion events with consequences that would permanently inflict change on two individuals who had felt confident that their perverted ways of life and past crimes were for ever immune from public scrutiny. Amedeo would no longer be an anonymous figure in a relatively small city right down in Italy's heel. He was all too aware that his rash bravery could make him the target for serious reprisals. His life would never be dull again – assuming that he remained alive to enjoy the sensation. Gabriele admired Amedeo's courage but expressed great concern for his safety and security. 'It's the price that I may have to pay,' said the judge resignedly.

* * *

Even from the outset, the return of the reborn and revitalised Amedeo Grassi to his familiar surroundings in Lecce had not been quite what he had expected.

What had struck him as soon as he had arrived home was that Antonella's anxiety about the recent threat to their daughter's life did not seem to be shared by Teresa herself.

'But where *is* Teresa?' Amedeo had asked as soon as he had arrived and warmly embraced his wife, whose returned hug, he had had the impression, lacked outright spontaneity.

'Where do you *suppose* she is?' Antonella had retorted almost crossly. 'She's busy ignoring any threat to herself and her family, tidying up the mess in her shop so she can get it up and running again before next Tuesday. She's like a dog with a bone. She has become even more determined to defy the mob than she was before.'

'She takes after her mother, then,' replied Amedeo chiding her gently. 'I don't believe that can be considered a fault, can it *mia cara?*'

'You've changed, Amedeo Grassi!' stated Antonella as if this observation had been intended as an accusation. 'And I don't just mean that track-suit,' she added with a note of asperity in her voice.

'I think it was high time, *amore*. And *I* am not referring merely to the way I am dressed.'

'That priest has cast a spell on you, Ame.'

'Ordained priests do not cast spells, Nella. Rather they invoke the Holy Spirit, I assume,' replied Amedeo smilingly, in an attempt to defuse the hostility in his wife's voice. She had started visibly when he had used the affectionate abbreviation of her name perhaps for the first time this century. Amedeo correctly deduced that his wife was venting the pent up anxieties that had accumulated over the week. He suspected, too, that she might slightly resent the fact that he seemed to have grown attached to another group of people who did not belong to *their* clan.

This impression was confirmed on Easter Sunday when, after mass at the church of *San Matteo*, Gabriele and an apologetic Marta had invited the Grassi family down to the *masseria* to celebrate *Pasquetta* – Easter Monday. Amedeo and Teresa had accepted the invitation with alacrity, especially when they were told that Elena-Rosaria and family would be there too.

'It's by way of asking your forgiveness, Antonella,' Marta had pleaded simply. But, although, the exchanges were polite, it was obvious that Antonella and her son, Aurelio were not willing to change their plans. So the family were divided. Amedeo decided that he would follow the wisdom of the local philosophy which said simply: *Natale con i tuoi, Pasqua con chi vuoi.* (Christmas time with dads and mums, at Easter time you take what comes). Marta's distress was very obvious despite Antonella's assurances that it was not a personal issue. Amedeo had been poignantly reminded that he was taking a step into a different kind of future. But, he reassured Antonella that the whole family would be back together again in Lecce that same evening. So an uneasy truce had been agreed upon.

It nevertheless detracted from the sheer joy of Gabriele's 'last' sermon. His unexpected appearance had been greeted with applause. He had launched into his Easter 'Resurrection' sermon with enthusiasm by asking the congregation: *Hands up all of you who would like to go to heaven.* Naturally, nearly everybody's hand shot up enthusiastically. Gabriele continued: *Now hands up all of you who would like to go to heaven NOW.'* There followed the usual smothered giggles from the children, who kept their hands firmly in their laps. One old man in a wheel chair, who must have been about ninety-five, broke ranks and put his hand up to everyone's amusement. *You will be welcome there, I am quite certain, signore,* Gabriele had said kindly. The monk had then delivered an almost metaphysical sermon about a timeless, parallel dimension that our veiled sight cannot comprehend. *God has created one universe within another which we will only be able to perceive as it truly is when we have passed away. Only then will our spirits be free to roam uncluttered by notions of time and space.* By the time he had finished, he had taken the fear out of the notion of death - if not the pain of dying. He had recreated a sense of the mystery inherent in Man's presence on Earth.

When Amedeo, Teresa, Cinzia and Emma had returned to Lecce on Easter Monday evening, it had been all too obvious which party had enjoyed itself more. Little Emma, in particular, had rubbed salt in the wound by relating how she had made new friends and eaten the best *antipasti* that she had ever had. 'And Chiara taught us how to dance the *pizzica*, grandma!' she had concluded exuberantly.

Late that night, Amedeo had made peace with Antonella in bed. They had lain awake until past midnight while Amedeo told her in great detail what had happened during his week's absence. The affection that he showed her and his account of the pitiful details of Chiara's years of suffering had finally mollified Antonella and they had fallen asleep in each other's arms. The subject of finding a replacement for Marta had been discussed and shelved. Antonella confessed that, despite understanding Marta's intentions and liking her as a person, she felt that the privacy of her home had been violated. 'Maybe you will have to put up with my cooking for the rest of your life,' she had said, probing her husband's loyalty to its limits.

'I shall be happy to share the intimacy of our home with you alone, *amore*,' he replied warmly – thereby avoiding passing judgement on her culinary skills; a nuance that did not escape Antonella's notice as she bathed in the pleasure she was feeling at the compliment paid.

During the week following Easter Monday, Amedeo had provoked a mild reaction of disbelief when he had informed Antonella what he intended to do with the €450 000 that had sat untouched in his second bank account for ten years. He had caused quiet consternation, but not a great deal of surprise, when he had explained its provenance. Antonella tended to be pragmatic about the more corrupt side of Italian life. 'I always knew that something like that must have occurred,' she said. 'I would have spent it already but I see that you are determined to become a do-gooder in your declining years. I suppose I should approve, *Ame*,' she said with secret admiration. And thus the matter was concluded between them.

Antonella's reaction to the news that he was going to relinquish all that wealth was mild compared to that of the bank manageress,

Annamaria Santucci, who nearly had an apoplectic fit at the news that her client was asking to transfer such a sum out of her branch. 'It will be put to better humanitarian use where it is going than sitting in my account for years,' explained the judge quietly. 'And, *cara signora,* it is quite simply money that was paid to me as a *tangente* – a massive bribe - to cover up a case of sexual assault that, albeit unwillingly, I allowed to happen. Now, do you really want *that* on your professional conscience?' And so the sum of money was duly transferred into Marta's account. It had been Marta's turn to be contacted by an astounded and highly suspicious provincial bank manager, who could hardly belief his good fortune. Suddenly, this good-looking but relatively unimportant woman would have to be treated like a Roman lady of high birth. Marta had shaken her head in sorrow and said to the little balding man: 'Ah, the tenacious power of money, *signore!* I am still exactly the same person as I was before.' His reply acknowledged the sentiment expressed but Marta could see the glint of unholy glee in his eyes as he considered the beneficial effect on his status in the eyes of his masters. And so Marta took sadistic pleasure in telling him that the money would soon be allocated to various projects which, she was sure, he would greatly approve of. She took pleasure in watching the look of glee evaporating into thin air.

Amedeo had presented himself at the offices of *Il Quotidiano* and had been warmly welcomed by the editor, Claudio Sabatini. How differently Amedeo felt on this occasion to the cantankerous, confused Judge Grassi who had sat in this self-same chair but a few days previously.

'Unfortunately, there are aspects of my little adventure that will have to be kept out of the public domain,' Amedeo had begun. 'There is a young woman involved – no, don't misunderstand – who is the victim of the worst case of sexual abuse that I have ever come across in my life. She is still very fragile and public exposure would most certainly destroy her for ever. You may, however, print that Judge Grassi confesses to having accepted a considerable sum of money on one occasion only and that this sum has been duly reallocated to an entirely deserving cause. Do I have your word of honour, *Signor Sabatini*...Claudio... that you will not attempt to print anything about my disappearance other than saying that I accepted an unexpected invitation from a friend?'

The editor nodded and said, like a chastened schoolboy: 'You have my word, *signor giudice.*'

'I will give you the full story if and when I consider it safe or in the public interest to do so,' added the judge. 'And now, let us talk about what you *can* publish.'

Amedeo told him in some detail that his daughter and other *commercianti* in Lecce had banded together with the aim of defying the local mafia by refusing to pay their protection money. 'My daughter's shop has suffered minor fire damage and she has received anonymous text messages – in very badly spelt Italian – explaining what will happen to her if she continues to defy the mob. I, personally, am intending to mount a public campaign to support her and the other shopkeepers. May I count on your help?'

Claudio Sabatini thought about it for a minute and then he said simply: 'Yes, *Signor Grassi.* You may. It is high time that this threat

253

to our civilised way of life was faced up to.' The editor was fully aware that he was putting himself in the firing line by agreeing to the judge's appeal for help. But, in the end, what was a free press for if not to stand up for the truth?

'Do not be too concerned for your own safety, Claudio,' added the judge. 'I intend to take direct action by confronting the individual who is ultimately responsible for this despicable form of repression and intimidation. Any recriminations will be aimed at me personally.'

'You are a very courageous man, *signor giudice*. I admire you for what you are undertaking.'

Before leaving, Amedeo had handed a printed sheet of paper to the editor saying: 'And this is my next article about our local wines.' In the article, he had apologised for his previous harsh criticism of the *viticoltore* in Matino, totally revising his earlier comments about the quality of their wines. *'And look out for a brand new wine due to appear next year from a producer near Soleto called La Masseria Marelica,'* the article concluded.

His week had also included a vital visit to the Greco private investigation bureau, where he had outlined his plan of action to an open-mouthed duo of private investigators.

'Amedeo, if I may call you that,' said Alessandro. 'Are you sure you have thought this through? You are treading a most perilous path.'

'You two are going to help me,' said Amedeo smiling benignly. 'Elena's skills and contacts are going to be invaluable in the next few weeks. Naturally, we shall have to talk about further remuneration...' Alessandro waved a dismissive hand.

'We'll be pleased to help you, Amedeo, won't we Elena?'

'Absolutely Alessandro,' replied Elena, thinking hard about how Rosaria, mother of two children, would fare in a situation where the local mafia was to be evoked – or rather provoked.

'I could enlist the aid of my friend in the *carabinieri*, *Colonnello* Marco Scarpa,' said Elena, hoping that such a high-ranking officer would minimise her personal involvement in the judge's newly conceived anti-criminal crusade. Inside, she was hoping that the epithet 'friend' was justified.

'How exactly do you intend to involve us, Amedeo?' asked Alessandro Greco. 'May we call you, Amedeo, *giudice?*' As he had not had a reply the first time, he thought that they should clear up the matter.

The new Judge Grassi looked at him and said without a smile: '*Amedeo Giudice* sounds a bit of a mouthful to me. Why not just call me Amedeo?'

Alessandro had not quite caught on to the judge's attempt at humour so Elena aimed a kick at him under the round table and said: 'Thank you Amedeo. We shall consider it an honour.'

Highly amused at his little charade, the judge merely added:

'Unless, of course, we devise another first name for me altogether; I have always deplored my parents' choice from the moment that I was baptised.'

'Oh, we've become used to your name,' said Alessandro. 'Besides, it does have suitably Mozartian overtones. Now, as we were saying... What exactly did you have in mind, Amedeo?'

'If things pan out as I imagine they will, over the next few weeks or months, I believe that we should ensure that the *carabinieri* are in a position to be able to monitor phone calls between a certain individual, with whom I have had dealings in the past, and the outside world.'

Both Alessandro and Elena knew that Amedeo was referring to the local underworld *boss* and, presumably, the arms dealer from Milan.

'But even a *colonnello* will need authorisation from a GIP before he can carry out phone-tapping. It's a very vexed question in this country, isn't it Amedeo?'

'You can leave the GIP to me,' replied Amedeo. 'I know the judge in question; a pernickety little bureaucrat who will want every step of the process to be gone through with a fine toothcomb before he agrees to let me put a tap on even my green grocer's phone. But, don't worry, I'll convince him. In the meantime, Elena, would you be prepared to monitor unofficially any activity from Don Augello Parzanese, the mafia boss here?' Alessandro and Elena had winced visibly at the open declaration of the local boss's name. He was usually referred to reverentially as 'La Volpe', the Fox, because of his extraordinary ability to avoid being trapped by the due processes of the law. 'I would like you to keep tabs on Aprea, the arms dealer too, as far as possible,' he added.

'You have certainly picked two formidable opponents, Amedeo,' said Alessandro.

Elena loved a challenge but had severe, unexpressed doubts about her abilities at the level at which she was being asked to perform. But she dutifully smiled and nodded her willingness to try. After all, she knew the mafia boss's daughter. That contact might prove to be very useful.

Judge Grassi made out another cheque before he left the Greco agency amid genuine protests from the pair of investigators. He waved a deprecating hand and finished the proceedings by explaining that he was leaving for Rome with Gabriele and Chiara in the next few days.

'Chiara is going to some private sanctuary in the hills outside the City to complete her recovery,' explained Amedeo. 'If you believe in the power of prayer, you two, then please start praying the moment I leave you.'

'She's a lovely girl,' was all Elena added.

Amedeo had spent most of that week in the company of his daughter, initially setting her shop to rights again but, once order had been restored, the premises cleaned up and the insurance company contacted – it had taken all of Amedeo's judicial weight to prevent the insurers worming out of their obligations by citing some invisible clause which purported to exonerate them in case of mafia involvement – their whole conversation revolved round setting up their campaign to stamp out the protection racket imposed by the local clan.

Teresa had hugged her father warmly and thanked him a thousand times for his love and support. She did not need to point out the danger that he was exposing himself to. They both knew that already. Amedeo trusted that his own judgment was sound. He was hoping to divert all the attention on to himself by paying a personal visit to *La Volpe*. It was a risky strategy. But he would cross that bridge when he returned from his pilgrimage to Rome.

Amedeo's final visit had been to his art gallery acquaintance, taking with him the portrait of himself that Chiara had painted. The lady took one look at the picture and said simply: 'When can I see the rest?'

During the six-hour journey to Rome, Amedeo kept falling asleep, lulled by the movement of the train. He had had an exhausting week in Lecce. Chiara took delight in nudging him playfully back to wakefulness each time. Amedeo apologised and hoped that he had not been snoring with his mouth open – one of the most undignified sights in the world on public transport, he commented. The unusual little group attracted the covert looks of the other passengers. Gabriele, who had reluctantly donned his priestly garb, retrieved their packed lunch from the rack above their heads and the passengers adjacent to them had been amused to see the priest, a beautiful dark haired girl and a distinguished looking man in his mid-sixties huddle together to listen to a rapidly intoned grace before tucking into their sandwiches. In a country where the incongruous regularly passes for normality it was difficult to work out what the relationship between the three people might be.

Outside Roma Termini, the group, laden down with Chiara's luggage, was met by a new, brightly painted minibus. It had the words *Santuario della Madonna delle Grazie* painted in orange lettering. The bodywork was decorated with the sun shining over trees and little hilltop towns. The Madonna, smiling at them with hands raised in greeting, was uncannily divided into two halves as they opened the rear doors of the minibus and loaded Chiara's luggage into the vehicle. The journey through Rome to the hilltop sanctuary was smooth. Chiara had looked out of the window in wonder at her first glimpse of the bustling city with its antique buildings rising out of the ground like solid ancient oak trees in a forest of saplings. Gabriele promised that he would take his sister sight-seeing as soon as possible.

Chiara hugged her brother and Amedeo in turn when they arrived at the beautiful old converted convent in the hills above and beyond the city of Rome. It was a very different paradise to their *masseria* in Puglia. The mountain air was clean and cool and the sound of birds singing in the garden was a new and enchanting experience for Chiara. She looked as if she was going to cry as they said goodbye. Cry! She had not shown that emotion for years, explained Gabriele on the way back to Rome. Before she could change her mind about embracing this next stage of her new life, Chiara was led away arm in arm by two cheerful nuns in white garb chatting animatedly to Chiara. It was the two men in her life, standing forlornly by the minibus watching her departing figure, who needed each other's moral support. Amedeo would have to wait several months before he would see Chiara again. He could not have imagined at that moment in time the transformation that would be wrought.

17: Walking a Tightrope

'But, Gabriele, have you forgiven your father for what he did?' Amedeo asked Gabriele during one of their daily phone calls. The judge was back in Lecce and was preparing to set in motion his planned assault on Antonio Aprea. He could hear Gabriele letting out a deep sigh.

'No, not really, Amedeo. I know I should have forgiven him but the enormity of what he did to my sister gnaws away at me every day. It is easy enough to say the words 'I forgive you', even possible to make yourself believe that you mean it. But it is quite impossible to eradicate the memories of a decade and more of suffering at the hands of someone like him. I think nowadays though that I am prepared to leave his punishment to God.'

'That is what I hoped you would say, Gabriele. I have been thinking that the only way to bring him to justice would be to involve Chiara. And that could prove fatal for her.'

'Yes, Amedeo, I agree with you absolutely.'

'Therefore, I shall content myself with ensuring that your biological father is kept permanently on tenterhooks by the threat of public exposure. He truly represents the dregs of humanity - Elena and Alessandro have provided me with information from Milan that suggests he indulges in every act of sexual deviance that money can buy. So I shall have no hesitation in rendering his life as uncomfortable as I can.'

Another deep sigh from the Vatican-bound monk, so Amedeo changed the subject, asking about Chiara. Gabriele's voice brightened audibly.

'The nuns have told me that I should leave her in peace for the time being, Amedeo. She needs to settle in first. Too much contact with her past life could slow her recovery, they say. It is hard to bear, Amedeo. But they are right, of course. In any case, they assure me that she looks amazingly serene. She has already begun painting again – inspired by mountains, it seems.'

'That is very encouraging, Gaby,' said Amedeo using the abbreviated form of his name for the first time. Marta always used this familiar form whenever she spoke to her son. 'You sound a bit distracted today. Is there something troubling you?'

'Theological matters, Amedeo. There was a lecture given two days ago at La Sapienza by an American professor. She was giving a lecture based on a piece of papyrus that she had unearthed in Egypt which purports to show words of Jesus referring to 'his wife'. It has thrown the whole of the Vatican into a state of turmoil.'

'I saw that on television, Gaby. It is almost entirely speculation on the lady professor's part. You know how Americans love to dramatize everything. They will have churned out a film about it within a year. Nothing to worry about, I would say.'

'Ah, Amedeo, that is not the problem for me. I dared to suggest to my brothers here that I see nothing wrong in the idea of Jesus having been married. I know that someone will whisper what I have said in the ear of some cardinal or other. And then... They love a bit of unholy gossip and intrigue here.'

Amedeo kept his own counsel. He was firmly convinced that Gabriele's decision to become a priest had been dictated as much by his own adolescent suffering in reaction to his father's evilly perverted sexuality as by a calling from God. He privately believed that Gabriele had misinterpreted the direction which his path through life should lead him. He even entertained the thought that Gabriele might be unconsciously exposing himself to the risk of expulsion from holy orders by expressing thoughts which bordered on the heretical, so that he would not have to make the decision. He channelled the conversation back to less controversial matters, as subtly as he could.

* * *

Monday, 30th April

'I trust that this line is a safe one, *Signor* Aprea – for your sake rather than mine,' began the judge ominously.

Are you threatening me? Nobody threatens me and gets away with it, I should warn you. How did you get this number? Who do you think you are?

'So many questions, Antonio! Which one would you like me to answer first?' replied Amedeo Grassi who was being as provocative as he possibly could be.

I do not have time to waste talking to some crank who thinks he can get away with crossing my path. Now get on with what you have to say or get lost – whichever occurs to you first.

'My name is Amedeo Grassi, Antonio. I was the judge whom you bribed ten years ago to let you off the charge of sexually abusing your own daughter. Now, I am sure you must remember *that* episode in your life with the greatest clarity.'

You would do well to choose your words with care from this point on, signor giudice, or else I will simply expose you for what you are – a corrupt judge.

'You can do my reputation no harm. What I did wrong I have admitted publicly, thus removing any barb from such a puerile threat as you have just uttered.'

I am becoming very bored with this conversation, Judge. I was acquitted of any sexual misdemeanour ten years ago – by you! Remember that Judge Grassi!

'But, Antonio,' continued Judge Grassi sweetly, 'you have not yet been brought to trial for raping your daughter *after* being acquitted. That is a separate offence. A trial for that particular crime would see you behind bars for a decade or more. Now, sir, do I have your full attention?'

Amedeo did indeed have this diabolically arrogant man's total attention for the next five minutes, during which time he explained exactly under what circumstances he, Amedeo Grassi, would refrain from dragging the man through the law courts; Antonio Aprea was to triple the allowance that he paid to maintain his daughter and family – from immediate effect, stressed the judge. He also told the arms dealer that he should buy himself a ticket to anywhere in the world outside the European Union. 'Although I hesitate to be instrumental in inflicting your presence on *any* specific country on this planet,' added the judge cuttingly. 'It is a shame that we have not yet discovered a planet outside our solar system where you could be dispatched to.' Amedeo informed the arms manufacturer that he was not to set foot on Italian soil again under any circumstances.

'This banishment into exile is for life,' added Amedeo. 'You should have plenty of time to ponder on the number of lives you have wrecked. If you ever return to Italy, I shall hound you to extinction for the horrendous crime that you committed against

Chiara. You must leave within sixty days. And consider that a generous offer!' asserted Judge Grassi and hung up. He received a round of applause from Elena and Alessandro sitting in their studio in a side street of Lecce.

* * *

Friday, 4th May

As Judge Grassi had anticipated, the GIP behaved in character - a bureaucrat who instinctively adopted a position of suspicious caution whenever any request for his authorisation was required. If Amedeo had offered him a cup of coffee, the GIP would have been faced with a moral dilemma quite out of proportion to the nature of the offer. 'What favour would you be expecting in return, *signor giudice*?' 'Well, I was really hoping that I could have one of your chocolate biscuits, *signor giudice.*' 'Ha, I knew there was a catch in it somewhere!'

Amedeo had amused himself inventing such silly conversations in his head while he was waiting, in the company of a fully briefed and uniformed *Colonnello* Marco Scarpa, to persuade the GIP that it was in the interests of public security to be allowed to tap the mafia boss's phones. Elena Camisso had given the colonel a full account of the situation concerning the Aprea family and had told the officer about Judge Grassi's moral crusade.

'What a remarkable woman!' Amedeo had said to Marco Scarpa, who had proceeded to give the judge an account of Rosaria Miccoli's determined campaign to track down the Calabrian *mafioso* who had murdered her cousin, Diletta, all those years ago.

'Intelligent and very determined – apart from any physical attributes that she may have,' added the *colonnello*. As they both knew her real name, it had been pointless to go on using her pseudonym during a private conversation.

'I am immensely grateful to you *Colonnello* for your support,' said Judge Grassi.

'On the contrary, *signor giudice*, I am deeply moved by your courage in taking on such a challenge – and doing our job for us, it seems.'

As expected, the GIP had dutifully put up as many objections to the phone tap as possible. 'But exactly whose life is being threatened in the circumstances that you are describing to me, *signori?*' he had asked in one last ditch effort to sabotage their efforts. There had been a significant pause whilst the *carabiniere* officer looked at Judge Grassi and Judge Grassi looked straight into the eyes of the GIP.

'Mine, *signor giudice!*' he said simply.

The GIP grudgingly allowed them to set up the *intercettazione* for a period of two weeks. It was the best they could hope for, so Amedeo and the uniformed *Colonnello* thanked the GIP and left. Invasion of privacy, it seemed, was a more serious offence than exacting protection money from innocent citizens.

* * *

Tuesday, 8th May

Judge Grassi's encounter with 'The Fox' had required a great deal more diplomacy and cunning to arrange than his brief telephone conversation with Gabriele and Chiara's father. The meeting had been achieved through the mediation of Elena Camisso who had in turn contacted her old school friend, the daughter of Don Augello Parzanese. The main snag had been that the underworld boss's daughter was reluctant to have dealings with her own father even if she was happy enough to accept his munificence when it was offered. In the end, a meeting had been arranged at Parzanese's country estate. Thanks to Elena and Colonel Marco Scarpa, who was throwing his whole weight behind this affair, Amedeo had been driven to his rendezvous by the young police officers who had previously come to the Grassi household in Lecce in response to his 'abduction'. Amedeo was very grateful for their presence even if he suggested that they remained discreetly parked outside the gates of the Parzanese territory during the 'negotiations', as the judge had termed this meeting.

Amedeo was ushered into the atrium by one of the permanent house staff and made to wait for twenty minutes before the underworld *boss* deigned to appear, still wearing a silk dressing gown to give the impression that Amedeo's visit was not sufficiently important to interfere with his normal routine. The judge had been quite prepared for this ploy and exhibited no signs of impatience or nervousness when the gentleman finally walked into the open central area with his hand outstretched, inviting a handshake. Now the judge would have to initiate the first move in the complex opening gambit of the game that was to be played out in the next half hour or so. He had anticipated correctly that the mafia boss's first gesture would be precisely the challenge of the handshake, so his decision to decline to shake the proffered hand was accompanied by a rueful smile looking straight in to the man's eyes.

'I shall be happy to shake your hand, Don Augello, at the end of our meeting, on the assumption that we shall have reached an agreement by then.'

Don Augello's mouth managed what most people would consider to be a friendly but knowing smile, followed up by the words:

'I am convinced, *signor giudice,* that we are both well able to appreciate the other person's standpoint without crossing swords, drawing blood or creating bad feeling between us.'

The smile had seemed so genuine, the words so sincerely meant. But Amedeo had continued to study his opponent's cold, unnerving eyes, still a steely grey despite the signs of ageing skin around them. There was not a jot of kindness there. Amedeo could see only a reflection of the power of a profound malevolence that was busy and invisibly at work inside Don Augello's mind. There came back vividly to Amedeo's mind the conversation that he had had with Gabriele in the garden of the *masseria;* the presence of evil in a man is much better explained by the workings of Satan than by all the phrases invented by all the psychoanalysts put together. Amedeo felt he was witnessing the evident truth of what the young monk had said. Amedeo shuddered inwardly with a sense of dread, which required a supreme effort to master.

'May I offer you some coffee, *signor giudice,* before we begin?' the mafia boss was saying.

Amedeo knew the rules instinctively; *never* accept a gesture of hospitality if you knew that you were about to oppose your adversary; your moral stance is instantly compromised.

'That is most kind, Don Augello,' the judge managed to say silkily, 'but I have already drunk two coffees this morning. I find that too much coffee tends to make my heart beat too fast.'

Amedeo noticed, with interest, that Don Augello tended to move his head slightly to one side when he was listening to Amedeo's words. He realised with something approaching joy, that the man had a human weakness; he was deaf in one ear.

'I believe,' continued Don Augello, 'that we have a common interest that you wished to discuss.'

The preliminary skirmish was over. Amedeo forbore to tell this man that they had about as much in common as Attila the Hun with Mother Teresa.

'We certainly have one thing in common, Don Augello; we both have a daughter whom we care for deeply.'

The mafia boss nodded curtly. The smiling mouth had changed shape and had assumed the appearance of a scar just below his nose. 'The connection?' asked the scar-like slit gracelessly.

'None at all, Don Augello; I was merely attempting to find some common ground,' replied the judge with deep irony. He could see that the first parry of the foil had hit its mark.

'My daughter,' continued Amedeo informatively, 'runs a moderately successful boutique near the *Piazza Mazzini.* A short while ago her shop was set alight by a couple of low-level hoodlums – whose faces are clearly identifiable from the CCTV footage. Fortunately, there was little damage done to the shop or its stock on this occasion. She also received a text message on her mobile phone, threatening physical violence if she continued to oppose the notion that she owed money to a third party. The message was evidently composed by someone who was nigh on illiterate, but its meaning was clear enough.'

Don Augello felt that he was on home territory now.

'I fail to see how I am involved in your daughter's misfortunes, *signor giudice,* as much as I deplore any discomfort she might have suffered.'

'You are a man of considerable influence, Don Augello – in certain well-defined fields of activity, that is,' continued the judge whose heart rate had increased by a few beats a minute as he came as close as he dared to openly calling this man a criminal. The accusation was tempered by the hint of flattery that he knew would appeal to the man's enormous ego.

'I fear you may be exaggerating my influence somewhat, *signor giudice.'*

The man is so far gone down this path, thought Amedeo, that he is in a state of self-denial. Or, equally as likely, he is now so removed from the daily grime of drugs, prostitution, protection rackets, refuse collection and the merciless exploitation of immigrant workers in the tomato plantations in Salento that he can afford the luxury of believing that his hands are clean.

At Don Augello's words, the judge permitted himself a smile as if to convey the message that they could pass on to the next stage.

'We are in times of deep recession, Don Augello. One must not dwell upon a past that may never be recaptured, economically speaking. Small shops are seeing their profit margins being reduced to a few percentage points. People are up in arms at having to submit to their living standards being eroded even further by this extra – and totally non-productive – expenditure. They are in revolt, Don Augello. I am sure you will agree that it is in *nobody's* interest to see them going out of business.' He paused to give the criminal mind a moment to digest this point of view.

'Assuming for a minute, *signor giudice,* that I were in the position to be able to bring my influence to bear on this matter, what solution might you be proposing?' said the mafia boss in the softest, smoothest of voices.

In for a penny, thought the judge.

'A truce, Don Augello, a truce lasting seven years,' said Judge Grassi quietly; 'time for our faltering economy to recover.' Again he noticed the slight twist of the head as Don Augello strove to hear the words. But it was obvious that he had caught the essence of the judge's proposal; the look of surprise and outrage on the face of this man was unmistakable – however hard he tried to control his features.

'And if I decline to put your very audacious request to the parties concerned?' asked Don Augello with an edge of real menace in his voice.

Amedeo was spared the necessity of replying immediately by an incredible jangling noise coming from the mafia boss's dressing gown. What had at first startled Amedeo, finally reassured him that his theory had been demonstrably proven; Don Augello was deaf. Had the mafia boss left his mobile phone at the far end of his football-pitch-sized swimming pool, it would still have sounded like a fire alarm going off. The gentleman excused himself as he rescued the device from his dressing-gown pocket and headed for one of the rooms leading off the atrium.

Don Augello's Achilles Heel meant that the owner of the phone had not immediately realised that the device was in loud-speaker mode. Thus Amedeo heard the beginning of the conversation initiated by the caller.

'Ah, Don Augello, Buongiorno! Please make sure that you are alone for this conversation. I'm sure you know who I am...

Amedeo knew instantly that he should have recognised that distinctive voice but he could not place it because it seemed inappropriate in the context of this house. Unfortunately, Don Augello had realised that the loud-speaker was switched on and had, in that second of time, put the device back to silent mode. However, like most deaf people using a telephone, he was unaware that his voice was raised. Not that he had the chance to speak all that much. But Amedeo heard the occasional interjected word as if Don Augello was not sure that he had caught its meaning.

'Falcone? Non capisco... Ah sì! Bisogna tarpargli le ali! Va bene, ho capito, signore. Sì, sì, con piacere, signore.'

The rest of the conversation took place behind a closed door so, frustratingly, Amedeo was none the wiser. Why had they been talking about clipping the wings of a bird of prey? It frustrated him that he could not put a name to the voice on the other end of the phone. He shrugged. What did it matter? If all had gone according to plan, some young *carabiniere* should be monitoring the conversation a few kilometres away.

Don Augello emerged from behind the solid oak door a few minutes later. He looked pleased with himself in a gloating, sadistic kind of way.

'I have been thinking about your very bold suggestion, *signor giudice*. I understand your concerns and feel I can agree to your terms – for a three year period only, however.'

Amedeo had already allowed room for negotiation, knowing full well that the mafia boss could not afford to lose face by agreeing too readily to any proposal. Amedeo's argument had been that, even after a one year period of not paying protection money, it would be much harder for the mob to reassert its power. Amedeo was struck by two things; firstly, that Don Augello had agreed too readily to the terms which he had proposed and, secondly, that the mafia boss had forgotten to maintain the pretence that exacting protection money was not in any way connected to him. Amedeo knew that something was amiss. But his immediate concern was to get out of the house. So he managed a smile of gratitude and held out his hand to Don Augello. Shaking Satan by the hand was the most disagreeable and disconcerting part of the whole proceedings. It felt as if the hatred and malevolent force were being transferred to him up his arm and into his soul.

'I would offer to have my chauffeur drive you back to Lecce, *signor giudice*. But I see that you already have transport,' the man remarked with a leer, all pretence of friendliness having evaporated.

'Thank you for your time and cooperation, Don Augello,' concluded Amedeo. He was accompanied to the main gate by a young man wearing large sunglasses and an expensive leather jacket, restraining a muzzled Doberman on the end of a short leash.

By the time Amedeo had collapsed with relief into the back seat of the police car, his whole body was shaking with suppressed nervous reaction. The police officers were looking at him with unabashed admiration. He needed a *grappa* and the comfort of a hug from his wife.

18: In Satan's Embrace

Saturday, 12th May

The *Piazza Sant'Oronzo,* with its centuries' old Roman amphitheatre, was thronging in a modest way with banner-carrying shopkeepers out to celebrate their miraculous release from having to pay their *pizzo*. Their hero was, to their great surprise, a 'reformed' judge whose daughter had been leading their reluctant campaign against the local mafia. The banners bore a variety of epithets in praise of their local saviour: *'Thanks you, GGG!'* which was supposed to convey the meaning: '*Grande Giudice Grassi!*' whose appreciative slogan the banner bearer was shouting out enthusiastically. The words 'thanks you' had been written – almost correctly - in the world's universal language in order to double its impact. Other variations on the same theme were reflected on all the improvised banners.

Amedeo himself surveyed the scene on the television from the relative security of their home – almost permanently wearing his track suit. Antonella had strictly forbidden her husband to set foot outside the confines of their house and garden, suddenly fearful for his safety and alarmed by the consequences of his newfound defiance of the darker side of Italy.

She had good reason. On the day after his encounter with *La Volpe*, an anxious Alessandro Greco and Elena Camisso had telephoned the judge, imploring him to take a taxi – a driver who you can trust, they insisted – and come immediately to their *studio*. Antonella knew of no other 'taxi' driver that she trusted more than herself, so she had driven her husband to the Greco offices in person.

'You have really set the cat among the pigeons, Amedeo! We have just had a visit from a very concerned *Colonnello*. One of his smartest officers, who happened to be monitoring calls to a certain gentleman whom you visited yesterday, drew his attention to a particularly menacing communication.' Alessandro handed the judge a transcript of the telephone conversation which he recognised immediately as the one that he had partially overheard the previous day. It read:

Ah, Don Augello, buongiorno. Please make sure that you are alone for this conversation. I'm sure you know who I am... but please don't repeat my name out loud over the phone.

No sir, of course not. I cannot quite believe that you are who I think you are, however...

I AM that person, Don Augello. Rest assured.

What can I...?

Listen carefully. We have a grave problem with a... (pause) ... a falcon who lives near you. We would like your... professional help. He urgently needs his wings to be clipped - permanently!

Falcon? I don't understand... Ah yes! He needs his wings to be clipped. Of course! I understand you, sir. It will be a pleasure, sir. You may leave it to me.

But I want no trouble, no lurid publicity. It must seem unequivocally like an accident. Nothing dramatic, you understand. So take your time and do the job properly.

Certainly, Signor Bal...

No names, I told you! Now you will, of course, receive adequate compensation; two golden eggs, immediately, and three more when the job is completed. That is all, Don Augello. The transcript ended there, abruptly cut off.

Amedeo had turned a shade paler. Antonella was still looking perplexed.

'Of course, Amedeo, you know whose voice that was, don't you?'

'I overheard the beginning of that call yesterday while I was there. I thought the voice was familiar but...'

'The *carabiniere* who was monitoring the call recognised it immediately, Amedeo.'

'It was our beloved ex-prime minister,' explained Elena.

Judge Grassi continued the process of turning paler still whilst his wife was beginning to show the same symptoms.

'But what is all that about falcons, for heaven's sake?' asked Antonella, her anxiety making her sound impatient again.

'The young officer played the recording to our *Colonnello*, Amedeo,' explained Elena. 'He made the connection immediately. *Il Falcone* is an oblique reference to Judge Falcone – that other judge from Sicily who notoriously defied the mafia and was blown up for his pains. The person who needs his wings clipped is *you*, I fear, Amedeo.'

In a flash, Amedeo understood. He recalled the telephone conversation he had received ten years ago at the time of the Aprea trial. It was obvious, of course. Aprea had contacted his old political pal, Balducci, as soon as Judge Grassi had delivered his 'verdict' of permanent exile. Quite natural that he should turn to his powerful friends to seek redress – or vendetta, in this case. Quite natural, too, that the former prime minister should use his vast fortune to 'do a favour' for his old comrade-in-arms, Antonio Aprea.

'What a hornet's nest you have managed to stir up, Ame!' said Antonella, fearfully putting a hand on his arm. She noticed that he was trembling slightly.

'I suppose 'golden eggs' are code words for euros,' added Antonella with forced levity.

'I believe that one golden egg means €100 000, *signora*,' explained Alessandro quietly.

'Oh really, not even one million!' Antonella added sarcastically. 'Well, it is nice to know what the price on your head is, Ame – assuming that it remains on your shoulders long enough to appreciate the feeling,' Antonella said to her husband with trenchant irony. There was a heavy silence after her statement while everybody digested the implications of the words. It was Elena who broke the tension by saying:

'By the way, Amedeo, you may be interested to know that Antonio Aprea did not wait for your deadline. He has taken himself off to Ecuador, laden with several heavy suitcases. I have that piece of information from the *Colonnello.*'

'Poor Ecuador!' Amedeo remarked pensively.

* * *

Amedeo quickly became restless. He decided that, whilst housebound, he would complete the organisation of his 'pre-conversion' project of holding a food and wine festival in Lecce to promote the produce of the region of Salento. The idea had met with universal approval and a date had been fixed for the 23rd and 24th of June. It was to be held in the magnificent courtyard of the *Ex Convento dei Teatini* – a former monastery – just off the *Via Vittorio Emanuele*, a stone's throw away from the *Piazza del*

278

Duomo. He would have liked to finish his book on local Salento wines by then, but it would be impossible to meet the deadline. The event filled most of his time, contacting all the participants, organising stalls and getting posters and brochures printed. At the beginning of the month of June, Antonella had been frantically busy organising the 'Open Courtyards' weekend. She had decided that it would have been suspicious if their own garden had been closed to the public for no apparent reason. Thus, Amedeo was reluctantly confined to barracks for forty-eight hours as crowds of local tourists invaded their privacy.

The routine of his days was interspersed by telephone calls to Marta and – since he had just discovered the marvels of Skype – long conversations with Gabriele, who was deeply concerned by the direction that Amedeo's chosen path was taking him. One day in early June, Gabriele was full of joyous news about Chiara.

'She is well on the road to recovery, Amedeo. It is wonderful to behold. Yes, I have been to see her at last. She has done a portrait of almost everybody in the clinic, and she has done one really serious painting too. Her style is quite distinctive. It's almost the reverse of that painting which she called *Nelle grinfie di Satana*, you remember the one, I'm sure. She is really excited about the idea of an exhibition in Lecce – she is so grateful to you for all you've done. She asked about you too. I didn't dare even hint to her that your life is in danger. What else? She is teaching the inmates how to dance as well. The nuns tell me that her greatest therapy is helping the other patients.'

'I'm so happy to hear this, Gabriele. Please tell her I think about her and pray for her every day.'

'I will, Amedeo. And if all that was not enough,' continued Gabriele avidly, 'I believe that she has fallen in love – with a young doctor at the clinic. In fact, if I am not mistaken, so has the doctor.'

Amedeo, to his alarm, felt a twinge of jealousy at this piece of news. Shamefully, he had not felt at all jealous when his own daughter had announced her engagement to Leonardo. It was merely a sign of how deeply affected he had been by Chiara's troubles, he attempted to convince himself.

Gabriele and Amedeo spoke at length most days – like father and son.

'I'm fed up with being constrained to stay at home all the time, Gabriele. I actually went for a walk yesterday while Antonella was out. It did feel a bit unnerving at first, I have to admit. I found myself looking behind me to see if any fast, black cars were about to run me down. I had decided to walk down the centre of Lecce's little side streets – just in case *they* were thinking of throwing chunks of masonry down from the roof tops. But walking in the middle of the road made me feel even more vulnerable. I am just going to have to trust in the powers above, I think, and hope that I shall have as many lives as the proverbial cat.'

'I shall be praying for your safety every day of my life,' said Gabriele, the monk. 'Remember that you can always go into hiding in our *masseria*. That is probably going to be the safest place in the world for you to hide in one day.'

'Prescience again?' wondered the judge.

Antonella, when told by her husband that evening that he had ventured out on his own, hurled a plate at his head, only narrowly missing it. She told him in no uncertain terms that, if he wished to walk through the streets of Lecce, then she would come with him every time.

'I don't want to be a widow, Amedeo. I would rather be dispatched into the next world at the same time as you if that is how things have to be.'

That night they made love. Afterwards, lying with Antonella in his arms, he asked her quietly the question which had been nagging him for weeks:

'Have you ever had a lover, Nella? You never answered my question last time.'

'Because it did not deserve an answer, Amedeo Grassi. I have only ever had one lover, *mio caro...*'

Amedeo felt a lump forming in his throat at what he thought he was about to hear. '*You!* Now go to sleep!'

Saturday, 24th June: Amedeo's Food and Wine Festival, Day 2.

If the truth were told, admitted Judge Grassi to himself, he had become just a little blasé about his own safety as the uneventful days had unfolded with no apparent threat to his life. A dangerous assumption on his part, Antonella had assured him. But here he was, on the second day of his festival, walking openly round the ancient courtyard of the former monastery, where a host of stalls had sprung up bearing a veritable cornucopia of products from all over Puglia: wine producers, big and small, were encouraging the numerous passers-by to sample their wines from generous, wide-rimmed glasses; olive oil producers were doing the same, offering pieces of bread to dip into the green or golden liquids displayed in little dishes constantly washed clean and replenished for the next samplers; local restaurants had been invited to display a huge variety of *antipasti* to whet the appetites of even those who had already eaten beforehand. By eight o'clock in the evening, a local group of musicians called *Schiattacore,* who had been invited by Amedeo at his daughter's suggestion, to add local colour to the event, were setting up in the centre of the paved courtyard. The group of musicians were accompanied by their own dancers who expertly demonstrated the *pizzica* and other traditional dances. At one point, they began to play the same song that Chiara had made them dance to in the moonlight. *'Luna d'argentu quante cose viti, quandu la notte sula sula stai...'* Amedeo, to his embarrassment, had to hide behind a pillar whilst he regained control of his emotions before rejoining the throng of people milling around.

But then a black cloud cast a sudden shadow over the lively proceedings which, for Amedeo, turned a celebration of the best aspects of life in Puglia into something altogether more sinister. He saw Don Augello Parzanese, *La Volpe,* standing apart from the crowd, flanked by two dark-suited figures whose faces were half hidden by large sunglasses with reflector lenses. Amedeo, despite his sudden fear at this menacing apparition, decided to face the challenge head on. He walked over to where the mafia boss was standing and accosted him directly with the words:

'This does not seem an appropriate place for you to be, Don Augello. I suggest that you consider leaving.' Something about the two men standing stock still by the man's side was quite unnerving. He knew that they were studying him carefully despite his only being able to see four identical versions of his own tensed up face reflected in the mirror-like coating of the lenses. His instinct told him that these two were not local hoodlums; maybe they had been imported from Bari. That was a bad sign. Amedeo took out his mobile from his coat pocket and flipped open the lid in what he hoped was a meaningful gesture. Apparently, Don Augello took the hint. He became effusive and smiling.

'If my presence here disturbs you *signor giudice*, I will most certainly not inconvenience you any longer. But I was hoping that our truce would lead to... a closer association between myself and our community.'

Judge Grassi was outraged at the presumptuousness of the man as he slipped his phone back into his pocket. In the instant that followed, his outrage had turned to revulsion as the mafia boss took one step towards him with arms outstretched and gave him a hug. The force of the gesture took Amedeo's breath away as he instinctively tried to draw away. He was only vaguely aware of the surreptitious movement of Don Augello's companions and then it was all over. The Fox was shaking Amedeo's hand in both of his and saying: 'I respect you for what you have done, *signor giudice*. Not many men would have had the courage to do what you have done.' And he turned round, flanked by his henchmen, and walked towards the door leading on to the street. He had a slight limp which Amedeo had not noticed previously. Once more, he felt reassured that this man was only mortal after all.

Amedeo felt sullied by the contact, shaken by the suddenness of the mafia boss's gesture. He had to shake himself to be free of the residual sensation of the pressure of Don Augello's arms locked around his body.

He was relieved to spot 'Elena' with her partner, Adam, and their two children accompanying Alessandro and his *fidanzata*, whom the judge had never met before. Introductions were made and polite conversation ensued. The group was about to leave,

Elena explained, because they had bribed the children with the promise of a pizza.

'Will you be alright, Amedeo?' asked Alessandro anxiously.

'Yes, fine. Teresa is coming to pick me up as soon as I phone her,' replied the judge. 'Thank you all for your support.'

'Are you really sure that you don't need a lift home, Amedeo?' asked Elena-Rosaria anxiously.

'I'll manage. Even if Teresa lets me down – which is unlikely – I have devised an escape route taking the back streets behind the cathedral,' said the judge with an airy wave of his hands, taking malicious delight in the effect that his words produced.

Elena had looked at Alessandro with a distinctly alarmed expression on her face. The group walked off, laden down by bags of the goods that they had purchased.

Amedeo spent a further half hour or so walking round chatting to the various stall holders, including a grateful couple from Matino. He felt a wave of tiredness pass over him. Time to go, he thought. That was the moment in which he discovered that his mobile phone was missing from his coat pocket. Now the mafia boss's gesture made sense. He kicked himself inwardly for his naïvety. Don Augello's street-wise gangsters had nimble fingers. He felt bereft, isolated. He now knew that the threat to his life was real. At least, they will not be able to take me by surprise, he thought. He headed directly for the main door and out on to the street. Miraculously, a taxi drew up just as he stepped over the threshold. 'Need a lift, *signore*?' asked the taxi driver. There was something furtive about the man's attitude that put the judge on his guard. He shook his head and headed off smartly in the opposite direction to his home. Let me reach the side streets quickly and disappear from sight, he thought. As he walked, he thought how cutting Antonella would be when he got home. 'How many people were left at the food fair when you left, Amedeo Grassi? Don't you think *one* of them would have let you use their mobile phone?' When he got home! What was he saying? It was quite likely that he would never make it home.

The taxi driver, Amedeo had noticed, was on *his* mobile phone as soon as he had begun to walk away.

* * *

Teresa was looking at a text message purportedly sent by her father. It read: *Don't worry about coming to pick me up. Some friends will take me home. Tuo papà.* It was her father's phone number that showed up on the screen, no doubt about that. But the message did not ring true. Her father always referred to himself as Amedeo when speaking to her. Somebody was trying to be clever and had miscalculated. Her father was in trouble. A quick call to an increasingly anxious Antonella confirmed that she had received a similar text message – a clumsy, but sinister attempt to leave Amedeo isolated and bereft of a lift home. Teresa cut her mother's speculation short.

'Stay at home *mamma* – or at the very least, keep a look out for him in the street. Now I'm going to contact Elena.'

* * *

Elena and family, Alessandro and his *fidanazta*, Isabella, had just plunged their knives into their crusty pizzas bubbling with mozzarella cheese when Elena's phone sounded shrilly from where it was lying on the table top as if it had been a part of the necessary accoutrements for eating a meal. It was doing a sort of injured bee dance across the table top in vibration mode. Elena's face told everyone instantly that there was something wrong. They could all hear the anxious high-pitched tones of a woman's voice.

'No, *I'll* phone the police, Elly,' she said. 'You go round to your mother's. Sorry, everybody. It's an emergency.'

Alessandro was already on his feet still chewing a mouthful of pizza. They were out in the street in an instant running towards the place where they had parked the cars.

'*My* car, Elena. I know the streets of Lecce better than you do,' said Alessandro in a voice that brooked no argument from his partner. For once, he was unequivocally in charge of the duo. 'Phone your *carabiniere* friend,' he ordered. 'Let's pray that he is awake.'

As soon as they were in Alessandro's car, he shot off down a side street. He remembered what Amedeo had said in what had seemed half in jest about 'taking a back street route' home. Within minutes, he had reached the bottom end of *Via Cairoli,* where Amedeo's house was, and was heading up the nearly empty street at speed in a direction which, he hoped, would intercept their client. Elena had barely finished talking to Marco Scarpa – thank God for his existence – when her phone rang again.

'Yes?' she snapped, impatient at the interruption. To her utter amazement, it was the Angel Gabriel in Rome.

'Amedeo is in danger,' said the voice of the messenger from God. Elena quickly pressed the key that put the phone on to loud-speaker mode so that Alessandro could share this seemingly paranormal intervention. 'I see Amedeo running away from a big black car with headlights ablaze. He's in a poorly lit side street crossing a little square with an unusual looking church in it.'

'We're out looking for him, Gabriele. I'm leaving the phone on so that you can be with us,' replied Elena without thinking how absurd the words might have sounded to anyone listening.

'I think I know which route he's taken,' shouted Alessandro. He swung his Citroën C3 into an even narrower street half way up *Via Cairoli* with the words: 'Let's hope we're not too late.'

* * *

Amedeo had reached the old church of *Santa Teresa* in *Via Giuseppe Libertini* and had dived left towards *Via Marco Basseo* which was ill lit and deserted compared to the main street, still bustling with Saturday evening strollers. He quickly turned right into Via Morelli, which was a one way street barely wide enough for a single vehicle. His stubborn independence and refusal to enlist the aid of the stall-holders, who would have leapt at the chance of helping him, now seemed like an act of sheer folly. He had turned left again at the little *Piazzetta Fiorentini* and was about to cross *Piazza Tancredi* when he heard the sound of a vehicle behind him. He looked fearfully over his shoulder and saw a large black Audi Q7, headlights full on, a hundred metres or so behind him.

How on Earth had they managed to follow him, he thought immediately. He must be mistaken. He was being paranoid. But there was something menacing about the purposeful, slow progress of the vehicle, as if the driver was feeling his way around the corner, taking aim before firing. Amedeo was filled with dread. Too late for evasion! Impossible to call for help! He plunged his hands in to his overcoat pocket and increased his pace like a man, fleeing from a pursuing tiger, who does not want to break into a run for fear of unleashing the full power of the beast in pursuit. That was when he found the small hard disc in his pocket. He pulled out the alien object and knew at once that he was on the wrong end of a tracking device – even though he had never seen one in his life before. 'That pair of slimy pickpockets from Bari!' he thought hurling the device down on to the cobbled street, irrespective of the gesture being quite redundant.

He had turned into *Via Caracciolo*, the narrow one-way street that led to *his* road. Too late! The Audi was closing in on him. His main feeling was not so much fear as anger at himself. He felt upset that he would never see Chiara again, angry that he had not completed his book. He could now hear the vehicle behind him revving up its engine. Now there was another pair of headlights heading towards him at speed. So that was how they would make sure he wouldn't escape his fate. They would crush him between two speeding...

'Get in, Amedeo, for the love of God!' a woman was shouting at him at the top of her voice. People were coming to their windows to see what was happening and a front door opened. It took him several seconds to realise that salvation was at hand. The Audi had stopped about five metres behind him blinded by the full headlight beam of Alessandro's Citroën. Elena had to run and shake Amedeo as if he was a stupefied rabbit mesmerised by the beam of the headlights. The two hoodlums in the Audi could not risk outright assassination – they had been told on penalty of death that the job was to look like an accident. However, they apparently still thought that they might be able to redeem the situation by staging a simple mugging. Only Alessandro, sitting impatiently at the wheel of his car, with reverse gear already engaged, was able to appreciate the dark comedy of two blatantly obvious gangsters, who had seriously misjudged the width of the road, trying to open the doors of their oversized Audi wide enough to be able get out. They had effectively trapped themselves in their own vehicle with no chance of reversing out of their predicament because a little old FIAT had pulled up behind the Audi and was tooting ineffectually at this monster blocking its rightful path.

Alessandro reversed the C3 quickly and skilfully, to the admiration of his partner, until they had reached the narrow crossroads on *Via Cairoli*. The flashing blue lights from two police cars stopped him going any further. Amedeo's two assassins had had no choice but to follow the C3 slowly – right into the arms of the *carabinieri*. One of the cars had been patrolling around under orders to try and stop an assassination. The second one had arrived because a neighbour had immediately telephoned 112 on seeing the suspicious goings-on down his narrow *vicolo,* thus confirming to the drivers of the first patrol car that they had arrived at the right place.

After a bit of manoeuvring, the ancient FIAT, driven by a seventy-year-old lady, shot off angrily into the night. The *carabinieri* extricated the mafia henchmen from inside the Audi. Years of practice had made the mafia henchmen adept at protesting their innocence in suspicious circumstances. Judge Grassi managed to give the policemen a brief description of what had happened from where he was slumped in the passenger seat of Alessandro's C3. An officer had been dispatched along *Via*

Caracciolo and had managed to retrieve the tracking device where Amedeo had cast it down. 'And one of these gentlemen will still be in possession of my mobile phone,' he added. Alessandro and Elena were dispatched back to the waiting 'family'.

'We'll take your statements tomorrow, *signori*. And well done! You have saved our judge's life. *We'll* make sure he gets safely home.'

Amedeo had got out of the car. He was still visibly shaken by his near encounter with death. He silently hugged both of his rescuers.

'I'm sure you must be like the cat with seven lives,' Alessandro reassured Amedeo.

'You should go to England, Amedeo,' added Elena. 'Adam tells me that English cats have a longer life expectancy. They get nine lives.'

On the way back to the restaurant, Elena remembered that her mobile phone was still sitting on the dashboard with the Angel Gabriel, who had lived up to his name and beyond, waiting on the other end of the invisible thread of electrons linking them together.

'Are you still there, Gabriele? It's alright, he's safe – this time at least.'

They arrived back at the restaurant to find Adam, Anna, Riccardo and Isabella picking in desultory fashion at the remains of their pizzas. In point of fact, the pair had been absent for little more than half an hour. Fresh pizzas were ordered and Alessandro and Elena sat down and swallowed a few resuscitating gulps of beer while they related in colourful detail how they had plucked Judge Grassi from the jaws of death at the very last moment.

'How brave you are, *mamma!*' declared Anna in admiration. 'I want to be like you when I grow up!'

'Where did you leave your Superman costume, Sandro?' asked Riccardo cheekily, finally breaking the tension.

Isabella, Adam related later on to an amused Rosaria, had been far more concerned about her *fidanzato* shooting off into the night with a beautiful woman than any danger that he might have been exposing himself to.

* * *

Amedeo was in the kitchen with Antonella and Teresa looking accusingly at him. He had immediately taken off his suit, had a shower and put on his grey tracksuit again. He was sitting at the table fondling a glass of *grappa* whilst the two women were standing on the opposite side of the table, obviously having to restrain themselves from saying what was uppermost on their minds. Amedeo had just related the events of the past hour – even managing to make light of his having to be rescued by Elena whilst he stood like a pillar of stone in the middle of the road. He laughed as he told them about Don Augello's henchmen trapped inside their own vehicle.

'Just as well that they were not familiar with our narrow roads,' commented Teresa. 'That might well have saved your life, *papà.*'

'Oh no! It was those two who saved my life – plus your quick thinking, Elly.' Amedeo did not yet know about the telephone call to Elena from the Angel Gabriel. When, eventually, he was told about it the following day, a new dimension to his miraculous rescue was added to the equation.

'I still blame that monk,' said Antonella, finally breaking her silence. 'He has altered your way of thinking to such an extent that you are more concerned with the next life than the present one. *'Who would like to go to heaven NOW?'* he said in his sermon. I don't know why *you* didn't put your hand up like that poor old duffer in the wheelchair, Ame. On Monday, I am going to the police station and demand to be issued with a pair of handcuffs. They are bound to oblige when they realise how much police time will be saved if they know that you are safely attached to the kitchen radiator. I will spoon feed you your pasta – *my* special recipe pasta – rather than let you loose again on the streets of Lecce.'

In the end, Amedeo walked round to where the two women were standing and hugged them both warmly with an arm round each one of them. It helped to chase away the memory of that diabolical embrace of a couple of hours previously.

'I promise to be more careful from now on...' he promised. And he slept from pure exhaustion dreaming only of his guardian angel who appeared to be perched on top of the lofty *campanile* looking down upon Lecce's ancient, narrow streets from on high.

19: Reclaiming Chiara

Next day, Judge Grassi and Antonella received a visit in person from *Colonnello* Marco Scarpa, dressed in full regalia, his only concession to the informal nature of his call being to hold the stiff, golden crested kepi under his left armpit rather than wearing it on his head.

With a cup of *moka* coffee in front of him and his kepi on the table, he began to talk, first of all congratulating Amedeo on his courage and then on his lucky escape.

'*Caro colonnello,*' piped up Antonella, 'please do not encourage him. Explain to him the difference between courage and foolhardiness.'

Amedeo had the grace to smile and shrug his shoulders by way of admitting the truth of his wife's accusation. Antonella was looking at the *carabiniere* colonel in the same way as she had stared at the Angel Gabriel while he was delivering his sermons, Amedeo observed.

'I promise not to waste any more police time,' said a repentant Amedeo.

'On the contrary, *signor giudice* - Amedeo,' he said, changing his mode of address because Amedeo had mouthed his first name silently in the colonel's direction by way of correction. 'I am putting two officers at your disposal should you ever need to go out anywhere in public – especially at night time. It will be the same two young officers as before. They volunteered to take on this duty before we had even requested an escort for you.'

Amedeo felt touched by other people's unexpected kindness. What a pity that human life could be threatened so effectively by a few rotten apples in the barrel - the black scorpions hiding under the stones.

'Oh, by the way, Amedeo, here is your mobile phone. Unfortunately, we won't be able to charge those two thugs from Bari on anything that will stick in court. They were not carrying any weapons. They even claimed that they were under orders from Don Augello to make sure you got home safely and that they had your phone with them because you must have dropped it. Their Bari dialect was so strong that even our most down-to-earth officers found them difficult to understand. We are fairly sure that they can speak Italian but had chosen to make things harder by speaking in *barese* dialect. In the end, we took them to the station and put them on an Intercity train back to Bari under threat that, should they ever set foot in Lecce again, they would be instantly arrested – a more effective punishment than you might imagine, Amedeo, because we are almost certain that they arrived by car, which they will have left at Don Augello's place. They will have to come back down and face Parzanese again to pick up their Porsche, or whatever it is. In fact, I wouldn't put it past Don Augello to 'borrow' their car permanently in retribution for the failure of their mission.'

'More coffee, *colonnello?*' interrupted Antonella. He nodded and Amedeo noticed how she stood as close as possible to the police officer whilst pouring the coffee as carefully as she could. Did she merely fancy this good-looking man, wondered Amedeo, or was she making sure that her husband would suffer pangs of jealousy to punish him further for her ordeal of the previous evening? It could quite easily be both, he conceded.

'There have been some interesting developments, Amedeo, since, thanks to your efforts with the GIP, we put a tap on Parzanese's means of communication. We have, as a result, begun to get to the bottom of this gentleman's latest scam which involves flour of all things. We understand he's been importing low grade flour from Asia, milling it to make it finer and then packaging and marketing it as the high-grade double zero quality stuff 'produced in Italy' in his chain of local supermarkets throughout Salento – you know, the group which calls itself *Amo-Shopping*. We've been able to pass the investigation on to the *Guardia di Finanza*. Quite a little money-earner for the clans we understand.'

Amedeo merely shook his head in horror at the growing deviousness and dishonesty in the modern world in general.

'I'm telling you this, Amedeo, because you deserve to know that the phone tap has proved to be a vital tool in helping us get the better of the local mafia, but also to ask you to restrain yourself from any rash action that might occur to you which would involve you challenging Don Augello face to face again over your attempted assassination.' The *colonnello* had a broad smile on his face but a shrewd look in his eyes. 'It is vital that we do not run the risk of alerting the man that his calls and messages are being intercepted, you see.'

'I shall be keeping him under strict surveillance, *colonnello*,' promised Antonello.

'Now, Amedeo,' continued Marco Scarpa, smiling as he imagined the likely restraints on Amedeo's future movements, 'as to the threat on your life; in view of the identity of its main instigators, we must continue to be very vigilant. It is unlikely that

Parzanese will set up anything so elaborate and expensive again, thereby risking a second failure. He is more likely to employ a 'stalker' to follow you around and take advantage of an unexpected opportunity or a lapse in your concentration. If you see the same person following you around, then be extra careful. And make sure you always have someone with you. The one thing in your favour is that Don Augello stands to lose more than money if your demise is anything other than an apparent accident – so avoid driving your own car. I do not consider that any member of your family is at risk,' concluded Marco Scarpa.

'He won't be going out alone, *colonnello*. Rest assured!' stated Antonella categorically.

* * *

The net result of Marco Scarpa's visit was that Amedeo Grassi finished writing his book. That was one directly positive aspect of his confinement. On another level, he grew closer still to Antonella, called her 'his treasure', made love to her some nights and held her hand as they walked round their secret garden. They discussed every aspect of his new life. He told her that they had once again become like the two centuries old olive trees in Gabriele's garden whose deep roots were invisibly intertwined, drawing strength from their common subterranean source of energy.

'Are you trying to imply that I look old and gnarled, Ame?' she asked cuttingly. But inside she felt that warm glow of someone who feels desired and needed by her partner. Amedeo had even told the Angel Gabriel what he had said to Antonella.

'She still refers to you as 'that monk', Gaby. But I know that she secretly feels a deep debt of gratitude towards you.'

'Ah, women, Amedeo! They want to save us from ourselves but they also want to be unique in playing their part in our salvation.'

'Thus speaks the Man of God,' said Amedeo reluctantly.

'You are still hoping that I will renounce my orders, aren't you, Amedeo?'

The judge, yet again, was astounded at this man's insight.

'I have *never* said a word about ...' he began to protest.

'Ah, but admit you have often wished it,' said the Angel Gabriel, amused.

* * *

In the city of Lecce, Judge Grassi had become an overnight celebrity – the judge who had defied the mafia and almost become a victim of his defiance of the mob. Even Umberto Incazzato was forced to publicly sing the judge's praises. Since Amedeo was forbidden to go out, his family came to see him regularly. Elena and Alessandro appeared once or twice a week complaining that life had become very dull as they were reduced once again to investigating tedious cases of infidelity – of which there was no shortage. 'We need a new challenge, Amedeo,' said Elena. 'It will be the school holidays soon and I shall have to be with Anna and Riccardo – and my long-suffering partner, Adam. But after the holidays...'

'I might be able to help you there,' said Amedeo. 'I was talking to Leonardo the other evening – you know, Teresa's husband. You know that his department has some very advanced nanotechnology projects on the go. But he is becoming increasingly convinced that information about their research is being leaked out. Maybe that would be a suitable challenge for you two?'

Elena's eyes were alert with interest.

'In addition,' continued Amedeo, 'when I am finally allowed out again, you could spend some time shadowing me to see if I am being tailed. Your Marco Scarpa seemed very sure that Don Augello will have me tailed by a 'stalker' looking for an opportunity to push me in front of a passing lorry. Someone whom I would never think of suspecting,' he added.

'Like that couple of cigarette smoking junkies who are loitering around in the street outside your house, at the moment?' said Elena, out of the blue.

Antonella froze. 'I saw them there yesterday and the day before, come to that. A boy and a girl - I assumed they were students from the school of music. Come to think of it, they did look more like members of the great mass of unfortunates who have no purpose in life.'

'Just the kind of people whom the local mafia likes to recruit – on the cheap,' added Alessandro.

'Who is coming out with me to have a look?' said Amedeo already heading for the door.

'Oh, Good Lord!' exclaimed Antonella. 'He's going to be courageous again. Somebody stop him, please!'

'Amedeo,' said Alessandro tactfully. 'It might be better not to alert them that you are aware of their presence – if indeed they are your stalkers. Confronting them will only serve to put them on their guard. Better the devil you know. Let Elena and me see if you are being followed next time you go out shopping.'

Alessandro's counsel of caution prevailed. After two weeks of careful tailing, it seemed that indeed they were being followed by a couple similar to the man and young woman that Elena had spotted outside their house. The couple usually kept their furtive distance. Only once did they seem to close the gap and come up right behind the judge and his wife.

'It's as if they were rehearsing,' said Alessandro ominously.

'Maybe we are being paranoid,' said Amedeo.

'Maybe with good cause,' added Antonella.

Elena was silent for once – the mother of two young children sensing danger.

* * *

'Will you come to Rome, Amedeo, and keep Chiara and me company on the way home?' asked Gabriele. It was already the end of July and the Judge was becoming restless again.

'Yes, of course, I will come to Rome, Gaby,' he replied without consulting Antonella. She agreed to let him go on condition that his two uniformed escorts accompanied him to the railway station and put him safely on the train.

'You must be prepared for a big surprise, Amedeo. Chiara has found herself again,' added Gabriele.

To the judge's secret relief – and to Antonella's open joy - the two young *carabinieri* informed him that they were to accompany him all the way to Rome and back. 'We are not taking any risks with you, *signor giudice.*' Their names were Adriana and Massimiliano – Max, for short, he insisted. The judge decided to run the risk of taking these two into his confidence rather than sit through the long train journey either in silence or making trivial conversation. 'What I am about to tell you is for your ears only, Max, Adriana. Not even your *colonnello* knows the full story. But I want you to understand why we are going to Rome and who Chiara really is.'

'You can rely on us entirely, *signor giudice,*' they replied in unison. By the end of Amedeo's story they were both appalled and fascinated. Whenever the train came to a standstill, Amedeo paused in his narrative so as not to be overheard. The only thing Amedeo left out were the identities of Chiara's father and the involvement of a certain notable politician. If they were smart, Amedeo considered, they would make the connection on their own.

A moment of light relief was occasioned by a small boy eating a sandwich who had stopped at their table to stare at the unusual group, fascinated by the uniformed police officers.

'Are you taking him to prison?' asked the boy who was about six. 'Is he a dangerous crinimal? He doesn't look like a crinimal.' The boy was at that age when his powers of speech were fully developed but still lacked the social restraint that would come later. The three adults laughed and Adriana told him that they were there to protect him. 'What does he need protecting from?' asked the boy. They were saved from further explanations by the arrival of the boy's mother who apologised and led her son away protesting.

* * *

To Amedeo's further surprise, the group was met by a police car and he was taken swiftly and safely to the clinic whilst his young escorts, modest holdalls in hand, said they would meet

Amedeo, Chiara and Gabriele outside *Roma Termini* the following morning for the return trip to Lecce.

Amedeo had been prepared to see changes in Chiara. He was not ready for the total transformation that he witnessed within the first few seconds of seeing her. In fact, he confessed to Gabriele later, he would not have recognised her had she not been standing next to her brother. From a nervous adolescent just emerging from her shell, she had become an animated, talkative young adult. She greeted him with a warm embrace and a kiss on both cheeks. How strange that essentially the self-same gesture from Chiara should feel so warm and compassionate compared to the malevolent contact with Don Augello – clear proof of the invisible power of human emotions, Amedeo considered.

'Thank you a thousand times, *papà,* for coming to take me back home again.' But she had said the word *papà* with a hint of irony in her voice, almost regretfully. The transformation of Chiara into this new person was explained in part by the fact that she was speaking in Italian – a change which Amedeo did not bother to comment upon.

'But thank you above all, Amedeo, for everything that you did to help me along on my road to recovery.'

'I am happier than you will ever know that I have been able to help you, Chiara. But I really do not know how...'

'You remember the time when Gabriele was about to say grace and you were already about to eat your first spoonful of soup? Something clicked inside by brain... I don't know. It was exactly like clicking a light switch on. I was suddenly aware of something comical happening. It all began from that moment.'

Amedeo felt like shedding tears of joy but just managed to stifle the reaction. At that moment, another man approached and stood by Chiara's side. She hooked her arm through his. Amedeo realised immediately who was about to be introduced to him but in the split second beforehand he experienced the uncanny feeling that he was seeing double. It was as if a second, slightly taller version of Gabriele had materialised out of thin air.

'Yes, I know, Amedeo. They look like brothers, don't they? This is my *fidanzato*, Roberto,' said Chiara proudly. The judge wanted to take his *protégée* to one side and advise her not to be so hasty about such an important choice in life, but realised in the same instant that he was acting precisely like a jealous father resenting the intrusion of another man. So he stepped forward and shook Roberto warmly by the hand, holding his 'rival's' hand in both of his.

'I'm very pleased to meet you, Roberto. You could not have made a better choice.'

'Oh, I know it, Amedeo,' he replied. The judge realised with a sensation of pride that Chiara must have spoken about him to her *fidanzato.* 'I've been waiting for most of my life to meet Chiara,' he said simply. The judge was struck by the fact that he had not said that he had been waiting 'for someone *like* Chiara' – a good sign that! He was also instantly struck by the soothing, reassuring quality of the man's voice, gentle like Gabriele's but quite a bit deeper.

'You're not a hypnotist by any chance, are you?' asked Amedeo.

The three people facing him burst out laughing in a mixture of surprise and admiration.

'You see, Roberto? I told you that the judge was a man to be reckoned with,' said Gabriele.

'You are absolutely correct, *papà,*' laughed Chiara lightly. 'He hypnotised me and then stole my heart.'

From that moment onwards, all tension vanished. They spent the rest of the evening together. Chiara did not want to wait before showing Amedeo her latest paintings and told him how excited she was about exhibiting them in Lecce the following week. There were two pictures that left Amedeo reeling as soon as he looked at them. The first was the picture that Gabriele had spoken about; it showed a beautiful, dark-haired girl standing on a cliff top looking radiantly down on the cowering figure of a dark and twisted male figure on the rocks below. Gabriele had been right – it was the exact reverse of *Nelle grinfie di Satana.*

'Have you thought of a name for it, Chiara?' asked Amedeo.

'No, I was waiting for you to suggest a name, Amedeo.'

Amedeo did not hesitate. *'La Nascita della Gioia,'* he proposed without needing to think at length -'The Birth of Joy'.

'That is brilliant, *papà,'* she said, kissing him on the cheek.

The second painting had an altogether different feel to it but was equally striking.

'I used oil paints for the first time,' said Chiara proudly. The picture once again showed a beautiful, radiant woman. Her head seemed to be high up in the stars. She was pregnant but her swollen belly was half of the planet Earth, showing oceans and continents. There were two African children clinging for dear life on to a tree that was bending under their weight, threatening to cast them into the void of space. Amedeo could not take his eyes off it.

'It's quite something isn't?' said Gabriele quietly.

The following morning, Gabriele and Amedeo were standing a discreet distance away from Chiara and Roberto while they said their clinging goodbyes. 'It's alright. Roberto is coming down to stay with us in August,' explained Gabriele, who once again, was dressed in civilian clothes, Amedeo noticed.

'I've been given dispensation for my holidays, Amedeo,' the Angel Gabriel explained with a knowing smile in the judge's direction. 'How does he do it?' thought Amedeo.

'I shall have to train myself to stop thinking, Gaby, just in case one day you really catch me out thinking evil thoughts.'

In the minibus, Amedeo warned his adoptive daughter that they would be travelling back to Lecce in the company of the two young *carabinieri* officers. She looked alarmed.

'What have you been doing in my absence, *papà?*' she asked.

'He's been upsetting the local mafia boss,' explained Gabriele.

Chiara was looking deeply concerned so Amedeo briefly explained how Teresa had been threatened and her shop set on fire – which she had remembered. He omitted to say anything about the roundabout connection with her biological father. When they arrived at the railway station, Max and Adriana were not wearing uniforms but dark blue overalls. They had not wanted to overawe Chiara, they explained to the judge. Their holdalls were bulging at the seams. 'Thank you for being so thoughtful,' said Amedeo quietly. The extra pairs of hands were needed as they loaded the carefully packed pictures on to the train plus what seemed double the amount of luggage that Chiara had arrived with. Chiara did not appear to be in the least overawed by their presence and was soon chatting happily with them.

At Lecce station, Amedeo was taken home while Chiara and Gabriele were met by an overjoyed Marta, tears of long pent up emotions pouring uncontrollably down her cheeks.

'See you in Lecce next week,' said Amedeo embracing brother and sister warmly.

'*Grazie papà, grazie, grazie, grazie.*'

* * *

After only one day of exhibiting her paintings, it was obvious that Chiara would soon become a recognised artist. At one point, there were so many people standing in front of her picture of the pregnant girl, that those at the back could not see it properly. The ability of the image to express the miracle of birth, sullied by the suffering and vulnerability of the third world, provoked a poignant stab of emotion that made it impossible to feel complacent about the image portrayed. At that point, nobody had succeeded in finding a suitable title for the painting. Later on, somebody suggested that it be called 'Falling Angels'. Much later on still, Chiara would be paid handsomely by an international children's charity to be allowed to use it as publicity. It was to be Elena who helped Chiara take advantage of the Internet to publicize her work.

It was also a fact that she could have walked away a richer woman by the end of the first day. But while she categorically refused to sell a single picture, she was more than happy to enjoy the enthusiastic praise.

'I simply *cannot* part with them,' she explained to the gallery owner, a friend of the Grassi family. 'They represent my salvation, my return to life!' Carlotta, the gallery owner, suggested that they make limited edition prints of her paintings as a compromise. Several people proposed that she should paint portraits of their children or grandchildren on a private basis. Amedeo saw that Chiara was overwhelmed by the attention and took her aside to reassure her that she had all the time in the world to think about her life. 'Get used to being Chiara again first,' he told her.

'That's not all, Amedeo. I want to tell you that Roberto and I are going to ...' she said but was unable to finish the sentence because someone else came up to congratulate her.

* * *

The following week, Antonella and Amedeo held a garden party at their home to celebrate Chiara's return home and her rediscovery of herself. Everybody was there who had been involved in the events of the last few months. Antonella forgave Marta and even drove down to Soleto to invite her in person – incidentally begging her to help with the catering. Marta was, in any case, too good-hearted a person to hold a grudge.

It was just like a big family party - everybody was talking to everybody else, the children were playing with the children and stealing food from the table before it was time to eat, Elena and Alessandro were talking busily to Teresa's husband, Leonardo, about his work in the nanotechnology department and the Angel Gabriel was telling whoever he could what a good man Amedeo was.

Chiara approached Amedeo at one point, taking his arm and leading him away from the other guests. 'I want to talk to you, papà. I do hope you don't mind me calling you papà. I know that you are not really my father – but I wish you were! I shall always

306

think of you as being my father for the rest of my life, because you saved my life. I want you to promise that you won't allow yourself to get into any danger. I couldn't bear to lose you.'

'I shall be very careful, Chiara. I promise.'

'Because,' she continued, 'I have a favour to ask you.'

'Anything,' said Amedeo.

'It's nothing bad, Amedeo. I want you to be godfather to my child.'

'I shall be more than happy to do that, Chiara, when the time comes.'

'No, you don't understand, Amedeo. The time *has* come. I'm expecting a child. I haven't told anyone except you yet. I only found out yesterday for certain and I wanted to wait until Roberto comes down next week to tell him in person. It's wonderful, isn't it? It makes everything right again.'

Amedeo felt a lump of emotion constricting his powers of speech as he said, holding Chiara tightly round her waist: 'Yes, Chiara. It is the best news in the whole world. And I, too, would be the happiest man alive if you were my daughter.'

They each went their separate ways back towards the expectant onlookers in order to conceal the encroaching tears from the other – shed from very different perspectives.

20: The Demise of Amedeo Grassi

'I think, Ame, we should sell the holiday house down near Leuca.'

Amedeo had been expecting this declaration sooner or later, ever since he had felt morally obliged to tell his wife that the interior renovations had been heavily subsidised by Don Augello and company when he had been 'persuaded' to reduce the sentence of one of the Parzanese cousins all those years ago.

'I feel the house is tainted in some way. Apart from which, after your rash attempts to defy the mob, it is probably the least safe place in the world for you to stay. What do you think, *mio caro?*'

Amedeo had to agree with what she was saying. The house on the cliff-top was, after all, a part of his compromised past life – and its position was indeed isolated.

'Besides which,' continued Antonella, 'I feel that we should be more adventurous from now on.'

'What did you have in mind, Nella?' He prayed that she was not going to suggest a cruise. He suffered from sea-sickness and claustrophobia, hating the idea of being constrained to the deck of a ship or a cramped cabin.

'I would love to go on a Mediterranean cruise,' said Antonella mischievously, enjoying seeing the agonised expression on his face as a wave of nausea shot across his stomach. She laughed gaily. 'No, I was being facetious, Amadeo. I really have not decided where I would like to go. I have always fancied going to Cornwall, Scotland, or even further afield.

And so, it was decided that they should sell the house near Leuca and Antonella proceeded to contact the estate agent who had sold them the house some time during the previous century.

They made an appointment to meet the estate agent at the house the following morning. As Antonella drove out through the massive, wooden doors, they both checked, out of habit, to see if there were any strangers hanging about before Amedeo stepped out of the car to close the doors again. There was nobody; not even the 'student-looking' couple who had seemed to be following them some days previously.

It was a beautiful drive down south through the Salento countryside along the *superstrada* that runs from Lecce down to Leuca. They passed olive groves, old stone *masserie*, herds of goat-like sheep tended by wizened old men who could almost be mistaken for the olive trees that they were sheltering under. Time stood still as soon as one averted one's gaze from the ribbon of road which had incongruously invaded the tranquillity of centuries of unaltered existence. Both Amedeo and Antonella were having the same misgivings, wondering if they were making the right decision.

'It isn't set in stone,' was all Antonella said.

There was little traffic at that time of day. Yet, however fast Antonella drove, and she was no slowcoach, there was always some male driver who felt the need to prove that he could cover the distance between Lecce and Leuca even more rapidly than she could. The same road carried local farmers riding push bikes wobbling perilously along with shopping baskets, laden with bread and vegetables, slung over the handlebars. The racier locals were sitting astride old *Vespa* scooters, with shopping bags wedged between husband and wife; the latter perched precariously on the pillion seat. Very often, if it was not shopping jammed between them, it would be a helmetless child. Antonella often expressed her despair at the casual faith that possessed parents who put their children's lives at risk in this manner. Amedeo and Antonella overtook a couple of jean-clad youngsters, astride a *Vespa*, whose helmeted heads made them look more like aliens compared to the country people whose slow progress along the road belonged to a different time warp altogether.

When Amedeo and Antonella arrived at their house, exactly on time, the estate agent had not arrived. They opened up the house overlooking the vast expanse of turquoise blue sea, sparkling in the sunlight, stretching as far as the eye could see, where Albania and Greece were shrouded in hazy mystery. They sat out on the veranda and waited. Amedeo remarked on the scooter which buzzed past on the road down below.

'Look, Nella. It's the aliens again!' he joked.

After twenty minutes, Antonella was becoming mildly impatient at the non-arrival of the estate agent. After thirty minutes, she had decided in advance that whoever turned up to deal with the sale of the house was going to be given a hard time. When forty-five minutes had elapsed, she had decided that she would approach another agent altogether.

'Why don't we ask Alessandro to advertise the house for us?' suggested Amedeo. 'It's become quite a successful sideline for him. And he doesn't whack on the huge percentage on top of the real value of the property that all the estate agents do.'

'Why not?' agreed Antonella. 'We should have thought of him before.'

Antonella had brought food and a bottle of wine. Amedeo said he would take a walk down to the cliff top where he could sit and meditate on whether this was a paradise that they were really willing to give up.

'Twenty minutes, Ame,' said Antonella. 'We'll eat out on the veranda.'

Amedeo walked down to the road and across to the steep cliff-top where he sat down on a rock overlooking the sheer drop to the waters below. He was careful not to go too close to the edge where the sensation of giddiness always took hold of him. He noticed the scooter parked a bit further down the road. Of the aliens, there was no sign. He fell into an uneasy trance as he usually did when looking out at this seemingly tranquil stretch of water with the sunlight dancing on the surface of the water. It was hypnotic in its effect. There was an impossibly tiny boat, so it seemed, out to sea. He screwed up his eyes to try and make out why the white robed figure appeared to be standing up. Yes, there was no doubt about it. The figure was waving its arms. Amedeo had the uncanny sensation that it was the Angel Gabriel. 'Stop being so fanciful, Amedeo Grassi,' he muttered. He looked again at this apparition. There was no doubt about it. The white figure was looking directly at him and he wasn't waving in greeting. Amedeo stood up to be able to focus his attention better. The figure was making a gesture by thrusting his arm forward and jabbing a finger at something behind and beyond Amedeo. 'Ridiculous!' thought Amedeo turning half round to see what the figure was pointing at. After that, everything happened with breathless speed. He could see the figure of the female alien standing above him on the edge of the road-side with a hand over where her mouth would have been had she not been wearing a helmet. It was a gesture of unabated horror. The male alien was bearing down on him at great speed only about ten metres away from where he was standing precariously near the edge of the cliff.

What Amedeo did next was purely instinctive since he had less than three seconds to save his life. He threw himself forwards into the path of the alien. He did not immediately feel the pain of landing on the sharp rocks. The rapidly approaching youth did not stand a chance. His own impetus carried him over the edge of the cliff and he flew into empty space and vanished with a heart-rending shriek that would stay with Amedeo for ever. The girl was screaming hysterically, her helmet still firmly in place making her keening lament sound eerily muffled.

Antonella heard the shriek and the subsequent cries of anguish carried with crystal clarity on the warm easterly wind. Her heart was pounding with utter dread as she careered down the drive to the level of the road. Her first illogical gesture was to batter the helmet on top of the girl's head repeatedly, shouting: 'You've murdered my husband!' She had instantly made the connection between the two riders and the two stalkers. The girl's reaction was to wail even louder with an element of protest in her scream added to the horror. The whole helmet was shaking from side to side and her outstretched left arm was pointing down the sloping cliff top.

Drawing huge gasps of air into her lungs, Antonella saw with total disbelief and overwhelming joy the unmistakable figure of her husband, with his distinguished head of wavy grey hair, sitting on the rocky edge of the cliff. He was holding his head between his hands and she could see his body shaking even from that distance. She left the girl standing where she was, finally trying to release her head from the helmet, and scrambled as fast as she dared down to where Amedeo was sitting. She was shocked to see that his hands were bleeding and blood flowing steadily from a gash on his forehead. Amedeo was muttering words which made no sense to her. He kept on repeating: 'Where's the boat gone, Nella? There's no boat!'

'It's the shock!' she thought. She put her arms round his shoulder urging him to stand up. She led him shakily up to the cliff path to where the girl had collapsed, sitting and sobbing to herself. Without pity, Antonella kicked the helmet viciously down the cliff whence it bounced with increasing speed towards the edge, spinning crazily before it plummeted downwards out of sight.

'Get up!' she ordered the girl. 'You're coming with me.' The girl obeyed without question and followed Antonella and the intended victim up the drive to the house. She had fallen silent at last apart from an occasional, sobbing intake of air.

Antonella got out a rudimentary first-aid kit from one of the cupboards and cleaned and swabbed her husband's cuts, which seemed to be moderately superficial, and applied bits of sticky plaster on his forehead and the palms of his hands. She then retrieved a bottle of *grappa* from another cupboard and filled two small glasses with the clear fiery liquid.

'And one for her,' said Amedeo gently.

'She has just tried to kill you, Ame! You want me to offer her hospitality?'

'Forgive thine enemies, Nella – and she *has* just lost her boyfriend, you know.'

'That damn monk again!' declared Antonella, nevertheless fetching another tiny tumbler and filling it to the brim and handing to the girl who, without her helmet, looked quite pleasantly normal except for a shifty, suspicious look about her eyes.

'I didn't want to do all this,' she whined between chattering teeth. '*They* made us do it.' There was no need to ask who '*they*' were.

'How did you know we would be down here today?' asked Antonella.

'*They* told us to be here; something to do with selling a house.'

'*That* makes sense!' stated Antonella. 'That would explain the non-appearance of the estate agent.'

'What's your name?' asked the judge almost kindly.

'Ada Grimaldi,' she answered shakily. The poor kid is going to have nightmares for a long time to come, thought Amedeo.

'Why is it that *everybody* involved in this drama that your life has become, Amedeo, has the initials **A.G.**?' proclaimed Antonella impatiently.

The judge gave his first shaky smile. 'I didn't think of that,' he said. 'Maybe because the whole series of events seems to show evidence of the invisible hand of...a deity,' he said almost inaudibly. 'I haven't told you about the boat yet, *amore mio,*' he added hesitantly, not being quite able to come to terms with his narrow escape from a terrifying death.

'What boat, *caro*?' asked Antonella a little less aggressively.

'Precisely,' said Amedeo. 'What boat? A boat that was never really there,' he added. He refused to be drawn any further – until he had had time to think about it, he explained. There followed a protracted silence while the three people present pondered over what would happen next.

'There is only one place for you to go, Amadeo – now that you are dead! I'm sure you know where I mean. It is the only way out of this dilemma.'

Amedeo nodded. He had been following a similar train of thought.

Antonella looked hard at Ada. Ada looked fearfully back at Antonella, her eyes avoiding the penetrating stare.

'You will have to be made to disappear, young lady,' said Antonella pitilessly, fully realising how her words would be interpreted.

'No, please, *signora*,' she pleaded with a look of terror on her face – fearing this time for her *own* life. 'I didn't want anybody to get killed. I tried to tell him but he wouldn't listen. He said it was that or being killed by the mob...'

'Who, no doubt, kept you supplied with drugs,' said Antonella viciously. 'You do not deserve to live, *signorina*.'

'Please, *signora,*' whimpered the girl called Ada.

Amedeo made a gesture in his wife's direction meaning that the girl was already scared out of her wits.

'Where's your family?' asked Antonella with only a hint of concern in her voice.

'I left home two years ago, *signora*.'

'You know what will happen to you if ever the mob find out that it was your boyfriend who died instead of my husband, don't you, Ada?' she said using the girl's name for the first time. Ada nodded. She knew too much and would be surplus to requirements.

'What are you going to do with me?' whispered Ada, now entertaining a glimmer of hope that she would not be dispatched into the next world by this formidable woman.

'We are taking you to a place where you will have a chance to turn your life around, my dear, before it is too late.' It had been Amedeo who had spoken softly to her. The echo of the words that had become part of his existence over the past months had returned to haunt him with their persuasive appeal: 'Judge not…!' This girl, Ada, was more sinned against than sinning.

'You don't seem to be all that upset about your boyfriend, Ada,' noted Antonella abruptly while they were driving up towards Otranto and across towards Soleto.

Ada was thinking, possibly surprised herself, that she had stopped crying.

'I know he was a bad person,' she said mournfully, 'but he was the only one who ever cared for me… sometimes.'

How deeply saddening, thought Amedeo, that life could become such an undervalued commodity that the memory of bereavement could be set aside so casually.

Antonella was about to warn her beloved husband about taking lame ducks under his wing – as she suspected was his intention. Any words of advice that she was about to utter, however, were prevented by the fact that she suddenly brought the car to a violent halt, throwing Amedeo against the restraining force of the seat belts. The unfortunate Ada, who had not attached her seat belt, was hurled forward hard on to the back of the driver's seat, the mobile phone that she had just put to her ear being flung on to the floor by Amedeo's feet.

'You won't be needing *that!*' Antonella stated categorically to the shaken girl as she picked the device up off the floor and put it permanently out of the girl's reach by chucking it out of the window with all the energy of her pent up anger.

317

Amedeo, Chiara, Marta, Gabriele, cousin and uncle – and even a slightly less intractable Ada – were watching a televised memorial service in the church of San Matteo in honour of the late Judge Grassi, mercilessly assassinated by the local mafia. His body had not been recovered. They were gathered around the TV set in the kitchen of the *Masseria Marelica.* The ceremony and the talk delivered with reverential respect by his son, Aurelio, and his daughter, Teresa, might have been ironically amusing had it not been for the obvious and genuine distress on everyone's faces - especially Antonella, who was sobbing into a handkerchief with what was undoubtedly a genuine display of emotion. Apart from Rosaria, Adam, their two children and Alessandro Greco with his fiancée, Amedeo was overwhelmed by the number of ordinary citizens who had turned up at the church.

'You see, Amedeo, you are a true celebrity,' said Chiara in a cross between irony and genuine admiration.

'I would rather be free to come and go as I please,' sighed Amedeo. Nobody took his comment amiss.

As soon as the little group had arrived at the *Masseria Marelica*, a week previously, Amedeo's belief in supernatural intervention and the non-locality of certain sub-atomic quantum particles had been confirmed by Gabriele's opening words.

'I have just had the most vivid dream about you, Amedeo. I was having a siesta and I dreamt that I was standing up in a little boat, trying to tell you that you were in danger. I could see two shadowy figures behind you – they looked more like aliens from a sci-fi film...'

'It wasn't a dream, Gaby. You saved my life,' said Amedeo in total awe at the words he was hearing coupled with disbelief in the words being uttered by his own mouth. Judging by the pallor of her face, Antonella's faith in solid reality was obviously shaken to the core. 'Allow me to introduce you all to one of the aliens,' said Amedeo. 'I think she might qualify as your first lost soul to be saved.'

The judge had, of course, embraced his return to life with his second family, who had welcomed him, literally, with open arms. There was a lot to be done – early in the morning and later in the afternoon, since the August heat made work impossible during the daytime. Dario and Enrico had purchased rudimentary bottling equipment and, more importantly, the vats in which the wine would ferment. The additional income from the fugitive Aprea, not to mention Amedeo's contribution, had made a lot of difference to the comfort of the family's country home. They were overjoyed that Amedeo was 'back home' as Chiara put it.

Ada was made to feel welcome from the outset, in the same way that Amedeo had been before her - without reservation and with the unquestioning acceptance that a human being with different needs had chanced upon them. It was not that Ada proved easy to live with – if only because she spent the early days suffering withdrawal symptoms from her regular 'fix' of drugs, cigarettes - and her mobile phone. At one point, she had taken a ladder from the workshop area, propped it up against the perimeter wall and had scaled its heights with no thought as to how she was going to descend the other side to affect her 'escape from prison'. She had not been strong enough to haul the ladder up over the wall. Ada had displayed a naked fear of Argo, who, cruelly, took full canine advantage of her phobia to bark at her whenever possible. The German shepherd dog had stood at the foot of the ladder and barked, tail wagging, for nearly half an hour, until Marta took pity on her. It was a salutary lesson for Ada, since everybody had merely walked by and waved at her in a friendly manner, whilst patting the dog amicably. The humiliation put her in an altogether more favourable frame of mind towards her new companions. She volunteered to help with the washing up for the first time that same evening.

Chiara, who only months before had been imprisoned in her own tormented world, had gone into Ada's bedroom later that evening to try and initiate the healing process of friendship. She had expected sullen rejection and was thus agreeably surprised that Ada had merely looked a bit suspicious as she, Chiara, had sat down on the bed beside her and had asked her how she was settling in.

'I've never had a room to myself before,' began Ada pathetically and so obviously unaccustomed to kindness being shown to her that she felt awkward and ignorant as to how she should react. Chiara started talking to her about her past life and became increasingly sympathetic towards her, especially when Ada, in veiled language, began talking about how she had been abused by an uncle who lived under the same roof. After that, the doors to friendship were open in a way that can only happen between two women.

At one point during the conversation, which continued well into the early hours, Ada said, out of the blue:

'You're pregnant, aren't you Chiara?'

Chiara was astounded at the girl's perception since there were barely any visible signs of the magic swelling of her belly.

'How did you know?' she asked Ada.

'I just felt it. I was pregnant once too,' she said with tears welling up in her eyes. Chiara told her a little about her own suffering and how she was now with a wonderful man – whom Ada would soon be meeting. By about two in the morning, the bond had been formed. The following day, Ada offered to help Marta with the cleaning and the cooking. Marta and Chiara took Ada shopping to buy her some new clothes. Amedeo had been rescued for a second time in his life by the covert delivery of a large suitcase full of clothes to last him as long as his exile was deemed necessary for his safety. Even having clean pyjamas did not spare him from the nightmare images that besieged him whenever he lay down on his bed and tried to sleep. He usually had to wait until the small hours before merciful slumber overtook him.

* * *

Events unfolded much more rapidly than Amedeo could have wished for. Roberto had arrived the following week and Amedeo had had to overcome the initial shock of taking third place in the ranking of men who were important to Chiara. He had to admit, albeit reluctantly, that his 'paternal' jealousy was quite uncalled for; the man was just perfect for Chiara. Roberto displayed quiet joy and deep contentment at the news that he was to be a father.

'It's what I've always wanted,' he confided to Amedeo.

The text message from Elena Camisso came as a shocking reminder that the outside world was still functioning in all its sordid destructiveness. Antonio Aprea had been informed by his 'associate' that it was safe to return to Italy without fear of prosecution. He had not wasted any time. Elena had been contacted by Marco Scarpa - who was, naturally enough, fully aware of Amedeo's whereabouts – and been told that there was a strong possibility that *Signor* Aprea was on his way down south. 'Tell the judge to contact me immediately on my private number, if the man shows up at the *masseria,*' the *colonnello* had insisted. 'This time, Aprea Senior might even give us grounds to convict him.'

Enrico had taken the car to get supplies from Galatina. Thus, when they heard a toot from a horn outside the closed gate, Dario had assumed that it was Enrico returning and begun to open the gates. For once, the usual advantage of people on the outside not being able to peer into the grounds of the *masseria* was turned on its head; the occupants could not see who had just arrived until it was too late.

A warning shout from Dario rang round the courtyard and brought everyone outside, Amedeo appearing last of all. He had keyed in the number he had been given by Elena but realised that an explanation would take too long, so he had merely left the phone switched on before going outside to face the unwelcome visitor. He had feared that something like this would happen although not so soon. However, it was maybe for the best that this risky encounter should be faced up to sooner rather than later. The man had not changed, although his mop of hair was looking greyer. He swaggered down the path calling out his daughter's name. Chiara was standing erect, looking defiant, with Roberto's arm held tightly round her waist. The rest of the group, Ada included, were standing like a solid wall protecting the front entrance to the *masseria*.

Amedeo broke free and, fully track-suited, walked up to face the arms dealer squarely before the villain could get any nearer. 'Be careful, Amedeo,' said Marta.

'Stop right there, Signor Aprea!' called out the judge across the intervening space. Aprea, as he remembered, was quite a bit taller than himself and certainly no weakling.

'Oh, what have we here?' exclaimed Aprea with dismissive sarcasm. 'Are you the family *buttafuori,* or something?' *(bouncer)*

'I am Judge Grassi and YOU have broken the terms of your agreement with me!' declared Amedeo in a clear, bold voice.

Aprea checked his advance in surprise.

'Judge Grassi is dead. I have it on good authority, *signore,'* he stated with less assurance.

'Your trust in the ex-prime minister is sorely misplaced, Antonio Aprea. I am very much alive and I shall now have the pleasure of dragging your name and reputation through the mud in the gutter where you belong.'

The two men were separated by less than ten metres. A revolver had appeared, as if by sleight of hand, in Aprea's right hand and was pointing directly at Amedeo's heart. The shock that he felt was palpable. There was a collective gasp from the group standing behind him. Amedeo's heart rate had increased suddenly. There was no mistaking the ruthless hatred on his adversary's face. He would use the gun without hesitation and have no remorse about killing anyone who stood in his way. His faith in his own immunity from laws which only affected other people was obscene.

'You have five seconds to stand aside if you value your life – *Amedeo!*' he said coldly. 'Five, four ....'

Surely, thought the judge, it was not going to end like this - not after the miraculous manner of his escape on the cliff top. No, there would be no divine intervention this time – God had left it too late.

'Three...'

Amedeo was convinced that the thumping noise that he could hear was his own wildly beating heart. Aprea's attention was diverted at the very last minute by the pounding feet of a charging German shepherd dog heading for him at breakneck speed, teeth bared in a furious snarl. As Argo leapt up in the air, a shot rang out. The dog let out a yelp of brief agony. But his forward impetus had been so great that the full weight of his body knocked the assassin to the ground. Everybody heard the crack of bone as Aprea's skull struck stone. Antonio Aprea lay dead under Argo's now motionless body. Amedeo felt light-headed and realised that he was about to faint. The driver of the car in which Aprea had arrived had driven off hurriedly at the sound of the shot.

* * *

When Amedeo regained consciousness, his first impression was that he was in paradise; his head seemed to be resting in the downy lap of an angel – whilst another angelic figure was holding a glass of crystal clear water to his lips. The angel in whose lap his head was placed resolved itself into Ada and the one offering him the water was Chiara. No, if it had been paradise, it would have certainly been the other way round, his mind told him perversely. 'You're so brave, Amedeo,' said Ada. 'I'm so happy that the man didn't kill you!' Chiara was smiling in sympathy.

He could not identify immediately the deep emotional pain that he felt as he became aware of what had happened. Then he realised that it was for Argo. When, later on that day, the family buried their faithful pet in the grounds of the *masseria*, Amedeo felt guilty that the animal had died in his place. He also realised vividly that the loss of life, be it man or beast, represents the departure of something uniquely precious and fragile. He told the assembled gathering his inner thoughts on the matter. They nodded in silent agreement.

'Argo was only a puppy when *he* was still here,' said Gabriele. 'He hated being taunted by our father. Today, Argo exacted his own form of justice.' It had never occurred to Amedeo that the dog would have been alive at that period.

The police arrived as Amedeo was recovering from his fainting fit. They went about their business quickly and efficiently. *Colonnello* Marco Scarpa, who arrived some twenty minutes later, came up to Amedeo and spoke to him:

'I understand you have been very courageous again, *signor giudice!*'

'Please call me Amedeo,' said the judge in a hoarse whisper.

'One curious thing, Amedeo; the revolver was not loaded – that is, there had only been the one bullet in the gun. We suspect that Aprea thought he was bluffing. He must have been very surprised when the gun fired. I'm sorry. You must be in a state of shock. We'll leave you in peace and deal with statements at a more appropriate time.' Marco Scarpa shook Amedeo warmly by the hand.

To Amedeo's surprise, Chiara had taken events in her stride and did not appear to be devastated by what had happened. Her future was securely tucked away inside her body and standing by her side in the shape of Roberto. It was Gabriele who was more affected by his father's violent death. 'He died in sin and hatred without any chance of redemption,' he whispered to Amedeo later on as they walked around the darkened garden arm-in-arm before supper.

'I suppose you did not foresee the nature of my third miraculous escape in a few weeks, Gaby?' enquired Amedeo curiously.

'No, Amedeo. Your salvation was out of my hands completely. There was barely time to think on this occasion. But I have not ceased to thank God since that awful moment.'

* * *

It was Roberto's idea to set up a long table in the garden the following evening, and subsequently, the extended family ate their meals outside in the olive grove. They had begun to absorb the shock of the previous day's events and the evening meal began in a more light-hearted manner. Gabriele stood up and spoke the words of grace in Latin – a habit that had slipped since Ada's arrival. In a gesture identical to Amedeo's all those months ago, a starving Ada was about to ladle her first fork-full of pasta into her mouth before she realised what was going on and her fork, with spaghetti hanging precariously in mid-air, froze in surprise before her open mouth. She turned red with embarrassment when the whole table laughed at the gesture, until Amedeo explained that he had made precisely the same mistake when he had first arrived. It was uncanny that the self-same gesture unlocked the barriers in Ada's mind. She began talking freely, having quite spontaneously decided that she was at home with these people; she had a family for the first time in her life.

'Are you really a priest, Gabriele?' she asked

'Yes Ada, for my sins,' he replied smiling.

'Do you do confessions and all that stuff?'

'Only during siesta times,' he said jokingly.

'You mean when *you're* asleep, Gabriele?'

Everyone laughed at this unexpected display of wit from a girl who had hitherto seemed so sullen and withdrawn. The small miracle was at work again, thought Amedeo.

That evening, at Chiara's instigation, they danced again in the enchanted garden, as the night air cooled down and a crescent moon hung low in the summer sky. Ada, Amedeo noticed, moved with surprising grace. The little group looked thoughtful, each person digesting the recent events according to their own perspective as they danced in a circle, an arm on the shoulder of the person next to them. Amedeo was thinking about the act of loyalty and courage displayed by a dog, which had granted him precious extra time on this earth. He recalled what Elena – or had it been Alessandro - had said about Italian cats having seven lives. If this applied to him, then he only had four left. He hoped that they would not be used up as quickly as the first three. It was best not to conjecture about what fate awaited him. His future was no doubt written in the stars above.

Luna d'argentu quante cose viti? Quandu la notte sula sula stai... they sang as they swayed in time to the music in the eternal circle of life.

Epilogue

There had been a clause in Antonio Aprea's will that stipulated that he should be buried in a cemetery in Galatina. It was ironic, therefore, that his trip to Salento was to have been his last defiant gesture. Only Marta and Gabriele attended apart from a scattering of Aprea's cousins.

The consequences of Antonio Aprea's death were far-reaching; Marta, Gabriele and Chiara became wealthy overnight. It was an unlooked for outcome in their lives and one which led to lengthy discussions about the moral implications of accepting 'blood money'. Judge Grassi was there to act as their judicator at the family's behest. He persuaded them that they had a unique opportunity to convert the arms manufacturer's ill-gotten gains into a force for good; a chance given to very few people in this life, he added. Gabriele resisted more than any other member of the family and accepted the situation on the sole condition that they never used a cent of the money to purchase anything that altered their social status in the slightest way. 'No red Ferraris, then!' joked Chiara with an expression of mock disappointment on her face.

It was Ada who suggested that they set up a cookery school and train young unemployed people – such as herself, she added – how to prepare Salento dishes and become chefs. Amedeo considered it was a brilliant idea and thought they could combine the cooking with training young people to become sommeliers too. 'Marta's a fantastic cook,' added Ada. 'She could teach young people to cook properly – couldn't you, Marta?' Her enthusiasm was infectious. It really was a good idea. 'It's worked before,' added Amedeo. 'An English TV chef once set up a cookery school in London to train unemployed youngsters. I saw it on Rai Uno. It was decided to buy up and equip another run-down masseria nearby rather than encroach on the sanctity of the Masseria Marelica.

Chiara and Roberto went back to Rome where Chiara gave birth to a baby boy whom they called Matteo. She wanted his middle name to be Amedeo but the judge in question persuaded her that it was not a good idea to inflict such a ponderous, old-fashioned name on any child – especially one who was going to be loved dearly by his parents. After a year or so, Roberto found a post in Lecce and the couple returned 'home'. A second child was on the way.

Marta discovered a stray Golden Retriever hanging around outside their masseria one morning and she immediately took it in.

Gabriele, back in Rome for a short time, confided in Amedeo that he had conceived the idea of building and establishing a school in Ecuador, in some remote village where the Catholic Church was struggling to hold on to this outpost of Christianity. 'A wonderful idea, Gaby!' said Amedeo. 'Why don't you come out with me for a year or so, Amedeo? By the time you get back, any risk to your life will surely have been removed by the passing of time. You know that you wanted another challenge in life.' In a rash moment of despondency, after his near assassination by Aprea, Amedeo had told Gabriele that he had rather envied Jesus, who had not had to worry about growing old and having to face retirement. 'By the time you return to Italy,' Gabriele had argued, 'Don Augello will have been deposed by the younger members of his family and your daily cup of espresso coffee will seem like manna from heaven.' It was a tempting idea but Amedeo put off the day when he mentioned it to Antonella, fearing her reaction.

Amedeo thought it was time he went back to Lecce and spend time with his wife and family. It was Ada who offered to 'change his appearance' to make it safe for him to return incognito to be with his wife. 'It would mean cutting your hair off,' she announced gaily. She did such a good job on him that Antonella had difficulty relating to him for the first few days. 'I see you've got yourself a new man, signora!' exclaimed one of her over-curious neighbours in somewhat disapproving tones. 'Oh yes! He's my new man all right,' answered Antonella and put a stop to any further speculation by giving the neighbour one of her imperial stares – usually reserved for recalcitrant employees.

Elena-Rosaria and Alessandro thought that they had a new client when Amedeo entered their offices one day to thank them for all they had done for him – which included an undertaking to sell the house near Leuca and making sure that a high-ranking civil servant in the pensions department knew that the judge was in hiding. The charade played out by the family had been very convincing indeed, the official had commented. Elena was excited because, as Alessandro was at pains to point out, she was to be 'temporarily seconded' to the university under the auspices of Amedeo's son-in-law, Leonardo, to discover who the mole was in their midst leaking out vital information about their top-secret nanotechnology projects.

Apart from that, Amedeo spent precious time with his family and grandchildren for the first time in ages. Emma and Alessio had been sworn to secrecy and told that their grandfather's life would be in danger if they blurted out anything at school. So effective was Amedeo's disguise that young Emma had serious doubts as to whether she even had the same grandfather as before. Not only was *his hair cropped but he had grown a beard too. When out of doors, the sunglasses became de rigueur, whatever the time of day.*

One day, just after Christmas, Amedeo dared to tell Antonella about Gabriele's project in Ecuador. 'It's a splendid idea!' declared Antonella. 'I suppose he wants you to go with him?' 'How did you know that, amore?' asked Amedeo. 'Because I read you like a book, Ame.' 'And do you mind if I go to Ecuador for a few months?' 'Not at all, mio caro - I'm coming with you. I have always wanted to visit South America.'

There was nothing that Amedeo could say to that – so he didn't.

1st March 2014   (Amended version)

Glossary of Italian terms and cultural references:

Chapter 1:

1: Primitivo di Manduria: Manduria is a town well to the south-west of Lecce where this full-bodied red wine is produced. It is made from the variety of grape called *Primitivo*.

2: 'Star-shaped ceiling:' The traditional shape of interior ceilings in Puglia. The mouldings meet at a point in the centre and radiate outwards and downwards like a star. The style is known as a *soffitto a stella*.

3: Salento: The southernmost province of Puglia, of which Lecce is the capital city. The *Salento* region is largely flat. It has a distinctively red, iron rich soil which supports the production of vines and olive trees in great profusion. It grows a cornucopia of fruit and vegetables too.

4: viticoltore: The man – or woman – who makes wine.

5: Il Quotidiano: Lecce's own regional newspaper. The words just mean 'The Daily'

6: cantine: A *cantina* is a wine cellar or a wine producing establishment. *'Cantine'* is the plural noun.

7: analasi: A complete analysis of blood and anything else that can be tested. As you grow older, you are encouraged to carry out these tests every six months so that you may measure the process of physical degradation as it happens. Something of a national obsession!

8: Leuca: (Pronounced LAY oo ka); the town called 'Santa Maria di Leuca'. It is situated right at the bottom of Italy's heel, where the Ionian Sea meets the Adriatic Sea. Like Penzance in Cornwall, it is nicknamed 'Land's End'.

9: mio caro: my dear - generally a term of endearment. Used frequently amongst friends too, sometimes with a hint of irony intended.

10: Melissino: A fictitious name for a real up-and-coming old town to the south of Lecce where Antonella's pasta company is based. There *is* a pasta factory there which produces superior dried pasta.

11: Cantine Le Due Palme: Situated in a town called Cellino San Marco. The wines produced in this *cantina* have established themselves as among the very best wines from Puglia. If you are in the area, try a bottle of *Selvarossa*. It will make you a lifelong devotee of Puglian wines. Another excellent *cantina* is *Candido*.

12: 'signor giudice': Italians are obsessed by calling everyone by their professional title as a mark of respect.

13: campanile: A bell tower.

14: La Piazza del Duomo: 'Cathedral Square'. Lecce's deserves to be ranked among the most beautiful in Italy.

15: Telenorba: Puglia's regional TV station. Local TV stations abound in Italy.

16: 'Buona domenica': The standard greeting to wish people a 'Happy Sunday'. Since children attend school on Saturdays in Italy, the only day off each week is on Sunday.

17: crema: The creamy light brown top layer of an espresso coffee if it has been properly made!

18: La Guardia di Finanza: The specialised Financial Police – who are never unemployed in Italy! They wear a smart grey uniform with a yellow stripe running down the trouser leg.

19: padrone / padrona: Meaning the owner (of a bar etc). M/F

20: crepare: An informal word meaning 'to snuff it', 'to kick the bucket'.

21: dottore: A general, all-purpose professional form of address. It does not necessarily imply that the bearer is a medical doctor. There exists the feminine form *dottoressa* too.

22: papà meaning, of course, 'dad'. Not to be confused with the words *'Il pàpa' (different stress)* meaning 'the pope'.

Chapter 2:

23: San Matteo: Saint Matthew – a beautiful, baroque church in the old town, near *Via Cairola* where the judge and Antonella live.

24: The Sermon: The sermon given by the young priest is based on an actual sermon that I was lucky enough to witness. The sermon was 'performed' – that is the only word for it – by the parish priest in the cathedral of Gallipoli. The children were overjoyed at being able to participate. I wondered what some of the more 'traditional' members of the clergy thought of it!

25: La Corte Santa Lucia: This is a real restaurant in the town of Nardò. Am I advertising too much? No – it is a remarkable and inexpensive restaurant where you can enjoy traditional *Salentino* cooking. It deserves its reputation.

Chapter 3:

26: tribunale: The highest level of criminal court in Italy. The *tribunale* is the last resort court for cases that have gone to appeal. Judge Grassi would have presided in this court.

27: 'L'abito non fa il monaco': As it says in the story, this proverb means 'The habit does not make the monk'. The correct English equivalent is: 'You can't judge a book by its cover.' The young priest/monk in the story takes the proverb literally and turns the judge's accusation back on him.

28: 'Non meniamo il can per l'aia', says the judge. 'Don't let's beat about the bush.' The literal meaning is: 'Don't lead the dog around the farmyard'.

29: Il Castello Carlo V: A magnificent medieval castle in the centre of Lecce. It can be found on the web. The inside of the castle is more beautiful than the outside – which is, nevertheless, solid and imposing.

30: INPS : L'Istituto Nazionale della Previdenza Sociale; the body responsible for paying out state pensions in Italy.

31: Oscar Wilde. Whatever criticisms can be levelled against Italians, they are certainly well ahead of us in matters cultural. Every reasonably educated Italian has read, or at least heard of, *The Picture of Dorian Gray* – even if only in translation. I once bought an A4 lever arch file in Italy which had nothing but quotes from Oscar Wilde on its inside covers. So it would be normal for Judge Grassi to know this quote – which was recently used on *Rai Uno's* most popular quiz show, *L'eredità.*

Chapter 4:

32: pizzo: The word for 'protection money' paid to the mafia.

33: 'Bravi tutti voi!': 'Well done all of you!'

34: Carabinieri: The national police force

Chapter 5:

35: Adam and Rosaria: The two main characters from the previous novel, *'Dancing to the Pizzica'.*

36: fidanzata: Untranslatable! A cross between 'girl-friend' and 'fiancée'. *'Fidanzato'* is the masculine form of the word.

Chapter 6:

37: pizzica: A traditional dance which, like the Tarantella, was originally danced frenetically to cure a bite from a tarantula.

Chapter 7:

38: signore d'onore: A euphemistic term for a mafioso – a 'Gentleman of Honour'.

39: Palazzo Chigi: (Kee Gee) The 'palace' in Rome where the Prime Minister resides – the equivalent of 10 Downing Street.

40: 'in gamba': An expression that implies a person is mentally alert. It translates literally as 'in leg' – a very typical and much used idiom.

Chapter 8:

41: masseria: A traditional farmhouse in Puglia.

42: Melpignano: A small town near Soleto where the annual *Notte della Taranta* is held one night every August.

43: cornetto: A croissant.

44: un bacio: A friendly kiss on the cheek – pronounced 'bat-cho'

45: Palazzo di Giustizia : Law Court.

Chapter 9:

46: '...finances for the renovation had not come directly from his pocket'

When a mafia boss is 'returning a favour', it is often paid by services rendered to avoid traceable payments in cash.

Chapter 10:

47: nonno = granddad

48: maresciallo = marshal – a rank in the police force.

49: Don Matteo: A popular TV series about a priest, Don Matteo, who always solves the crime just before the police do.

Chapter 11:

50: zitella = a derogatory term for a spinster

51: La Piazza Sant'Oronzo: Lecce's main public square, where there is the well-preserved remains of a Roman arena.

52: capo = 'chief'

53: 'In bocca al lupo!' Best of luck! (Literal meaning, 'In the mouth of the wolf' to which the standard reply is *'Crepi'*. Don't ask me why, though!

54: tangente = a bribe or a back-hander

Chapter 12:

55: Piacere! = My pleasure! (When you are introduced to a new person)

56: Mi dispiace tanto = I'm so sorry.

Chapter 13:

57: Ci penso io, mamma = I'll take care of that, mum.

58: Te sai balli propiù bonu = Tu sai ballare proprio bene. 'You dance really well,' says Chiara in dialect.

Chapter 14:

59: It is easier for an Audi Q7 to pass through a keyhole…' Gabriele deliberately misquotes Jesus's saying 'It is easier for a camel to pass through the eye of a needle…'

Chapter 15:

60: Pope Clemente: I chose this name so as not to put words in the mouth of the present pope! There has not been a *Clemente* since the 249th pope who took office in 1769.

61: Ti voglio bene, papà. 'I love you, dad,' says Chiara to Amedeo. *'Ti amo'* is said when there is sexual attraction involved.

Chapter 16:

62: By Italian law, *un'intercettazione,* a phone-tap, has to be authorised by a special judge known by the initials G.I.P. *Giudice per le Indagini Preliminari;* an examining judge in England.

Chapter 17:

63: Don Augello Parzanese: The 'title' Don is applied to priests and mafia bosses alike! The mafia bosses regard themselves as 'virtuous leaders' – so great has their self-delusion become.

Chapter 18:

64: Thanks you GGG! Not a typing error! Italians believe, by using English, that they are increasing the impact of their message! The confusion between 'thanks' and 'thank you' is rife. They invariably say things like: 'Thanks God my little boy is better!'

Chapter 19:

65: 'barese' dialect The dialect spoken in Bari is totally different to that spoken in Salento. It is much coarser and almost impossible for an outsider to understand.

66: 'I was talking to Leonardo the other evening...' says Judge Grassi. His son-in-law is in charge of the university's nanotechnology department. The University of Salento (Lecce) does, in point of fact, have a worldwide reputation in this scientific field.

Chapter 20:

67: 'the non-locality of certain sub-atomic particles' I claim in all seriousness that the constitution of God's universe is nowhere nearly as fully understood as scientists would have us, or themselves, believe. How else could we get occasional glimpses of other dimensions or perceive the presence of the spiritual world around us? I have seen people and things that should not be there – as I am sure have countless of those of you reading this book. There has to be a 'scientific' explanation for such phenomena, doesn't there!

Epilogue:

68: A judge escaping to South America? That might seem far-fetched. But in point of fact, my fictional judge, who decides to accompany Gabriele to Ecuador to build a school, has an unexpected counterpart in real life. I understand that one of the judges who worked alongside Judge Falcone in Sicily, Judge Antonio Ingroia, has accepted an invitation to go to Guatemala to help the police incriminate mafia gangs operating in that country.

My grateful thanks to friends in Italy, France and Great Britain who have kindly read this novel chapter at a time, offering me their enthusiasm, support and critical appraisal. Without their help and encouragement, the process of creation might well have stalled along the way. RW

About the author

Richard Walmsley lived, loved and worked for eight life-changing years in Puglia – the 'heel' of Italy. From 2002 until 2005, he taught English at the University of Lecce until age forced him reluctantly into retirement. At present, he spends his time writing novels and short stories. His novels and many of the short stories are born of his vivid experiences during the time spent in that contradictory region of Europe. Apart from writing, the author loves Italian cuisine and wine, walking and classical piano jazz. He gravitates towards the countryside rather than life in the city.

Although written ostensibly as tales of intrigue, mystery, romance and the influence of the mafia, his stories are laced with humour; it is impossible, he maintains, to live in Italy without being struck by the Italians' anarchical relationship with the world around them. His modest ambition is to provide an enjoyable reading experience to as many readers as possible, regardless of age, gender or any other category which you can think of.

Printed in Poland
by Amazon Fulfillment
Poland Sp. z o.o., Wrocław